HERE TO STAY

SUANNE LAQUEUR

CATHEDRAL ROCK PRESS

NEW YORK

2015

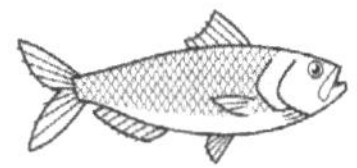

Suanne Laqueur/Cathedral Rock Press
Somers, New York
www.suannelaqueur.com

Book Design by Ampersand Bookery

Cover Design by Tracy Kopsachilis

Here to Stay/ Suanne Laqueur. — 2nd ed.

978-1-7372649-7-2 (Paperback)
978-1-7379814-2-8 (Hardcover)

To AJ,
Who always asks, "What are you writing?"

"But oh, my dear,
Our love is here to stay.
Together we're going a long, long way..."
                    —George and Ira Gershwin

"Draw a line and get on one side or the other."
                    —William M. Kaeger

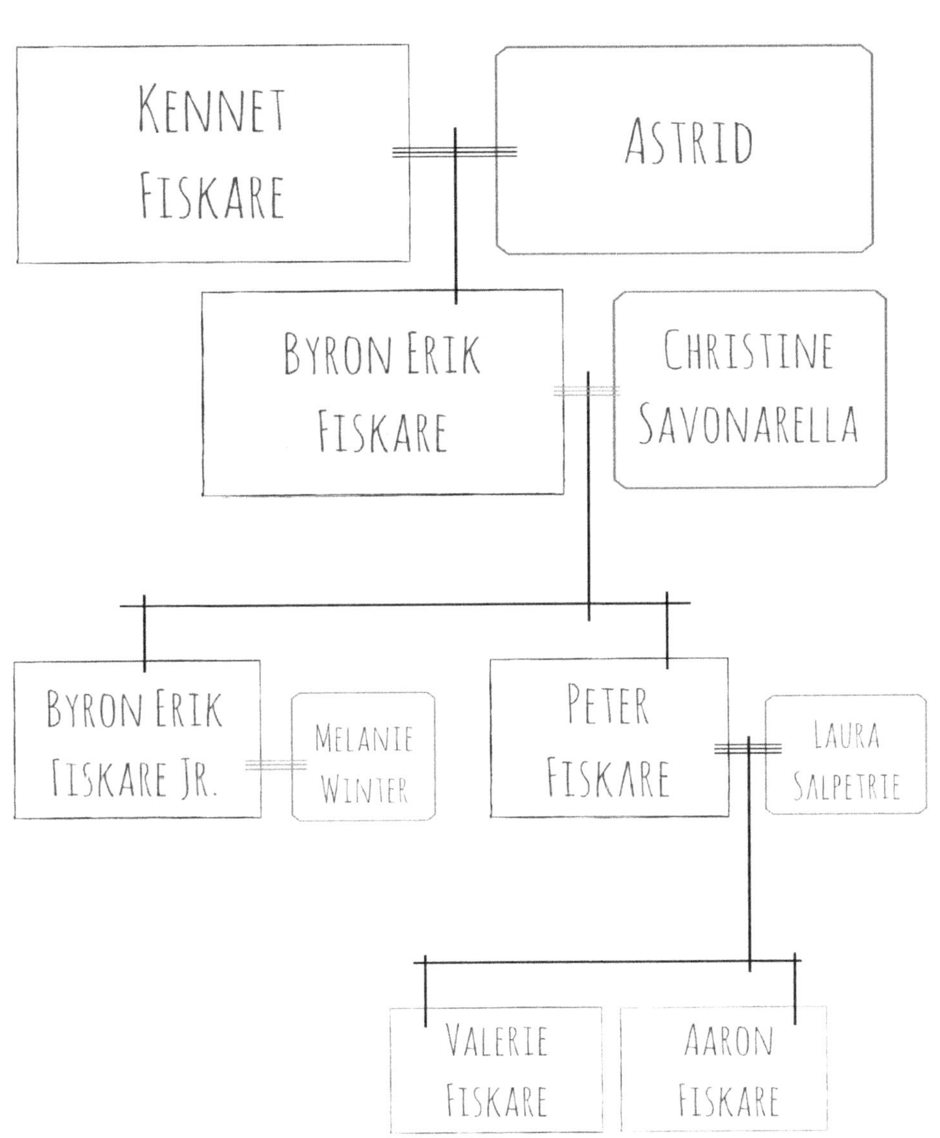

Kennet Fiskare
Astrid
Byron Erik Fiskare
Christine Savonarella
Byron Erik Fiskare Jr.
Melanie Winter
Peter Fiskare
Laura Salpetrie
Valerie Fiskare
Aaron Fiskare

Part One: Pearls

BORN TO LIVE 

IT'S A STRANGE THING to find a lost lover in your hands again. Like finding your childhood baseball glove in an attic box of memories. You're sure it won't fit. But the heat of your palm, a flex and a bend. A cautious knead of the leather and a tentative reach into the furthest recesses... It knows you. It remembers you.

It fits you.

"Do I feel the same?" Daisy asked, her voice a silken caress.

After twelve years, Erik thought, of course not. He had loved a girl. It was a woman's body up against him now, with the heft of wisdom and the weight of experience. He ran his fingers up her backbone and felt all the bits of new fused steel, overlaid with the strong assurance in her muscles and the soft aplomb of her skin. She was a hundred times more beautiful. A thousand times more thrilling.

And as her blue-green eyes stared into his, he was keenly aware of her vulnerability.

"You feel more," he said, his hands moving along her body, trying to remember how she felt when he last touched her. Thin. Beyond ballerina thin—she was drugged thin at the end of their days in college. Yet beautiful to him. Never anything but stunningly easy on his eyes and liquid in his embrace and sweet in his mouth.

"You feel right," she said, her own hands gliding along his limbs, in and out of him. "Maybe a little thinner."

"I probably am. I lost and gained weight over and over. Depending on how I was feeling at the time. When the dark came around, I'd stop eating."

"I know, but..." Her delicate, arched eyebrows flickered in her brow. "I think over the years, in my head, I made you bigger than you were. Or maybe I beat myself down into something smaller. But now I remember your body. I remember mine with it."

She was kissing him, pulling him to roll on top of her again. The digital clock on her bedside table read 2:06 in the morning. They had been going at it like possessed demons for hours now and no matter how tight he held or how hard he clung, Erik could not get both arms around making love to her. Too much feeling grabbed at him, clamoring for attention and precedence. Euphoria, lust, guilt and sadness were four wild stallions chained to each limb, intent on tearing him apart. Yet at the center of the jerking, pulling emotion, his heart was calm and accepting. Quietly riding out the storm, safe in the knowledge he was living his truth, living the life he was born to live.

"Don't leave me," she whispered under him.

"I can't," he said. "I'd never breathe again."

MADAME HAD COMPANY

THE SUN SHONE SOFT yellow through the frosty windows and it threw a square of light on Daisy's skin. Propped on an elbow, Erik ran his hand over her bare back, looking for scars. One by one he found the fine, raised lines in the curve of her waist and along the hollows of her ribs. He counted them. Cataloged and memorized them. Sighed as each was tallied under his fingers.

"What," she whispered. She lay on her stomach, arms around a pillow. One brilliant blue-green eye looking up at him.

"Nothing."

The eye closed once and opened. It was her thirty-fourth birthday and she was no fool.

"Tell me," she said.

"I feel like I pushed you to this."

"I made a choice," she said.

"I know. But I own part of this. Maybe one day I'll feel differently. Right now, I feel responsible."

His fingers traced and his mind pulled back through the years, imagining her alone in her dark apartment. In the darker dark of her mind. Her fingers curling around pieces of broken glass. His name in her mouth as she cut into her skin.

"You're not responsible for all of it," she said. "Pick one. You can have one. You can own it and hate it or heal it or touch it however you want."

He leaned his head closer to her back. He touched the thick ridge of healed skin that curved at the bottom edge of her right shoulder blade. He thought of the twisted courage it took to push past the revulsion of self-harm and lean on a sharp edge. Lean hard until it sank into the layers of skin and sinew.

He almost did. Once. On his darkest day, he sat on the floor of his lonely apartment with the phone in one hand and his Swiss army knife in the other. He started dialing and stopped a half-dozen times. Opened and closed the blade a half-dozen times, pressing it to his left wrist where the daisy was tattooed. Then stopped and closed the blade. Over and over, he dialed and stopped, opened the blade and stopped. Feeling he had to cut Daisy out of him or he would die. Feeling he'd rather die than cut her out of him.

Somehow his fingers had dialed one last time and not stopped. Help came and the knife was taken away from him.

"I never got it back," he said.

Daisy's eyebrows flickered. "What?"

"Nothing." He touched the scar beneath her shoulder blade again. "I pick this one. It's mine."

"All right, then." She rolled beneath his hand, turning to face him. "Hold me."

He wrapped his arms around her. Their legs wove and twined and they yanked tight like a knot. Soon their mouths touched and they were melting together. Soft and hard. Vicious and tender.

"It will never be enough," he whispered against her mouth, his hands coming up to cup her breasts. Pinky to thumb, he pulled his hands to their widest span, the most square inches he could lay on her skin, and he still couldn't feel her. Skin to brain and back, the message was garbled with a surreal static. After twelve years of estrangement, she was live flesh and blood to be touched and held again.

"Never enough, ever again," he said. "I'll never be able to touch you enough."

Her arms went up around his neck, her back arching. "Try," she whispered.

The square of sun crept across the mattress and the frost on the window panes melted as they made love, frenetic and sloppy. And fast, because Daisy had to get to a rehearsal. Not even a reconciled love affair could stop the tide of *Nutcracker* crashing onto December's shores.

He listened as Daisy splashed around in the bathroom. The scrub and spit of teeth being brushed. Faucets run, toilet flushed, towel rack rattling. Hating how she was wiping him off her skin and out of her mouth and he'd have to start all over again.

He watched with a tired arousal as she dressed. The flex of her leg muscles as she balanced on one foot and pulled a pant leg over the other. How she still hooked a bra backward around her waist then swiveled and pulled it into proper place. Drawing her hair back into a loose bun, she crouched by the edge of the bed and kissed him. Her sugar smell filled his head.

"I'll be back in a few hours," she said.

"Hurry," he mumbled against her neck, already getting sucked back down into sleep.

He woke again when the jingle bells on the front door rang out. Conditioned as a Pavlov dog, his erection stirred. The radiators were clinking and hissing and the room was warm. He moved the sheets and quilt off him, ready for another round. He felt the bit of desire settle between his teeth and a smug, itching need to prove himself.

Come and get it, woman.

She seemed to be puttering around downstairs. She was teasing him. Fine. He waited twelve years. He could wait another five minutes. Still...

"You're killing me," he said against the pillows.

Now she was coming up the stairs. Slowly. His toes curled.

The bedroom door creaked open, accompanied by a strange, mechanical-sounding roll.

"Oh. Bonjour, monsieur."

Erik yanked the covers over his skin and rolled in a panic. A woman stood at the foot of the bed, grey and bosomy in leggings, T-shirt and a long apron, her hand on the handle of the vacuum cleaner. One of her eyebrows went up and the opposite corner of her mouth went down as they regarded each other and their place in the situation.

"Bonjour," he said.

She set her bucket of cleaning supplies down and walked through the tossed and flung clothing on the floor, over to the windows to open the drapes.

"I regret," she said through a thick French accent. "I not know Madame had company."

"No problem," he said. "I'll just…"

"No, no," she said, picking up a pair of jeans by the waist and giving the legs a brisk thwack in the air. "I begin downstairs today."

She set the jeans on the dresser, sniffing deeply as she looked around the rest of the wardrobe on the floor. She brushed one hand against the other, then took her vacuum and her bucket and retreated.

His heart pounding, Erik reached for his phone and texted Daisy.

I believe Madame's cleaning lady is here.

She replied a minute later. *FUCK. I switched her day. I totally forgot. I'm so sorry…*

No worries, he typed. *A little embarrassing when I met her at the door naked. But I think she's laughing about it now.*

Don't even…

She brought me breakfast in bed. Nice lady.

She's fired.

He got out of bed, scratching and yawning. He picked his jeans and T-shirt off the floor, shook them out and got dressed. In the adjoining bathroom he swished some toothpaste around his teeth with an index finger, rinsed and spat, and smiled in the mirror as he dried his mouth.

"This is happening," he said to his reflection.

ALPHABETICAL ORDER

HE WENT DOWNSTAIRS, skirting the cleaning lady in the living room. In the kitchen he lit a burner and pushed the kettle onto it. He found tea bags and the sugar bowl. The third drawer he tried had spoons. Opening all the cabinets to look for a mug, he found in one a pharmacy.

If you were in pain, Daisy was your girl. Tylenol, Advil, Aleve, Motrin. Various generic cousins for all. A plethora of vitamins and herbal supplements. She had a distinct preference for anything available in gummy form.

Her prescription meds were clustered together, separated in a dignified white-bottled grouping. Conscience and curiosity did a quick face-off in Erik's head. Curiosity body-slammed conscience and he turned each bottle to the front. Zoloft. Wellbutrin. He knew the names well. Another bottle had Clonazepam. He laughed under his breath. Captain Clon. The real vitamin C. He had his own bottle in his shaving kit back at the hotel.

"Never leave home without it," he said.

He flipped open a flat, buff disk to find birth control pills, that day's blister empty.

He thought about last night.

"Come back to me," she had cried over the phone. And he could deny her no more. Couldn't deny himself another minute without her. He had no more time to throw away. He pulled jeans over his bare skin, zipped a jacket over his thin T-shirt. Without socks, gloves or a hat, he burst out of the hotel, careened into the bitter Canadian night and drove back to her house. She was waiting for him and took him upstairs to her room.

It began.

Yet it couldn't begin.

Not until he was done with one last thing. Not until he was on his knees on her bedroom floor, untying the drawstring of her soft pants. Not until he pushed down the waistband and the flash of red letters was in his sight. Red letters spelling *Svensk Fisk* and forming the shape of a fish in the hollow of Daisy's hip bone. Forming the shape of him, for he was that Swedish fish inked forever in her skin. Fiskare the fisherman. And he wasn't done grieving the past yet. Not until he pressed his fingers to the red letters. Then wrapped his arms around the backs of her legs and pressed his mouth against her skin. Tasted the ink of himself on the canvas of her body. Found he was still there. She hadn't erased him.

It was on him then. The dam of his heart broke. His throat dissolved. His lungs gave up the last of their poisoned misery and he sobbed.

She slid down the wall to sit and gathered him close, her hair falling down on either side of their heads. She didn't shush him or soothe him with words. Only held him tight in the strong circle of her arms and let him dump the rest of it into her lap.

Then it was done.

Then it began.

They didn't even get to the bed the first time. Down on the cold floor they grappled. Kissing and seizing. With all the grace of a pair of chainsaws coupling. They remembered and forgot. He zigged and she zagged. His head clocked hard on the floorboards, then rebounded into her forehead. They grabbed brows, groaning in pain, then grabbed each other again, groaning in need and tearing at their clothes. Her earring got tangled up in the neck of her shirt. His jeans got snagged on an ankle. He was trying to get his mouth on her. She was trying to get her mouth on him. Neither seemed willing to calm down and take a minute or take turns.

They wanted everything at once, their kiss sliding around words and words smashing between their lips and tongues. Teeth and skin and tears and breath all fought for a chance. He was harder than a fifteen-year-old virgin and just as doomed: one touch and he would explode. This was not going to be his A Game. But Jesus fuck, it was Daisy in his arms. After twelve years in his head, shaping him from afar and haunting him in the night. Now she was on him, naked and crazed, crawling up the length of him. Planting her knees on either side of his hips and she had his cock in her hand—*twelve fucking years and she's putting me in her*—as her mouth sank deep in his. Her hips hovered over him, rising a bit, then lowering as she held him in place and let him feel a touch of her damp heat, like another mouth to sink into.

Give it to me.

Wait a minute.

No give it to me now put me in you now I need in you want in you now.

Wait a minute wait a minute wait a minute.

"Dais, wait." He stopped her. Pushed his palms against her hip bones, held her still and asked, "Do you want me to use something?"

She drew back a little, staring. Her eyes flicked from one side to the other, mouth parted, as if thinking.

He closed his eyes.

Fuck I don't care my cock in you now put me in you now...

Then she leaned down again. Her hand squeezed and the tip of him touched pink satin.

"No," she said. "I don't."

And she settled her weight into his lap.

He slid in deep, touched down in that smooth molten heat. His eyes opened and his throat unleashed a howl into the magic night. Daisy sat up on top of him, her thighs hugging his sides, her face in her palms. As she rocked her hips, her hands curled into fists and dragged down her cheeks.

"Oh my God," she said, shaking her head.

"Dais." His voice was a hollow shell against the jubilant screaming in his head, *I'm inside you, I'm in you, it's you, I can feel you, I got you back...*

Her fists at her collarbones now, she rose up along the slick length of him and sank down again. "Erik," she whispered. "Is this real?"

He wrapped an arm around her, pushed off the floor, rolled her down onto the rug and got her underneath him where he had always loved her best.

"It's real," he said. His fingers gently moved a piece of hair out of her face before he pinned her with his mouth and his body. Her arms and legs clutched him as he pushed into her. Her hand tight in his hair and her teeth at his earlobe as he reared back and plunged again. Further. Harder. Deeper. Groaning and crying. Nothing like a lover, just some deranged lunatic fucking her back into his life.

His phone pinged an incoming text.

I miss you. What are you doing?

He put the birth control pills as he had found them and shut the cabinet.

Snooping, he typed back.

Did you find the porn?

Not yet.

You suck at snooping then.

I do. Better text me when you leave so I can put everything back.

Alphabetical order, please.

You keep your underwear in alphabetical order?

Hello? Have we met?

A clearing of a throat. Erik looked up to see the cleaning lady in the kitchen doorway. He smiled, took his mug and headed back into the living room. He felt in the way and useless. And cold in his short-sleeved T-shirt and bare feet.

He texted Daisy again: *Is there anything resembling a man's sweatshirt on the premises?*

Sorry, I've only had women lovers since I moved in. You can wear that fur coat in the front closet if you want.

He drank his tea and considered. *I think I'll go back to the hotel and get some warmer clothes.*

Kindly leave your house keys on the piano, she replied.

You think I'm running away again?

I think you should run your ass to the hotel, check out, bring your stuff to my place and put your ass back in my bed. Any other questions?

He wanted to ask if she loved him. Instead he asked where he could get an egg and cheese sandwich.

Sorry, we don't have those in Canada.

Do you love me?

A few agonizing moments passed.

Kate's Bakery is a couple blocks down from your hotel. I love their egg and cheese sandwich. But not as much as I love you.

DIFFERENT COLORS

"NO MORE REHEARSALS after this," she said the next morning. "Tomorrow we'll sleep in."

It was hard to let her go, the reluctance even keener because they were starting to find their groove again. Sighing like a small thunderstorm, she slid out of bed. Erik let his hand run down her arm, holding onto her fingers and staying suspended in mid-air as she headed for the bathroom. His throat grew warm when she stopped to look back over her shoulder and extend her own hand.

"Is this real?" she asked, fingers reaching.

"It's real," he said. He curled his fist around the air and let it drop onto the blankets.

After the jingle bells on the front door rattled to stillness, he fell back asleep and dreamed he was busily sandpapering his forehead because he needed to repaint himself in different colors. He woke up to Bastet, Daisy's cat, licking his face. He grimaced under her rough tongue and gently pushed her away. "Morning."

Undeterred, she nudged her silver brow against him, purring. Daisy had declared the cat a standoffish bitch, but the bitch seemed to like Erik. Which he appreciated.

He got up and made some tea, moving easily around the kitchen now and finding things on the first try. Bastet perched on the counter and watched, still purring, her tail wrapped primly around her feet. He poured her a little milk into a saucer then took his mug into the living room, looking around the furnishings and fixtures with increasing familiarity.

Daisy bought a house, he marveled to himself. She had him beat—he and his wife were still renting when they separated. He couldn't swing the rent on just his salary and it was too much square footage for a single man anyway. And too depressing. He moved back into one-bedroom digs in the business district of Brockport and spent as little time as possible there. He only unpacked a quarter of the boxes. Just the essentials. All along, it seemed something was telling him he was in a holding pattern, and he wasn't to commit to a living space until certain decisions were made.

And a phone call placed.

He built up the fire. Straightened the couch pillows which were still lopsided and crunched from last night's lovemaking. The memory of cries and moans echoing in his ears, he folded the two wool throw blankets and laid them across the chairs in front of the hearth. One was upholstered in rust chenille ("Edith," Daisy called it) and the other a handsome brown leather ("Archie.")

Daisy liked to name her world. Her car, her favorite cast-iron skillet, the washing machine. A child of European parents, she grew up in houses with names. This one was called Barbegazi, after legendary Swiss gnomes beloved to the previous owner. Erik rolled the word around his tongue like a piece of candy as he wandered the first floor, looking at and gently touching Daisy's things. Books and music and pictures. An upright piano the previous owners had left behind. Erik sat and played a little, then got up and smelled the blossoms on the Meyer lemon tree, which, oddly, didn't have a name. ("It hasn't told me yet," Daisy said.)

He put on jacket, hat and gloves and went outside. It was an unnecessary inspection—she had been taking care of herself for years, still he felt the need to take a good look at the place and make sure she was safe. He walked the property and could find no fault. The house and its two outbuildings—a detached garage and a small shed—were solid, sound and shipshape. The gardens were rock hard and barren, filled with dead branches and clumps of decaying, toppled-over foliage. But he could imagine them in their spring and summer glory. He crunched over the frosty grass to the long dock at the edge of the frozen lake and stood staring for a long time.

Inside, he made more tea. Headed upstairs to get his phone, figuring he could sit in front of the fire and make a few calls. A handful of people knew he was here and probably would want to know how it was going.

Sell everything, he imagined saying. *Transfer all funds. Never coming back.*

He paused in the stairwell, fascinated by the gallery of photos Daisy had hung there. Pictures of her at all stages of her career. Partnerships with men Erik didn't recognize. Some pictures were matted and Daisy had written captions with pencil, giving provenance. Erik read things like *Rakewind debut, Cleveland, 1997, with Gabriel Ostin* and *Primo Vere debut, New York, 1998, with Anouar Bourjini.* Strange to see her partnered with someone other than Will Kaeger, who had been Daisy's exclusive cavalier at Lancaster University, and Erik's best friend.

Or was it ex-best friend?

Probationary best friend, he decided, and wondered if Will would get a kick out that. Maybe in time. You couldn't waltz back in after a twelve-year estrangement and expect to get many laughs.

Here was a picture of Daisy and John Quillis in partnering class. Looking like a young Ron Howard and branded as Opie in college, John was now a ruggedly handsome young man and, according to Daisy, a rising star with the Boston Ballet. He and Daisy started dating when they both lived in New York City, and eventually moved in together.

Balanced on the edge of a tread, Erik peered close at the picture. The photographer must have snapped the shutter at the precise second John caught Daisy in his arms: his shirt rippled out behind him and a spray of sweat arced off the back of his head. Daisy's eyes were closed, her mouth open in a smile, her body both taut and trusting. Further up the incline of the wall was another picture of them dancing. A real life shot. Dancing as lovers, not as performers. Out at a swing dance club venue. Hands joined, their bodies rearing back in mid-step, but their eyes locked and loaded. Joy etched every line of their bodies and Erik felt a pang in his chest.

She lived with him. He was her lover.

This wasn't news. He found out long ago, when he reached such a nadir in his isolated existence, he felt compelled to pick up the phone and call Daisy. John answered. Then Erik's stagnant world started spinning out of control and he became aware of just how deep one's rock bottom could get.

I'll tell her you called, Fish. But I'd appreciate if you wouldn't make a habit of it.

Fingers resting on the glass of the picture frame, Erik put his forehead a moment in the crook of his elbow. He could feel sorry for himself all he wanted but one irrefutable fact remained: John saved Daisy's life.

John first saw the scars and clued in to the ritualized cutting. It was John who found her in the bathroom after she stepped out of ritual and blindly slashed her skin in a desperate frenzy. He was the one to see what Erik didn't: the Lancaster shootings had thrown Daisy's mental health onto a trajectory with disaster. She was in trouble long before Erik left. The desertion only compounded the issue.

Erik wasn't there when Daisy reached her own nadir, a bottom littered with broken glass, not rocks. John found her. John called for help. And all through Daisy's recovery—the stay in the psych hospital and the months of therapy afterward, battling anxiety and depression and, above all, a pervasive unresolvable guilt for what she had done to Erik—John was there.

You left when she was weakest. He stayed.

Erik exhaled heavily and moved up a step. Here hung a picture of Daisy and a tall silver-haired man. Erik guessed it was her last boyfriend, Ray. They were dancing at a wedding or some occasion. Ray in black tie. Daisy in a pale cream dress. Ray had her thrown back in a deep dip and she was wide-mouthed laughing, hanging onto his shoulders.

A picture of Daisy and Lucky Dare, now Lucky Kaeger, Will's wife. In the picture she was in her wedding dress, her crazy blonde curls curbed into a neat bun but one or two errant spirals spilling around her face. Daisy, maid of honor, beside her in a pale blue gown, all gorgeous arms and shoulders, her blue-green eyes like two jewels. Another photo of Daisy dancing with Will, the longtime partners showing everyone how it was done. Will looking sharp and bad-ass in a tux as he twirled Daisy under one hand, the other at her waist.

Who was your date to their wedding? Were you with Ray then?

He moved up and down the stairwell. The pictures were hung in no order, leaving him confused and slightly fretful.

Here was an obviously post-performance Daisy—hair up, stage make-up, arms full of flowers—cozied up to a man in suit and tie. Erik had gone through life being told he could stand in bars and take numbers, but next to the strapping hunk of dude in the picture, Erik was the bar's invisible busboy. The picture was labeled only *Rakewind, 1997, Washington, D.C.* No names. Daisy was smiling at the camera but the man was smiling at her. Chemistry oozed out of the frame and dripped down the wall.

Interspersed with the couple pictures were ones of Daisy alone. Studio shots in class or rehearsal. Solo performances. Warming up in the wings for *Phantom of the Opera.* An adorable portrait of her catnapping beneath a grand piano, one hand closed around her pointe shoes, the other pillowed beneath her cheek. All up and down the wall she smiled and dazzled and laughed with old and new friends.

Who were these people?

I missed all this. She had a life all these years I know nothing about.

He'd reached the small landing where the stairs made a quarter turn. A narrow window, its top half a stained glass mosaic. A skinny table with a potted fern. And more pictures, including one of the Lancaster gang. Obviously taken at the memorial ceremony in 2002, marking ten years since the shooting incident in Mallory Hall. It left six people dead, over a dozen others wounded and innumerable lives changed.

Erik took the frame down from the wall and his finger touched it, taking attendance. Daisy. Will. Lucky. John. And good Lord, was that Neil Martinez? He was a giant compared to Erik's memory, all brawny bulk. Next to him stood David Alto. Bald from chemo. Fragile in the shadow of Neil's muscle, his hands stuffed in his pockets.

All of them were crowded up with Cornelis Justi, the conservatory's beloved director. He stood center of the group, his arms thrown wide to gather them all in. He was bald too, but he had always been. Bald, black and beautiful, Kees Justi owned center stage of every situation. Not an attention-seeker, he simply came with an irresistible pull of gravity, drawing in everything and everyone. He'd even been an unknowing beacon for Erik, who drove down to Lancaster on a whim a little over a month ago.

He hadn't set foot on the campus in twelve years. He was sure he was only going to look around and maybe visit his old technical theater professor. Instead, his feet had walked him straight into the theater of Mallory Hall, straight down the aisle past the ghostly echo of gunfire and into Kees's waiting arms. They went for beers. They talked a long time. About the shooting. About Daisy. About Daisy sleeping with David and Erik leaving without a backward look. Until now.

"You left," Kees said, his direct gaze on Erik both loving and stern. "You chose to leave. Sit there and own it. You turned your back on her, man. Now what the fuck do you *want?*"

And at the time, in that place, in Kees's uncompromising company, it was surprisingly easy for Erik to distill what he wanted down to a single thing and give it a name:

"I want to turn around," he said.

Four days later, he picked up the phone and called Daisy.

He hung the picture back up and took down another from the same timeframe. The circle of friends now on the porch of Daisy and Lucky's old apartment on Jay Street. Will with his arms around a pregnant Lucky. John standing behind Daisy with his arms around her shoulders, his cheek on hers. David alone in the middle.

Gazing down at his tribe, Erik's hand wandered up to touch the gold chain on his neck. The heirloom charms of fish, boat and saint's medal glided through his fingers. Like the tribe, it had been lost to him for years. The discovery of David in bed with Daisy had led to a brutal fist-fight in the kitchen of the Jay Street apartment. In the mêlée, the gold chain broke off Erik's neck and, unknown to him, was kicked beneath the stove. It remained there nine years, until the gang discovered it on their return visit in 2002.

He stared at the group on the porch, looking for evidence of himself.

Was this before or after they found my necklace? Is it in Daisy's purse or Will's pocket? Did they find me yet? Am I here?

He looked down along the entire gallery of the stairwell.

Am I anywhere on this wall?

His stomach was starting to hurt.

A picture of Lucky in a hospital bed with one of her babies. A blue cap so Erik guessed it was Jack. Will squashed on one side, Daisy on the other.

I missed all this.

Just off the landing was one last black and white shot of Will and Daisy from the college years, practicing in Mallory Hall's theater. Lighting instruments and technical mess were scattered across the apron of the stage. A ladder was in the background, with a boy in a baseball cap halfway up the rungs, looking over his shoulder at the dancing couple.

Erik squinted. A smile broke through and relief cascaded over his shoulders.

Here I am.

Close by, he found another black and white of Will, dancing alone on the same stage. And in the background was Daisy, sitting on the floor with her back up against the proscenium, reading a book. Erik lay on the floor, his head pillowed on her outstretched legs. His ankles crossed, his hands folded on his chest, the bill of his cap pulled low.

He touched the picture, still smiling as the knot in his stomach loosened. He was here. He was allowed on the wall. Not front and center—but when was he ever? Even in the background, he was here. She allowed him to be here.

His feet were happy up the three remaining steps. He unplugged his phone from the charger and dialed. Two rings. Three.

"Tell me something good," Kees Justi said on the other end.

"I don't got good," Erik said. "I got great."

WARRIOR'S BREAKFAST

THE NEXT MORNING THEY slept in until ten. Then they had Warrior's Breakfast. Daisy made bacon and fried potatoes and sunny side up eggs. She toasted half a loaf of raisin pecan bread and filled her biggest cups with strong tea. The kitchen was chilly, so they sat kitty-corner at the small table in the living room, nearer to the fireplace. Their ankles twined beneath the feast.

"Happy?" she asked.

He was too happy to answer. He pushed his plate away and pulled her into his lap. His arms wrapped around her slender body and he laid his trusting head on her heart, held her tight while she fed him the last crispy bits of potato, the burnt buttery raisins and the toast crusts. His hand worked its way up the back of her shirt or inside a pant leg, caressing her softness.

"Let's go back to bed," she said. "Let's lie around in bed all day. Sleep and make love. We'll only get up to pee or eat."

"Let's do that," he said into her neck, his hand moving slower underneath her clothes.

They stayed where they were, kissing longer and deeper. She swung a leg over to straddle him. He pulled her shirt off, gathered her breasts in his hands, hungry for skin, to suck and lick and fill his mouth with her response.

She slid his shirt over his head, slid her hand down his heaving chest and trembling stomach and into his pants. His erection rose up long and hard into her palm and pulled back along the length of his spine, drawing him in both directions, a taut wire. He jerked and strained and crackled beneath her. His fingers slid into her mouth, then took the savory wet down between her legs. Past the warm pink and deeper to the hot red. Up to his knuckles in her velvet depths.

"Want to go upstairs?" she whispered.

"No," he said, pulling her pants down her hips. "I want you right here."

He kicked his own sweats free and turned her away from him. She pulled on the clip at the back of her head and let her hair fall past her bare shoulders. Reaching behind to help guide him in, she settled down snug in his lap.

"God," she said, hunched a moment over the table, her fingers white at its edge. "Nobody fucks me like you."

Through the muck and mire of emotion collected in his chest came a sword of masculine affirmation. A smug, bright blade cutting through the fog to show the sunshine of his maleness, bright and powerful and blinding.

"Nobody," he said, his voice hoarse with longing, his hands sure and strong, drawing her to lie back on him. "Nobody will ever fuck you like me."

And there in a wooden chair, with Daisy sprawled back on his chest, her knees open, her arm hooked around his head, her mouth wide and wanton, he finally felt the needle of his sexual compass swing around and find its true North. His wet, syrupy fingers felt the length of him gliding into her and he remembered. Remembered what it was like to throw out the hook and feel it *dig* into her edge. The tension of the line steady and perfect as he reeled her in to him. The tectonic plate of *her* rumbling into the plateau of *him* and the buckling heave of *us* as climax erupted like a new mountain chain. Coming like a cataclysm, a spine of jagged rock thrusting up into her. She went limp and liquid in his arms, the back of her neck damp on his shoulder. A nearly-silent scream through her open mouth and his eyes blurred at her beauty *oh, mine, you are mine, you are me, I am you, and we and us and this, only this.*

I am home.

Home by the fire and the feast with his naked lover in his lap. Plates rattling, napkins and forks clattering to the floor and the cat fleeing for more civilized company. The pendant light swinging over the table, throwing them in and out of shadow.

"Now let's go back to bed," he said. They abandoned dishes and clothing and went up to sleep like death, wrapped up in each other.

"Is this real?" one kept asking.

"This is real," the other would answer.

They loved and napped the afternoon away, falling into each other, talking afterward and then falling back asleep.

"I keep nodding off," Daisy said. "It's crazy."

"Who knew getting back together would be so exhausting," Erik said, yawning.

"Do you feel all right?" she asked. "I mean...overall?"

"I don't have one word for what I feel," he said. "It's a thousand things at the same time."

"I know. I'm so happy and my throat has such a lump in it," she said. "I can't believe you're here." She slid closer to him then moved to lie on top of him, her heart against his. "I can't believe you came back to me."

He folded his arms around her, dug his hand into the tangle of her hair. "I had to."

"I'm sorry," she whispered. "I'm sorry about what I did."

"Me too," he said, a little catch in his voice. He ran the back of his hand over his eyes once, then again and pressed it still. "I'm so sorry."

So the time passed in sleep, sex and apology.

"I'm sorry," one whispered during lovemaking, coming together in joy and sorrow.

"I'm sorry, too," the other whispered.

KING COLE

BY DAY FOUR, they were both chafed below the belt. Sore and stinging, they agreed to get out of bed, get dressed and cool it a while before they did irreparable damage.

"You look hot," Daisy said. "Boxer briefs are the best thing to happen to men's underwear."

Standing in his best things, Erik swallowed, staring at the sight of Daisy in nothing but a pair of pink boy shorts. She was stepping into her jeans, pulling them up over her hips.

In college she was slender as a blade, with a ballet dancer's uncompromisingly narrow silhouette. Clothing further diminished her. She was five feet five but looked taller and fuller when she was naked. Unclothed or not, she fit to Erik like a made-to-measure dream. The top of her head rested against the bottom of his chin. His arms could wrap neatly around her body like the bow on a present. Her small breasts and tiny butt cleaved to the curves of his hands. Her frame was spare yet it possessed a wicked, seductive strength.

With her performing career behind her, she'd gained soft weight in her breasts and a leaner weight in her legs and hips. She was sculpted and lithe, like a young jaguar. Mouth-wateringly beautiful from every angle.

"Stop staring at my ass," she said.

"I can't," he said. "You never had an ass before."

"Too bad you missed me in the nineties," she said, opening drawers. "When I was wearing thongs all the time."

Groaning at the visual, he sat on the bed, palm coming to catch his brow. "I am such an idiot."

She laughed, hooking her bra backward around her waist.

"Tell me you still wear them occasionally?" he said.

"Here." Bra fixed, she stretched a black thong around her fingers and sling-shotted it into his face. "You can take that home with you. Souvenir."

He threw it back at her. "Wear it later so I can take it off you. Then I'll take it home. Do you know nothing about souvenirs?"

Dressed, she picked up his shirt from the floor and walked over to him, turning it right side out. She sat across his knees and pulled the neck hole over his head. Kissed him as she fed one arm, then the other through the sleeves.

"Come on," she said, running her fingers through his hair, messing it up. "Off the bed. Out."

Barbegazi had three bedrooms upstairs. Daisy slept in the largest with its adjoining bathroom. The second was a guest room. The third had a barre and mirror along one wall, and her desk and file cabinets in a corner. The windows were uncovered, allowing bright, southwestern sun to stream in and throw two large rectangles on the hardwood floor.

"Is this where the magic happens?" Erik said, running his hand along the barre.

A corner of Daisy's mouth went up, then she pointed across the hall to her bedroom. "All magic happens in there, babe."

Smiling, he pointed at a set of double doors in one wall. "What's behind those?"

"Ah. A tiny bit of magic," she said, crossing the room and opening the doors. They revealed a galley room, no more than four feet wide. Ostensibly a closet, but Erik saw no clothing rods or shelves. Just the long narrow space with a porthole window at its end, sectioned like a compass rose, looking out through the branches of a tree to the lake.

"You don't store anything in here?" Erik asked.

She was looking out the window. "No. The attic has tons of space with a cedar closet. I was thinking it would make a sweet place for one of Lucky and Will's kids. A little hideaway. You could put a tiny desk in it. Or even build some kind of bed under the eaves."

"Absolutely," Erik said, tapping on the plaster walls. The studs were right where they should be. It wouldn't be hard.

She squeezed by him and took his hand. "Come on, I'll show you something else."

Outside the kitchen door, a concrete foundation was along the back of the house, facing the lake. But nothing was yet built. Erik noticed it yesterday during his walkabout but forgot to ask her about it. Sex made him stupid that way.

"Was this supposed to be something?"

"A screened-in porch," Daisy said. "It was their last planned project, but it never got past the foundation. They left me the plans they had drawn up. It was going to be pretty spectacular." She gestured to one side of the kitchen door. "All this side would be a table and chairs area so you could eat out here in summer without being bitten up. Then over on that side, wicker furniture. Three ceiling fans along the length of it."

"Strings of lights around all the windows," he said, seeing it manifest before his eyes.

"A door out to the yard here," she said, pretending to open and close one. "A path down to the water. And then on either side, all below, flowers." Hugging her sides, she paced the length of the concrete slab, tracing imaginary curved beds. "Drifts of color."

"Daisies," he said.

She grinned up at him. "Of course."

He looked out at the icy lake, squinting into the past. "Being on the water like this, it reminds me of where I grew up."

"That's right, you were on the river."

He nodded. She waited to hear more, but his train of thought sat idling in the station and he shook his head. "I don't know where I was going with that."

Shivering, Daisy came back inside and shut the kitchen door.

He folded his arms around her. "What should we do?"

"I need a Christmas tree," she said.

A window shade snapped up in his heart, flooding him with joy. "Yes, you do."

They took a ride. Sunglasses on, music blasting, they drove up Route 101 toward Fredericton, singing their faces off. At Heighleau Farms, Daisy picked a tall Douglas fir and Erik cut it down. As it was wrapped in netting and trussed with twine, Daisy bought an apple pie, chatting in French with the proprietor as she paid.

Erik had been hearing a lot more French out here in the rural areas of New Brunswick. But even when they drove closer to Fredericton to get some lunch, his ears continued to pick up the language. In parking lots, on the streets, on overheard cell phone conversations. Hostesses, waitresses and bartenders trilling a double greeting, "Bonjour. Hello." Always the bonjour first.

"This must be a treat for you," he said, as they sat in a booth at a café. "Speaking French all the time."

"It's not the French I grew up with," she said, laughing. "I call home and my mother is appalled at my accent."

He spun his spoon on the tabletop. "What did your parents say when you told them I called?" He looked up at her. "I mean, I assume you told them."

She set her chin on the heel of her hand. "Are you worried when you see him Pop will sic the proverbial dogs on you?"

"Yes." He smiled. "But I like 'when.'"

Her other hand slid across to twine with his. "They're happy for me," she said. "For us." But then her fingers were tight between his and he saw some of his own unease mirrored in her eyes. "What did your mother think of this trip?" she asked.

He let go of her hand and slid his palm along her cheek. "She told me love doesn't give a shit about geography. It's not a thing you can abandon at will. She said what I had with you deserves a second chance. I should come here and take it. And then we'd both be free."

She smiled, but her lips were pressed too hard to make it much.

His hand kept caressing her face. "It was long ago," he said softly. "And everyone sees a lot of things we didn't see back then. Including our parents."

She nodded. "So many young relationships... They exist in a vacuum. A little self-centered bubble. We were never like that. Do you know what I mean? To me, it always felt our little love story was part of a larger epic. Which sounds really smug and big-headed except so many people told me when you and I broke up... It broke a lot of other things." She leaned against his palm. "Not that us speaking again is going to fix the world, but..."

He nodded, adoring her. "It's going to make my little world feel a lot better," he said. "I know what you mean. What you did hurt my mother as well. And what I did hurt your parents. And I hurt Will bad. I really need to make time to talk to him alone. Or listen."

She took a deep breath and let it out along with her full, beautiful smile. "We'll get to it all."

They sat back so the waiter could put their plates down.

"Bon appétit," he said.

Back at Barbegazi, they wrestled the tree into its stand. Erik brought a stepladder up from the basement and Daisy brought boxes of ornaments down from the attic.

"A little mood music?" she asked.

"Sure."

She opened a CD case. "Pop burned this for me," she said. "It's all the oldies."

"I'm warning you, if Nat King Cole is on there, it's going to be ugly."

She slid the disc into the stereo and hit the play button, then held out her arms. "First track. Let's get it over with."

With the opening wail of violins, Erik's chest constricted. "Ugly," he said, drawing her tight against him.

"Evil," she said against his shoulder.

Chestnuts roasting on an open fire.

Jack Frost nipping at your nose.

And then Erik was back in time, to a 1992 Thanksgiving at Daisy's Pennsylvania home. La Tarasque in all its hospitable glory. He, Will, Lucky and David guests at Joe and Francine Bianco's table. More than guests, cherished sons and daughters. Through the long weekend they ate, drank and laughed. Stayed up late and slept in. One night they decorated the Christmas tree while all the vintage holiday standards played. And for a short magic time, the shooting had been forgotten.

The weekend imprinted in Erik's mind as the last of the great times, before he and Daisy began to spiral down into the dark.

"Fuck this fucking song," he said.

"I never forgot," she said, lifting her tear-stained face off his chest. "I never knew anything like it again. I didn't decorate another tree for years."

This tree would go undecorated for twenty-four hours. They started kissing and kissing made them spiral up into the light and back into her bed. Soft, careful touching under the covers, bringing each other around. Coming gently as falling snow and melting into deep sleep afterward, relaxed and warm and safe. Just as they had that long ago winter weekend.

They woke around four o'clock to the tone of an incoming text on Daisy's phone.

"It's Will," she said, yawning against the back of her hand. She turned the screen toward Erik.

Tell Fish to put some clothes on. I'm taking him out for a beer and a beating. Not necessarily in that order.

THE SIZE OF THE GRUDGE

Walking Down Prince Street, shoulders hunched against the wind, Erik saw Will waiting by the pub. His back and the sole of one foot were against the brick building. Bare-headed in the cold night, his breath exhaled small clouds as he looked down at his phone.

Erik met both Daisy and Will on the same day his freshman year of college. It was like being struck by lightning twice. In Daisy's case, he sat still and let the bolt hit him because one look and he wanted her. When Will crackled onto the scene though, Erik backed away. Keeping a distance measured in equal parts distrust and fascination.

A son of New Brunswick, a quarter Native American, a uniquely talented ballet dancer and a black belt mixed martial artist on the side, William Kaeger was incapable of being ignored. Erik watched him, at a loss how to process this strange, charismatic presence. Will wasn't a clown, he didn't demand attention. Like Kees Justi, Will simply had a compelling gravitational force. Wherever he went or was, that was the place others wanted to be. Erik hung back and observed through curious, narrowed eyes, realizing Will knew this, yet treated it as a responsibility, not an entitlement. He was decent to everyone and demonstratively loving to those he held dear.

"What's up, asshole," Will said, pushing off the wall.

They shook hands and Erik waited for an accompanying touch of some kind. Will's brand of affection was unapologetically physical. Hair ruffling, head locking, shoulder patting. Nudging, shoving, hugging. And often coupled with suggestive remarks.

Nothing about Will ever struck Erik as effeminate. Even within the context of ballet, Will's demeanor exuded masculinity and strength. Yet he was openly bisexual and he occasionally flirted with Erik. You couldn't call it anything else. Rather than dissecting it, looking for intentions or threats, Erik found himself teasing right back, firing innuendos and verbal side-jabs from their arsenal of inside jokes. Keeping up banter on who was checking out whose ass.

Tonight? Nothing.

Will finished texting something and slid his phone in his inside pocket. Then he looked at Erik with undisguised expectation.

"How's it going?" Erik said.

Will raised his eyebrows.

"Swing away," Erik said, offering one side of his jaw.

Fast as a cobra strike, Will reared up, fist curled. Erik stepped back, a little slower, forearms coming up to shield his head.

"God, you've gone soft," Will said, relaxing. He opened the pub door and with a curt flick of his head, said, "After you."

"After you."

"Go so I can look at your ass."

"It's not what it used to be," Erik said over his shoulder.

"What is?"

"Bonsoir, good evening," the hostess said, gathering menus. "Deux?"

She seated them in a booth where they shrugged their jackets off and ordered a round.

"All right," Will said, rolling up his shirt sleeves, showing his tattooed forearms. "Since it's our first beer in over a decade, I propose we do this speed-dating style. No gory details. You get sixty seconds to go from our last phone call to today."

Erik inhaled against the guilt of that long-distance argument. Friendshipicide. Twelve years and some of the things Erik said on the call still filled his chest with shame. It was a heated, top-of-the-lungs exchange that went beyond the severing of diplomatic ties into emotionally economic sanctions. Other than a brief conversation a few days ago, they hadn't spoken since.

"Sounds fair," Erik said.

"You go first."

"Your idea. You go first."

"Fine. Time me. I got a job with National Ballet of Canada. I danced in the corps for a year. In ninety-four, I got an offer from the Frankfurt Ballet and decided to get the hell out of North America."

"Where was Lucky?"

"In New York. We finally split up because I..." Will trailed off and touched his brow with his left hand. It was missing the ring and pinky fingers that were blown off in the shooting. He wore his heavy gold wedding band on his index finger.

Erik gently cleared his throat. "Because no details."

"Right. So I was in Germany the next four years and that's where I had my spectacular mental breakdown. No details. I got my shit together, headed to London for a spell. Then my dad started having some health issues, ended up having heart surgery and—"

"Time out," Erik said. "Is he all right?"

Will smiled. "All good. I took some time off to be with him and did some teaching workshops with New Brunswick Ballet Theater. They offered me a principal contract and I decided to take it. I started seeing Lucky again. We did the long distance thing. Then Daisy came up to audition and the company made her an offer. The girls moved up here in ninety-nine. Luck and I got married in two thousand. We had Jack. We had Sara. Number three to be determined. I went over to the theater to do a little work. I looked up and saw your ugly face. The end."

The waitress delivered their beers and they drank. Will shook his wrist out and looked at his watch. "Go."

"I left Lancaster. Sulked for a few months then went back to finish my degree at SUNY Geneseo. I stayed there about four years after I graduated. Worked at the Playhouse. Cobbled an existence from a bunch of little jobs. Perfected the art of shutting down. Then I had my spectacular breakdown. I think a year going into it and a year coming out of it. In ninety-seven I got a job at SUNY Brockport. Moved there. Met a woman. Dated her two years. Got married..."

"No details."

"Marriage fell apart. I got divorced. I headed to Lancaster and saw Kees. I picked up the phone and made a long overdue call. I bought a plane ticket. I showed my ugly face so everyone could smack the shit out of it. I ordered a beer. The end."

"All right then."

They sat in awkward silence, drumming fingers and spoons, avoiding eyes.

"Did I apologize for that phone call?" Erik asked.

Will shrugged one shoulder.

Erik forced himself to be still. "I'm sorry."

Will ran his three-fingered hand through his hair. In college, it had been an impressive mane, falling below his shoulders. He shaved it down to the scalp after the shooting. Now it was a short and shaggy cut that framed the strong T of his nose and eyebrows, and the slanting accents of his cheekbones. Erik could stand in a bar and take numbers as long as Will wasn't anywhere near.

Now Will smiled, rubbing the back of his neck. "Dude," he said. "I got so much to say, I'm kind of paralyzed. I don't know where the fuck to even start."

"I hear you."

Silence. Will drained the rest of his beer and plonked the glass back onto the table. "Jesus, if this actually were a date, I wouldn't call you again."

Erik killed his own draft. "Wouldn't blame you."

The waitress came over. "Une autre tournée, messieurs?"

"La même chose," Will said, sliding the glasses toward her. "Merci."

Erik echoed his thanks to her back. "Tournée. Does that mean a round?"

Will nodded, his fingers fidgeting around the table. Which was odd. Will was, in Erik's memory, preternaturally composed.

"I quit smoking," Will said, taking a deep breath and linking his hands on the tabletop. "Never mind the nicotine addiction. It's crazy how dependent I got on that bit of business to occupy my hands. I've never had to pay this much attention to holding still before."

"I'm thinking this conversation might be easier if we had a cord of wood to split and stack."

Will laughed. "Too bad I already have my winter supply laid in."

"Where are you and Lucky living now?"

"We're west of the city." He turned a placemat over. "You got a pen? You must. You always had a pen."

Erik had a pen and Will grinned as it was handed over. "I always had smokes, you always had a pen."

"What do you carry now?"

"Fucking gum. It's pathetic. Merci," he said to the waitress who set down the next round. He drank as he sketched a quick map of Saint John, putting his house and Daisy's house into perspective. "We love the place but it's small. And with this third kid coming we really need to think of moving. I'd rather do it before the baby comes than after."

"What's parenthood been like?"

Three slow chuckles in Will's chest. "Dude, that's not small talk. We'd need a camping trip to discuss parenthood."

Which was fine with Erik, who had severe fertility issues and wasn't yet ready to talk about them. He fished around for a topic and finally asked, "Do you miss dancing? Performing, I mean."

Two years earlier, Will and Daisy retired as principal dancers with New Brunswick Ballet and took up reins as co-artistic directors.

"I do," Will said slowly, as if taking the admission for a test drive. "But it was time."

"How so?"

Will reached behind to touch the left side of his back. "Scar tissue from the bullet wound, for one thing," he said. "Didn't bother me until I turned thirty, then every other day it seemed my back was giving me grief." He held up his maimed hand, flexed it back and rotated it around. "But more than my back it was this. Sounds fucked for a dancer, right? But all the compensating for my lost fingers over the years was doing a number on my wrist. Bad tendonitis. It started to affect my ability to partner safely. I came close to dropping Daisy in a performance one night and I knew I'd have to make a decision soon. So I made it before anyone else could. You know—leave the party while you're still having a good time?"

"But you miss it."

Will nodded. "It was a good party. Sometimes I'll be in rehearsal or watching a performance from the wings and I feel a bone-deep envy I'm not doing it anymore. But in other ways, I'm glad to be out. I can indulge my carb addiction. I wake up in the morning without my first thought being whether or not I can plié. Things like that."

"You like running a company?"

"I like running this one. And I like running it with Daisy."

"I wondered if your onstage partnership would lend itself well that way."

"Same kind of seamlessness. I start, she finishes. She jumps, I catch. I'm where she needs me to be, she stays out of my way. I don't really like teaching class, she loves it. She hates the administrative and marketing shit and I actually enjoy it. So it works."

"But who didn't see that coming?" Erik said.

"It's good," Will said, folding and unfolding his napkin. "It's been a good life."

Silence settled between them again. Erik drank his beer and tried to relax into it. Will's phone pinged from his jacket pocket and he checked it.

"Well, well, well," he said. "My wife has invited you for dinner."

"Really?"

Will squinted at the phone, running a hand through his hair. "Unless she means she's serving you as the main course."

Erik laughed weakly. "She's pissed at me, isn't she?"

Will bobbled his head around. "You have different shit to work out with all of us," he said. "She was pissed, but you know Luck. She'll bitch you out, have her say, make it clear. And then she'll put it behind her. She's not a grudge-holder."

"I'm just worried about the size of the grudge," Erik said.

"Size doesn't matter," Will said as he texted.

"Easy to say when you're well-hung."

"How would you know?"

"I lived with you for three years," Erik said. "Baron von Casual Nudity."

Will grinned and put his phone away. "Come on, finish up. Dais is already heading to our place. We'll have some dinner, we'll talk, we'll get drunk and screw. What do you say?"

"Just like old times," Erik said, killing the rest of his beer. "Minus the dinner."

BANG THE MANNY

"HOW MAD WAS LUCKY?" Erik felt compelled to ask again as he and Will walked to their cars.

"Well," Will said. "She and I had only just started up again when Columbine happened. And that day she was emotional in general but particularly angry at you."

"Me?"

"Angry you didn't call us. That not even a shooting could move you to reach out to Dais at most. Me at least."

Erik tucked his chin down into his jacket collar, swallowing around a cold empathy. He lamented almost the identical thing to his therapist years ago but in regard to his father.

Byron Fiskare had abandoned his family and disappeared without a word. Erik couldn't make the slightest conjecture if the man was even alive. The shooting incident at Lancaster, splashed across national media with Erik's name in countless articles and news reports, hadn't even flushed him out. Leading Erik to wonder if his father was indeed dead.

"Would it help to know," he said, "I spent most of that day in a drugged stupor because I saw the news coverage and passed out on the floor of the student lounge?"

Will glanced at him. "For real?"

"For real. One minute I'm watching the news with all my peers. Then I'm lying on the floor with my heart exploding through my chest. One of my more spectacular panic attacks."

"Huh. That sucks."

"I woke up in a woman's bed so it wasn't all bad."

Will laughed. "Did you bang her at least?"

"I married her."

He followed Will's car out of Saint John, west over the river into the suburbs. The beers were heavy in his stomach and he kept sighing around the tight thumping in his chest. Lucky could be even more outspoken than Will. Like him, she hated drama and preferred people voice the brutal truth so shit could get done. Her love was unconditional but it was often tough.

Erik never denied the reason he could tolerate Will's flirting was Lucky. She was the safety net under all the carrying on. The same time Erik was falling in love with Daisy, Will was falling in love with Lucky. The four of them went everywhere and did everything together. Will remained open about his bisexuality, but Erik had never seen him seriously engage with men on a sexual plane. He had only seen Will with Lucky, a guy in love with a girl. Erik was comfortable with the teasing, with the winks and cracks and insinuations because in his personal experience, to his observant eyes, Will was straight.

But when James Dow came to Lancaster in Erik's junior year, and Erik began to see first-hand the other side of Will's coin, it was another experience. James disturbed the precious status quo and reversed the polarity of Erik's carefully-ordered universe. The affair with Will raised Erik's hackles in all kinds of ways, none of them pleasant. It both repelled him and made him jealous. It started to pull threads out of the fabric of daily life. The second semester of 1992 felt like a pot about to reach the boiling point, the tension rising up to the surface and starting to break in bubbles of danger.

Then it boiled over.

And it nearly got them all killed.

Will turned into the driveway of a low-slung bungalow with a stone facade. A couple spotlights lit up a tiny porch and a yellow door. Daisy's car was already parked at the curb and Erik pulled his rental in behind it.

"It's nice," Erik said.

"It's small," Will said. "Soon to be even smaller."

Lucky met them at the front door. She kissed Will and shooed him inside, then stepped onto the porch in front of Erik and pulled the yellow door shut behind her. She crossed her arms and looked at him. His brain drained of words. All he could think was how much she resembled Glenn Close in *Fatal Attraction* and how much he felt like a rabbit about to be boiled.

"I'm sorry," he said.

She took a step and hit him.

"I know," he said. "I'm sorry."

Her open hand smacked him again, hard against his upper arm. She planted her other palm in his chest and shoved him backward. "Get the fuck off my porch, asshole."

"Finally some refreshing honesty," Erik said, stumbling down the steps.

"You fucking punk." She followed, backing him down the walk toward the driveway, punctuating her lament with a volley of slaps. "You son of a bitch, I hate you. You stupid, stupid, stupid thing. I could *kill* you."

She wasn't fooling around. He couldn't recall being hit this way since his pissy adolescent days, when his mother wouldn't hesitate to swat him for being fresh.

"I love you too," he said, shielding his head.

She had him up against the car now, still letting him have it. After a few more good slaps, Erik started dodging them. He got a hand around one of her wrists, then the other, pulling her in, too close to hit.

"Don't fucking hug me," she said, her voice thick with tears.

"I'm not." He drew her against him, where, finally, she crumpled and sobbed.

"I hate you."

"I'm sorry," he said against her head, taking a handful of her blonde spiral curls and holding them to his face. His own eyes watery and burning.

"You broke his heart," she said through her sobs, her fists pounding weakly on his back. "You broke Will's heart, do you know that? Do you know what you did to him? You stupid, stubborn ass."

"I know," he whispered. "I was wrong. I'm sorry, Luck."

Now the hands that punched and slapped him turned tender, holding his head, caressing his shoulders, and all the while she was weeping, "Oh why, Erik, why? Why'd you do it?"

"I'm so sorry." He held her tight, sniffing hard against memory. Lucky crawling around in the blood on the stage floor after the shooting, in a frantic race against time and veins. Will was shot through the side and had his hand nearly blown off. Daisy's femoral artery was severed. Together Erik and Lucky pressed their hands against the wounds and held back the tide until help arrived. And it didn't stop there. Another night, another bloody floor, and Erik holding onto Lucky as she miscarried a baby at Jay Street. So much blood over all those years. Blood that permanently stained so many memories.

Our little love story was part of a larger epic.

And Erik had closed the book and left it all behind.

"I hate you," Lucky said, laying her cheek against his jacket and exhaling.

"I hate me too," he said, slowly becoming aware of a presence that eclipsed their emotion: Lucky's belly, hard and curved against his. He had never hugged a pregnant woman before. It surprised him, the persistent and pervasive heat. It even vibrated slightly, like a little engine in the cold night. Above that awesome warm sphere, Lucky's shoulders began to shiver.

"You're cold," he said. "Go inside."

"All right," she said, wiping her eyes on his scarf. She turned to head up the walk but Erik stayed where he was.

"Can I come in?" he asked.

She turned, dragging the back of her hand across her face, sniffing and considering. Her magnificent cloud of curly hair backlit by the porch lights. A deep breath and at last her smile. "Yes, asshole, you can come in."

"Neither got Lucky's hair," Erik said, looking at Jack and Sara Kaeger, who were both dark-haired, sleek and slim like their father.

"I know, right?" Lucky said. "But hey, I'm not complaining. Hair like mine is a bitch. I wouldn't wish it on anyone."

"I love your hair," Will said, burying his face in it before coming to sit next to Erik on the couch. Beers and potato chips were passed while domestic chaos raged. A little overwhelmed, Erik shrank back into himself, observing.

Daisy apparently was Jack's property and the boy was throwing Erik some appraising looks over his shoulder with an expression far beyond his four years. He leaned on Daisy's knees now, speaking French as he showed her a myriad of things, his back firmly to Erik's gaze.

Sara, who was just past two, kept up a constant stream of chatter to anyone who would turn an ear in her direction.

"Does she ever take a breath?" Erik said, laughing as he was handed dolls, blocks, stuffed animals and crayons under a narrative volley that seemed part French, part English and part Swahili.

Not laughing, Will shook his head. "She never shuts up," he said quietly. "Dude. I'm not even kidding. She talks in her sleep. I mean she never. Shuts. Up." He slumped into the cushions and his last word dissolved in a small moan of despair. He exhaled heavily and for a split second, his head touched Erik's shoulder.

"It's all right," Erik said, smiling, his hands full of toys.

Sara did take a breath then, pausing to look from her father to Erik and back again. She said something Erik couldn't understand and Will laughed and pulled the little girl onto his lap.

"She asked if Lucky spanked you before."

Erik nodded at Sara, pushing his lower lip out a little. Looking sympathetic, she handed him another crayon.

Finally the Kaegers' nanny herded the kids upstairs for baths and bed and the four friends were able to sit at the small kitchen table and eat. Over beef stew and buttered noodles, Erik remained slightly disengaged. It could hardly be helped when conversation kept slipping into work mode. Lucky, after years in private practice, was now the physical therapist for New Brunswick Ballet. She, Will and Daisy were friends and co-workers and their lives rotated around the theater and their houses accordingly. Unfamiliar with either, Erik ate, listened and watched. Beneath the table, Daisy's calf crossed over his, and as Lucky passed dishes, she would often caress his arm.

It was enough for now. He was happy to just be included.

The nanny looked around the kitchen doorway and waved goodnight. "All prison cells secure. Nine o'clock tomorrow?" she asked Lucky.

"Ten's fine. Thanks, Sofia."

To another chorus of goodnights, Sofia let herself out.

"She Italian?" Erik asked.

"Spanish," Will said.

"Basque," Lucky said.

"Whatever," Will said. "The kids like her. After the string of au pair nightmares we've had, she could be from Mars for all I care."

"They all come from Europe?" Erik asked.

"Most of them," Will said.

"And always girls?"

Will nodded.

"They tried the manny thing once," Daisy said.

"Can we not get into that?" Will said.

"Manny?" Erik looked around the table.

"Male nanny," Daisy said. "Manny. What was his name, Alonzo?"

"Alessio," Lucky said, getting up to clear the dishes. "He was the Italian. That got out of hand fast."

"What," Erik said, handing Lucky his plate. "He was hitting on you?"

Daisy and Lucky pointed to Will and Will pointed to himself.

"Jesus," Erik muttered.

Daisy laughed and got up to help clear. "It was a train wreck."

"Hey." Will spread out his hands. "I behaved. Right, Luck?"

"You were a paragon of restraint," she said, running a hand over his head. "And we're all so proud of you."

When her back was turned again, Will winked at Erik.

"Don't wink at me," Erik said.

"What?" Daisy looked over the top of the refrigerator door.

"What?" Will said.

Lucky turned around. "William."

"What?"

Lucky threw a dishtowel at him. "Did you lie to me about banging the manny?"

Will deflected it back to her. "I didn't bang the manny."

"You totally banged the manny," Erik said.

"You weren't even here," Will said. "All right? We're talking 2004 BEC. Before Erik Came...Back. And I'm still mad at you."

"I'm sorry," Erik said. The mood was light, but he was painfully aware of the lines still drawn and only how far jokes would get him. How some things might not be ready to be joked about.

Will folded his napkin and tossed it on the table. "Suck my cock and we'll talk about it."

"I won't be able to answer."

Will stood up and pointed a finger at Erik. "I didn't miss you. At all."

"Nope," Lucky said. "He didn't cry one tear."

"None of us," Daisy said, coming to sit in Erik's lap.

He slid his arms around her waist, laid his forehead then his cheek against her. "Well, I did," he said. "Cried every night. Buckets."

"Poor you," Lucky said with a little snort. But as she leaned to collect more dishes, her hand settled soft on the back of Erik's neck.

AT HOME

ERIK TURNED IN THE rental car. The *Nutcrackers* were finished, the Imperial Theater was dark and Daisy was off from work until January. He didn't need his own ride.

They made a few plans. They'd spend Christmas Eve together, and Christmas Day with the Kaegers. If a babysitter could be found, the two couples might go out for New Year's. Maybe. For the most, Erik and Daisy let the time come to them unplanned. Erik found the joy of being with her and doing absolutely nothing wasn't something he could take for granted ever again.

She did take him on small tours. It was cold for outdoor sightseeing, but she drove him up to see the Reversing Falls, where the Saint John River squeezed through a narrow gorge before emptying into the Bay of Fundy. Every twelve hours, the tides of the Bay forced the river current to reverse itself, resulting in a series of impressive rapids.

"You get much snow here?" Erik asked.

"Sure. But it rains a lot in winter, too, so the snow doesn't stay around for long."

As he wandered with her around Saint John, he was introduced. To the bartender Nick at the Wharf Tavern. To the owner of Kate's Bakery, where Daisy always got her breakfast. To company members and friends they passed on the street. The proprietor of a tiny restaurant greeted Daisy like a countess. "Madame Bianco, bonsoir," he said, kissing her cheeks. And then turned to Erik with a smile and a hearty handshake. "Et monsieur. Bienvenue."

Erik liked the sound of monsieur. He felt welcome in this pretty city on the water, dressed up for the holidays. He liked being out and about, hearing the mix of English and French. But mostly, he liked being at Barbegazi. Just being.

Daisy had never been an adventuress or party girl. "I like to be dancing," she said when they first met. "Or I like to be at home."

As such, she lived at opposite ends of the physical spectrum: full out to the extremes of her capability, in magnificent movement, or still, doing small peaceful things. Still wiped out from all the emotional catchup, Erik was content to join her at the quiet end of the range. He played the piano. Daisy read. Something was always cooking on the stove or baking in the oven. They drank an obscene amount of tea. They built up the fire and did dopey things like play board games or tackle a thousand-piece jigsaw puzzle. Sometimes they curled up on the couch and watched TV. But more often they were in the two mismatched armchairs, Edith and Archie, with their mugs of tea and snacks, talking and talking and talking.

He moved easily through her house. When his suitcase was depleted, he did a couple loads of laundry. When they ran out of kitchen staples, he knew how to get to the corner market. He brought in wood and took out the garbage. Turned off lights and locked doors before they went to bed.

Bed. Bed. When the sun went down they swung to the other side of the spectrum and made love like monsters. Desire was a subtraction, leaving them with less than what they had started with, desperate to connect again. One more time. All night long. Erik couldn't get enough.

Sometimes Daisy growled and clawed at his body, wanting him to make her scream. Other times they made nearly no noise and the skin of one melted to the other. Feelings and the words to describe them piled up like boulders at the back of Erik's mouth. Too big for description or definition. He lay with Daisy in his arms, mute and choking on his own experience. Simultaneously pulled apart and pressed together by euphoria, despair, longing, pining, celebration and grief.

One rainy day he passed a couple hours in the upstairs office, talking first with his mother on the phone, then with his brother on the computer. Signing off, he inhaled at the yummy smell wafting upstairs. Something was in the oven. Hoping it was roasted potatoes, he followed his nose down and heard Daisy talking in the kitchen. He presumed she was on the phone as well.

She wasn't.

"It's not a question of talent," she said, opening the oven. "Her technique is supernatural but she has no imagination. This ballet requires a sense of drama she simply doesn't have."

Amused, Erik shrank back from the doorway, watching as Daisy pulled the oven rack out and ran a spatula through whatever was on the baking tray. Listening as she kept talking.

"Nice girl, don't get me wrong." Daisy slid the rack back in with a bang. "She's beautiful in the classics, but for this kind of passionate, edgy work, she's not who we want." She shut the oven door and tossed the potholder mitt on the counter. "She can't carry the music."

She turned around and jumped back as she saw Erik. He was leaning on the jamb now, arms and ankles crossed. His stomach filled with an amused, goofy love.

"Hi," she said.

He smiled.

Her tongue pushed at the inside of a cheek as she took a bunch of parsley and set it on the cutting board. She picked up her favorite chopping knife. "How much of that did you hear?"

He shrugged. "It was adorable."

She cleared her throat and started running the blade through the leaves. "I'm used to living alone," she said. "And I talk to myself a lot."

Something in her manner was beyond embarrassment and he downgraded his expression from teasing to kind. "I get it."

"I kind of forgot you were here," she said, her voice tight around the words. "I mean, I didn't forget but I…"

"Dais, come on," he said, walking over to the island. "It's no big deal. I talk to myself too."

"I know." She tried to smile, but her mouth constricted at the corners, fighting to fall down. She forced a laugh as her eyes overflowed.

"Actually, no, I don't know what this is," she said, turning to wipe her face on her shoulder but only getting her chin. "I really don't. Shit." She put the knife down and picked up a dishtowel, swiped it at each cheek.

"Dais."

"This is stupid."

"Not it's n—"

"I don't know what this is," she said, her voice now filled with alarm. "You overheard me nattering to myself, so what? Why the fuck do I feel like crying?"

She was crying.

"You're here," she said, picking up the knife and toying the point through the pile of parsley. "You can catch me talking to myself and think it's adorable. That's awesome. I should be happy."

He moved to her side. "Are you?"

She sniffed. "I don't know what's happening. I don't know why I'm so emotional."

He reached and set the backs of his fingers on her tear-tracks. His other hand dropped onto hers on the knife and made her let go the handle.

"I think it's because I can hear you," he said softly.

She turned into him, face in her palms, knuckles against his chest. His arms folded around her, his hands sliding into her hair. He made his body a tight hard scaffold around her quaking limbs. Knowing now she was weeping for the years of silence, when she talked at him, not to him. Talked into the air because her voice was the only company she had.

"Do you love me," she said into his heart, skinless and defenseless.

He pulled her hands from her face and took her head. He kissed her. Forehead. Each cheek. Nose. Chin. Mouth.

"I love you," he whispered. "And I can hear you."

ERIK COULDN'T FALL ASLEEP that night. He lay awake, staring at the ceiling and silently mouthing, *I can hear you.* Thinking about the power of the human voice. Thinking about his brother.

Peter Fiskare had been left profoundly deaf in infancy, when both he and Erik suffered a bout of mumps. After later contracting meningitis, the deafness was near total. Pete was learning to get by with hearing aids and extensive speech therapy when Byron Fiskare abruptly and mysteriously abandoned the family.

Erik's mode of survival was shutting down large swathes of his memory. Even now, at thirty-five, parts of his childhood were redacted in thick black ink, erased from the record. Pete chose silence. He tore off his hearing aids and with rare exceptions, refused to speak. He remained electively mute through his young adulthood. He went to college. He took a year off to travel, moving easily through the world with sign language and guide dogs. He was barely twenty-four when he married. He and Laura ran a large dog shelter in Rochester and trained rescue canines for service therapy.

After his kids were born—a daughter, Valerie, and a son, Aaron—Pete gradually began using his voice again. He got fitted for new aids and worked with a speech therapist. Four years ago, he elected to participate in clinical trials for a new type of cochlear implant.

"Why now?" Erik asked, excited for his brother but curious about the decision.

"Because I'm ready," Pete said.

Pete flew out to Chicago for the surgery and missed Erik's wedding to Melanie. Three weeks later, Erik and his mother were invited to watch when the implant was activated. They squeezed into a little room with Laura and the kids as the device was ceremoniously turned up.

Sitting in a chair next to the technician's desk, Pete's expression was one of wide-eyed anticipation, but he wasn't terribly emotional. At points, he looked overwhelmed, partly from the onslaught of sound, and partly from all eyes being on him. For the most part, he kept his gaze on the technician, Beverly, who urged him to be patient as the device worked with his brain to sort out all the new stimuli.

"What's that?" he said as Beverly shuffled some papers around.

"These are the insurance forms which—"

"I mean, what's that sound?" he said.

"It's the paper." She moved the sheets through her hands, then separated one out and crumpled it. Pete stared as if she'd made a hundred dollar bill manifest from thin air.

"Paper makes noise?"

Beverly looked back at the family. "Every time," she said. "Every time they ask and every time it blows my mind. Yes," she said to Pete. "Paper makes noise."

She took a scrap and slowly tore it in half for him to hear. Pete took a half and tore it himself. Then crumpled the pieces and laughed. Stopped short. Laughed again.

"That's me laughing," he said, putting fingers to his head. Then he touched his chest. "I can kind of hear my heartbeat," he said. "It's so weird." He smiled at his small audience and took a deep inhale. "And I can hear my breath. How do you get anything done with all this noise?"

Christine was crying, trying to hide it with laughter. "I'm sorry," she said, her voice a mess. "It's just..." She gave up and pointed at Pete with the tissue box, almost as if she were about to throw it at him.

"God, Ma, you sound worse than I do," Pete said.

Then Christine did throw the tissues. "I'll spank you. I mean it."

Pete deftly caught the box and drummed his fingers on it. Cocked his head and drummed them again, listening. He smiled at his wife. *Can't wait to hear you in b-e-d*, he signed.

Laura smiled back. "You know the kids can s-p-e-l-l?"

Erik had stayed quiet all this time, cross-armed in a corner of the room. Out of the way and observing. Finally, Pete set the tissue box aside and looked over at him.

"What's with you," he said. "You never shut up."

Erik smiled but couldn't think of anything.

"Say something," Pete said.

At a loss, Erik swallowed and managed, "Hello?"

Eyebrows wrinkled, Pete gestured *louder.*

Erik cleared his throat. "Can you hear me?"

Pete seemed to draw back a little. He nodded, his eyes welling up, staring at Erik like a little boy would at Spiderman.

"You can hear me?" Erik said, taking a step closer.

Pete nodded, hands twisting. "I can hear you," he said. Every wall was down. He looked small in the chair, staring up at his brother.

"How do I sound?" Erik said.

The tears started to track down Pete's face. Laura turned away. Christine, tissue-less, buried her face in her hands. Aaron and Valerie looked wide-eyed from their father to their uncle.

"It's me," Erik said. "This is me."

"I can hear you," Pete said.

Erik crouched between his feet, his hands on Pete's upper arms. "This is my voice."

Pete was crying then, bent over double in the chair. Erik shifted onto his knees, babbling nonsense just to keep his voice present.

"I can hear you," Pete said, his shoulders shaking, his hands fisted around Erik's shirt. "I can hear you."

Now Erik rolled toward Daisy, conscious of the creak of springs and the whisper of cotton and quilting against skin. The watery click in his throat when he swallowed. His heartbeat muffled in the ear that was pressed into the pillow. The tiny sigh in Daisy's chest when he touched the back of her neck.

"Can you hear me?" he said.

She sighed again.

"I love you," he said. And even after he knew she was asleep once more, he kept whispering little nonsense things. Just to keep his voice present.

MY GOOD DEED

WILL TEXTED ERIK THE day before Christmas Eve.

Want to grab a beer and a steak? And my ass?

Erik replied. ***Is this the second date? I thought I blew it.***

Yeah, well, I've always been kind of stupid when it comes to you.

As they drove into Saint John, their conversation flowed a little easier. Will played Jimi Hendrix on the stereo, which filled any awkward gaps with air guitar.

"This is *Are You Experienced?*" Erik asked. "I don't think I've ever listened to this album in its entirety."

"I rediscovered it when I was in Germany," Will said. "I choreographed a solo to 'Fire.' Lately I'm thinking I could add to it. You know, like a rock ballet set entirely to Hendrix."

"Huh," Erik said, air drumming now.

They parked in a municipal lot and walked down King Street toward Market Square. The streets were lined with lighted trees and the air smelled of snow.

Will's phone pinged as they passed Lawton's Pharmacy.

"How does she do that?" Will said. "I swear, Lucky has a sixth sense for when I'm passing a drug store. And she always needs something."

"Maybe she's put a tracker app on your phone."

"I wouldn't be surprised. Sends her an alert anytime I'm in range."

While Will collected his goods, Erik hung out in the magazine aisle, flipping through *Sports Illustrated.*

"Dude. Check it out." Will materialized by Erik's shoulder and was pointing discreetly to the next aisle over.

Erik glanced over the top of the display shelves. A third of the adjacent aisle was the family planning section and a young teenage boy was facing down the condoms. Clearly overwhelmed by the selection and ne rvous from the presence of a middle-aged woman two feet away, comparison shopping fiber supplements. The boy kept looking up nervously, shuffling his feet, then trying to study the display again.

"Watch this." Will walked briskly down their aisle, rounded the end and headed toward the boy. He stopped and regarded the shelves a few seconds.

"Excuse me." Without making eye contact, Will made a confident choice and walked off toward the registers. Erik flipped pages and watched the boy stare after Will. Then the boy reached and took the identical brand. Erik put the magazine back and headed to the front.

"He get them?" Will said.

"Yep."

"Same kind?"

"Yep."

"My good deed for the day." He held the bag up as they headed outside. "You got need of rubbers, my friend?"

Erik shook his head. "No. But if you're ready for some gory details, I got a story for you."

"So," Erik said, when they were seated in a booth at the steak house and had ordered. "My marriage started disintegrating when we started trying to have kids."

Will held up a palm. "Time out. Let me just say I'm glad it didn't happen. I suck and I think I'm about to suck even worse but go on."

"Well, nothing was happening so I got tested first and turns out I'm shooting blanks."

A long stare. "Do they know why?"

"It might have been from the mumps when I was a kid. Might've been just a flukey thing. At the end of the day, they couldn't point to any one reason. And I don't exactly shoot blanks. My counts are low and whatever can be counted doesn't swim. We tried to do IVF, but I had about four different procedures to extract sperm and they just never got anything viable."

He knew the general luxury of spilling your guts to a buddy. But he'd forgotten the particular comfort in slicing off a bit of a problem and handing it to Will to hold. Something in his chest seemed to both jump up in remembered joy and pass out in relief at the same time.

I missed him.

"Dude..." Will sat back, rubbing his forehead. "That sucks. I'm sorry. I don't know what to say."

Erik started to shrug it off. But this was the new him. He worked through the impulse to dismiss and held still. Took a taste of sympathy. Let the idea of sterility sit down next to him and properly introduce itself. He looked at Will as a father of two. Two and a half. An extension of his blood and his name. A manifestation of his and Lucky's love. A legacy. The most elemental part of being a human being.

As he thought, Erik felt the links of the gold chain around his neck. The necklace had been handed down through generations of Fiskare men. Eldest son to eldest son. But Erik was the end of the line. A branch of the tree that might not bear fruit. If he died with no son, he'd leave the necklace to his nephew Aaron.

Which ought to have consoled him but didn't.

It kind of sucked.

And it hurt.

"Believe it or not, I think I'm taking it in for the first time," he said.

Will nodded. "Holy fuck, you really did shut down."

"Yeah."

"Maybe... This is probably the shaman in me talking, but maybe you were so good at shutting down, you shut down on a cellular level."

Erik looked across at Will, met his eyes and held on tight. "I could get behind that."

"What was Dais' reaction when you told her?"

Erik swallowed. "I haven't yet. I'm kind of paralyzed between it's too soon and it's too important."

Will checked his watch. "Yeah, give it a few more hours. You just met."

They laughed into their beers. "When," Erik said, "I mean, if Dais and I ever get to that point—"

"You will."

He blew out a sigh. "I can't look that far. I'm still learning how to feel what I feel as I'm feeling it. All I know is it's going to matter."

Will nodded. "I'm really sorry. I have no reference point."

"When I called Daisy on Thanksgiving? She made a crack about how you'd sneeze and Lucky would be knocked up."

Will smiled, rolling his eyes as if embarrassed at the virile feat. They pushed aside their drinks and silverware as the waitress set a strip steak in front of each of them, arranged dishes of creamed spinach and sautéed mushrooms. "Bon appétit," she said.

Will speared a mushroom and ate it. "When I said 'you will' before? I meant you will get to that point. Or at least to that conversation. She wants a family. It's why her last relationship fell apart."

"Ray?"

"Oh, you know about Ray?"

"I know she was with him a few years and it was pretty serious." He took a bite of steak. The charred, peppered sear gave way into melting pink goodness, forcing a small grunt of pleasure from his chest.

"It was definitely the happiest I'd seen Dais since college. And Ray was a great guy. I got nothing bad to say about him. But..." Will took a bite of his own and closed his eyes. "Jesus, that's good. Sorry, what was I saying?"

"Nothing bad to say about Ray, but."

"Right. It actually feels good to talk about this because Lucky and I were all smiles to Daisy's face and then we'd lie in bed at night and moan about it. *Think she'll marry him? Why wouldn't she? She should. He's great to her. Yeah, but if they get married, it'll be the end.*"

"The end?"

"That's how we felt—if she married him it wouldn't be the beginning of a beautiful life but the end of some crazy little dream we had that you'd come back."

Their meals were demanding attention and talk died away while they ate. The food was outstanding. Erik kept closing his eyes in appreciation, his stomach yearning like a dog who wanted the belly rub to go on forever.

"Ray was older than her," Erik said.

"By like fifteen years. He was in a totally different place. He'd gotten married young, had his kids while still practically a teenager. He was about to become a grandfather. His empty nest was beautifully arranged and Daisy wanted to fill it with babies."

Erik had been wolfing the last bit of steak, but "babies" made it go cold and tough in his mouth.

Will went on. "And we sucked so bad. We felt like shit, lying around sighing about it. *I hope she doesn't marry him. God we suck, why shouldn't she be happy, she should marry him. Oh God, don't marry him, it's the end of hope...*"

Erik managed to laugh in the wobbly security of how things turned out.

Will glanced up. "Just out of curiosity?"

"I know where this is going."

"What would you have done if you called and she was married?"

"Dude." Erik carefully scraped together the last forkful of creamed spinach. "It's a good thing I'm still an expert at not thinking about shit. Because I can't even think about that shit."

"You thought about it. Come on."

Busted, Erik gave it a try. "It would have been...not a good thing."

Will wiped his mouth, revealing a grin. "I would've helped you steal her."

"Shut up."

"Telling you."

"Jesus fuck, I don't know what I would've done."

Will pushed his plate away. "Would you still have called me?"

Erik tried to rearrange events, fold time into a different origami ornament. A different scenario. "I like to think so. I had it in my mind that my shit to work out with you was entirely separate from Daisy. I had things to put right with you no matter what happened with her. I could only do one thing at a time though. And no offense, but she smells nicer than you."

"Fair enough." Will folded his napkin and tossed it on the table. A bit of silence as Erik finished eating.

"You haven't told Dais about the fertility thing yet?" Will said. "For real?"

"For real. Why?"

Will laughed a little. "Nothing."

"What?"

"It used to tickle the shit out of me when you'd come to me with a problem. Feels like old times."

Erik set his silverware across his plate and pushed it aside. "I missed you," he said, wiping his mouth.

Will caught the waitress's eye and signed the air with an invisible pen. He rubbed his hands together, then back through his hair. "I have some Christmas shopping left to do," he said. "You got time to come with?"

"Time I got," Erik said.

ANXIETY TRAVELS

SNOW WAS FALLING AS they walked back to the municipal parking lot. Will had a handful of gift bags. Erik had looked for something for Daisy, but nothing moved him to a purchase.

"Who'd you sleep with all those years?" Will asked. "Before you were married."

"Too many people."

"All female?"

"Shut up."

Will laughed. "We always said you could stand in bars and take numbers."

"Well it wasn't in bars. And I was picky about what numbers I took. I didn't want anything serious. I barely wanted to talk. I ended up nailing a lot of older women. It was easier."

"You whore."

"I plead the Fifth."

"What did they look like?"

"What do you mean?"

"The chicks I dated after Lucky? All of them tall and brunette with straight hair. Not one little, curly blonde. Couldn't do it."

"My ex-wife is black."

"Shut up."

"Hand to God."

"You really went to the opposite pole."

"It was funny when it happened though. I went so long thinking my heart was shut down for good, but I came across her in the theater one day. This little voice inside started tugging at my sleeve. *Hey. Girl. Look. See? Girl. Pretty girl. Fetch.*"

"I hear you, I couldn't believe when I felt attracted to another woman after Lucky. Anyway, back to her being black... What was that like?"

Erik shrugged. "It honestly wasn't anything until we were trying to have kids. And then it...showed up like a snake. Somehow. We had some ugly arguments, man. One in particular." He shook his head hard, diffusing the memory. "I was a shitty husband at the end. She called me out on a bunch of behavior. I was defensive at the time but looking back now, she knew me better than I knew myself. Which sucks."

Will grunted. "Self-realization usually does."

"Did you have anyone serious? At all?"

"Not really," Will said. "Anytime something started to turn serious, it started to rub me wrong. Love made me anxious. Then again, everything was making me anxious at that point. So I did the obvious thing and ran away to Europe."

"Anxiety travels in your luggage."

"No shit."

Erik waited for Will to take the bait, maybe talk about his breakdown in Germany. But the hook went untouched.

"So what will you do now?" Will said. "About Dais, I mean."

Erik dug his hands further in his pockets. "Half of me wants to resign by phone and let my landlord have a yard sale. The other half knows I can't just bail. So I'll stay for Christmas. Ring in the New Year if she'll have me. Then decide what next."

"Stay through New Year's, then go home? Try it long-distance?"

"I can't see that being too sustainable, but... I mean, you tell me. Am I insane to just drop my life in Brockport and come here?"

"Is your life really in Brockport?" Will asked.

"True."

"You want to wait another year or two while you guys *date* or some shit? Just because it looks sensible on paper?"

"I could say I should stay close to my mother, but she's in Florida half the year and she has Fred. I could argue I want to be close to Pete, but he has Laura and the kids. Nobody in New York is depending on me to stay." He looked at Will for validation but Will wasn't there.

Erik turned. Will had stopped at a storefront and was peering into the window. He looked over at Erik and beckoned with his chin.

Erik went. It was a jewelry store. Will touched the glass with a gloved fingertip, pointing to a white mannequin head. Its chin was turned aside to show off a thin gold chain at the neck, off which hung a tiny gold fish. Not a carved bob like Erik's charm but flat, no bigger than his little fingernail. Next to it hung a single freshwater pearl.

Erik looked at his friend, then back at the necklace.

"I don't believe in coincidences," Will said.

The bell on the jamb tinkled as Erik pushed the door open and walked into the perfumed warmth of the shop.

"THINGS GOING ALL RIGHT with Will?" Daisy asked that night in bed.

"Yeah," he said. "Yeah, it's good."

"What do you talk about?"

"Oh God, all kinds of shit. You. Me. Us. Life. Parenthood." He told her about the boy and the condoms in the drug store.

"You know he and Lucky didn't plan this third baby," she said. "After Sara, they were done. One boy, one girl, they were set. So Lucky got an implant. Eighteen months later...surprise."

"Holy shit. Will must have sneezed really hard one night."

She laughed. "It wasn't exactly joyful when they found out. It was definitely a decision to have it, not a no-brainer."

He turned onto his side. "Lie against my back?" he asked.

She snugged up to his shoulder blades, her hand coming around to rest on his heart. Bastet jumped on the bed and settled between their calves, kneading the mattress and purring.

Erik took a deep breath. "Something I want to talk about."

"All right," she said.

"The other night?"

"Which night. We have several now."

He threaded his fingers with hers. "The first night I was here. When I asked if you needed me to use something."

"I'm on the pill."

"I know. But what if you hadn't been?"

"Ah." She kissed his head and gently closed her teeth on the top of his ear. "You mean would I trap you into staying by getting pregnant?"

"Well, I'm staying anyway," he said, while his mind bit its nails.

Quit fucking around and tell her.

He sighed. Did he have to?

Yes. Now. Everything on the table.

"That's your troubled sigh," Daisy said.

He smiled. "You remember."

"Qu'est-ce qui se passe?"

He rolled over to face her. "My marriage began to fall apart when we tried to have kids," he said, taking both her hands. "The shortest, simplest story is I have some major plumbing issues and I probably couldn't get you pregnant even if I wanted to."

The room raised its eyebrows. Even Bastet looked up from washing a paw and stared at him. *Really?*

He squeezed his eyes tight then opened them. "That sounded better in my head than it did out loud."

"Shh," she said, her own eyes closed. "I'm rearranging my personal narrative."

He pressed the clump of their fingers to his mouth and waited.

The room went away on tiptoes.

A click in Daisy's throat as she swallowed. When she opened her eyes, the blue-green of her gaze was blurred and wet.

"I'm so sorry," he said.

"Sorry for what?"

"I know why things ended with Ray."

Her smile flickered. "Will told you?"

He nodded.

Her chest filled up, then slowly deflated. "Ray wasn't you," she said. "And this conversation isn't about me."

"Isn't it, though?"

"It's about us." A single tear tracked diagonally from one eye to her nose. Her hand settled soft on his face. Her thumb moved along his lower lip. Her breath became his breath.

"Erik, I'm in love with you," she said.

"Still?"

"It never stopped." She leaned up and brushed her mouth against his. "I've rearranged now," she said. "And the shortest, simplest story is I still want you."

"Even if it's not your dream?"

"You are my dream. I want us."

"You want a family, too."

"I know a lot of different ways to have a family."

He made and discarded a half dozen sentences. "It's hard to say what I want to say without getting way ahead of myself."

"Tell me."

"I was ambivalent about kids with Melanie. But with you... If the time comes... I mean, when it comes...it's going to matter. I already know it's going to be different. Because it's you. And it's us."

She nodded. "When it's our time," she said. "I'll do anything. Right now, all I want is you. And to know where you are."

He nodded, lost in her eyes. Perfect peace drawing over him like a glove welcoming cold fingers. He ran his hand soft over her head, remembering all the nights he reached into the empty dark beside him and made her materialize under his touch. Laid his palm on a cheek that wasn't there and felt the loving weight of her gaze settle on him and press him into stillness. Both marveling and lamenting how no other woman ever made him feel as complete and content.

"Dais, I love you," he whispered.

He sat up then, got out of bed and went looking for his jacket. Dug in the inside pocket for the gift box with the necklace. His plan had been to give it to her on Christmas morning.

Plans changed.

She lifted the lid from the box. Stared at the necklace a moment. Then closed her mouth up in her palm. He took the chain from its nest of white cotton and undid the clasp.

"I'll have to go back home soon," he said, fastening it at her nape. "But this is so I can stay here with you."

Daisy released the hair she had been holding out of the way. Cupping the charms in her hand, holding that hand against her collarbones, she turned into his arms.

"You came back," she said.

"I'm staying," he said.

She pressed her face into his chest and cried.

EXTRACTION

THEY IGNORED THE DAYS that fell away faster and faster. The New Year was nigh. They made dinner reservations with Will and Lucky at The Supper Club. Erik had nothing suitable to wear so he went with Will to buy a shirt and sport coat.

"I've waited years to dress you," Will said.

"Just so you can undress me?"

Will pointed an empty hanger at him. "I didn't miss you. At all."

Will insisted Erik get a new pair of shoes. They were, Erik had to admit, perhaps the finest shoes he'd owned in his life. He felt three inches taller in them. If asked to dance, he might even say yes.

As he packed his bag his last night in New Brunswick, he left the shoes in Daisy's closet

"Are you crazy?" she said. "Take them."

"Nope," he said. "These stay here."

"I trust you, if that's what this is about."

"I know you do. And they're staying here."

He led her around Barbegazi that night, intent on making love in every room. From the obvious to the absurd. Laughing up against the linen closet door and then shivering on the basement steps. He overlooked nothing.

"I want you to walk around this house and see me everywhere," he said, pressing her to walls, floors, piano keys, cushions and counters. Marking his territory with a vengeance.

"This is your home now," she said, leading him back to her bedroom. "I want it to be your place, too."

The candlelit air pulled apart, gossamer threads of aching need stretching across the hours.

"God, honey," she said, stretched out on her back at the corner of the mattress, her arms long over her head. Her silky legs rested on his shoulder. He curled an arm around them like a cello, running his mouth along her calf.

"You're so good," she whispered, pulsing around him.

"Only with you," he said. "I'm best with you."

Their shadows danced across the walls and ceiling. The flickering light caught in the tender curve of her throat and the gold fish curled in its hollow. The coiled heat in his belly reversed direction and spiraled down, heading for the warm wet that had no name. His awareness swelled, pressed against his eardrums. A wave of furious release tumbled down from his head as the intense, squeezing pressure rocketed up his spine. He checked the impulse to thrust, to force it over the top. He held still. Let it rip through him like a slow-motion bolt of lightning.

"Erik," she said, one last time before her voice disintegrated. The spiral threaded out and his insides caved in after it. Teeth clenched, eyes screwed shut and the world exploding behind his eyelids, he dropped his head down on his chest as he came into her and she came down on him.

"Stay awake," she whispered in his arms afterward. "Let me fall asleep first."

He'd been about to ask for the same thing. Sleep was too much like leaving and he didn't want to be awake without her. So they tried hard to fall together, breathing and blinking and eventually drifting away.

The morning dawned grey and chilly and they moped over tea in the kitchen, picking at toast.

"Don't come with me to the airport," Erik said. "It'll be like fucking *Casablanca* and I can't handle it. I don't want you driving home upset afterward. Let Will take me."

"All right," she said, drawing a deep breath. "I guess I'll take the tree down."

"Oh, that's not depressing," he said, grimacing. "At all."

She shrugged. "Why be miserable when you can be wretched?"

The last minutes slipped through their fingers like sand. He kissed every inch of her face. It was twisted up with bravery and despair and he was positive he was going to die walking out of here.

"We'll be all right," she kept saying, her smile fighting to stay ahead of the tears. "We'll figure it out. I know where you are now."

He touched her necklace, then her ears where the matching pearls he bought her for New Year's hung from her lobes.

Don't leave me, he thought, even though he was the one going.

How am I even doing this?

He had come back to her, given her his heart, showered her with his love and his gifts, and now he was walking away again. He hated his life, wanted to trash it like a hotel room. The years thrown away were sour on his tongue. Regret was an iron cannonball in his stomach. Every hair on his forearms up like a barb and wailing *don't want to don't want to don't want to don't want to...*

Both Will and Lucky came to Barbegazi to orchestrate the extraction.

"Say goodbye now," Lucky said gently, after one last hug on the porch, after the last one, after just one more. She put a firm arm around Daisy and took her inside. The door closed.

Bag in hand, Erik trudged down the porch steps with the macho stoicism of a revolutionary going to the wall to be shot. It was starting to rain. Naturally.

He got in the car, his face a stone. Will didn't offer a word as he put it in gear and drove them away. For two miles Erik stared out the window, listening to the smeary scrape of the windshield wipers.

"One of the rear tires on Daisy's car looked low on air," he said. "Remind her to fill it?"

Will looked at him with a curt nod.

Erik exhaled heavily and turned on the radio. The rest of the drive he made some innocuous chit-chat, but mostly he looked out the rain-beaded window and let all the songs make him feel like shit.

"I'm tempted to put on Barry Manilow," Will said. "Let it get really ugly."

Erik chuckled. "I'd open my jugular right here. Ruin your upholstery."

Will started to sing under his breath. "When will our eyes meet...?"

"Shut up."

Will sang louder, leaning over the arm rest. "When can I touch you?"

"Shut the fuck up," Erik said, laughing. "You put that song in my head, I'll fucking kill you."

"Oh Mandy..."

Erik smacked the back of his hand against Will's arm. "Asshole."

"You know you can't smile without me, Fish."

"That's always been my problem." And Erik was smiling. Still miserable and moody and contemplating throwing himself off a bridge. But smiling.

Will pulled up to the departures terminal. They both got out, hugged and pounded each other's backs at the curb.

"Did I apologize for that phone call?" Erik asked the air over Will's shoulder.

"About thirty times."

"I'm sorry."

"I know." Will stepped back. "Now don't try anything funny because I'm circling this airport until I see your plane take off."

Erik smiled. "Watch my ass as I fly into the sunset?"

"You wish." Will's hand landed in a soft swat on Erik's face. "Bring that ass back soon or I'll kill you."

"I will."

"Promise?"

"I promise," Erik said. "I'm back."

Will ruffled Erik's hair. "All right. Don't fucking call me."

"Believe me, you miserable bitch, I won't."

Will gave a stern flick of his jaw toward the airport doors. "Go."

Erik went. Feeling he hadn't done enough and was leaving the best of himself behind.

Part Two: Diamonds

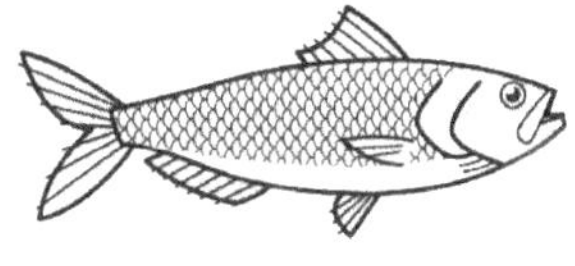

ON THE LADDER

"DON'T BE NERVOUS," Daisy said, laying a hand on his forearm.

"I'm not nervous," Erik said, his stomach burning.

I'm flat out scared, he thought.

The sun was starting its descent over the rolling hills of Lancaster County. The day had been suspiciously mild for January: one of winter's smartass attempts to get you to drop your guard and think it won't be so bad after all. Then she'd swoop in for the kill.

"Remember where you're going?" Daisy asked.

"I remember," Erik said. It was surreal how little directional prompting he needed. Left at the crossroads. Bear right at the gas station. He smiled at the yellow barn with the beautiful compass rose hex signs on its façade. He raised his fingers off the steering wheel at the huge *Amish Quilts* roadsign and its patchwork design.

Hello. It's me. I'm back.

His heart kicked up as they cruised along a half-mile of split rail fence and another familiar road sign loomed ahead: *Bianco's: Farm to Market.*

He turned up the road, eyes sweeping the land. The Christmas trees were full-grown—they were saplings when Erik first saw them freshman year of college. More acres of them sprawled on his left. The bare orchard trees on the right looked bigger and more numerous. The grapevines were cut down to the ground, leaving only the supports lining the slopes like stunted telephone poles.

A mailbox marked the Biancos' private driveway. At its base squatted a funny little stone statue, like a small dragon pretending to be a turtle. La Tarasque: both the name and the sentry of Daisy's parents' house.

Erik turned up the drive, his chest pounding hard. He parked, switched off the engine and clutched the steering wheel another nanosecond. Then found his balls and got out of the car. He straightened his shoulders and told his heart and stomach to knock it off. He was only seeing Daisy's parents for the first time in thirteen years. After he'd walked out on their traumatized daughter and ignored her as she descended into a near-suicidal darkness.

No big deal.

"Welcome back," Daisy said, closing the passenger door.

To Erik's staring eyes, La Tarasque looked unchanged. A beautiful farmhouse with a front porch that wrapped around both sides. Black shutters neat against grey shingles and a sunny yellow door. Three gable windows along the second story roof.

Joe Bianco was sitting next to one, hands clasped in his lap. Looking like a small Buddha.

"Dad?" Daisy said, laying a hand across her eyebrows and squinting into the sun's rays.

Joe freed one hand and raised it. "Hello."

"Dad, what are you *doing?*"

"I'm laying an egg, what does it look like I'm doing?"

"Are you stuck up there?"

Joe flicked a thumb over his shoulder. "Ladder fell over."

"Where's Mamou?"

"At her book club."

"You were up on the ladder alone? Are you insane?"

"Bon dieu de merde, this is going to take forever."

"You don't have your phone with you?"

"It's in my tool bag."

"Where's your tool bag?"

"Hanging on the ladder."

"Oh for fuck's sake, Dad. How long have you been sitting there?"

"Stop asking him questions," Erik said.

"Thank you, Erique," Joe said. "Perhaps you can get me the hell down from here before my wife returns? I've already pissed once off the roof and I think I splattered the patio."

Erik had already started walking around the side of the house to the back where, sure enough, the long extension ladder was lying on the ground.

Here we go again, he thought.

Daisy helped him get the ladder righted and braced properly against the roof.

"All set," Erik called, getting a foot on the bottom rung and his hands on the struts. To Daisy he said, "How about you give me a minute?"

Daisy glanced up at the roof, then back at Erik.

"I got this," he said, and leaned to kiss her. Shaking her head and muttering, she walked off around the corner of the house.

Joe started scooting down the roof's incline on his butt. "Not one of my brighter ideas, hé?"

"At least it didn't fall while you were on it."

"Let's not talk about that." Carefully, Joe maneuvered himself backward and, with Erik's guidance, got his foot on the top rung.

"How the hell did you plan to do this yourself?" Erik asked, the sheer idiocy finally sinking in.

"Shut up."

Erik closed his teeth around his tongue, shaking his head. He stepped aside as Joe neared the lower rungs, keeping one hand on a strut until Joe had both feet on the ground.

Joe whacked one hand against the other and brushed off his jeans.

"Laying an egg," Erik said. "Good one."

"You like that? I had a couple hours to think up my lines. And reflect on my life in case my wife found me."

He seemed a little shorter than Erik remembered. The hair was all silver grey, combed back from a peaked hairline, and he was sporting a goatee. He took hold of the ladder as if to bring it down, then stopped and pointed at Erik.

"Not a word of this to Francine."

"No, sir," Erik said.

For a moment they stared at each other. Then Joe's pointing hand reached out and his palm came onto Erik's face with a firm, familiar pat. Thumb and forefinger taking hold of Erik's ear and tugging.

"I'm sorry," Erik said.

"I know," Joe said. "But you showed up just in time, Franci would have killed me. Now let's put this ladder away and get the piss off the pavers."

"Dad." Daisy was calling from the side of the house. "The patio is like a latrine. Did you even *attempt* to aim?"

"Who's this?" Erik asked Francine.

She came closer, pulling her glasses from the top of her head onto her nose. Leaned and looked at the picture Erik was pointing to. A group shot of Francine, Daisy, Joe and a young man Erik didn't recognize but felt like he should.

"Oh," Francine said. "That's Joe's son, Michel."

"You found him?" Erik said.

Francine laughed. "He found us. Tombé du ciel, he rang on the telephone last fall, looking for Joe. We nearly dropped dead. He's in the States now, working as a chef, and he came here for Thanksgiving." Her hand reached to rub circles between Erik's shoulder blades. "The same night you called. Isn't that funny?"

Erik smiled beneath her loving caress, studying the picture, noticing Michel had the signature Bianco eyes. His mother had gotten pregnant with him just before Joe left for Vietnam. Joe intended to marry her, but when his tours were up, he returned to France to find she had married someone else. Her husband made a campaign of cutting Joe off from his son. All communication was sporadic and secret—letters and pictures snuck in and out of France by a sympathetic grandmother.

Now here he was, framed in silver and set proudly on an end table. Relaxed, confident and smiling under the drape of Joe's arm. As if he had always belonged there.

"And look at this," Francine said, picking up a picture of Joe with a little blonde girl on his lap, reading a story. "Joe gets a son and an instant granddaughter. Isn't she adorable?"

"Did you eat her?"

"Shamelessly," Francine said, patting him again. "Not a scrap left."

"What's it like having a brother all of a sudden?" Erik asked Daisy as they unpacked in the old carriage house. The upstairs had been converted into an apartment and it was always where Erik and Daisy slept during the college years.

"Weird," she said. "And wonderful. I'm still getting to know him but from the little time I've spent with him, I think he's a lovely man. And it's made Pop so happy."

"Talk about happy," Erik said, pulling her tight against him. "I can't believe I'm back in this room."

She wound her arms around his waist and set her cheek against his chest. "Neither can I," she said. "I haven't been up here since you left. Never slept in this room again after we broke up. John and I came to Pennsylvania for Christmas one year. I made my mother put us in the guest room."

"Really?"

"To me, this was our room," she said.

"It's still ours." He tilted her chin up and kissed her. "I'll prove it…"

SPATCHCOCK

THEY DIDN'T MAKE ANY long-term plans. Didn't discuss any scenarios of one of them moving to the other. They phoned every night, texted throughout every day. Arranged and rearranged however they could to get to each other.

Daisy came to New York for a long weekend. Erik picked her up at Rochester airport and drove them over to his mother's house for dinner.

"Remember when I teased you down at my parents' place? For being nervous?" Daisy asked as they got out of the car.

"Yeah?"

"I apologize."

He laughed and put his arm around her. "It'll be fine."

And it was. Fred greeted them in the little front hall. Fred was always so smooth and unflappable. An effortless host who could make a corpse feel at home. He took their coats to hang away and they went into the kitchen.

Christine, her hands in the soapy dishwater, looked over at the two of them standing in the doorway. Then looked up at the ceiling, blinking rapidly.

"Jesus Christ, I'm bawling already."

"Great, Ma," Erik said.

"Look at you," Christine said, drying off her hands and not looking at Erik. She walked over, her arms reaching. "Look who's here..."

She and Daisy hugged, rocking side to side a little. When it was clear neither was letting go, Erik retreated behind the refrigerator door, pretending to look for something.

"So good to see you," Christine said over and over.

Daisy said something Erik couldn't quite hear, but he was sure it was *I'm sorry.*

"It was long ago," Christine said. "Another life. You're here now and he's so happy. And that's all I care about. All right?"

Erik shut the door and straightened up. Fred strode into the kitchen and clapped his hands together. "Who wants a gin and tonic?"

"Forget the tonic," Daisy said, wiping her face with the dishtowel Christine handed her.

The emotional scene concluded within one drink. Ten minutes later, Daisy was in an apron and showing Christine how to spatchcock a chicken.

"Come again?" Fred said.

"You cut the backbone out," Daisy said. "Press it flat and roast it that way."

"She did this the first weekend Erik brought her home," Christine said. "I had a chicken dinner all planned, then my hours got screwed up and I was going to be late getting home. I told them to order pizza. Instead, I get home and Daisy's made the whole meal. But she did *this* with the chicken."

"I was showing off," Daisy said, grimacing as she cut through a joint with the kitchen shears. "I'd watched my mother do it all the time but I never tried. So I called her up and she talked me through it. Erik was holding the phone to my ear with one hand and signing to Pete with the other, trying to explain what I was doing."

"You had him at spatchcock," Erik said. "He had to make up a new sign for it. It was like his favorite word for a year."

"I think it's mine now," Fred said. "What's the benefit of doing it this way, rather than roasting it whole?"

"The skin," Erik and Christine said at the same time.

"The skin," Daisy said, smiling.

"Every inch of it is crispy, salty and perfect," Christine said. "We stood over the stove and tore it off with our fingers, remember? So disgustingly good."

"You want to make stock with this?" Daisy asked, indicating the excised backbone.

"No," Christine said. "I'll never use it before we leave for Florida."

Daisy regarded the scrap regretfully before tossing it in the garbage. She looked over at Erik, blinked her eyes once then returned to her work.

EMOTIONAL SLAUGHTER

IN BROCKPORT, IT WAS Daisy's turn to be shown around Erik's world and introduced to friends and co-workers. They had lunch with Miles and Janey Kelly, the couple who had all but adopted Erik as their own. Afterward, Daisy asked to see where Erik lived when he was married to Melanie. He thought it a strange request, but he took her past the old Victorian in the historic district. She looked at it from the passenger side window, saying nothing for a long time.

"Where did you get married?" she finally asked.

"In Rochester. At the courthouse."

She nodded, still looking out the window.

He took her hand and squeezed it. "What are you thinking?"

She looked over at him. "I'm glad I didn't know until now. Every time I thought about reaching out to you one more time, I just... I didn't want to find you were with someone. It was easier not to know." She looked out at the house again, drew her breath in and let it out. "I don't want to pretend it never happened though. So I wanted to see where."

A slight unease glazed the visit. Their newfound love didn't seem to fit into Erik's turf. Perhaps because his apartment was so sparse and unwelcoming. Perhaps because, truth be told, he didn't have much of a life outside work, whereas Daisy was so integrated and active in her community. Without it being discussed, the rest of the visits in January and February were in Saint John, where both of them felt at home.

Erik spent the long March break there, even though New Brunswick Ballet Theater was coming to the end of its winter season and Daisy couldn't take much time away. Neither could Will. Erik ended up hanging out a lot with Lucky and the kids, which wasn't always fun.

Jack still didn't seem to care for Aunt Daisy's new beau, and Sara's constant chatter made Erik's eyes glaze over. Driving with Lucky and the kids to a movie one morning, Erik calculated that Jack and Sara asked Lucky thirty-six questions in forty-five minutes. He would have gone batshit, but Lucky calmly fielded one inquiry after another, never losing patience. At least not to the outward eye.

"You're like Answer Girl," he said during a rare lull in the interrogation. "What will you do when the third one comes along?"

"I plan to become quite stupid then," Lucky said.

Erik got back to Barbegazi in a strange mood. Just as unease had glazed Daisy's visit to Brockport, this week felt suffused with a slight boredom.

Daisy's car was in the driveway—with Sunday's matinee performance over, the theater would be dark until Wednesday. Getting out of the car, Erik noticed the flag on the mailbox was still up so he went to collect yesterday's post. He flipped through it, as if expecting something for him.

His fingers stopped, backtracked and drew out a plain white envelope, hand-addressed to Daisy. The postmark was Virginia Beach. The return address read *David Alto.*

A sinister warmth coiled in his stomach and his bored mood pounced on it. He looked up at the house, down at the envelope. Up at the house again. Drew a long, concentrated breath in through his mouth and blew it out.

"Be a grownup," he said as he walked up the steps of the porch and let himself in.

"Hey," Daisy called. She was curled in her chair by the fire, reading. "Have fun?"

He kissed her head and set the bundle of mail in her lap. "You got a letter from Dave," he said, rather loudly. Bastet stopped washing her ears and looked at him.

Daisy set her book aside. Erik leaned his elbows on the back of her chair as she worked her thumb under the flap. A single piece of paper, folded in thirds, which she unfolded.

Naturally it was in fucking French.

"Dear Marge," she said. And then twisted to look up at him. "Or would you rather I not...?"

He gestured for her to go ahead. A pair of dark hands settled on his shoulders and he gave an involuntary squirm beneath them.

March 12, 2006

Dear Marge,

Last round of scans and ultrasounds showed something weird on my liver. Could be an abscess, could be nothing. Could be a thing. I go in for a biopsy today so I'm up before sunrise listening to Beethoven and brooding. It's what I do best.

Virginia Beach Playhouse is putting on On Your Toes *and I'm lost in the "Slaughter on Tenth Avenue" ballet. Remember when you and Will danced this—spring concert, 1991, I think. It's bringing back a ton of free-association memories and I'm sort of a nostalgic mess right now. All over the place.*

Lydia's pregnant and I'm the one crying all the time. Maybe all the regret for being such a callous asshole all those years is catching up with me. It was all fear. You know that. You of all people have to know that. I was a scared kid trying to become a scared man. Acting like losing my parents hadn't scared the shit out of me. Pretending the shooting didn't touch me, that destroying you and Fish didn't imprint, that cancer wasn't terrifying.

Impending parenthood has managed to break through the bullshit like nothing else. I'm scared out of my mind. Scared I don't have a fucking clue how to do this and I'm going to die before I figure it out and leave my kid a scared mess to repeat the cycle.

It's the typical emotional slaughter at four in the morning. I hate it.

I don't know why I'm telling you this.

HA! We both know why.

I'm sorry.

I hope you're all right. Staying warm and smelling good. I hope... I still hope a lot of things. You know what they are.

I'm sorry. I'll stop now. I'll let you know how things turn out.

Hope for me, okay?

Dave

With a small, sympathetic noise, Daisy set the letter on the table. "God, I hope it was nothing." She unfolded her legs and stood up.

"Does he write you often?" Erik asked.

The phone rang. "Every few months," she said, reaching for the cordless. "It's been a while, actually. Hello?"

Then she was speaking French and picking up her empty tea mug, heading into the kitchen. Erik sat down in Archie, the leather chair he'd come to regard as his. He picked up the letter and skimmed the lines. A familiar irritation filled his chest. It had been a common tactic of Dave's back in the day: sitting at a table where Erik and Daisy were and launching into French, deliberately excluding Erik. Daisy never stood for it. She would either respond in English or not respond at all.

Now the sound of her French from the kitchen was rubbing against the nap of his peace. As if it were Dave on the phone and she was indulging him. Deliberately excluding her lover.

What's going on?

Is this happening again?

His eyes tried to pick words out of the letter. He saw Fish written out. *Carnage emotionnel.* Was that emotional slaughter? Had she read him everything David wrote or just the safe parts?

Knock it off. For fuck's sake, it's a letter from a friend worried about dying from cancer before his kid is born. Don't be an asshole.

He folded the paper and jammed in carelessly back in the envelope. Got up and put his head into the kitchen.

"I'm going for a run," he mouthed. Over the phone Daisy smiled at him, nodded and gave a wave. All of which his mood translated as dismissal.

He went upstairs, stomping past the picture gallery of Daisy dancing in the arms of other men. With each tread, the steps morphed into the stairs of David's old apartment, and he'd get to the top and see them in bed.

This is old pain, he told himself.

But it felt fresh.

Why is this showing up now?

"Because you didn't deal with it then," he mumbled.

As he shucked off his jeans and sweater, he felt like throwing something.

I dealt with this. In therapy. I went through the day. I threw things. I likened it to a firing squad. I did this. I dealt with this.

"You didn't deal with it in front of Dais," he said, pulling on sweats and a thermal T-shirt.

He caught sight of himself in the mirror over the dresser. Held out his hands in an exaggerated shrug. "Dude. I got nothing. Go run it out."

He found earphones and his music. Thumped back down the stairs, shouldering past the pictures like he didn't give a shit. He sat on the bench in the little front hall while his head filled with the images of David rolling over, Daisy appearing from under. David over. Daisy under.

I did this. I'm done with this. Don't do this.

As he picked free the knot in his laces, he noticed his hands were shaking.

"The fuck is wrong with you?" he said, stamping a foot down into a sneaker.

"Glad I'm not the only one who talks to themselves," Daisy said, appearing out of nowhere on her little silent feet. Bastet trailed behind with a smug expression, as if she had tattled.

He gave a token chuckle as he tied his laces. "Private conversation."

She leaned her shoulder against the closet door. "It's going to get dark soon so please don't go too far."

"I won't."

"Are you in the mood for anything in particular for dinner?"

"No."

"Is something wrong?"

"No."

Silence as he threaded the cord of his earphones down a sleeve and zipped his fleece jacket. He opened the door. Shut it. Without turning around he said, "I think I'm mad at you."

The silence swelled like a water balloon behind him.

"About David?"

"Yeah."

"Please turn around."

Hand still on the doorknob, he turned. "It's not the letter," he said, addressing her ear because he couldn't meet her eyes. "I think this is twelve-year-old anger showing up. I think. I don't know. I'm not sure what to do with this. So I'm going to go for a run and take the edge off and put some distance between me and...the letter. Which is obviously bothering me."

He met her gaze then. Her arms were crossed over her middle, holding onto opposite sides of her cardigan. Her face was composed but her eyes blinked rapidly. Her chin rose and fell a few times. "We never had this fight," she said. "We never dealt with it in the moment."

"And that's on me," he said. "I don't want a fight now. This is residual shit and a weird moment. So I'm stepping out. I'm going to feel what I feel and organize my thoughts a little."

She nodded. "All right."

He nodded. Then stepped onto the porch and shut the door behind him. Immediately, he opened it again and put his face in, with the closest thing he could get to a smile. "My keys are on top of the piano."

Her mouth made the approximate shape of a smile in return. "I trust you."

FOREST PRIMEVAL

HE LET TWELVE BARS of a single song play and then shut off the music. Listened to the slap of his feet on pavement and the sound of his breath falling into a cadence. Let his thoughts wander in and out, trying not to be surprised at any of this. Tried to look at all the layers within, let every thought have its turn to talk.

Come take a run. We'll have a conversation.

He turned off the lake's rec path and took the trail through the woods instead, wanting to get far away from civilization and into the forest primeval of feeling.

Where he could talk out loud.

"All right, what's bothering you?"

She fucked him.

"Yes, she did. That hurt."

David. Of all fucking people.

"I know. It was a betrayal on all kinds of levels."

He put his cock where only mine had been.

"Yeah, you liked being her first. You got off on being the only one."

So what?

"Just saying."

He fucked her. He took what was mine.

"He did."

And she let him.

"It sucked. It was traumatic."

What else did he do to her?

"Is that what's really bothering you, bro?"

What did she do to him? Who started it? Where did it start? How did they get upstairs?

"And was she even thinking about you?"

God fucking dammit. What did she do to him up there?

"Does it matter now? Never mind. It does. Go ahead."

Did she touch him? Did he lick her? Did she blow him? What? What did they do?

"Dude, I don't know about you, but I don't need the play-by-play."

Well how much play are we talking about? What did I walk in on? The first time? The third? Fourth?

"You could ask."

Fuck that.

"You could. She'll tell you. As long as it's a conversation."

The fuck was she thinking?

"Probably not much. She was high."

He stopped running in a grove of tall pines, pacing around, panting, pulling his hands back through his hair. He was pissed. Twenty-two years old again, shaking and murderous, his hands itching for violence.

"Fuck you, Alto," he said through clenched teeth. Then he released his jaw and bellowed it out loud to the trees. He broke a few sticks against the trunks. Hurled some rocks. Paced until finally his lungs unfolded, shook their fists at the sky and he fell on his knees with a last cry of frustration.

A flurry of wings made the air suck back through his lungs. A murder of crows screeched over his head, fading further into the trees.

Get a load of him, the crazy man in the woods, scaring the birds.

Feel better?

"A little."

She hurt you bad.

"Yeah."

The letter reminded you.

"Brought it back."

Yeah.

"She saw him at Lancaster."

I know.

"What did they talk about?"

You have to ask her.

"I know."

Sulking out here in the woods won't get you your answers.

"I fucking *know*, okay?"

You're doing great, feeling your way through this.

"Fuck off." He sat on the ground, his back against a pine tree. He was cold and it was getting dark. He promised her not to go too far.

He promised she would always know where he was.

He stared up at the tall trees, and before his eyes they morphed into the image of the cathedral he always imagined in his heart. The structure of his love, now covered in scaffolding, yet beneath it he could see arches and scrolls and stained glass. A restoration in progress. A lifetime project.

What are you going to do? Tear it down? Or build it in? The night you came running back to her, you told her the past was going to be part of it all. You weren't going to pretend it never happened.

He exhaled, running his hands through his hair. "I know."

She made peace with the past. Including David. She finished that business. You're just starting. So turn around. Go back. Explain the letter made you emotional. The old you ran off to have a fit in the woods. The new you is coming back to have a conversation. This is a huge improvement, dude.

"Thank you."

She loves you.

"She fucked up and she loves me."

You fucked up, too, and you can't breathe without her.

He took his phone out and texted her: ***I went a little further than I expected. I'm turning around now.***

K, she replied.

He stared at the single, terse letter. Waited for more but she had none.

I love you, he typed with cold, cautious fingers.

Just come home.

He shook his head. "Might be a loud conversation, dude," he said. He stuffed the phone in his pocket and took off running through the woods.

TRIGGERS WITH TRUST

"I FULLY APPRECIATE HOW that letter could have thrown you off," Daisy said. "I completely understand you needing to step out and collect your thoughts. And you may joke about leaving your keys on the piano, but those keys fucking matter to me. Those keys tell me you're coming back."

"I know and—"

"No. You don't know. You don't know what I went through when—"

"I see the scars of what you went through every damn day," he said. "I've counted them. I can find them in my sleep. Every time I look at your body I'm reminded of what I did. Maybe I don't know everything about what you went through, but I don't know nothing."

The stove hissed like an angry cat as the soup boiled up and bubbled over the edge of the pot. Daisy seized a dishtowel and dragged the pan off the burner, muttering, "And now my fucking soup is burning."

Reaching for a wooden spoon, she tipped the crock of utensils over. Erik righted it just in time. He crouched to pick up spatulas and spoons while his back molars ground together.

"I'm getting chilled off," he said. "Can I jump in the shower five minutes?"

"No," she said.

"Jesus Christ, Dais."

"I don't like when you disappear," she said, banging the spoon on the rim of the pot. "It upsets me."

"I'm not disappearing, I'm going *upstairs*,"

"Hey," she cried, pointing the spoon at him like she was going to skewer him with it. "You fucking know what I mean. And if you say you know what I went through then you know why I'm in the middle of an anxiety attack right now and I need to talk to you." She swiped the back of her hand across her eyes and drew a breath. "I need you right now."

"Okay, calm down," he said. "I'm sorry."

"Don't tell me to calm down like I'm some overwrought bimbo looking for attention."

He took a breath of his own. "I'm sorry," he said again, slower. "What can I do? What's making you anxious?"

Her shoulders shivered. "It's a kneejerk reaction. I admit it's not rational but it's there. You deserted me. With good reason—I cheated on you, I disappointed you, I let you down. And you disappeared. Now, tonight, you pretended you weren't upset by David's letter when clearly you were. You slammed out of here in a moody sulk and it set me off."

"I told you as I was going what I was doing. What was in my head or not in my head. I went for a run and then turned around. Last time I left for twelve years. This time I left for an hour. Can I get a little credit here?"

A smile made half her mouth curve up. "I give you a ton of credit, honey."

"Yeah, but do you trust me," he said. "Do you trust I want you and I want us? Do you trust I'm here to stay this time?"

"I do," she said. "And while I was trusting you, my stomach was still in shreds. Ninety-five percent of me trusted you. The other five percent was cowering under the bed feeling like I fucked up again and you were gone. I can't help that, Erik. I can't help it and I can't keep it from you. I'm going to tell you everything. I'm going to stamp on every damn eggshell. I'm not going to fall to pieces every time you walk out the door but if you walk out upset with me, it's going to trigger my residual shit. Especially if it was something to do with David because he's your trigger."

His eardrums flinched against her raised voice. Much as he tried to stay calm, some instinctive involuntary impulse in his gut was bristling, baring its teeth and looking around frantically for an escape.

"I suck at this," he said.

"Suck at what?"

"I don't know how to have an argument with you," he said. "I can't remember ever fighting with you."

"Because we didn't," she said. "We didn't do this twelve years ago. This is way overdue. You were insanely angry at me and never let me see it."

"I was angry at David. I don't know what I was with you. Angry never fit the definition. All the talking out loud I did, none of it was confrontational, not with you."

"Then what was it?"

"Denial. Holding it frozen in place so it could keep being perfect. If it wasn't perfect it was useless. Sometimes I pretended you were dead because it was easier to maintain the illusion. These weren't my finest moments but they're the truth."

"Well, I'm alive," she said. "And imperfect. I have my flawed, weak moments. I have my dark times and my anxiety attacks."

"Hello? Have we met?"

She went on as if she hadn't heard. "I have ex-boyfriends who stay in touch with me and to an extent, I have David. I made my peace with him. He's married now, he's having a kid. His health is fragile and we keep in touch. We're not best friends, but we have our inside jokes and our history and our regrets and our guilt. We saw each other at Lancaster. We went for coffee and we forgave each other. He writes me. Do you want me to tell him to stop? Because I will. If it matters to you, I will and I won't think any less of you."

"Dais, I don't know what the fuck I want when it comes to Dave," he said, looking up at the ceiling with his empty palms up. "As little as possible. That's what I want."

She nodded, stirring the soup again. "Do you trust me?" she said. "I already know you trust me with your heart and your love and your goodness. But I want you to trust me with your darker moods. I want you to trust me enough to be annoyed or irritated with me. Or even flat-out angry with me. I want to be able to tell you David wrote me without it raising your suspicions. And I want you to be able to go back to New York and trust I'm going to be faithful to y—"

"Stop it." He stepped and took her by the shoulders. Hard. Her spoon clattered into the pot as he pressed his forehead to hers, pulling air in through his teeth. "Just stop," he said. "I never once thought you'd cheat on me ag—"

"I can't stop," she said. "I can't not think it. You wanted to kill him, I watched you try to do it. I wanted you to turn around and throw all that rage at me where it belonged. I kept waiting and waiting for a fight that never came. Empty mailboxes, no messages on the machine, the sound of you fucking breathing on the other end of the phone but never saying anyth—"

"Because it killed me," he cried, letting go of her. "What was I supposed to do? You were the one thing I had left. The one fixed point in my life and I found you fucking David and it was ruined for me. I didn't want to know, didn't want to hear, didn't want to see. It was changed forever and nothing would get it back the way it was."

He had paced away during the rant but abruptly turned back now. "Is this really what you want?" he asked. "Me yelling at you? You want me to get in your face, call you a whore, shove you around?"

"No," she said. "No, not now. But back then I would've taken anything but the silence."

"Well this is now and I'm not that guy."

"I know."

"But I was," he said. Their eyes caught and locked. Inside his damp clothes, his legs were quivering. "I did trust you with my dark side. Up in your room at Jay Street, all those nights we were high and insane. I was more than a little rough with you. I made you cry. I made you bleed. I tied your hands, scratched and bruised you, fucking pulled your hair out. We got off on making each other hurt in bed. You've seen me at my worst, but not once while I was beating up David did it occur to me to turn around and belt you one."

She was shaking her head, staring at the tiled floor. "This conversation isn't going where I wanted it to."

"Take it somewhere else then," he said. "I feel like we're not telling each other anything we don't already know."

"What would you have done if I came to your room that night?"

"I can only answer that in hindsight. It's easy to say now I would've let you in and talked to you. Would I though? I honestly don't know. I might have locked you out and ignored you. I might have let you in and sat there like a stone. I might have thrown you up against the wall and fucked you and then made you go. I might have just cried. I don't know."

She nodded, hugging herself, one of her palms moving up and down her bicep.

Erik's arms were crossed as well. "This is old pain."

"But it matters. Don't tell me it doesn't, otherwise why did you need to get out of here so fast?"

"The letter brought it all back," he said. "I didn't want it to but it did. Wondering why you did it. Wondering how you could do it. What did he have that I didn't." The words fell in a tired vomit on the floor. No commitment was in them, but they were squatting illegally in his heart and he evicted them. Turned them out on the street, yanked them loose like rotten teeth and let the bitter taste flow through his mouth.

"I didn't know how to get past it. I didn't want to get past it. I was too tired. I had no fight in me left anymore. David took the last of it. He took you and he took my will to keep going. I felt used and useless. I told Will I couldn't pretend it never happened. I couldn't get back with you and act like we weren't changed. No matter what I did or said or forgave or forgot, from that day on you and I were different. And I hated it. I didn't want us to be different. If it couldn't be us, it was no use to me. So I left. You know this, Dais. We've talked about this. What can I tell you you don't already know?"

With an exhaled sigh of frustration he sat down on one of the kitchen stools, leaned on an elbow and ran his hand through his hair. His other hand reached to take hers and they held still a long while. No sound but the tick of the clock and the low murmur of bubbling soup.

The tension eased up in his gut, unwound like a severed vine and fell away. His love for her stirred in his heart. An easing in his crowded mind, knowing this was part of the fight. And the fight was good.

He drew her closer to him, bringing her between his knees. He slid his arm around her waist and laid his head against her. Her heart was kicking hard against the wall of her chest, but the hand caressing his hair was calm.

She was wearing her oldest, sloppiest jeans. The ones that hung loose on her hips. His fingertips ran along the waistband, pushing it down a little, until the red-lettered fish emerged. He touched it. Ran the ball of his thumb over it. Then pressed the daisy on the inside of his wrist against it.

"I know you," he said. "I know you like I know myself. If it had been me—me who slept with someone else and you who walked in on it. Much as I tell myself you would have left me the same way, I know in my heart it isn't true. Sure, maybe you would've gotten out of Dodge and gone home to let the shock dissipate. But when I called the house or showed up at the door, on my knees begging to explain, you would have answered. You would have given me something. A few words. A timeframe. A status."

He looked up at her. "Sometimes the pain of you sleeping with David is so insignificant when I put it next to the time I threw away. I could have fixed things so long ago. Or at least closed things. One phone call or letter. One cup of coffee. I don't know if the regret for that will ever go away. I hate what I did."

"I know you do," she said.

"But I guess today was a day when you sleeping with David hurt more. Still..." He put both his arms around her waist, holding his wrists in the small of her back. Her eyes filled his vision, drawing him up. His heart slowly turning about, preening in the mirrored reflection of her love, viewing itself from all sides.

"This is now," he said. "I'm not holding over your head something you did when you were twenty-one and traumatized. Not anymore. Will it bug me if he writes you? Sure. I'm human. Do I trust you'll be faithful to me? Yes, I do, and what's more, I'm intent on fucking you so good, you won't want it from anyone else. Furthermore, I— Stop laughing."

Her hands were over her face, her shoulders quaking. He sat up, took her wrists and pulled them away. "Stop laughing."

"I'm not laughing," she said, sniffing.

"I never fell out of love, Dais," he said, his thumbs smudging the tears from under her eyes. "I fell out of touch. And I know it killed you. I'm here now. I'm back and I'm here to stay. I'm fighting triggers with trust. I got a ton of fight in me now but not enough to keep secret grudges or keep score on who screwed up and who was the screwed. This is the new us and it's the us I want. Whether I go out for a run to clear my head or I go back to New York, my keys are on top of the piano. If I could detach my dick, I'd leave it on top of the piano, too."

She blinked at him.

"You were supposed to laugh at that," he said

She tried, but her face crumpled and a fresh stream erupted from the rims of her eyes.

"Come here," he said, pulling her into his lap. "It's all right."

"I'm sorry," she said, curling into the circle of his arms.

"Shh..." He held her tight, feeling the world shift back into proper place. "I love you more than I ever loved anything in my life," he said, sliding his jaw along her head, a bit of her hair twined about his fingers. "I didn't come back to fight you. I came back to fight for you."

"You don't have to fight too hard." A long breath cascaded out of her chest. The weight in his lap turned soft and pliant. "You're the one," she said, her thumb gliding over his tattoo. "You're still the one I can tell anything. You're still the one, when my sentences run out of words, you finish them by looking at me. But at the same time you're surprising me. I still get to discover you. I love who you've become. And I love that who I've become still works with you."

He reached to touch the hollow of her throat where the gold fish and the pearl nestled. "You're the best thing to ever happen to me twice."

THE THIRD OPTION

THE SPRING BREAK VISIT was the turning point. In the wee hours of the night he returned home, Erik's cell phone rang. Adrenaline sliced through his chest as he fumbled for it on the bedside table, thinking, *Mom*. He squinted into the stabbing light from the display. It was Daisy.

"Hey," he said, falling back into the pillows.

"Hi," she said. A single wretched syllable and her voice disintegrating into four kinds of despair.

"What's wrong?" he said, alert but still slurred with sleep. "What is it?"

She was crying. Hard. Words slipped through the weeping but he couldn't grasp them.

"Honey, what's the matter," he said. "Tell me."

"I can't," Daisy said. "I can't do this anymore."

He sat up. "Do what anymore," he said as his heart kicked up another few beats.

"I miss you," she cried. "You weren't even gone an hour and I fell apart. I miss you so bad."

"I miss you too, and I—"

"I want you," she said. "I want you here all the time." Her voice splintered apart as she laid herself bare to him. "I want you here all the time, Erik. I want you here with me. I can't keep saying hello and goodbye to you. I can't be away from you anymore. I can't. It's breaking my heart. Erik, I can't..."

"I know," he whispered. "I know it's hard."

"I love my necklace, but it's not helping me get through. I love texting all day and talking on the phone all night but it's not helping me. I love that I always know where you are, but it doesn't help because you're not here. And I just want you here. I don't want to wait another bunch of years to be sure of what I already know. I'm sorry, Erik, I just..."

"Don't be sorry," he said. "I need to know this."

She was weeping again. "I want you here all the time."

"Dais," he said. "I'll come."

Her sobs hitched to a stop. Her breath was still choppy over the line but she was quieting down. "I don't mean drop everything tomorrow and move," she said. "I just need to know you—"

"I'll come, Dais," he said. "I'm done with this too. It's pointless. It's making nobody happy. Nothing is keeping me here. My life is with you. I belong with you, and I don't have any more time to throw away either. All right, honey? This is it. No more long-distance crap. I'm coming to live with you in Canada and we're going forward."

She sniffed hard, let her breath out. "All right."

"I love you," he said. "And I'm coming home."

"I love you. Come back to me."

He texted Will the next morning.

If you got room at your feet, I got a really big problem to lay there.

He sent it and shoved the phone in his back pocket. Took it back out and added, ***Help.***

Will rang him a few minutes later. "Talk to me."

"What's it going to take to get me to Canada? How did Lucky do it?"

"She got student papers," Will said. "She applied for a master's program at UNB and got in. That's one of two ways you can come here and stay longer than six months. Student papers or working papers."

"Okay," Erik said. "So I either go back to school or I get a job."

"A job with an open-ended contract," Will said.

Erik started writing things down.

"Actually you have a third option," Will said. "You marry Dais and come here as a non-working spouse. Stay home and take care of the kids."

A wincing pause.

"Fuck, my bad," Will said. "Sorry."

"I can stay home and take care of your kids," Erik said. "You can fulfill your dream of banging the manny."

"You're flirting with me," Will said. "That's what this is."

"You wish."

"You fucking tease. Where was this attitude back when I could've done something about it? You're hurting my feels. I should let you rot there in New York."

"Don't," Erik said. "Help me. Let's just table the third option and let me try getting there on my own."

"All right, all right. Let's see." An exhaling sigh. "Technical theater jobs up here are so heavily unionized. You barely have a chance unless you have an uncle or a godfather who's already in."

"Doesn't have to be the theater. I'll wait tables."

"Dude, you need something long-term to get working papers. Let me think."

"What about citizenship?"

"You're way ahead of yourself. Lucky's not even a citizen. She's a permanent resident. That's a ton of bureaucratic bullshit but it won't kill you. We need to get you here first."

"All right," Erik said, scribbling again. "Stupid question but am I going to have to speak French?"

"Oh yeah," Will said. "New Brunswick is officially bilingual. You'll definitely need French to get your papers."

"Fuck. Really?"

A long, sober moment of silence.

"You can't sort of do this, Fish," Will said. "Draw a line and get on one side or the other."

"All right," Erik said. "I guess I can audit some classes here the rest of the year. Dais will help me."

Will burst out laughing.

"What?" Erik said. "Son of a bitch, are you fucking with my head?"

Will responded with a string of French.

"Goddammit, Kaeger," Erik yelled.

"I *had* you," Will said. "Aw fuck, I shouldn't have laughed. I totally had you."

"How do you say asshole in French?"

"Mon tabarnak," Will said, howling laughing. "J'vais te décalisser la yeule, calice."

"I didn't miss you," Erik said. "At all."

"Oh man," Will said, chuckling. "All right. I'm sorry. I'm hanging up now. I'm going to call in every favor I can think of. Someone has to know somebody who knows somebody."

"If you owe anyone blow jobs, now would be the time to deliver."

"No way, I clear all oral debts immediately. You don't want that bad credit following you around."

Credit made Erik think of financial details. A long road of paperwork and hassle and stress rolled out in front of him like an ugly carpet.

But Daisy.

Waiting at the end.

She answered the phone. She wasn't married. She was free and you were free and you got another chance.

Draw a line and get on one side or the other.

He scraped his toe on the floor in front of him and stepped across. "Help me," he said to Will. "I want this."

"So do we. We'll move the Earth."

SAID NO WOMAN EVER

IN A PERFECT WORLD, the technical director of the Imperial Theater would have retired or quietly expired of a heart attack, leaving a vacancy for Erik to step into. And he and Daisy would have spent their working days under the same roof.

Unfortunately the director was young, hale and hearty, and any vacancies at the Imperial were under union stronghold. Will didn't dare pull a string for fear of making enemies. Pipe dreams were extinguished and other avenues explored.

The entire province of New Brunswick had not one graduate theatre program. Erik would have to go back to school in an entirely unrelated field. Now chasing down thirty-six, he didn't feel enthused about starting from scratch.

The Fredericton Playhouse was his most promising lead. He interviewed twice and got on famously with its board. But they had no openings. They kept his resume and his number and promised to be in touch.

Night after night, through the spring of 2006 when he came to Canada every few weeks and his time left at Brockport dripped away, he and Daisy held onto each other and talked the problem to shreds.

"You and me," Erik said. "Eye on the prize. I don't care what it takes. You and me. It's all that matters. It'll work out."

"Worst case, I'll leave here and we go back to the States," she said. "We have a ton of options. It'll work out."

They reassured each other and made love, and then tossed and turned through the night.

Acadia State Playhouse. Theater New Brunswick. The Capitol Theater. They loved him. They had no work.

Erik found himself making wishes when the clock read 11:11 or 12:34. Searching the evening skies for the first star. Looking for signs and auguries as he entreated the universe: *Please, let me find work.*

Salvation came from the most random and unlikely of places. He was in Brockport's library, researching jobs, when a spicy orange perfume slid around his nose and a woman spoke over his shoulder.

"Well, look who's here."

"I know that voice," he said, not turning around.

"I hope so," she said, her breath a warm whisper on his earlobe. "You slept next to it for six years. Four of them legally."

Erik turned and looked up at his ex-wife. A smile spread across his face at her fine, noble features and long cornrowed hair. Then his gaze dropped.

"Well, look at you," he said. He put out a hand and gently touched her pregnant belly.

"Don't touch me, Erik Fiskare," she said. "Said no woman ever."

The scrape of his chair cut the silence of the library as he got up and embraced her. "Look at you," he said again.

"Look at me," she said, laughing. "In a fix."

"How far along?"

"Five months. It's a girl."

He slid his hands down her arms to catch her fingers up. They were bare.

"No, you conservative twerp, I'm not married," she said.

"Conservative? Have we met?"

"What are you doing here?"

"Book report. What are you doing here? Do you have time, you want to get coffee?"

She sighed. "I'm so sick of coffee. Soon as I give birth, I'm getting drunk. Yes, let's get coffee. Fucking *decaf,* this is what it's come to."

Her catchup took ten seconds. She was still teaching music at a private school in East Rochester. She met a man. She got pregnant. He bailed. She made a decision. "Happily ever after," she said. "To be continued. The end. All of the above. Fuck it."

"I'm thrilled for you. You look beautiful."

"Thanks, baby," she said. "As usual, it hurts to look at you. What's giving you that decidedly masculine, non-pregnant glow?"

He smiled, his cheekbones warm with a guilty joy. "One guess?"

She leaned her cheek on her hand and studied him a moment. "Oh, for fuck's sake, you finally called her."

He gave her the condensed version, ending with his current predicament. Through it, Melanie made small, precipitating noises. Nodded. Shrugged. Laughed. And now her cheek was back on her hand and her eyes blinked over a crooked smile.

"Wouldn't it be ironic if my sister's best friend's cousin's husband had a friend who knew someone who was opening a dinner theater in New Brunswick?" she asked.

He stared at her, his utter unworthiness heavy in his lap. "Oh, Mel, don't tease me."

A WEAK PLACE

THE DINNER THEATER WAS in Moncton, a two-hour commute from Saint John. Being part of a start-up venture would mean long, grueling hours. But it was open-ended work and it got Erik his papers.

Moncton, fortunately, was Will's hometown. He got his hands on strings and started pulling. The Acadian Ballet Academy was putting together its summer intensive program. They needed guest teachers. Madame Bianco from the New Brunswick Ballet was invited. She accepted.

Maurice and Ségolène Kaeger owned an apartment in Riverview, a pretty community across the river from downtown Moncton. They rented it to graduate and doctorate students at the university. Now they offered its summer lease to Erik and Daisy. At the same time, Daisy arranged to rent Barbegazi to the guest conductor coming in for Symphonie New Brunswick's summer program.

Emptying his office, saying goodbye to friends and colleagues and packing up his apartment left Erik drained. The twelve-hour drive from Brockport to Saint John was a bear, including an enchanting delay at customs when he had to unload the entire U-Haul, explain its contents and his intentions, and then load it again.

"You know I can stand in bars and take numbers," he muttered under his breath as he lugged boxes back into place. "I'm not the kind of terrorist you're watching for."

"Reason for your visit?" an official asked him for the hundredth time.

Tired and punchy, Erik looked the guy dead in the eye and replied, "Because I love her."

The official raised his eyebrows. A corner of his mouth went up then the other joined it, showing a wide smile with a gold tooth.

"That's the best reason I've heard all day," he said, signing Erik's papers and handing them back. His fingers touched the bill of his cap. "Good luck, my friend."

Erik had three days to unload his boxes and clobber and load up on sleep and sex. He sorted out what was going into the attic at Barbegazi and what was coming with him to Moncton. Then he packed up again and headed to the Riverview apartment. Daisy would finish the spring season, see to Barbegazi's tenants and join him in two weeks.

They agreed later spending the summer in Moncton together was the best decision they could have made. It allowed them to be a couple right away. They were both clocking long, hard hours of physically demanding work, but they could sleep together every night and be the first thing they saw in the morning. Saturday nights and Sundays were all theirs and they made the most of Moncton's offerings, all the while assessing Erik's new job and how it was going to work for them come fall.

Almost immediately, it was obvious the two hour commute was not sustainable. Not on a daily basis and not with Erik's schedule. Swallowing disappointment and manning up, they faced the idea of a commuter relationship come September.

"We're in the same time zone," Daisy said.

"And on the same timetable," Erik said.

They both would work Wednesday to Sunday. After Sunday's matinee performance, Erik could drive back to Saint John, spend Monday and Tuesday, then head back to Moncton on Wednesday. The Kaegers would let him continue the lease of the apartment, at an embarrassingly generous discount.

The future sorted out, they leaned into the joy of the present. The summer was beautiful that year, with mild weather and not too much rain. The days passed in a blur of work and love. They discovered the Trans Canada Trail, the world's longest rec path, went right through Riverview. They rented bikes and explored it on their days off, even making little overnight trips to Prince Edward Island and Nova Scotia to pick up the trail there.

On the fourth of July, Jacqueline Grace Kaeger was born. Erik and Daisy headed back to Saint John.

"She's all you, Luck," Daisy said, looking down at the baby in her arms. Jacy had little wisps of nearly-white hair, some of it already curling up. Her wide cheeks and pointed chin were an exact, almost eerie replica of Lucky's face.

"Finally I get some representation," Lucky said from her hospital bed. She looked worn-out, as did Will. Erik couldn't help feeling concerned for their well-being.

"You guys all right?" he later asked Will over beers.

"We'll be fine," Will said. "You make a plan and God smiles, right? But everything happens for a reason."

"No shit," Erik said, knocking the neck of his bottle against Will's. They drank deeply.

"In other news," Will said. "I'm not allowed to look in Lucky's direction until I get a vasectomy."

"Yeah, I'd book that immediately," Erik said.

His foreboding turned out to be accurate and as July wound down it became evident Lucky wasn't doing well at all.

"She's so depressed," Will said on the phone. "Dude, it's bad."

"I hear Dais on the phone with her in the middle of the night," Erik said. "It sounds bad. Has she seen her doctor about it?"

"She finally went and he wrote her a script for antidepressants, but she's balking at it."

"I know," Erik said. "I did the same."

"I'm going to leave Jack and Sara with the nanny this weekend. Take Lucky and the baby up to stay with my parents. I need to get her out of here and Lucky needs Dais."

"Good idea. Come to us."

"And listen," Will said. "Will you help me talk to her? About the meds?"

The four friends gathered close.

Mostly Lucky talked.

"I feel like such a shit," she said, tucked in the circle of Will's arms and weeping. "I have this beautiful life and I'm such an ungrateful bitch."

"Stop," Will said against her hair as he rocked her. "Don't beat yourself up like this, babe."

Lucky cried harder. "I don't understand. She's so good. She's such a good baby. She's a piece of fucking cake. Jack and Sara are being amazing. Our nanny is an angel. We have a roof over our heads, we have work, we have fucking government-mandated parental leave. What the hell is wrong with me?"

"Don't," Daisy said, coming to sit on Lucky's other side. "This isn't something you're doing. It's something that's happening to you."

Lucky gulped and sniffed. A flicker of understanding seemed to cross her flushed, swollen face.

"Nobody thinks you're doing this on purpose," Erik said. "Look around the table, Luck. You got three breakdowns in front of you. We've all been there and it's not something you choose to do for kicks."

"We're the jury of your peers," Daisy said, smiling as she smoothed Lucky's hair. "Not the judges."

Lucky exhaled. Took a deep breath and exhaled again. "I love you guys. I'd be fucked without you..." She looked across to Erik and held out her hands. As he caught them tight and squeezed, he noticed for the first time Lucky wore her gold wedding band on her left index finger. To be one with Will, who had no choice but to wear his there.

"I just want you to feel better," Will said.

"I do, too," she cried, letting go of Erik and slumping against her husband. Will rested his forehead on her temple, his love for her etched in every line of his face.

"Take the meds," Daisy said softly. "They won't make it all go away, but they'll help you feel yourself again."

"It makes me feel so weak," Lucky said.

"You're in a weak place right now," Erik said, smiling as his own therapist's words came out of his mouth.

"Life is too short to go around feeling like you're dying," Daisy said.

Lucky dropped her head on Daisy's shoulder. "It sucks."

"A cesspool of sucking suckage," Daisy said, twirling one blonde curl around her finger then tucking it behind Lucky's ear.

"It won't suck forever, honey," Will said. "This is only right now. Fish is right—it's not weakness, it's just a weak place. So go on the meds a month. Try counseling a month. Four weeks. Just to get out of this place and into a better one."

"I'll go back on mine, too," Daisy said, which got a chuckle from Lucky.

"Me too," Erik said. "We'll do it together."

"The friends that medicate together, stay together," Will said.

Lucky laughed for real then. Lifting up her chin she looked around the circle. The tears were falling again, but a little light was back in her grey eyes. "All right," she said. "All right, I'll try."

JUDY'S PUNCHING BAG 

AS MUCH AS THEY planned the logistics and anticipated the pitfalls, it was hard when September came and Daisy went back to Saint John. They looked for the bright side: two hours apart wasn't twelve hours apart. Two solid days together was better than a scattered handful of hours over a week. It was far from perfect but it was better than before.

And it was hard.

"At least Lucky's glad to have Daisy back," Will said on the phone. "From the department of silver linings."

"How is she doing?" Erik asked.

"All right," Will said, a sigh in his voice hinting she was far from all right.

"Truth, please," Erik said.

Another sigh. "It's slow to come around and I don't need to tell you therapy can make it get darker in your mind before the light comes on. But she's definitely more engaged. Starting to crack jokes about depression rather than crying about it. Which is good. I mean, if you can laugh at a shitty situation, you have the upper hand."

Erik hesitated. "Any insight as to what's behind all this?"

Will gave a short chuckle. "One guess?"

"Begins with a J, rhymes with moody?"

"Fucking Judy," Will said. "You know, dude, I don't hate people. I don't have the time and it isn't in my nature. But when I say I hate my mother-in-law, I mean I *detest* my mother-in-law."

"I take it not much support coming from her."

"Zero."

"She doesn't call at all?"

"Oh, she calls plenty. To tell Lucky all the wrong things, invalidate her feelings, belittle her accomplishments and undermime any progress she's made. I'm at the point now where I run interference on the calls and it's a fucking chore just to be civil."

"But it's not the lack of support that drove Lucky over the edge. It goes deeper than that, right? It's older."

"It's as old as Lucky." Will paused. "Hang on a sec, I'm going outside. Too many ears around."

Erik sat on the couch, putting his feet up on the coffee table. If he were at Barbegazi, Bastet would have immediately jumped in his lap. Out of habit, his hand reached, looking for the dome of that silvery head nudging at him. The empty air beneath his curved palm made the dull ache of missing Daisy rear up like a startled cobra.

"Sorry," Will said. "Anyway, you know Lucky's family pretty much mirrors our situation. Two kids and then Lucky was a surprise third."

"When did her parents divorce?"

"She was six. And the unspoken skeleton banging on the closet door is Rich was already kicking around the idea of separating when Judy got pregnant with Lucky. Either accidentally or on purpose."

"Did he have someone else?" Erik asked. "Or he'd just had enough?"

"Not sure. Somehow Judy shamed or manipulated him into staying. He came back home and stuck around for the kids' sake."

"So basically, Lucky was Judy's pawn in a loveless marriage?"

"Yeah. And when Rich left anyway, she became Judy's punching bag."

"Because she failed to serve her purpose."

"Exactly. Plant that seed in Lucky's subconscious and fast-forward to when we find ourselves pregnant for an unexpected third time. What do you get?"

"Rattling bones."

"Whether Lucky saw Jacy as herself and Lucky was going to turn into Judy. Or both..."

"You're not Rich, though," Erik said. "And your marriage is anything but loveless."

"Doesn't matter, I guess. It obviously triggered something."

"Weird how it's nothing you consciously do or decide," Erik said. "When an instinctive, free-associated idea gets into your mind, it gets into your DNA. You just start living it."

"Yeah," Will said, his voice dull and tired. "She's working through it. She likes her therapist and the meds seem to be evening her out. She's getting up and getting dressed and getting through the days. But..."

"She's not herself," Erik said. "And you miss her."

"I hate seeing her so lost. I hate that half her candles are blown out. She's here, but her eyes are just...gone. God, it fucking kills me. Especially since I know how bad it can get and I'm helpless to fix it. I want to go in with a wrench and duct tape and make it all better. I suck at patience."

"You're the most patient person I know. Are you kidding?"

"It's a cleverly-crafted illusion," Will said. "I want the world yesterday. Always have."

"Huh."

"I can't do anything about it," Will said. "Directly, anyway. It's all indirect support—managing the kids and the house, trying to carve out time just for us, wrapping my arms around her every chance I get. Blah blah."

"Hey, they sound like little things but they're huge."

Will gave a grunt. Erik caught the keen edge of frustration within it, and only hesitated a few seconds before saying, "Probably not much sex going on, huh?"

"Shit," Will said. "I feel like a douche for being bothered by it but Jesus *Christ*."

"This is entre nous," Erik said. "Douche away."

"Same sob story," Will said. "She's here. She's present. She doesn't initiate, but if I want to, she lets me in. But her head is just somewhere else. It feels so empty and it makes me sad. I miss her jumping my bones. God, I suck."

"Come on, you do not," Erik said, laughing. "Sex is your and Lucky's favorite hobby."

"Cheapest form of entertainment there is," Will said, a little humor back in his voice.

"It's a huge part of your relationship," Erik said. "Sucks to have it disappear. Sucks for anyone."

"Yeah, especially since we were back in a groove since Sara turned two. Before that we were just too damn tired to do more than sloppily grope. But once we got a routine going and the kids were sleeping through the night, we kind of had a Renaissance."

"Now it's the Dark Ages."

Will made a disgusted noise.

"It'll come back," Erik said, realizing a man had a dozen ways to feel impotent.

"I know," Will said. "I'm just impatient. And horny. But enough about me. You guys doing okay? Your teeth must ache from missing her."

"We're all right," Erik said. "I make no illusions about patience. The circumstances suck balls and I want to be living with her for good. Yesterday. But so far we're managing. And joking about it."

"Joking around and jerking off."

"Twice today."

"Same. Ever look at so much porn you depressed yourself?"

"No."

"Yeah, me neither. All right, I need to go. It's the evening meltdown."

"Have fun. Say hi to everyone."

"Love you," Will said. "Don't fucking call me." He hung up.

Erik tossed his phone aside and sighed, arms crossed tight over his chest. Teeth aching. The lonely cobra still stirring in his gut and the silence of the little apartment pressing on his ears.

"It'll be all right," he said softly.

But he awoke in the thin, wee hours. Crying out into the dark, ripped from dreams of blood pouring off the stage in Mallory Hall. A gunshot like a punch to his chest. His insides caving in, not from pain, but the despair of helplessness. Paralyzed and dying, unable to stop James from going back to shoot Daisy dead.

His voice echoed off the bedroom walls in a strangled yell. T-shirt stuck to his back with sweat, heart writhing within his chest. Holding his head, he pulled in breath after breath. Putting the world back in place, remembering when it was and where he was.

It's all right, he thought. *This is now. She didn't die. You found her. She's safe.*

He stripped his damp shirt off and threw it on the floor. Moved over to the other side of the bed which was dry, but cold. He pulled the covers high, letting his shaking breaths warm him.

You're safe.

He shouldn't be surprised. The nightmares of the shooting always came to him in the fall. Something about the turn of season and the shortening of days triggered them. Still, he thought having Daisy back in his life might have kept them at bay this year. His stomach twisted in a strange disappointment. Almost a reproof. As if he had let himself down.

You can't help it, he thought. *It's not something you do, it's something that happens to you.*

He hesitated, looking at the phone on the bedside table. Daisy's words in his head.

I want you to trust me with your darker sides.

Pushing against the notion that calling made him weak, he reached. His eyes squinted against the glare of the phone's display as his thumb picked out the number. Two rings. Half of a third and then Daisy's voice in his ear. Sleepy, but not surprised.

"Hey," she murmured. "You all right?"

He curled into her comfort. "I had a bad dream..."

ALWAYS STOP FOR COFFEE

DAYS FOLDED INTO WEEKS. They laughed through the misery of separation. They bitched and moaned to the world at large but never to each other. They came to easy agreements about money and domestic affairs. The house was in Daisy's name, but she included him in the maintenance decisions and transferred many into his hands. She never treated him like a guest. Barbegazi was his home. And when he pulled into the driveway Sunday nights and the porch light went on, it always filled him with joy. Rain or snow, frigid or mild, Daisy always came out to meet him, running the last few steps and jumping into his arms.

It was hard not to ask for more. But he wanted more. Often to a desperate and frustrated distraction. Phone sex was a red-hot novelty the first few times, but it left him empty and blue afterward. He suffered through the work week, rubbing sulky ones out in the shower, volleying back Daisy's lewd texts with his own obscene intentions. Not soon enough it was Sunday, when he was dropping his backpack in the front hall and pushing Daisy up the stairs with a sailor's agenda.

"Jesus," she said, gasping as she crawled up the mattress toward the pillows.

"Come here," he said, catching one of her ankles. "I'm not done with you."

"No. My brains are gone. I can't."

"You can," he said, dragging her back. "And you will."

She did.

"You are a hundred times the lover you were in college," she said later.

He pressed his face into her breasts. "A hundred."

"Yes. I counted."

"Counting means you still have brain cells left," he said. "Which means I'm definitely not done with you."

He was done exalting the past, though. The gilded monument to the college era was unceremoniously toppled and a new regime of magnificent sex ruled the bedroom. They made love with an astonishing freedom. Physically fearless and verbally uninhibited. Confident with their desires and needs.

"It's so different," he said in the drowsy aftermath. "But I can't put my finger on why."

She yawned against his chest. "Well, you fuck like a grownup now."

He chuckled into her hair. "I do my big boy fuckies."

They rolled away, laughing. Rolled back, clonked heads and snorted, laughing harder. Their utter joy in each other's company piled up on the bed like extra throw pillows. The dark of the bedroom shimmered around them, suffused with laughter and passion.

"I love you," he said, his voice hoarse with happiness. "And I love fucking you..."

The spires of the cathedral sparkled against candlelit walls. Buttressed and vaulted and arched, their bodies ringing like bells within. Her arms unfolded, her legs beckoned and he came to her any way she would have him. He reached high and far into her body, her love spooling out like a ribbon and wrapping around his limbs.

He had three nights to wind himself up in her scent and feel and taste. Too soon it was Wednesday and they had to pry their fingers off what they'd made and let it go another week.

Missing Daisy did make his teeth ache. Yet Erik genuinely loved working at the theater, which saved him from both the melancholy and the harrowing schedule. His fingerprints were on every inch of wiring, every lantern, every screw sunk in every strut. He did good work and made good contacts. He made friends with the cast and slowly earned the respect of his crew.

Most of his young minions were Acadians with a grudging understanding of English and a fierce, tribal mentality. Many had fought to get this job as an alternative to a lifetime of drudge work in the fisheries. One or two, Erik suspected, were closeted gays looking for a safer environment.

Impatient to overcome the cultural gap, he started listening to French language tapes on the drives to Saint John and back.

"Finally a legitimate reason to talk to myself in the car," he said to Daisy.

He made slow progress. Nothing he heard on the tapes sounded remotely like what came out of his men's mouths at work. Worse, most of the instruction was useless to him. Knowing how to pass the salt or discuss the weather wasn't helpful when he had to show a tech how to set the proper DMX value for the automated lighting fixtures.

He persevered, listening hard. He picked up technical terminology first, courtesies next, and finally curses.

"Listen to *you*," Will cried. "Swearing like a native."

Between the vehicular courses and the backstage education, he ended up with a ridiculous accent and a pathetic lingo that couldn't even be called pidgin. He got laughed at a lot. But the good kind of laugh. The stagehands slowed down their talk, gently corrected his mistakes and when they started calling him Fish, he knew he had arrived.

One Monday afternoon, late in September, Lucky called Erik's cell phone.

"Are you home?"

"I'm here. Dais is food shopping."

"No, I want you. Are you decent?"

"I am."

"I'm coming over."

"To kill me?"

But she had hung up. Erik shrugged and went back to his sandwich making. He pulled up to the kitchen island with chips and a beer just as Lucky yoo-hooed from the front hall. She walked into the kitchen carrying Jacy in her carseat. She set it on the counter and took her jacket off.

"Hey beautiful," Erik said, touching the tip of Jacy's nose. She was looking everywhere but at him. Babies didn't seem to dig him much. A newspaper was wedged between her squirming body and the side of the seat. Lucky took it, smoothed it out on the table next to Erik's lunch.

"I was waiting in line for my coffee and I picked up *La Presse*. Just scanning through the arts section. I nearly dropped dead when I saw this," she said.

"*La Presse* is in French. I can't read it."

"Neither can I but as far as I can make out, it's about a retrospective for deWrenne Atelier. They're one of the biggest jewelry houses in Montreal. But look. Here. You don't need to know French..."

Her finger circled one of the color photographs. In a nest of black velvet lay a gold fish, the end of a gold chain in its mouth. It was articulated in four sections and intricately carved, its eye a tiny red jewel. A few inches down from it on the chain hung a smaller gold fish.

An exact copy of the gold fish hanging around Erik's neck.

"Do you see what I see?" Lucky said.

"I see it." His heart pounding, Erik's eyes scanned the words printed below the photograph.

> *Le gousset, poisson d'or, environ 1887. Fabriqué par deWrenne comme cadeau de mariage pour Björn Fiskare de Clayton, New York. Bijou de montre, un cadeau pour commémorer la naissance du fils aîné de Fiskare, Kennet. Trois poissons supplémentaires ont été créés pour chaque enfant Fiskare, leur localisation étant à ce jour inconnues. (Collection privée)*

Erik reached behind and unclasped his necklace. He separated the gold fish from the rest of the charms and carefully laid it down next to the picture in the newspaper.

"It matches," Lucky said. "It's the same fish. And it says Fiskare. Right there."

"Jesus," Erik said.

Lucky took out her phone, zoomed in on Erik's fish next to the photograph and its French text. The shutter clicked. "Sending this to both Dais and Will," she said, her thumbs busy on the keypad. "One of them can read it."

She put her phone down, took Jacy out of the seat, held her up high and sniffed her butt before handing her to Erik. Jacy glared at him.

"She always looks at me like I owe her money," Erik said. He tried a couple of bounces, but she was having none of it. She squirmed and fussed in his hands. Lucky took her back.

"You big baby," she said. "Handsome hunk like him offers his lap, you say *yes*."

Erik smiled, and tugged one of Lucky's curls. "How you feeling?"

"Better."

"Good. You look better."

"You were right about meds cutting out the extreme ends of the spectrum," she said. "Which is good because it stops the free-falling anxiety. But on the other hand..."

"You don't get real jazzed up about anything," Erik said. "I remember."

"It's sort of surreally neutral. But I'm eating and sleeping again. I'm not crying all the goddamn time or having a panic attack at the thought of leaving the house. So I'll take it."

Her phone pinged. They both bent their heads to the display.

HOLY SHIT, Will had texted.

Erik's cell phone rang, it was Daisy.

"Holy shit," she said. "Is that another fish?"

"Sure as hell looks like it. I can't read the text."

"It's a chain for a pocket watch. Made in 1887 by deWrenne as a wedding present for Björn Fiskare of Clayton. And an accompanying watch charm, made to commemorate the birth of Fiskare's oldest son, Kennet. Isn't your grandfather's name Kennet?"

"It is. But eighteen eighty-seven? It's too early to be my grandfather. He was born in the twenties or something. It must be another relative."

"It says three additional fish were made for each Fiskare child, whereabouts unknown. This is from a private collection."

"Look at my arms," Lucky said. "Look at the hair standing up on my arms."

Every hair on Erik's body was standing up. His lunch forgotten, he snapped his own picture of the newspaper and texted it to his mother. ***Call me when you see this.***

She called him five minutes later. "I see your fish and I see Fiskare, what does the rest say?"

He told her.

"Holy shit."

"Right?"

"Well, it's news to me. I know nothing about that necklace other than it was a family heirloom."

"I want to dig into this."

"You should. This is exciting. Let me know what you find out."

Lucky had taken a pen and circled the byline of the article, Pavitra Mhendu. Her finger circled the phone number of the newspaper. "You want to call?"

He went through the switchboard, asked for Pavitra Mhendu and was transferred to voicemail. He told who he was and what he had, left his number, thanked her and hung up.

"This is the most excited I've been in months," Lucky said. "Can I keep watching?"

"You found it, clever girl. You're on the team."

"See?" Lucky said, kissing Jacy's fat cheek. "Always stop for coffee."

Erik finished his lunch and Lucky flipped through a magazine. They drummed their fingers on the table and tried not to stare at the phone. But after twenty minutes, Jacy was having a meltdown. Lucky left and Erik went out to cut the grass.

Pavitra didn't call back until four o'clock. "Mr. Fiskare," she said, her voice chirping and melodic. "I am pleased you called me. I was so surprised."

"You and me both," he said.

"Do you recognize any of the names in the article?"

"I do, but I'm afraid I don't know a whole lot about that side of the family tree so I'm not sure who they are to me. But I have one of those small gold fish. I'm wearing it right now."

"Well, the fob and the charm came from the private collection of Vivian deWrenne. I interviewed her for the article. She's head of the company now. It's always been family-run. Do you know of any relation between your family and the deWrennes?"

"No," he said, wondering if the connection were somewhere along his grandmother's side. Her name was Astrid but with a pang, he realized he didn't know what her maiden name was.

"Well let me hang up and call Madame deWrenne. She's quite busy, but I'm sure she'd want to talk to you. She pressed the point that the small fish charm was one of four made by her great-grandfather, and the other three were missing, so to speak. She'll be thrilled to know another has resurfaced. May I give her your telephone number?"

"Please do. Yes."

THE ROMANTIC INVALID

 to Barbegazi for dinner that night, with much discussion about the newspaper article and Erik's necklace passed around the table so everyone could examine it with fresh eyes. Christine called once to see if any new developments had surfaced. Erik could only relay the name Vivian deWrenne which Christine didn't recognize.

The Kaegers left and Erik was stringing his guitar when his cell phone rang with an unidentified number. His gut twisted in a hunch and he answered formally, "Erik Fiskare."

"Erik, this is Vivian deWrenne, from deWrenne Atelier."

"How are you?"

"Among many other things, I'm delighted to meet you."

"Same here. That article made the hair on the back of my neck stand up. It's still up."

"Well, I should say the name on my birth certificate is Vivian Fiskare. I use deWrenne professionally. And if you're wearing one of those gold fish and it was passed down through your family then I believe you and I are cousins."

"We are?"

"Let me figure a few things out. Hold on, I'm pouring a drink. I'm exhausted. I just got in from Europe."

"You can call me back if you want."

"Oh no, I'll never sleep if I don't get to the bottom of this. I don't sleep anyway. I don't even know what time it is."

"It's ten-fifteen where I am."

"Is it? Oh dear, I'm calling you late. I'm so sorry."

"No, I won't sleep either so we may as well get into it." He looked up to see Daisy in the living room doorway, eyes wide. He gave her a thumbs-up. "Would you mind if I put you on speaker? My girlfriend is dying to hear this."

"Oh certainly. Am I on? Hello?"

"Hello," Daisy said.

"Hello there, I'm Vivian. I'm going to drink and ask questions. Your job is to write it all down."

Daisy held up pen and paper as though Vivian could see her. "I'm writing."

"Now, Erik, who is your father?"

"Byron."

A long pause. Long enough to make Daisy and Erik exchange glances.

"I know who you are," Vivian said. "I know exactly who you are."

"We've met?"

"You probably wouldn't remember. You were a little boy. I was maybe twenty-three and you couldn't have been more than five."

"Where was it? In Clayton?"

"Back up a moment, I need to fit us together first. If you're Byron's son, then Kennet is your grandfather, correct?"

"Yes."

"And Kennet is Emil's son."

"I don't know," Erik said. "I'm sort of embarrassingly clueless about my family history. My knowledge ends at Kennet."

"Kennet was Emil Fiskare's eldest son."

"Who was Kennet's mother?" Daisy asked, writing names and drawing lines on her pad.

"Oh God, what was her name," Vivian said. "Martha? Mary? Something with an M. She and Emil ran the hotel up in Clayton."

"I grew up across from the hotel," Erik said. "On Hugunin Street."

"Now Emil," Vivian said. "Here's where we connect the dots. Emil was one of four children. He had one older brother, another Kennet, who married into the deWrenne family. He was my grandfather. What does that make us?"

Daisy was drawing and mumbling under her breath. "I think that makes you and Erik's father second cousins. So you and Erik are second cousins once removed?"

"Sounds good on paper," Vivian said. "So my grandfather Kennet was the eldest. Then came Emil, your great-grandfather. Then the twins, Erik and Beatrice. Four children in all. Antoine deWrenne, the jeweler, made a gold fish at the birth of each child, for Björn to wear on his watch chain. And the big fish, the articulated one, that was a fob at the end of the chain. It kept the chain from sliding through his buttonhole."

"The article said the big fish was a wedding present," Erik said.

"Yes, exactly. It was made for Björn when he married Marianne Dupre. I don't think the photograph in the article showed it, but his initials are engraved in the tail fin."

"I have his Saint Birgitta medal," Erik said, reaching a finger up to touch it. "It's engraved with his initials on the back. B.K.E.F. And the date 1865."

"You have it?"

"I'm wearing it. And the gold fish and a third charm which is a boat. It has *Fiskare* engraved on the bottom."

"Hmm. I don't know anything about those. It sounds as though the saint's medal is personal. It could have been a christening present and come with Björn when he immigrated to the States. I don't know anything about the boat though. Could you take a picture and send it to me later?"

"I will."

"Obviously after Björn's death, the fish charms were distributed to his children. I have a fish and you have a fish. That's two. Which leaves the ones belonging to Beatrice and Erik, the twins."

"Do you know anything about them?" Daisy asked.

"I know Beatrice died in infancy, but I don't know what became of her fish. It could be she was buried with it. I tend to think it would be kept for sentimental purposes. As for her twin brother, Erik, I know nothing about him. I assume you don't either."

"This is all news to me," Erik said.

"Well at least we'll sleep now."

Erik paused. The woman sounded tired, but the small bits of information she had dropped about his father were too tantalizing. He'd never sleep. "You said you met my father?"

"Yes. You have to understand, I didn't go often to the Thousand Islands and then only under duress. I was rather obnoxious in my youth."

"Weren't we all?"

"But I remember the first time I met your father quite vividly. I was perhaps eleven. And he was fifteen or sixteen. He'd been injured in a terrible boating accident and when I came to visit, he was just home from the hospital. He was out on one of the verandas. Lying on a big wicker couch with a hundred pillows and a tray nearby, looking quite the romantic invalid. And handsome, oh, just the handsomest boy. I fell terribly in love, so I was paying attention to details. Funny how I can still remember. He was wearing a grey bathrobe over blue pajamas. His vision was still doubled—I think he'd had a severe concussion—so his brother was reading to him. He was easy on the eyes, too, and—"

"Wait, what?" Erik said. "Who was easy on the eyes?"

"Byron's brother."

"My father didn't have a brother."

"His half-brother. Andrew?"

"I don't know who that is."

"They had the same mother. Your grandmother Astrid married twice. Kennet was her second husband."

"Oh," Erik said. He looked at Daisy and shrugged, his bottom lip curling in cluelessness.

"Your grandmother was such an interesting woman," Vivian said. "She spoke, I think, four languages."

Erik's eyebrows flew up his forehead. "She did? I only heard her speak English and Swedish."

"She was fluent in Spanish."

"Spanish?"

"Oh yes, I remember it quite well. Anyway, back to the subject, the second time I met your father was at his brother's funeral. In nineteen sixty-eight. I was a senior in high school. It was another boating accident. Andrew and Elsa drowned on the river."

"Elsa?"

Vivian's silence seemed hesitant. "Another relative. It was a terrible tragedy."

"And you were at the funeral?"

"Oh yes. It was devastating for the family. They never found the bodies. Just the wrecked boat."

The hair was up on the back of Erik's neck again. On her sketched-out family tree, Daisy drew a new box under Astrid, labeling it *Andrew*. Nearby she wrote *Elsa?* and circled it several times.

"The last time I saw your father," Vivian said, "was some time in the early seventies. I was either a junior or senior in college. It was a quick passing-through. I was going from New York to Montreal and I stopped in Clayton with...oh, whoever I was wearing on my arm at the time. And I had dinner at the hotel. Byron was there with his wife. I remember a little blond boy running around which was you. It made an impression because it seemed you were the only thing that could bring a little light back into your grandparents' eyes. They'd become withdrawn and reserved since Andrew's death. But whenever you came close to them, they came back to life."

"What was my father like, do you remember?"

"At that time? Somber. Both him and your mother. Their second child—forgive me, I can't remember boy or girl."

"Boy," Erik said. "My brother, Pete."

"He was sick. Or something. I can't remember, but your parents were occupied with it."

"He'd gone deaf."

"I see," Vivian said. "It had just happened. Or just become evident."

"So," Erik said. "All three times you saw him, he was..." He ran a hand through his hair. "I'm not sure what I'm saying."

"You could say I always came into contact with him when he was down on his luck."

"Right. Exactly."

Vivian yawned audibly. "I'm sorry. The day is catching up with me. I'm so pleased to talk to you and know now at least two of the fish charms are accounted for."

"This has been really interesting. I've wondered a long time where this necklace came from."

"I'm so glad you got in touch. If you're ever in Montreal, do look me up. I'd be delighted to show you the watch and the other fish."

"I'd like that."

"Well, cheers, my dear. Until we talk again. Goodnight."

"Goodnight."

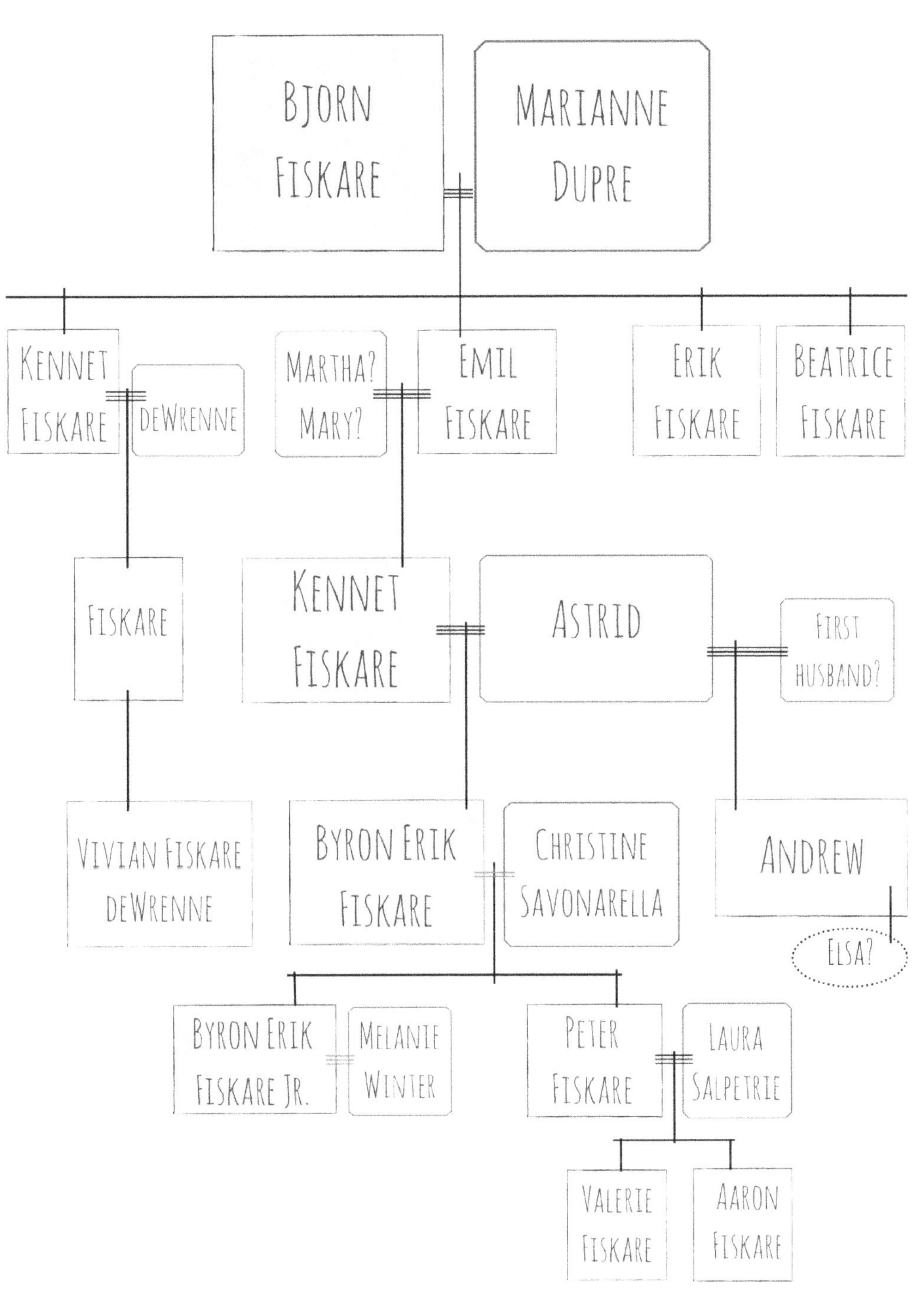

Bjorn Fiskare
Marianne Dupre
Kennet Fiskare
deWrenne
Martha? Mary?
Emil Fiskare
Erik Fiskare
Beatrice Fiskare
Fiskare
Kennet Fiskare
Astrid
First Husband?
Vivian Fiskare deWrenne
Byron Erik Fiskare
Christine Savonarella
Andrew
Elsa?
Byron Erik Fiskare Jr.
Melanie Winter
Peter Fiskare
Laura Salpetrie
Valerie Fiskare
Aaron Fiskare

SEARCH AND RESCUE

PUMPED UP WITH MYSTERY and intrigue, they signed up for a 30-day trial on an ancestry website. Erik laced his fingers and cracked his knuckles, then did a search on Fiskare in the riverside town of Clayton.

Census records were the top search results. He didn't know what to do with them so he scanned past, looking for...

"I don't know what to look at first," he said.

"Why not refine it on Andrew Fiskare," Daisy said. "Your father's half-brother."

He did, and the search results tightened to newspaper archives from *The Ogdensburg Herald.*

He clicked on one dated April 27, 1968. He dragged the digitally scanned copy until he saw Fiskare highlighted in yellow, and zoomed in. "'Search continues for Fiskare youths,'" he read. "'No hope for survivors.'"

"It's always April," Daisy said behind the fingers steepled over her nose.

> *Coast Guard officials confirmed the search and rescue has become search and recovery for Andrew and Elsa Fiskare, whose wrecked boat was found by Brush Island following Thursday's storm. Little hope remains anyone could survive in the frigid temperatures of the St. Lawrence for this long.*

Elsa Fiskare, 22, is the daughter of Emil and Marta Fiskare, proprietors of The Fisher Hotel in Clayton. Andrew Fiskare, 23, is the adopted son of Kennet Fiskare.

Andrew and Elsa were reported missing Thursday morning. Andrew's wrecked speedboat was located yesterday on the treacherous shoals by Brush Island. Pieces of clothing believed to belong to the two were also recovered.

A dredge of the river is not possible at this time due to the strong currents and dangerous riptides which plague the St. Lawrence after the ice melts.

"Marta." Daisy touched the screen. "It matches what Vivian said. Kennet's mother was Marta and Elsa was Kennet's sister."

"I'm confused." Erik squinted, doing some mental math. "She was my grandfather's sister, but she was twenty-two in nineteen sixty-eight? She'd be born in forty-six. She was my father's age."

Puzzled, he backed out of the article and clicked on the next one from May 14, 1968.

"'Search ceases,'" Daisy said. "'Fiskares presumed dead.'"

...the victims are presumed to have perished in the St. Lawrence River.

Elsa Fiskare was born in Clayton in 1946, the daughter of Emil Fiskare and his second wife Marta Toivonen. She graduated Clayton High School in 1964 and attended Cazenovia College for two years. In addition to her parents, she is survived by her half-sister Gertrude Fiskare Pettitte, and her half-brothers Kennet, Erik and Emil Fiskare. She was pre-deceased by another half-brother, Björn Fiskare.

"Second wife, Marta," Erik said. "*Half*-brothers."

"So Emil was married twice," Daisy said, erasing and re-drawing lines on the family tree. "Kennet's mother was someone else. He and three brothers and Gertrude had the same mother. Then Emil married Marta and Elsa was their daughter."

*Andrew Fiskare—Xandro to his family and close friends—
was born Alexandre Felipe Virtanen-Reyes in 1945, in St.
Petersburg, Florida. He was the son of Jose Alexandre
Davis-Reyes and Astrid Virtanen.*

"Well, Vivian said she spoke Spanish," Erik said, laughing a little.

"They speak Portuguese in Brazil," Daisy said, opening and closing drawers in her desk.

"But why would Astrid have been living in Brazil in the first place? That makes no sense…"

*Fiskare's biological father held dual American and Bra-
zilian citizenship. He fought with the Brazilian Expedi-
tionary Force in the Italian Campaign and died at Monte
Cassino in 1945. After the war, Mrs. Reyes married Kennet
Fiskare of Clayton, who legally adopted Andrew in 1947.*

*Fiskare graduated from Clayton High School in 1963
and from the Eastman School of Music in 1967. An accomplished violinist, he was pursuing his master's degree at the State University of New York at Fredonia. In
addition to his parents, he is survived by his half-brother,
Byron Fiskare.*

Daisy had found some graph paper and was drawing out the tree from scratch. Erik had his hands laced behind his head like a hostage waiting to be shot. "What the fuck," he muttered to the screen. He reached for his cell phone. "This is crazy."

"Who are you calling?"

"My mother."

"Don't you yell at her."

"I won't yell at her, I'm just going to ask why she never told me my father had a half-brother. Who was half Brazilian."

"Hey," Dais said sharply. She swung one leg over his knees and sat down in his lap, holding his hand with the phone up high. "It's possible she didn't know. You probably don't even know how she met your dad."

Erik's mouth fell open in protest, then shut.

"She may know nothing," Daisy said. "Or she may know everything but she chose not to answer questions you never asked. Both of you wanted to protect the other. If you're going to start asking things now then you can't just…"

"I know," he said, closing his eyes. "I know. I'll be nice, I promise."

She kissed his forehead. "It's not about being nice, it's about being tactful." She slid off him and back into her chair. "And speaking of tact, it's practically midnight in the States, so don't call her now. Stew on it and call her tomorrow."

He nodded, chewing the inside of his lip. He pointed to the screen again. "He was getting his master's at Fredonia. That's where my mother went to college. I wonder if she knew him."

HEIR TO A FORTUNE

"IT'S ME," HE SAID the next night.

"Hello, me," Christine said. "Did you talk to your cousin?"

"I did."

"Is there lost Fiskare treasure in her vault? Are you the heir to a fortune? Please say yes."

"No," he said, laughing. "You'll still be working until you're eighty."

"Crap," she said. "Well, what did she tell you about the fish?"

Erik told her the story of the watch and its charms. "She said she remembered us. From one visit to Clayton. It was just after Pete lost his hearing."

"I don't remember her. Honestly, Erik, at that time, I could've been introduced to Liberace and it wouldn't have made an impression."

"She remembers it being grim. And she told me a couple other things that have me curious. I'm wondering if…"

The rattle of ice in a glass. "If what?"

"Listen, I know I've never asked you much about him, but if I ask you now, will you tell me?"

"I'll tell you what I can."

"If anything is too painful for you to talk about, I get it—"

"Erik. I won two hundred bucks at bingo tonight. I'm on my second G and T and Fred is grilling me a steak. I'll probably get laid later."

"Nice, Mother," he said.

"Suffice it to say, I am in an outstanding mood. Ask away."

"Did you know Dad had a half-brother?"

A short pause. "I'm sorry, you can't ask me that. Whoops, dinner time. Talk to you later."

"Go home, Mom, you're drunk."

She laughed. "And you are such easy bait."

"You're killing me here."

"I'm sorry," she said. "You're trying to have a serious conversation with me, I'll cooperate. Dad's half-brother. Yes. Xandro."

"You knew him?"

"I met him when I was at Fredonia."

"You met him before Dad?"

"Yes, he was the TA for my music theory class and then I became his rehearsal accompanist. We went on a couple of dates. Romantically it wasn't anything terribly serious, but we worked well together. He was an incredibly talented musician. And then he died."

"In a boating accident. I found articles about it online. He was with another Fiskare, someone named Elsa."

"Their pocket aunt."

"What's a pocket aunt?"

"She was your grandfather's half-sister. Old Emil remarried to a much younger woman and she had this daughter, Elsa. So technically she was Byron and Xandro's aunt, but she was their age. The three of them grew up together like siblings. The accident was just a horrible tragedy. They never found the bodies."

"That's what I read."

"I went to Clayton for the funeral service and I met your father."

"I see," Erik said. "The newspaper says Andrew—or Xandro? He was called Xandro?"

"Yes."

"It says he was Farmor's son. And his father was Brazilian."

"That's right."

"How did I not know this?"

"About Xandro or about Brazil?"

"Both."

"Honey…" Her voice was gentle and patient. "I'm sure you knew about it. In the way little boys are generally aware of the details of their life. The details are present, but they're not vital. Plus you weren't a terribly curious child when it came to people. Pete was the nosy one. He liked to ask personal questions. You were a watcher and listener. And I think when your brain tried to do a selective memory erase, it probably wiped out all kinds of things it didn't think were important."

"I guess…"

Another rattle of ice cubes against glass. "Anyway, Astrid was the queen of shut mouths so even I don't know much of her story. It was hell getting that woman to talk about herself, but I know Astrid lived a good many years in Brazil and met her first husband there. In fact, I brought a friend up to Clayton with me once, when I was dating your father. My friend Carmen, who could speak fluent Portuguese, and I nearly dropped dead when Astrid started talking with her. I remember she blushed when she saw me staring with my mouth open. Like it was something she was embarrassed about."

"Huh," Erik said. "This is crazy shit. I mean, from a genealogy perspective."

"I just remembered something else: Astrid's father owned hotels. She grew up in the business, so to speak."

"I have one more question."

"One more, then I want my steak."

"Wasn't Dad also in a boating accident once?"

"Yes." A pause. "It was long before I met him, honey."

"But you knew about it?" he asked.

"Of course I knew about it."

Erik's eyes narrowed. Christine's voice had drawn in, gone just the slightest bit tight. An awkward silence wound between them, broken by Fred's voice calling in the background.

"Go eat," Erik said. "Enjoy. Love you."

"Love you, honey," she said, and hung up.

"She got weird," he said to Daisy.

Daisy turned from where she was paying the bills and put out her hands helplessly. It was weird to her. This was another language, these family secrets and mysteries and taboo subjects.

"I've gotten so used to not talking about him," Erik said. "Now I don't even know how to bring him up gracefully."

"You bring him up to me."

"Um, because you're the exception to every rule in my life."

Daisy smiled and turned back to her desk. He already knew paying bills made her fuse short and her patience tight. He let her be and sat at his own desk. Stared at the computer a few moments before he hitched forward and began to type in the internet search box, *Swedes in Brazil.*

He found several interesting articles about the Scandinavian settlement in South America, which began in the late 19th century. The largest Scandinavian population in Latin America was indeed Brazil, a fact he read out loud to Daisy.

"Learn something new every day," she said around the pencil held in her teeth. "I guess one bad winter too many and you'll head for the other side of the equator."

He hummed. He'd been hoping for more of a smoking gun. More grandiose evidence of *Your grandmother was here.*

He checked his scribbled notes, and for kicks he Googled *Virtanen surname.*

"Ah-hah," he said, rubbing the beard growth on his chin. "It says 'Virtanen is a surname originating in Finland—in Finnish, meaning *river*—where it is the second most common surname.'"

"Everyone knows that," Daisy said.

"Smartass," he said. He typed *Finns in Brazil.*

He felt his eyes light up as he clicked on the first search hit.

"'How the Finnish Utopian Colony of Penedo, Brazil, became a tourist attraction.'"

"Finnish utopian colony," Daisy said. "That's a thing?"

Erik didn't answer. He was reading.

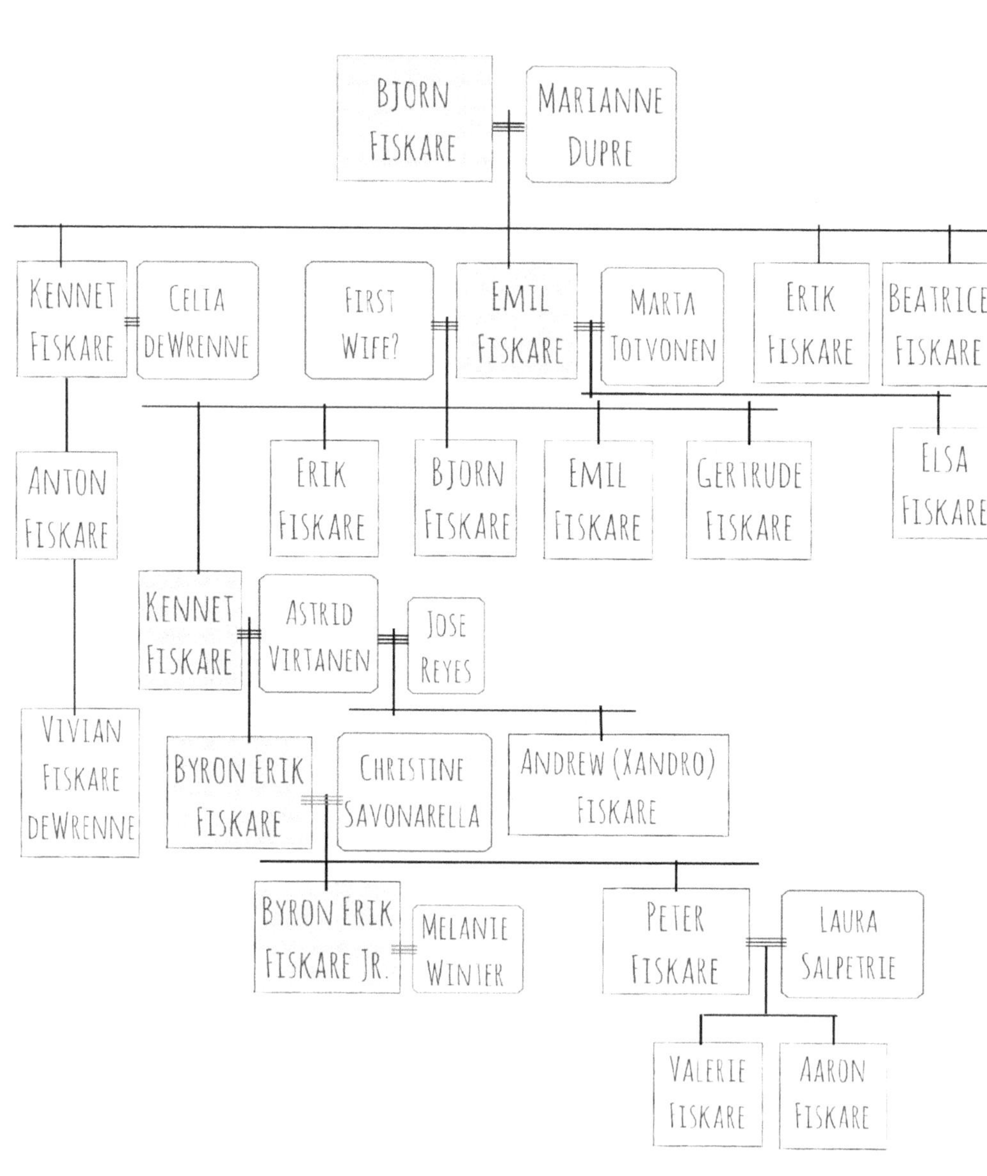

Bjorn Fiskare
Marianne Dupre
Kennet Fiskare
Celia deWrenne
First Wife?
Emil Fiskare
Marta Totvonen
Erik Fiskare
Beatrice Fiskare
Anton Fiskare
Erik Fiskare
Bjorn Fiskare
Emil Fiskare
Gertrude Fiskare
Elsa Fiskare
Kennet Fiskare
Astrid Virtanen
Jose Reyes
Vivian Fiskare deWrenne
Byron Erik Fiskare
Christine Savonarella
Andrew (Xandro) Fiskare
Byron Erik Fiskare Jr.
Melanie Winter
Peter Fiskare
Laura Salpetrie
Valerie Fiskare
Aaron Fiskare

A SPECTACULAR FLOOR

THE DAYS GREW SHORTER, darker and colder. The odometer clicked off the miles on Erik's car. He figured out how to manage possessions in two places, but he never got used to it. It occurred to him that since he'd been divorced, he had been living in temporary conditions, never fully settling in.

"I just wonder when I'm going to be *home*," he said, sighing. "You know? Home for good with you."

"I know," Daisy said. "I want it so bad."

Hand-in-hand, they ambled around Market Square. They passed a jewelry store, the bright lights in its window display making gold, silver and jeweled sparkles. Erik stopped. Daisy kept walking a few steps, stretching their arms out. He pulled her back to him.

"What do you like?" he asked.

"What do I like?"

He put his fingertips on the glass, above a white slotted tray holding diamond rings. "Which one?"

She glanced at him. "This is just conversation?"

"Let's say I'm getting to know you better."

She smiled and bent her head toward the glass. "Second row from the top. Third one from the left. I like."

It was a simple rectangular diamond in a plain gold band.

"That one?" he said.

"It's an emerald cut. I've always loved it. And I like the stone alone. No baguettes or any of that fancy stuff."

"Huh," he said.

"Which did you think I would like?"

He found the biggest, gaudiest ring in the tray and pointed it out to her. "But with more fancy stuff."

She swatted him. "You have so much to learn."

Canadian Thanksgiving came in October, along with Erik's thirty-sixth birthday. The weekend before Halloween, he made a short trip to Rochester to see his mother before she and Fred left for Florida.

In one of the great, mystical redundancies of his life, Erik found himself up a ladder, having a man-to-man. As he scooped dead, rotting leaves out of the gutters, he asked Fred why he and Christine didn't just sell the place and move down to Key West permanently.

"She still needs an outpost here," Fred said around the pipe in his teeth. The tobacco he smoked smelled of burning vanilla and Erik liked how it mixed with the autumn air.

"An outpost for who? Me and Pete? We're big boys now."

"Nobody knows that better than her."

Erik tossed the last handful and looked down at Fred. He was tall with a high, lined forehead and grey hair blowing around in the wind. He'd started dating Christine in Erik's senior year of high school. A retired town justice, Fred always reminded Erik of a pair of scales, perfectly balanced, weighing all sides of an issue. Erik hadn't taken many problems to Fred, but if consulted, Fred always gave good advice. He helped Erik negotiate buying his first car. And he was good to have around if you had a civics paper to write, or needed a guest for your high school Career Day.

"What do you think?" Erik asked, leaning his elbows on the top of the ladder.

Fred smoked a while before answering.

"Erik, I've been with your mother nearly two decades now."

"You ever going to make an honest woman of her?" Erik said, grinning. "You don't need my permission."

"Don't I, though?"

Erik tilted his chin. "You have it," he said. "If it's worth something to you, you have it."

"Well, thank you," Fred said, with a small bow. "I appreciate that. And maybe it's not my place to tell you why I think she won't marry me, but..."

"What?"

Fred rubbed the back of his neck. "Between you and me, I think she's still married to your father."

If he had kicked the ladder out from Erik's feet, the surprise couldn't have been greater. "No, she's not," Erik said. "They divorced. When I was ten."

Fred looked up at him, his face a blend of apprehension and conviction. "I don't think so," he said softly.

Erik stared.

"Promise me this stays between us," Fred said. "I've never voiced that thought aloud. I have absolutely nothing to back it up."

Erik nodded. The idea of judicious Fred making a statement without evidence made a nervous chill run down his neck. He came down the ladder and they manhandled it to the next section of gutter. The wind kicked up, blowing leaves around in a cloud of red and orange.

"I hear we're in for a hard winter," Fred said.

"You'll be far from it," Erik said. "I don't know why anyone would stay in Rochester through winter if they had an alternative."

"The way I see it is after your father left, your mother built a spectacular floor under you and Pete," Fred said. "Her pride in how she raised you was bound up in your house on Graceland Avenue. That house was the embodiment of everything she survived and everything she accomplished."

"But she sold it."

"And it was one of the hardest things she ever did. Leaving Rochester entirely would be even harder. The last tie severed. She's not ready to let go yet and I won't force it. Because you don't know hell until you've lived with a resentful woman."

Erik laughed. "You're good to her," he said. "I always thought so."

"She stays for you more than Pete," Fred said. "I know on paper you're the oldest but no doubt, you're her baby."

"You think?"

Fred tapped his pipe against the strut of the ladder then put it in his shirt pocket. "A watershed moment exists in every man's life," he said. "Sometimes it's profound, sometimes it's barely a blip. But every man has the moment when he stops being his mother's son and becomes another woman's man. When he goes from protected to protector."

Erik thought about that, looking down at Fred's gentle expression. "I wonder when mine was."

"I don't," Fred said, smiling. "It was when you crawled out of the lighting booth."

Flung backward in time, Erik stared into the air, nodding slowly. "You're right," he said. "I remember... When the glass was breaking over my head, I had this one clear thought. *My mother doesn't know where I am.* It was there, then it was gone. And from that point on I only thought of Daisy."

"It was your moment," Fred said.

"I can't begin to think what Mom suffered that day. All those parents."

"Well, when the news about Lancaster was on the TV and we couldn't get through to the school... It was about an hour window when your mother didn't know if you were alive. I'll face down a fleet of tanks rather than re-live that hour again. She looked me in the eye and said, 'If I lose him, I will die.' I didn't think for a nanosecond she was exaggerating."

WORTH SAVING

WHILE CHRISTINE CLEARED UP after dinner, Erik told her about the article he found on Penedo, the Finnish utopian colony in Brazil.

"It was almost like a religious movement," he said. "They thought God was in nature and they were going to build this communal farm and be entirely self-sufficient. Create a new society in the tropics."

"Shangri-La," Christine said. "Scandinavian style."

"The land turned out to be crap though. Coffee farming ruined it all. The only way to bring in money was to have paying guests in their homes."

"What guests?"

"Other Europeans," Erik said. "Looking for their own kind. Then Brazilians got hooked on the whole sauna thing and they started coming up to the area. Little by little, tourism became the main source of income."

"Isn't that interesting," she said. "I never would've thought."

"It doesn't prove Farmor was there," Erik said. "But if all this was going on in the twenties and thirties, it at least matches up with her timeline. She could have been there or been part of that wave of immigration. Do you want to wash these pots by hand?"

"Cram as much as you can in the dishwasher and we'll run it."

Erik hesitated, then said casually, "Daisy and I were looking at rings the other day."

Christine glanced over her shoulder. "Were you now?"

"Yeah."

"Did you buy anything?"

"No, I just wanted an idea of her style. She likes an emerald cut."

"Really."

"It's like a rectangle."

"I know what it is," she said, and he could hear the smile in her voice.

He squeezed detergent into the dishwasher, closed it and hit the power button. On the stove, the tea kettle began to wail. He turned off the burner and poured water into the waiting mugs.

"When did you first start making me tea?" he asked.

"I didn't," she said. "You drank it because your grandfather did. If Farfar drank warm river water with a sprig of algae, you would too."

"I wish I remembered more," Erik said, spooning a little sugar into his mug and a lot into Christine's.

Christine rubbed the back of her hand across her forehead, leaving her bangs damp. "Do you remember your Aunt Kirsten?"

Erik closed his eyes. "Kirsten," he said. "Farfar's sister? No, that was Trudy. Who was Kirsten?"

"Farfar's sister-in-law. His younger brother Emilio's wife."

"Oh." He didn't remember and it embarrassed him.

"I liked her best," Christine said, scrubbing her broiler pan hard. "She was a pip. Everyone loved her. She smoked, drank and cursed like one of the boys, but then out the other side of her mouth, she could discuss classical music, quote poetry or dictate a blueberry pie recipe. She was always laughing, always had a kind word for everyone. She and Trudy taught you to play poker one summer."

"She did?" Erik frowned into his mug of tea and tried to wriggle backward through the wormhole of time. He was sure he remembered a woman who played cards with him in a fug of cigarette smoke, but he always identified her as Astrid. Maybe his memories were a composite of all the women in the Fisher Hotel.

"She kept in touch a little while," Christine said. "After we left Clayton. Christmas cards and bits of news. Then it just trickled away. You talking with that new cousin of yours the other day got me thinking about it." Christine flicked on the faucet and began to rinse away the brownish foam from the pan. "I know your memory is choppy from those years."

"When I started to reach back and touch those memories," he said, slowly, for he had never shared this with her. "When I was in therapy. It was like they were feathers. I couldn't breathe heavy on them or grab at them. I had to let them come to me. Settle in my hands. If I held still they would come back."

"Sit down," Christine said. "I'll be right back. I want to show you something. Give you something, rather."

He took the mugs to the table and sat, put a cloth napkin on top of Christine's mug to keep the steam in.

Christine came back with a box and a folded packet of papers. She gave the papers to Erik, who unfolded them and wrinkled his eyebrows at the flourished letterhead reading LAST WILL AND TESTAMENT.

> *I, Astrid Martje Virtanen Reyes Fiskare, being of sound mind and body, do declare...*

"This is Farmor's will?"

"Yes," she said, and reached to turn some pages. "Here. Read this part."

> *To my daughter-in-law, Christine Savonarella Fiskare, residing at 94 Graceland Way, Rochester, New York, I leave the diamond from the engagement ring given to me by my first husband, José Alexandre Davis-Reyes (deceased) and the diamond from the engagement ring given to me by my current husband, Kennet Emil Fiskare. I make this bequest in the hope her sons, my grandsons Erik and Peter, will want to give them to a fiancée.*

Christine opened the box and took out two smaller velvet boxes. One royal blue, one black. She opened the black one and unwrapped a bit of tissue paper. Into her palm she tipped an emerald-cut diamond. Erik's eyes widened.

Christine set the tissue paper aside and gazed down at the stone. "This and the other one got me through the bad times," she said, smiling. "Astrid wasn't the most demonstrative of women. She was a practical old bird. She wrote the part about fiancées and it sounds romantic, but I don't doubt she thought I could sell them if I needed to. I kept them in my jewelry box. The last reserve. I'd tell myself, 'well, it's not so bad that I have to cash in Astrid's insurance policy. It's not so bad that the boys won't be able to give their girls a ring."

She held it up between her thumb and forefinger, let it catch the light. "Lot of love in this little bugger."

Erik held up his palm and she put the diamond into it. It shone along its two long edges and glinted along the two short ones. The light dropped down like a mirror into its faceted surface and reflected back in white and grey and silver.

"I'd love if you gave it to Daisy," Christine said.

Erik tipped the stone from one palm to the other. He took a taste of his mother's love and his heart swelled under his ribs.

So much Christine never told him. So much he simply never asked. Save for the necklace he wore, he had turned his back on Clayton and his name and dismissed it all.

Christine could have sold the diamonds. Said *to hell with love. Love is a pipe dream. Cash in hand is what sustains you.*

Instead, in her wisdom and grace, she chose not to throw the souvenirs of the past on the bonfire of spite, but keep them safe for a day that might not even come.

"Funny," Erik said. "For a time I thought all the women I loved made me feel useless. Like nothing I did was good enough. But now I see those women have always picked up the things I threw away or buried and kept them safe. They saved the best parts of me."

Christine slid her arm around his shoulders and pressed her lips to his temple. "Because you're worth saving, Byron Erik," she said.

"Did Dad give you an engagement ring?"

Her hand ran soft over his hair. "He did. But I sold it to help pay for Pete's cochlear implant. I have my wedding band, though. Upstairs in my jewelry box."

"You kept it?"

"I did." She pushed the tissue paper toward him. "Now wrap that diamond up tight. Take the little box, too."

IN THE BATHROOM

 marked a year since Erik picked up the phone and started turning things around. He and Daisy flew down to Pennsylvania to spend it with Joe and Francine.

La Tarasque was shrouded in fog Thanksgiving morning. Erik slipped from his and Daisy's bed in the carriage house. He walked across the yard and up the porch steps.

In the study, Joe was at his desk with coffee. Francine curled in her chair by the window with the paper.

The lemon trees were in flower.

"Frique," Francine said, folding down the pages and peering over glasses. "You're up so early."

"I wanted to show you something," Erik said. "Before I show Daisy."

Joe came around the desk. Francine pushed her glasses up on her head. Erik took the box from his pocket and opened it to show them the ring.

"Oh, darling," Francine said, clapping her hands together.

Joe's hand dropped on Erik's shoulder, fingers reaching to tug his earlobe.

"The diamond belonged to my grandmother," Erik said. "My cousin Vivian helped design the setting."

"It's beautiful," Francine said, running a knuckle beneath one eye before she reached up to take the ring from its velvet slot.

"I'm touched you wanted to show us first," Joe said.

"Well. You don't seem the type to grant permission for her. But I..." Erik rolled his lips in, thinking. "I left once. This time I'm staying. I guess that's really the point of me showing you first."

"Darling," Francine said again, holding the ring up to the window and letting it catch the light. The sun had broken through the fog and was slicing through the lemon blossoms. "The point isn't that you left," she said, making the diamond throw tiny rainbows on the sleeve of her blouse. "The point is you came back."

The ring stayed, shy and secret, in his pocket through Thanksgiving dinner. A half-dozen times he went for it, only to balk. Thinking irrationally, *what if she says no?*

Don't be stupid. She won't say no.

He didn't know what he was waiting for.

It's never going to be the perfect moment or the perfect place. Just fucking do it.

Will texted the next day. ***Have you fucking done it yet? I'm dying here.***

Finding out the ring was still burning the proverbial hole in Erik's pocket, Will called to give cheerful hell. Erik grabbed the compost pail and headed outside to talk.

"Good Lord, you're a wuss," Will said. "Where'd you propose to your first wife?"

"She proposed to me."

"Oh."

"In bed."

"Hey, bed is a perfectly respectable place to pop the question," Will said. "You're horizontal, you're most likely naked, you're in the most intimate room in the house save for the bathroom. Just do it there."

"Where'd you propose to Lucky?"

"In the bathroom."

"Shut up."

"I carved 'will you marry me?' into a bar of soap. Left it and the ring on the little ledge thingie just before she got into the shower. I waited. And waited. She's singing. She's jabbering away. I'm shaving at the sink and dying. Finally, I just yanked the curtain aside and pointed to the damn thing like *Hello?*"

Erik laughed. "I think the more elaborate the proposal plan, the more chance it has to bomb."

"Seriously. Go simple. Just ask."

Friday night they went to the bruschetta festival, hosted by the county's Italian cultural society. The parking lot of the volunteer fire department had been transformed into a Tuscan piazza. A long line of grills made from split oil drums held charcoal fires. On lopsided tables made from boards and sawhorses, volunteers were slicing loaves of bread. Others were dealing the slices down the long length of grill, or turning them to reveal the charcoal stripes. The toasted slices went into giant bowls where a third gang of workers drizzled them with olive oil, salt and pepper before setting the bowl out. The crowd grabbed and the bread kept toasting.

From booth to booth, Erik and Daisy followed the masses, trying all the toppings. Endless finger food, the ultimate cocktail party under the stars. Erik had the ring in his pocket and contemplated giving it as they sat eating on some hay bales. But a hundred people were around and his hands were a juicy mess, as were hers.

"You're so quiet," she said as they walked along the wine vendors' booths, tasting.

He shrugged and hooked his arm around her. "I'm just wordlessly happy."

A couple more times she asked if he was all right. On the ride home, she gave him a few sideways glances. Some puzzled. Some amused. He held her hand on his thigh. He played with her fourth finger but if she noticed, she didn't say anything.

Later, he sat on the bed, watching through the bathroom door as she washed her face at the small sink. Adorable in her underwear and his T-shirt. The fine hairs around her temples drawing up into little curls.

He remembered making love in there on a November day fourteen years ago. Up against the wall of the shower. Swallowing steam and conquering their demons. Finding themselves again. It had been one of the last good times before they spiraled down into the dark.

He got up and went in behind her.

"Do you ever think about marrying me?" he said.

She splashed her face and spit water out. "If I marry anyone, it'll be you," she said, and spit again. "Can you get me a towel?"

He set one hand on the ledge of the sink, and held the other with the ring in front of her. He watched the mirror reflection as she groped at him, eyes shut. Her fingers touched the diamond and pulled back. Her eyes opened.

"What is...?" Still bent over the basin, her breath caught in her throat.

Erik held the ring still and slid his other arm around her waist.

Her hand reached and stopped. She ran her damp palm along the front of her shirt, then reached again with shaking fingertips. She didn't take the ring. She just touched it.

"It's beautiful," she said. Water dripped off her chin.

"It's yours," he said.

Her fingers extended. Down the fourth one, he slid the shining gold band with Astrid's diamond. She pressed her hand to her chest and he covered it with his. Felt the beat of her life within.

"I love you so much," he said. But his voice was hoarse and the first two words got lost.

You so much.

It settled into his heart like a creed. He said it again. "You so much."

She turned her head up to him. "So much you," she said.

She turned all the way around, put her arms around his neck and kissed him. "The bathroom," she said, her mouth soft against his. "Seriously?"

Laughing, he picked her up. Laughing, she wrapped her arms and legs around him as he carried her to the bed. He set her gently on her back, still wound up in her limbs.

"Better?" he said, kissing her wet face.

"Not yet." She dragged his shirt over his head.

Her skin slid along his. He thought her kiss had never been so sweet. Swore he had never sunk so deep into her body or known what the word *wife* truly meant until her hand came up to caress his face and his grandmother's diamond caught the light.

"Will you marry me?" he whispered.

"Yes," she said. "It's all I think about."

HERE TO STAY

THE HOLIDAY SEASON ARRIVED and Erik fell into a state of celebration he hadn't known since he was a child. It was *Christmas.* The world frosted with snow and outlined in white lights. Daisy busy with *Nutcracker* rehearsals. Carols in the background and the smell of wood smoke and pine in the crisp, thin air. Loved ones to shop for and the tree to decorate—together, as a couple. Cards to send with their engagement photo. Both their names on the return address:

> *Erik Fiskare & Daisy Bianco*
> *Barbegazi*
> *Stevens Road*
> *Saint John, New Brunswick*

"You look happy," Daisy said, grating orange zest for pepparkakor, the Swedish spice cookies.

"I am." Erik leaned on his elbows on the counter top, watching her, in love with his life again. "Do you think you'll change your name?"

"To Fiskare? Do you want me to?"

He did, but at the same time, he respected how much investment she had in her maiden name. Thirty-five years as Daisy Bianco to her friends and loved ones. Her long stage career as Marguerite Bianco. And now Madame Bianco to her students. Erik knew the Madame was an earned honorific, not merely a French courtesy.

"Not professionally," he said. "I would never ask that."

"I actually like the sound of Madame Fiskare," she said. "It sounds a little Russian."

"Just marry me," he said, reaching to flick a bit of orange zest off her diamond. "I don't care what you do with your name."

She leaned and kissed him, laughing. "Yes, you do."

He smiled against her face and breathed in the scent of oranges. "Stop knowing me."

They had three weeks off from work, then Erik was heading to Riverview with a car full of groceries and clean clothes. The engine of the old routine reluctantly turned over and coughed back to life. It chugged along, feeling old now. Reluctant and grouchy in the cold winter months. Worried about no end to the situation. Would they be living like this when they were married?

They gritted their teeth and dealt with the separation, laughing at it, crying over it or bashing through it. Erik got his union card. His set designs were pulling excellent reviews in local papers. The dinner theater broke even then started pulling in a profit, to the point where Erik did a double-take at his bank balance one day. The euphoria died when he remembered he had to file taxes in both the United States and Canada.

"Fucked two ways to Sunday," he said to Will.

"Yeah, you're both countries' bitch now."

In February, the Fredericton Playhouse called. They had just secured a $2 million grant to replace all their production equipment: sound, lighting, the works. With the new equipment, they'd be able to stage full-scale Broadway productions. The technical director was in desperate need of an assistant, preferably someone up-to-date with the latest technologies. Was Erik still interested?

"Let me call you back," Erik said.

He hung up and texted Daisy: ***I'm coming home.***

For all his hard work and dedication at the dinner theater, Erik had been careful not to make himself too indispensable. He'd groomed his crew well and one young tech in particular was more than ready to take over at this moment's notice.

The dinner theater's owner could only wish his young, exhausted friend well. Still, wanting to tie up all ends, Erik spent an insane month working in Moncton two days a week and Fredericton the other three. It was the only instance when Daisy got short with him for the hours he was clocking. And when he arrived home badly shaken one night, after nearly nodding off at the wheel, she lit into him like a dragon.

"I didn't get through twelve goddamn years and the last six months only to have you flip your car into a ditch," she yelled, seizing two fists of his jacket and twisting them up toward his chin. "I will *kill* you if you die on me."

"I know," he said, too freaked out to do anything but slide down the front door to sit on the floor, taking her with him. He put his head on his knees. "I'm sorry. I feel sick enough already, stop yelling at me."

"I'm not," she cried, then clicked her teeth shut. "Yelling," she said in her normal voice.

"Jesus Christ," he said to his kneecaps. "I'm so done."

She put her own back up against the door and exhaled heavily. "You are. I'm drawing the line now. You stay on this side."

He fell sideways into her lap and agreed.

Spring takes its time coming to the Maritime Provinces, but one Sunday morning in late March was full of sunshine and promise. In only a light fleece jacket, Erik sat on the concrete slab outside Barbegazi with his big cup of tea, looking out over the water. Looking into his past and his future at the same time, leaving him in a perfect, present moment.

The sun had sliced through the bathroom window that morning and he'd frozen with a mouthful of toothpaste, shocked at how the light glinted off the silver in the hair around his ears. Surely he wasn't going *that* grey. He bent his head this way and that. No denying it: the stress of the past year had made its mark.

Daisy burst out of the shed with the wheelbarrow. Crappy jeans, mud boots and a fleece. Her hair in braids under her wool hat.

"Hello, fiancé," she said.

Erik raised his mug. "Hello, financier."

She laughed. "Damn straight." She parked by one of the large island beds, waded in and started clearing it out with a vengeance, throwing handfuls of grasses into the wheelbarrow.

Erik watched her, swelling with love. He was home on a perfect Sunday. Dais was doing her thing and leaving him free to unpack for good. Or he could just sit here and do nothing.

He finished his tea and went to get his boxes of tools and supplies which had been in the garage all these months. Finally he'd set up the workbench which ran the length of the rear wall. The previous owner had been a tinkerer. And slightly OCD. Shapes for tools were outlined all along the pegboard on the wall. Erik followed precedent and put his things in the pre-designated places. For now. In time, he'd make it his own space.

Plenty of time.

"You in here?" Daisy called from the doors.

"Here to stay," he called back.

Part Three: Gold

CALL ME MAURICE 

SPRING LAMB WAS ON La Tarasque's Easter table. Along with wedding plans.

Francine passed the bowl of new potatoes to her daughter. "Have you thought about where you—"

"Here," Daisy said.

Years ago, Joe and Francine had raised a beautiful new barn on the ridge overlooking the vineyards. Fully equipped and glossy with exposed wood, it made Bianco's a sought-after venue for all kinds of celebrations. Caterers could use the farm's produce and wines. For a nominal fee, Francine would do the flowers. Joe had amassed a collection of pedal tractors for younger guests. Brides and grooms often stayed in the carriage house on their wedding night.

"How convenient for us," Joe said, smiling. "But you—"

"Here," Erik said.

"Of course, we'd love it," Francine said. "But have you looked at other—"

"Here," they said.

Joe shrugged and poured more wine into everyone's glasses. "Here."

One April afternoon, Will's father lay down for a nap and never awoke.

Will was devastated, although he kept insisting, "If you have to go, that's the way to go. Eat a nice lunch with your wife, lie down in your own bed and just slip away smiling."

But he cried hard, caught up in the arms of his mother and sisters. At the funeral home Erik watched all the Kaegers weep over the loss of their beloved joker, while Erik himself mourned one of the kindest men he'd ever known.

A week passed in an exhausting blur of arrangements. Maurice was not only father and grandfather, but a popular and beloved professor at UNB. The line at the funeral home stretched for blocks with students past and present. The family had to extend two viewings to three. Runs were made to the airport, people needed to be shuttled here and there. Daisy covered the theater and Erik took time off from work to cover the home front.

Finally the chaos dissolved back into a semblance of routine. Ségolène Kaeger went out to Vancouver with one of her daughters for a spell. His filial duties wound up, Will appeared at Barbegazi with a six-pack under his arm.

"Mind if I use your dock?"

"Go ahead," Erik said. "You want company?"

"I want to get drunk and contemplate this gaping hole in my life," he said. "And I'd like to be looking at the water while I'm doing it."

"Take a blanket," Daisy said, handing him one.

He took himself out to the end of the dock where Erik and Daisy had set two Adirondack chairs and a little table.

Erik texted Lucky. *Have your husband in custody.*

She replied. *Keep him safe. If he gets plowed, give him a ride or a bed. Thank you for everything. We'd be fucked without you.*

Erik kept wandering past the east windows, looking out to Will's hunched silhouette. After one prolonged staring session, Daisy's hand slid gently up his back. "Go," she said. "He wants you, he just won't say so."

So as the sun started to drop and turn the skies to creamsicle streaks, Erik took another six-pack and went down to the dock. He lit the citronella torches and sat in the vacant chair. Popped a beer. Clinked the neck against Will's and they drank.

"Dig me not smoking," Will said. "Yet."

"Hand 'em over."

"Bitch." Will reached in his inside pocket and drew out a brand-new, still-sealed pack of Marlboros. "Fine, you hold them. I won't if you won't."

Erik set them by the leg of his chair. "Deal."

They sat in silence, drinking, watching the skies grow dark.

"I can't imagine doing this at eight years old," Will said, the words slippery and thick. "How did you do it?"

"He wasn't dead."

"He was *gone.*"

Erik tactfully decided not to debate the details. "I had my mom," he said. "And I was really good at shutting down. As we all know too well."

Will gave a chuckled grunt.

"Man, when that shit came out in therapy?" Erik said. "To just hold it in my hands and say out loud 'I missed him'? I thought I was going to die. I couldn't believe how fresh it was. I was like a little kid on the couch, bawling."

He went quiet. Tonight wasn't about him.

"Did I tell you," Will said. "That when I was having my breakdown in Germany, my dad came?"

Will hadn't told Erik anything about what had happened in Germany, but it was beside the point. "Did he?" Erik said as he took Will's empty bottle and passed him another.

"He came for me. It was like a fucking Elton John song. Not that I ever doubted my old man loved me, but he... Jesus, the next day he was on a plane. No questions. Just *hold on, I'm coming, everything's going to be all right.* Flew across the ocean and stayed three weeks."

"It's what you do," Erik said. "If Jack ever made that call, you'd be on a plane too."

Will took a long swallow and then handed the bottle to Erik. "Cut me off. I'm done."

Erik pushed it back. "Play through. I'll drive you home or you can take the guest room."

"Thank you," Will said, taking another pull before setting the bottle down on the dock. He ran his hands over his head then hunched forward, elbows on knees, fingers woven tight in his hair. "Thank you for coming back. You weren't at my wedding. You weren't here when the kids came.

But Jesus fuck, I needed you here now. Back when Lucky was in the dark and now Dad. I can't talk about this shit with anyone else. I need you because you get it."

Erik put out a hand and rested it on Will's shoulder. "I get it."

"Why'd you go?" Will said, his voice both hard with hurt and soft with sadness. "I mean, I know why you left Lancaster that night. Why did you stay away for good?"

"I didn't know any other way," Erik said. "I was out of skills. Out of resources. It was like another shooting and I couldn't... I didn't know any other way to survive except to desert it. I'm sorry."

"I know." Will exhaled and sprawled back in the chair, legs and arms flung wide. "I know all of this already. I'm just drunk and being morbid because I feel abandoned."

"I know."

"Check it out," Will said, rolling up his sleeve. "Had it done this morning." On the inside of his forearm was a new tattoo. A joker playing card, and beneath it the words *Some people call me Maurice.*

"That's awesome," Erik said, laughing.

"Nice, huh? Took me forever to find a joker image that didn't look evil."

This prankster, in his hooded, quad-peaked cap, was holding a finger to his lips with a sly expression. A small smile within a beard quite reminiscent of Maurice Kaeger.

"He'd love it," Erik said.

Will rolled his sleeve down, then pointed down the lake's shore to the property next door. "See that house?"

"I see that house every day, dumbass," Erik said. It was a pretty Dutch colonial with an impressive deck facing the lake.

"It's coming up for sale," Will said.

"How do you know?"

"Because the owner is a private client of my wife's. And my wife, God love her, has been on a mission of ingratiating herself to said client. And I think it worked because she's made an offer."

"Who made an offer?" Erik said. "The owner or Lucky?"

"The owner offered to Lucky to make an offer."

Erik burst out laughing. "Dude, you are lit."

Will smiled. "The point being," he said with careful enunciation. "How do you feel about me maybe being your neighbor? Not to get too ahead of the game, but for shits and giggles let's say it happened."

"You can afford it?"

"Maurice made sure of that."

"Really?"

"I saw his lawyer before I went to the tattoo parlor."

Erik twisted around, surveying the distance between the houses. "Would you be able to see my bedroom window from yours?"

"Oh, hell yeah."

Erik sat back. "How could I refuse?"

They sat in the quiet, listening to the lake lap against the dock posts and the song of the spring peepers, called tinkletoes in New Brunswick.

"Is it weird?" Will said. "The four of us?"

"What about us?"

"Wanting to live close together."

"No."

"It can't be, right? We need each other. I mean, don't tell me in the entire history of mankind, there's never been a friendship like ours. We're not weird. We're probably nothing but typical."

Erik gazed at the vista opening before him: his best friend living yards, not miles away. Nights out on the dock like this. Dinners on Barbegazi's screened-in porch if he ever got around to building it. The Kaeger kids running between the houses. Knowing if one family went away, the other would keep an eye on things. Help always at hand.

The four of them.

Doing it together.

"I don't care if it's weird," Erik said. "Buy that damn house."

OUR LITTLE SECRET

ERIK KEPT WORKING ON his French. He had a good ear and while he still struggled to put a sentence together, he at least knew what it was supposed to sound like.

"He has no game," Will said. "But it sounds like he has game, which technically is half the game."

Whenever Erik saw Francine, she took care to use slow, simple sentences and crystal enunciation. It drove Joe crazy.

"You're talking to him like Charles de Gaulle," he said.

"Charles de Gaulle spoke beautiful French," Francine said.

"De Gaulle addressed his wife as vous."

"So do you sometimes."

"When I'm begging for mercy."

"Well, that's every night," Francine said.

Joe glanced sideways at Erik. "Cover your ears."

Erik laughed. "I actually followed all that."

At home, Erik found it easiest to practice with Jack and Sara Kaeger. Their corrections didn't make him feel as stupid. They didn't show off or educate. They just talked to him.

At least, Sara talked to him.

"Sara will talk to a garden hose," Will said.

Jack was a harder nut to crack.

Erik and Daisy expected a lot of adjustments being back together. Nobody expected Jack Kaeger to have such a hard time with it. He didn't like Aunt Daisy having a live-in boyfriend. Didn't appreciate someone on the side of the bed he'd claimed as his own. Didn't care for this stranger in the midst.

Fini.

The engagement was a catalyst for a string of bewildering awkward moments. Sullen behavior and rude words at the communal dinner table. More than once Will ended up sending Jack to his room, then calling him down later for a forced apology that made everyone feel rotten.

Daisy tried to make extra special time alone with Jack, but it only seemed to make things worse. Erik walked a constant careful line, not being unapproachable but not being overly hearty and uncle-ish either.

"Dude, I'm sorry," he kept saying to Will.

"No, no. He has to deal with it. But damn, who the hell saw this coming?"

"He'll work it out," Lucky said. "Everyone just keep being nice. We have to keep up a united front. He doesn't have to love it, but he can't be nasty about it."

"When did your mother start to date again?" Daisy asked Erik. They were in the yard, edging the garden beds.

"I was in middle school, I guess," he said. "She went out more openly when I was in high school. Like when I was a sophomore, this guy she was dating came for Thanksgiving dinner."

"How did you feel about it?"

"I don't know. I didn't feel bad or angry. I guess by that time I was done with any fairytale notion my dad was coming back. And done with any jealous ideas she couldn't have anyone new. All her relationships seemed really casual. I don't know if they were or if that was the front she was projecting for me and Pete. They were all nice, but no one guy was on the scene long enough for me to get attached."

"Until Fred."

Erik rested his hands on the end of the shovel and set his chin on top. "Right away I sensed Fred was different. I liked him and I liked how he treated Mom. I remember playing basketball in the driveway with him one day and it was fun and relaxed. And I kind of exhaled and thought, *This guy is different. I got a good feeling about him.*"

"I wonder if your mother was waiting for that moment. Waiting for your permission. Kind of like you felt Fred was waiting for yours."

But Erik had lost his train of thought while looking at her. Her eyes were brilliant turquoise. Her cheeks were pink with fresh air and bits of leaf matter were stuck in her hair. He reached and picked them out, the moment vibrating in his bones.

"I got a good feeling about you," he said.

The Kaegers closed on the house next door. Two more Adirondack chairs appeared at the end of Barbegazi's dock. Jack and Sara ran back and forth freely between the yards, repeatedly slamming the pergola gate at the center of Barbegazi's wooden fence.

"That fence is infested with something," Daisy said. "I don't know if termites or carpenter ants, but every time the gate slams, you see a cloud of sawdust."

"The fence is fine," Erik said. "Whoever built the pergola didn't know what they were doing. It needs to be replaced."

"Well, get on it," Will said. "You're diminishing my property value."

Erik flipped him off. "Get on this, asshole."

Not a week later, Jack came tearing through the fence, letting the gate crash closed behind him. The pergola teetered back and forth before majestically toppling to its death. Luckily Erik was right there, cutting back the rose bushes. He yanked Jack out of the way, sending the two of them into a rolling pile just before the pergola hit the ground and disintegrated in a rubble of wood.

For a minute, neither of them said anything, lying on the grass breathing hard. Looking at the mess then at each other. Jack's eyes were doubled in size and he appeared on the verge of running for his life.

"You all right?" Erik said.

Jack nodded slowly.

"I think we best keep this our little secret."

Jack nodded harder. They got up, brushed off, and surveyed the mess.

"Well, that saves me the trouble of knocking it down," Erik said, kicking at the structure.

"What will you do?" Jack said.

"I'll build another one."

"You know how?"

"Sure." He went to the garage to get the wheelbarrow, not looking to see if Jack was following. He rolled back and started chucking the broken-up wood into the well. Jack reached for a piece.

"Ah ah," Erik said. "You'll get splinters. Go get your gloves."

Daisy had bought Jack and Sara little garden kits, including kid-sized gloves. Jack fetched his and helped Erik pick up every piece.

"Thanks for the help," Erik said, checking his watch. "Now I have just enough time to run out to Home Depot. See if I can get another kit."

He walked off, pushing the barrow, again not looking back. Hardly six steps when he heard the voice behind him, along with the sound of a tiny nut cracking.

"Can I come with you?"

Erik smiled over his shoulder. "Go ask your mother."

He built the new pergola during his next two days off. At first Jack just watched. But soon he was measuring and marking, holding and bracing. Erik tightened the straps on his extra pair of safety goggles until they fit the boy's head. Then he coached Jack with the Makita drill, keeping his hands on top. Jack flinched at the sound and the vibration only a few times before he was confidently sinking the screws.

"Let me do it alone," he said.

"Nope," Erik said. "Not until you're ten. That was my dad's rule."

"Where's your dad?"

Erik paused. "He went away."

"Where?"

"I don't know."

The screw dropped on the ground as Jack looked back over his shoulder. "He went to forever? Like my pépère?"

"Kind of."

"Were you sad?"

Erik nodded.

Jack looked down. He picked up the screw and set it carefully against the drill bit. They went back to work.

Jack stayed all day. As the sun slipped behind the trees, a rich garlicky smell drifted out of the house, beckoning.

"I made spaghetti and meatballs," Daisy called out the kitchen door. "You want some, Jack?"

Together he and Erik washed their hands in the mudroom sink and he had dinner with them.

"Want to sleep over?" Daisy asked afterward.

Jack made a show of thinking about it. "Where would I sleep?"

"In the guest room."

He was quiet and a little moody, but he slept over. The next morning, Daisy discovered Erik and Jack in the galley closet in the office, in deep consultation.

"What are you guys up to?"

"Uncle Erik says he can build a bed in here," Jack said.

Erik and Daisy exchanged a single telepathic glance.

"You can?" Daisy said, eyebrows high.

"I think so," Erik said. "Right under these eaves."

"I can lie in bed and look out the window," Jack said, standing on tiptoes to see out the compass rose porthole.

"A bunk bed?" Daisy asked, her elbow grazing Erik's side.

"I was thinking a loft bed with a desk underneath," Erik said, elbowing her back.

"It'll be my room when I sleep over," Jack said.

"It'll be your office," Erik said.

They sat at the kitchen table and drew plans. Then they built it together, hammering and nailing through a month of Sundays. Daisy went to flea markets and found a handsome patchwork quilt, a pair of reading lamps and an old radio. She hung a bulletin board over the desk and lined up mason jars with colored pencils and crayons. Erik put up tiny Christmas tree lights around the porthole window.

Jack's only request concerned the doors. He didn't like them shut. "Then it's too tight in here," he said. "It feels far away."

Erik took the doors off their hinges and Daisy hung heavy curtains in their place.

"'Night, Uncle Erik," Jack said, tucked up in bed. He leaned and hooked an arm around Erik's neck in a quick hug.

"See you in the morning," Erik said softly, rubbing the little boy's head. He backed through the doorway and let the curtain fall.

And exhaled.

I WANT THE STORY

THE TEMPERATURE DROPPED THAT night and Erik built a fire. He sat in the leather chair, his feet up and Jack's hug lingering on his neck. His fingers toying with the charms on his necklace.

He went to forever?

Were you sad?

Daisy was reading and eating oranges. The flames were fragrant with the peels she kept tossing into the hearth. When the kettle whistled in the kitchen, she put her book down and went in to make them tea.

Erik stared into the flames.

"Don't touch the drill, Erik." He could hear the voice perfectly. Accompanied by the woodsy smell of sawdust and the metallic heat of a still-spinning blade. He was seven and it was the summer his father knocked down the wall between Erik and Peter's bedrooms. Over days and weeks, a forest playground emerged in the shared space.

The memory settled in his hands. Not an elusive feather but a full, plump bird, warm and alive. His young legs crouched down amidst the mess of construction. He reached to touch the Makita drill, wanting it. Coveting its solid, manly power and the things it could construct. He was on the verge of picking it up, intent on curling a finger around the trigger and setting the barber pole spiral of the bit into action. Then he glanced up. Byron's sapphire blue gaze looked back at him. Amused, but firm.

The slightest shake of his ash-blond head. The light through the window catching the grey above his ears. The gold chain rolling at his neck.

"When you're ten," he said.

Erik took his hand off the drill and off the memory. The bird flew away.

"What are you thinking about?" Daisy asked, setting his mug down.

"My father," he said.

She settled in Edith, curling her legs up underneath her. "Do you want to find him?"

"I want..." Erik closed his eyes and let what he wanted float into his presence. Gently he pressed it down. "I want to know more about him. I liked hearing Vivian deWrenne tell me about him. I liked her stories. I guess I'd like to know what happened. Without having to have any contact with him. I want his story. Like if someone could just hand me a file folder and say 'here.'"

"See pages forty-two through fifty. Call with questions."

"Exactly. Let me hear the story, let me process it and see if any of it..."

"Resonates?"

"I guess. I don't know if I'll ever get to forgiveness with him, Dais. I know it's the noble and enlightened thing to do, but I don't know if I have it in me."

"Nobody can fault you for that."

"But maybe if I knew the story. And if I knew more about the Fiskares in general, so I could put the story into context. Then maybe not forgiveness but understanding?"

"Or simply to know. Finally stop wondering about it and have the truth. Be free of the unknown."

"Yeah."

"Are you afraid of what you'll find out?"

"Sure."

"What's the worst? What would be a story that just breaks your heart?"

"That... He left because he didn't love me. Didn't want me. I don't know, what the fuck, am I insane for making it about me?"

"What other perspective do you have?"

"I mean, Jesus, what makes a man leave? Not just leave but disappear, cut everything off and— All right, don't look at me like that."

Daisy hid her twitching mouth in her tea mug and kept her eyes away from his.

He laughed. "I walked into that bear trap, didn't I?"

"Well," she said. "Put it on the list. If we're going to brainstorm, let's brainstorm. What makes a man leave? He leaves because he's hurt and wants to escape."

"He leaves because he loves someone else," Erik said.

"He leaves to protect. His presence brings danger. Real or imagined."

Erik raised his eyebrows. "You're good at this. Maybe he was a spy?"

Daisy twisted her mouth, rolling her eyes a little. "I confess I sometimes wondered if he saw something he shouldn't have seen and went into the Federal Witness Protection Program. Far-fetched, I know, but I thought about it."

"Hurt," Erik said, ticking off on his raised fingers. "Love. Danger or to protect. What else?"

They both thought.

"Maybe," Dais said slowly, "he leaves because he feels unworthy. Somehow. It's sort of an offshoot of the protection theory. Not that he brings danger but he brings despair. No good can come of him being there. He's failed and they're better off without him."

Erik sighed. "I don't know, I can't get my head wrapped around that one. I just don't have any memory of him being a morose man. Or he and my mom being an unhappy couple. But God knows my memory isn't the most trustworthy thing. Just because I didn't see it doesn't mean it wasn't there."

He stared into the flames, lost in thought. After a few minutes Dais stroked his forearm and opened her book again. Letting him be.

He looked down, scooping up the boat charm on his necklace.

Where did this one come from? What does it mean?

Who am I?

He gathered up all the charms in his hand, remembering when his mother had given him the necklace. He'd been about sixteen. And he didn't want it.

"It belongs to your name," Christine said, laying it in his palm and closing his fingers over it. "It's an heirloom. Don't let one asshole ruin it for you."

He reached down and picked up his laptop. Opened an online maps application and typed in Clayton, New York. He zoomed in on the little peninsula jutting into the St. Lawrence River. Switching to satellite view, he scrolled northeast, looking for his block.

He found it, but didn't recognize anything.

Let it come to you. Don't grab at it.

Hugunin Street made up the block's southern border. Erik lowered a fingertip and touched the second house on Hugunin's south side. There. He lived there. He closed his eyes and remembered. Buff-colored shingles. One big triangular gable facing Hugunin and gables on the east and west sides. His window overlooked the driveway. On the other side of the driveway...

White feathers floated in his peripheral. His finger moved and touched Farmor's house. He remembered. He was allowed to walk there alone. If he wanted to cross the street, he needed permission and a pair of eyes on him. If he wanted to go to the water, he needed an adult.

"I need to know where you are," his mother always said.

With permission, his adult finger now crossed Hugunin Street. So many houses on its north side. He didn't remember so many. Only the one on the corner and the gravel path alongside it. Someone lived in that house, someone belonging to him. He was allowed to use the footpath, cutting through to the hotel.

His eyebrows knitted together. So much of the big block appeared to be parking lot. He didn't remember all this paving. He remembered grass and trees and flowers behind the hotel. It was still there, though, the L-shaped building. The map labeled it The Saint Lawrence Inn, which must be its new name. He closed his eyes.

The Fisher Hotel.

He held still and let it come to him. The building's north side, the short end of the L, facing the water. Verandas on both the main and second floor. Three wide steps leading up to the porch. Erik's chin lifted, as if looking up. He remembered the fish. Carved from wood and polished to a high gloss, it hung from two chains over the steps, welcoming the guests.

"Where are you?" Daisy said, her voice tiptoeing into his reverie. He blinked and focused on her hand, curled around the mug, the flames catching the edges of Astrid's diamond. He looked at her face. Her eyes caught his and held. The clock ticked.

"How would you feel about taking a little trip?" he asked.

THE FISHER HOTEL

"THREE OPTIONS," ERIK SAID. "We fly to Plattsburgh via Boston and drive three hours. Or we fly direct to Montreal and drive three hours. Or we fly to Watertown via Philadelphia and drive thirty minutes."

"Watertown has an airport?"

"Watertown *International* Airport. Which only flies commercially to Philadelphia. But if you're coming in from Europe on your private jet, you can land there. With two hours notice."

"I'm sure a ton of rich jet-setters fly to Watertown all the time." She put up her hands. "This is your expedition. You pick."

They flew to Montreal and met Vivian for dinner. They had tickets to see Alvin Ailey American Dance Theater—which Erik enjoyed more than he thought he would—and a room at the Intercontinental, which was impossible not to enjoy. In the morning, they picked up their rental car and headed southwest out of the city.

"It was so good last night," he said, squeezing her hand on his leg.

"Alvin Ailey?"

"Well, that too."

"Did you like *Revelations*?"

"I did," he said, playing with her diamond, feeling spectacularly fine. "I would gladly watch it again. In fact I'd like an entire replay of last night."

She leaned over the console and put her face against his arm. "It was yummy."

"God, when I had you... And you were... And..." His shoulders gave a little twitch remembering.

"That thing with the thing?"

"Oh my God."

"Yeah, I kind of lost my mind there," she said, and then yawned against her fist. "I'm really quite sleepy."

She always fell asleep on long drives, but he liked thinking he had something to do with her nodding off today. Once he negotiated his way out of Montreal and they were cruising along the A20, he turned on the radio and relaxed into the ride. By the time they crossed into Ontario and A20 became the Macdonald–Cartier Freeway, he had fallen into a zone which was half song lyrics and half stream of consciousness. With the occasional loving glance to the hand still curled on his leg and the sleeping face turned in his direction.

They stopped for lunch in Cornwall then continued along Highway 401 until the turnoff to Route 137, which would take them over the Thousand Islands Bridge and into New York.

"What's scarier," Daisy said, as they left border patrol. "That someone will recognize you or no one will?"

"Stop knowing me," Erik said.

She was carefully putting their papers away. They had to travel with both American and Canadian documents and tended to call the little folder they kept them in The Football.

"Are you nervous?" she asked.

He touched his chest. "I'm a little...thumpy. Yeah."

"When was the last time you were here?"

"I think I was twelve? Maybe thirteen? Probably a moody little fuck, not paying much attention to anything."

"Unlike now," she said.

Every nerve in his body was sitting up straight and taking notes. It was a straightforward drive. Down Route 12 into Clayton, two right turns and then they were parking on Riverside Drive. It was a postcard day, with stunning blue skies over the river and the bridge sparkling in the far distance.

"God, it's beautiful," Daisy said, her hand shielding her eyes. "This is a sweet little town."

Erik said nothing as he stared across the street at the double-verandas of the Saint Lawrence Inn. "Holy shit," he said.

The fish was still hanging over the stairs.

"It's still here," he said, catching Daisy's hand as they crossed Riverside. At the foot of the front steps, he took a picture and texted it to Christine.

She texted back: *Touch the tail and make a wish. Long tradition.*

Sure enough, as they mounted the wide steps, they saw the varnish on the tail was worn away and dulled from thousands of hands making wishes.

Erik's phone pinged again. *I remember two wooden carved planters by the front door. Like fish. Flowers in their mouths. Still there?*

The planters by the door were plain urns. Then Daisy pointed to the far end of the porch. "There's one."

In the corner by some wicker seating it stood. A beautifully carved fish perched upright on its tail fin. Its mouth full of geraniums. Erik snapped a picture and sent it. *Here's one. Don't see another.*

Your father carved his initials in the tail of one of those planters, Christine replied.

Rather than shove aside furniture and tip over private property to look for initials, they decided to go inside first. A cool dry breath of conditioned air greeted them.

"I have no memory of this place," Erik whispered hoarsely, like Gandalf. Daisy elbowed him.

The lobby—chairs and couches and friendly bookshelves—was empty. No one was behind the front desk. It was quieter than a library. The solitude allowed them a few minutes to prowl. Erik frequently stopped and looked around, trying to get his bearings. Daisy went in search of a bathroom.

The stairs were in the same place at least. He remembered those. But he couldn't seem to get the galaxy of the rest of the hotel to rotate around it the right way. He couldn't remember. Left was right. Up was down. Vaguely, he recalled the dining area being open to the rest of the space. Now it was firmly partitioned off. As was the bar on the opposite side.

Daisy returned from the ladies' room.

"Want a beer?" he asked.

"I do."

They went into the bar and perched on two stools. The woman behind was in her fifties, blowsy and bleached-blonde. She dealt coasters like they were playing cards and pulled two beers without taking her eyes off the TV. Her voice was friendly though. "You two visiting for the weekend?"

Erik nodded and took a long pull, wetting down his dry throat. "I used to live here."

"Where?" the woman said over her shoulder. "In Clayton?"

"Here," Erik said, gesturing around. "My family owned the hotel. I grew up on Hugunin Street."

"No kidding? When did you move away?"

"When I was nine."

"Oh." She made the single syllable into a song around her gum. She moved a bowl of popcorn in their direction and then returned her attention to the TV.

"Salut," Daisy said, touching her glass to his.

"I guess you can't go home again," he said in his klutzy French, weirdly disappointed. A part of him expected to be recognized. By whom? His face hadn't been seen in this building in more than twenty years, what the hell was he thinking?

The phone behind the bar rang. The blonde woman had a long conversation about a fish delivery. She caught their eye in the middle and, unexpectedly, winked at Erik.

"Hey listen," she said into the phone. "I've got a guy in the bar who says he used to live here. Says his family owned the place. What's that?" She put her hand over the mouthpiece. "What's your last name, hon?"

"Fiskare," Erik said.

"Fiskare," she said into the phone. "He says he I—... Hello? Hello? Can you hear me?" She held the phone away, then back to her ear, shrugged and replaced it in the cradle. "Weird. He hung up on me."

"Who were you talking to?" Daisy said.

"Phil MacIntyre. Old Phil. He bought the place back in the nineties. Phil Junior and his wife run it. Old Phil just barks orders and brings in the fish."

"Who would he have bought it from?" Daisy asked Erik. "Your grandparents?"

He shook his head. "They both died in the eighties and they didn't own it. Farfar had his boating business. Farmor worked here. In the kitchen, I think."

"You want to talk to Cassie," the bartender said. "Cassie MacIntyre, she's Phil Junior's wife. She's the heart of this place. And she's super active in the historical society. She loves this shit. Pardon my French."

"Your French is doing life, Roxanne," said a woman's voice behind them. "No pardon or parole."

"There she is," the bartender said.

"Here I am. Still. Please shoot me." A woman looking to be in her late forties, with greying red hair, plopped onto a stool and put her face in her palm.

"This guy's family used to own the hotel," Roxanne said, drawing another beer.

"I'm Cassie MacIntyre, I own it now. Do you want to buy it back? Please? Put me out of my misery?" She smiled and shook their hands. "I don't mean it. I love it the way you love a teenage daughter. I'm sorry, what's your name?"

"Erik Fiskare."

"The Fiskares, of course. My father-in-law bought it from them. He kept some pictures." Cassie slid off her stool and went behind the bar. "Weird thing about Old Phil. He's a total grouch in the present, but he has a soft nostalgic heart for the past."

On either side of the mirrored wall behind the liquor bottles were clusters of photographs and vintage ads for soda and beer. Cassie took a picture down, wiped it off with a bar towel and set it in front of Erik.

In a faded, black and white shot, a family posed on the front steps of the hotel beneath the fish. A man and woman, she holding a baby in her arms. Four boys lounging at their feet. A handwritten caption in the corner: *The Fisher Hotel, 1932. Emil and Ingrid Fiskare and children.*

"Ingrid," Daisy said. "This is Emil's first wife. Your grandfather's mother."

"The fish has been hanging over the steps all these years," Erik said.

Cassie nodded. "And Fisher Hotel is still etched into the front windows. Old Phil changed it to the Saint Lawrence Inn, though. Not sure why."

"Maybe his soft spot isn't that soft," Roxanne said.

"Do you recognize anyone?" Daisy asked, peering at the four Fiskare sons.

Erik shook his head. Not one of the boys looked especially like him, although in a weird generic way, they all looked like him. He could fall into the picture, sit down on the steps and fit right in.

Cassie brought down another picture. Four young men standing on a dock, holding up impressive catches. Another handwritten caption: *Fiskare boys, 1938.* Beneath each boy's feet a name was inscribed. *Kennet. Erik. Björn. Emil.*

Erik's finger touched the first boy on the left. The tallest. With the biggest fish. "That's my grandfather, Kennet," he said. "That's Farfar." He touched the last boy on the right. "And that's Uncle Emilio."

A man spoke behind them. "I bought this place from Emilio's widow." The voice was full of gravel. Erik spun on his stool. Two yellowed eyes stared back at him. Watery blue in creased, sunburned skin. Disobedient eyebrows and tufts of white nose hair.

"You're Kennet's boy?" he said.

Erik stared back, feeling young and in trouble. "I'm Byron's boy," came spilling out of his mouth and he felt Daisy glance at him.

"This is my father-in-law, Phil MacIntyre," Cassie said. "Be nice, Phil. He doesn't want to buy it back from you. Although I begged him to."

Phil MacIntyre didn't shake hands or sit. He went around the bar. Erik turned on his seat, following him.

"You bought the hotel from Emilio's wife?" Erik asked. "From Kirsten? Is she still alive?"

"She's alive," Phil said in a grunt, his back to the guests, perusing the photographs. He picked one down and used another bar towel to wipe off the frame. When he turned around, his face had transformed. He was smiling. As he laid the picture on the bar in front of Erik, his expression was pleased to the point of smug.

"Jesus," Erik whispered.

It was a black and white photograph, five by seven. Three men clustered at its center. An old man seated in an armchair. Bald with a mustache, dressed in a plaid sport coat and a tie. He held a blanket-wrapped baby in his arms. A young man was seated on one wide arm of the chair and a middle-aged man stood stiffly on the other side, hands in his pockets. Handwriting in the picture's corner—*The Fisher Hotel, January 1971: Four Generations.* None of the men were labeled, but Erik didn't need help. His finger reached and touched the man sitting on the chair's arm.

"That's my father," he said. Then he touched the standing man. "That's Farfar."

He touched the old man and looked up at Phil MacIntyre.

"That's Emil," Phil said. "Your great-grandfather."

Erik looked down. His finger hesitated and then pressed down on the baby. He looked up at Phil again. Who smiled and nodded.

"Look at me, I'm bawling," Cassie said, touching fingertips under her eyes.

"Oh my God," Daisy said, her hand curling around Erik's elbow and her finger joining to point to the baby in the old man's arms. "Honey, that's *you...*"

THIS IS YOUR LIFE

PHIL TOOK ONE MORE picture down from behind the bar. In it Kennet Fiskare stood as a soldier, sharp and creased in his uniform. One arm stiff at his side, the hand almost in a fist, wishing for a pocket to hide in. In contrast, the blonde girl next to him was all softness. Round, laughing face, young curved body, a foot kicked fetchingly up behind. One hand on her hip, the other around Kennet's shoulder, she draped on him like a blanket thrown over a straight-backed chair. *Kennet and Gertrude Fiskare, 1945* was written in the corner.

"Aunt Trudy," Erik said.

"He must have just come home from the war," Daisy said.

"Trudy married Louis Pettitte," Phil said. "He and I were school buddies. He died in oh-three. Trudy retired down to the Carolinas. Mike Pettitte's her oldest. He runs boat tours out of Alexandria Bay. You should give him a call."

Cassie already had a phonebook out on the bar and was thumbing through the yellow pages.

"Do you know him?" Daisy asked.

"Honey, everyone knows everyone around here," Roxanne said, putting out a fresh bowl of popcorn.

"You think he'll see me?" Erik asked, as Cassie picked up the phone and swung her hair aside to fit it to her ear.

"Of course," she said. "He's your cousin."

Daisy took the piece of paper with Erik's sketched-out family tree from her purse. She smoothed it on the bar and set an index finger in different boxes, matching up the generations. "He's your father's first cousin."

"Hey, is Mike Pettitte around?" Cassie said into the phone. "Thanks." She smiled at Erik, drummed her fingers on the bartop then ran them along the frame of the four generations picture. "I have a scanner in the office," she said. "Let's try to get this out of the frame and make you a copy."

"You don't have to," Erik said.

"Of course I do," she said. "This is your life. Mike? Hey, Cass MacIntyre over at the Saint Lawrence Inn, how are you? Good, good. Listen, I think I've found a cousin of yours. He's sitting right here at the bar. His name is Erik Fiskare. He's…" She moved the phone under her chin. "Byron?"

Erik nodded.

"He's Byron's son. And—" Abruptly Cassie moved the phone away from her ear and through it came a Miss Othmar squawk of unintelligible words. She put it back to her ear. "Yes, he's right here. Swear to God. And… All right. No, I don't think so." Again she moved the phone. "Are you guys staying locally?"

"We're staying here," Erik said.

"They're my prisoners. I won't let them get away. All right. Nine?" She looked from Erik to Daisy, who nodded. "Nine then. We'll see you here. Okay, Mike. Take care."

She hung up. "You are to report back here at nine and not a minute later. Mike's coming down."

"He remembers? I mean, he knows me?"

"Sure sounded like it. Nearly yelled my ear off."

Daisy's fingertips curled into his forearm. His own toes curled in his sneakers. "This is crazy."

"Finish your beers and we'll get you checked in," Cassie said.

"The beers are on me," Phil said, and finally extended his hand across the bar to Erik. "Welcome home."

"You, buy a round?" Roxanne said. "You must be dying, Phil."

Checked in, Erik and Daisy went down the front steps of the hotel and walked around the block.

"Look," Daisy said, pointing across the street. "Clayton Opera House. You can come home and get a job."

"Cute," Erik said absently, looking around his old neighborhood. He swore there had been fewer houses and more trees. As they moved further south down Merrick Street it grew shadier. The two houses at the far corner had tall maples on the property.

They turned left onto Hugunin Street. After a hundred feet, Erik pointed across the parked cars. "There."

"That one? That was your house?"

He nodded but made no move to cross the street. He didn't want to go any closer. They walked along and he viewed the house nervously, as if it were a bear he shot and it might not be dead.

It was still the same buff color. The little front porch under the triangular gable had been open when he was a boy. Now it was enclosed with louvered windows. Other than that, it looked the same. It looked *too* the same. He prayed no one would come out and see them gawking at it. Invite him in. He couldn't go in.

"All right?" Daisy said softly, her hand creeping into his. "Must be weird."

"Yeah," he said. His glance fell on the driveway along the left side of the house. His eyes lifted to the two upstairs windows, then down again. The driveway was paved. It was gravel when he lived here. From one of those upstairs windows he'd heard wheels crunching on stones as his father's truck backed down the driveway. Watched the sweep of headlights as the vehicle rolled into Hugunin Street. The red tail light eyes looking back at him from the corner as his father made a left onto Webb Street and disappeared.

He went to forever.

And I was sad.

He cleared his throat. Pointed again. To the house next door. "Farmor lived there." He turned around, looking up at the corner house on this side of the street. "And this was the original family house. I think. I know some Fiskares lived there, but I can't remember who. It was definitely part of my world, though. I could go inside. There used to be a path here and I could cut straight through from the sidewalk to the hotel. Except I think it was all lawn and gardens back then..."

Daisy made a soft noise in her throat and stood still, holding his hand. They didn't talk on the way back to the parked car. On the ride out of town, down Route 12, they stayed quiet.

The village cemetery was cool and green, with a small-town majesty. Neat rows of headstones dotted with a dozen tall monuments and few noble mausoleums.

The sexton was an old woman who apparently lived for visitors. A computer sat on her desk, but she ignored it in favor of the back-up leather ledger. She knew her shit, though, and in five minutes she had written names and locations on a slip of paper and was pointing them in the right direction from the step of her office hut. She waved goodbye after them as if they were off to climb Mount Everest.

"Nice people here," Daisy said.

The caught hands as they walked along a neatly manicured path. Dragonflies and grasshoppers jumped away from their steps. A breeze blew through the pines piled up at the cemetery's border. The world seemed to shrink and draw in tight around them.

My people are here, Erik thought, his eyes sweeping the stones, consulting his slip of paper.

"I see it," Daisy said, pointing.

He followed her finger to one of the monuments. A tall, stone obelisk, slightly mossy on its north side, where was carved *B. K. E. FISKARE, 1865-1924.*

"It's real," Erik said, touching the blurred and weathered letters. Hardly aware he was doing it, he reached up to his necklace and took the Saint Birgitta medal in his fingers. The flat square of gold with the identical initials and dates.

It was real. He was a real person. I knew he was real but he was here. He was mine.

On the opposite side of the base, in smaller, crisper letters: *Marianne Dupre Fiskare, His Wife.*

Cozied up tight to the marker was a smaller stone. Prim, white marble with green moss collecting around the inscription: *Beatrice Klara, beloved daughter. 1893-1894*

The marker and its companion held court in the center of the plot. Radiating around were more headstones.

Emil Erik Fiskare, 1891-1971.

Ingrid B. Fiskare, 1893-1940.

Close by these two was another stone with a bronze military marker at its base: *Björn Fiskare, 1924-1945*

"He must have died in the war," Daisy said quietly. "God, he was twenty-one. He was a baby."

"Look." Erik pointed to the top of the obelisk. Its pointed tip was softened by a round filial, and on it perched a stone bird.

"That's weird," he said. "I mean, with all the fish imagery attached to the family. Why a bird?"

"I don't know," Daisy said, her head tilted back. "Fish gotta swim, birds gotta fly?" She glanced at him. "I gotta love one man 'til I die?"

Erik laughed, but it petered out as over Daisy's shoulder, he spied his grandparents' gravestones.

Kennet Emil Fiskare, 1919-1987.

Astrid V. R. Fiskare, 1918-1981.

Daisy went up to them first. She crouched down, pulling a few weeds away from Astrid's stone. She brushed her hands off, stood up and looked back at Erik, who hadn't moved.

"I need a minute," he said. He had no idea why he needed her to go away but he did. He had to do this alone.

She smiled, nodding. And pointed ahead. "See that little garden? It has a bench. I'll be there."

He waited until her footsteps on the gravel trailed away before he moved closer to his grandparents. He crouched down, put his hand on Kennet's name. He felt utterly blank, like the back side of a gravestone. He reached up to touch his necklace again. He tipped back and sat on the grass, cross-legged, and waited.

A monarch butterfly tripped through the air, drawing drunk loops. It landed on Astrid's stone. Its wings swelled and contracted like tiny lungs. It breathed. Then flew away.

Erik glanced up the path. Daisy sat on the bench, her face turned up to the sun. Composed and patient. Gentle with him.

He looked back at his grandfather, a smile beginning to lift the corners of his mouth.

"You gave me the money," he said. "So I could go to school. So I could go to that school. I wouldn't have met her if you hadn't. So you changed my life."

He glanced at Astrid. "And you made Pepparkakor. You taught me broken cookies are still sweet."

He breathed in deep, let it out. Sure he could say so much more, but he was done for now.

"I came back," he said. "I'm sorry I'm late."

He got up. Leaving seemed so abrupt. He didn't think to bring flowers. He could pick some from the grounds, but it felt irreverent. He knew in Jewish tradition you were supposed to leave a stone on the grave to show you had come to visit. He went out to the path, poked around and found two small, identical white pebbles. He put one on each marker.

"I'll come back again," he said. "It's nice here. It feels good here."

He touched each stone again and turned to leave. His eye caught two last graves in the plot.

Alexandre V. R. Fiskare, 1945-1968.

Elsa M. Fiskare, 1946-1968.

He stood before Xandro's stone, hands on hips. His chin tilted, remembering the bodies were never found after the accident. He wondered what was beneath the ground, if anything.

"Hi," he said. "I'm your nephew."

He glanced at Elsa's stone, thinking about it. "I guess I'm your nephew, too."

The monarch butterfly fluttered past but didn't land. After a moment Erik left the plot, starting up the path to where Daisy waited for him.

OH HELLO, MICHAEL 

"WELL, I'LL BE DAMNED," Mike Pettitte said.

He and Erik shook hands and then stepped back a little, giving the once-over. Mike was in his fifties, sandy-haired with a beard framing his red, ruddy face. The eyes looking Erik up and down were dark brown.

"I'll be damned, too," Erik said.

Mike crossed his arms. Then uncrossed them and put his hands on his hips. "This is nuts," he said, running a hand through his hair. "You look just like..." He trailed off and scratched his forehead now.

"Like who?" Erik said.

"Like everyone," Mike said. "Everyone I've ever known."

Cassie came around the bar with a tray of beers. Daisy followed with a big bowl of freshly-made popcorn, which she tucked in one elbow so she could shake Mike's hand.

"Come onto the porch," Cassie said. "I lit the citronella torches so it's not too buggy. You can sit and be comfortable and nobody will bother you. Including me."

The three of them sat in the wicker furniture by the carved fish planter—Erik and Mike kitty corner, Daisy across from them. They raised glasses and clinked. Drank. Looked around at each other.

"This is just unbelievable," Mike kept saying.

"How is Trudy?" Erik asked.

Mike put his glass down. "My mother is well. She and Aunt Kirsten live down in South Carolina."

"Together?"

Mike nodded. "They've been best friends since birth, practically. Kirsten's mother died when she was little and her father was out fishing all the time. She was at the hotel every day after school. Like a sixth Fiskare. Until she actually became one. I'm told everyone in the hotel knew she and Emilio were in love before they did.

"Anyway, after Kirsten and Trudy were both widowed they decided to pool their assets and take over the world. I would have called them to tell about this little reunion, but they're on a cruise in the Bahamas. Do you remember them?"

"Not really," Erik said. "According to my mother, Trudy taught me how to play poker. I have a vague memory of a woman playing cards with me, but I always thought it was my grandmother. I guess I was wrong."

"Astrid, play cards? No, no, no. Astrid would kick your ass at Scrabble. Backgammon or chess—Astrid was your girl. Card games were beneath her. My mother was lethal at poker. So was Kirsten."

"Emilio and Kirsten were the legal owners of the hotel?"

"That's right," Mike said. "Old Emil split the deed between his sons, but Emilio Junior bought everyone out."

"Did he and Kirsten have kids?" Daisy asked.

Mike shook his head. "No. Which made Kirsten the greatest aunt in the world. If you needed a shoulder to cry on, twenty bucks or a body buried, you called her."

"People always call Erik when they need a body buried," Daisy said.

Erik smiled. "I'm good with secrets."

"And how is your mother?" Mike asked.

"You knew her?"

Mike laughed. "Oh man. Your mother... I got a story for you."

"All right," Erik said warily, wondering if they had dated. That couldn't have been possible.

"The first time I ever kissed a girl was at your parents' wedding," Mike said.

"My parents?"

"They got married here at the hotel. You know it used to be all gardens in the back?"

"It did, didn't it?" Erik said. "I keep looking at the parking lot thinking something's wrong. It was all land in there, I remember, like a courtyard."

"Exactly," Mike said. "Kirsten and Astrid grew all the flowers for the hotel, then they had their personal garden plots for vegetables. They even had chickens back there for a while. Anyway, your parents got married in the lobby by the fireplace and the party was out back. I was fourteen. It was my first suit. This was nineteen sixty-nine, so I'll let your imagination just run with it. God, what an ugly decade." Mike took a pull of his beer and crossed one ankle over the other knee.

"My brother and I, we were out back in the garden where the tables were set up. Where we weren't supposed to be. Every table was beautifully set and at each setting was half a grapefruit. With a maraschino cherry in the center. Can you guess where this is going?"

"Oh God," Daisy laughed.

"I'm guessing twelve tables were out there," Mike said. "I cleared one of cherries and Dan cleared the other eleven. Then he proceeded to upchuck grenadine into the hydrangea bushes. So being a good brother, I got the hell out of there because screw that, he dug his own grave. Anyway, I wandered around the hotel, itching in my suit and bored to death. I went past this little room in the upstairs hall. Almost like an alcove with tall windows. And I saw your mother. In her white dress and veil. Beautiful cool blonde, like Honor Blackman, and—"

"Hold up, time out," Daisy said. "Did you just compare my future mother-in-law to Pussy Galore?"

Erik choked on his beer while Mike gave a great belly laugh and high-fived Daisy. "I'm telling you, I stopped dead in my tracks and stared like an idiot. I'd never seen anything so beautiful in my life. She turned her head back over her shoulder and saw me. She said, 'Oh hello, Michael.' And if she had followed it with, 'Please saw your leg off for me,' I would have gone in search of a butter knife to do it.

"Well, the evening only got better from there because one of the party guests was just my age, cute little brunette in a pink dress and a little more accessible. Usually my brother was the one to charm the girls, but he was still retching on cherries. So I snuck off with her to the riverfront and she was the first girl I kissed. Never forgot it. Kind of got all mixed up in my head and after a while it was that girl's face superimposed on your mother in her white dress. You know, like it was all one combined female ideal."

"Are you writing this down?" Erik said to Daisy.

She tapped her temple. "I won't forget it. Trust me."

"But your mother," Mike said. "She's all right?"

"She's good. She's a speech pathologist and works with deaf kids. Lately she's been dividing her time between Rochester and Florida, following the good weather. She has part-time work in both places."

"Married?"

"No, but she's been with a really nice guy for a long time. You could probably consider them common-law spouses."

Mike nodded and drank his beer and a slightly awkward pause squeezed past them.

"You know," Mike said. "To continue on the theme of firsts, because your family seems to have a lot of mine, you were the first baby I held."

"Really?"

"At Old Emil's funeral. He died in early seventy-one. You were a tiny thing, when were you born?"

"October of seventy."

"Right, you were just a few months old. Your father was holding you, but he was one of the pallbearers and he had to go get in line with the others. We couldn't find your mother. So he gave you to me. I was all of fifteen. You give a baby to a fifteen-year-old boy, he holds it like it has leprosy."

"Did he cry?" Daisy asked.

"No, he was cool. I had on my wool overcoat. It had big buttons. He found the one on the collar and started chewing on that. And he closed his fist around my finger and then we were buddies." Mike looked over at Erik, looked through him. "At one point you kind of leaned your head on my jaw and I smelled your hair. A baby is pure heroin, man. When they grab your finger and lean on you and trust you. And their head is soft and it smells amazing. It was this small revelation of *All right, I see why people want to do this.* And I remember having to give you back to your Mom just when I was getting used to you." He drained the last of his beer, as did Erik.

"I'll fill these," Daisy said softly, taking the glasses and the tray and heading back inside.

"She's lovely," Mike said. "You been together long?"

"We met in college," Erik said. "We were together three years. Then we were extremely un-together for about twelve. Long story short, we found each other again."

"When are you getting married?" Mike said, lacing his hands behind his head.

"End of July."

"Fantastic. Congratulations."

"Thanks."

Mike cleared his throat. "I hope it wasn't insensitive, telling a story about your parents' wedding."

"No, not at all."

Mike put both feet down and cracked his knuckles. "Look, let me just put something out there. I don't know you from a baby I held once and what happened with your father was a horrible thing. If you don't want to talk about it or you don't want me to tell any stories about him, that's fine, I get it."

"No, I do," Erik said. "I came here to look around. To see if anyone was left here who knew me, or knew him, or knew anyone in my family. My memory is so full of holes and I want to see if I can fill some of them. Does that make sense?"

"Absolutely."

"I'm ready to hear stories about my dad but not from my mother. It's too painful for both of us. Hearing it from someone a little more removed is easier."

Mike nodded. "Your dad meant a lot to me. I'm born fifty-five. He was born forty-seven. So an eight year age difference. If my Uncle Emilio wasn't available to bury a body, Byron was my next phone call. He taught me about cars and boats. Taught me about fishing. He was the guy who drove me to the drug store to buy rubbers when I was seventeen. He made me go in there and buy them myself, said I couldn't cheat by buying shaving cream and a bunch of other stuff to hide them. 'Go in there and buy them like a man.'"

Erik gave a bark of laughter. "Jesus Christ, one of my mother's brothers did the same thing with me. 'If you can't walk into Rite-Aid and buy your own rubbers, you have no business having sex. Now get in there.'"

"Well, good, you grew up with some uncles. I feel better knowing that."

Daisy came back out with their beers. She seemed to stretch her antenna into the air between the men and make a decision. "It's a little chilly for me out here," she said, leaning to kiss Erik's face. "I'm going to hang with Cassie a bit then I might head up to the room."

"You sure?" Erik said, half getting up, as was Mike.

"Sit," Daisy said, reaching a hand to squeeze Mike's. "You guys talk. It's your time."

"SO," MIKE SAID. "I grew up looking up to your dad. When I graduated high school, my mom wanted to have a party out in the gardens, but then you and your brother got sick with the mumps. They had to quarantine the hotel. Your dad felt really bad about it and once things calmed down, he took me out to dinner."

Erik nodded.

"Then I joined the Coast Guard so I was down in Cape May, New Jersey, a couple years. Your dad wrote me a few letters. He was busy but he took the time. That's how I found out your brother had gone deaf. He shared his thoughts with me, said how hard it was to see your kid suffer. Hard when things beyond your control just happened. He..." Mike's hands groped in the air as he searched for words. "He let me see the harder parts of growing up. Know what I mean?"

"What else," Erik said, hardly daring to breathe. "What was he like?"

"Serious. Not that he didn't have a sense of humor, but his home base seemed to be thoughtful. He often faded into the background in a crowd. Listening more than he talked. Like he was recording everything. Sometimes he'd go away though."

"What do you mean?"

Mike's face twisted as if he weren't sure. "He'd get a faraway look in his eyes," he finally said. "Like he was listening to music no one could hear. I sometimes wondered if he was a secret poet. It wouldn't surprise me if he had a novel tucked away nobody knew about."

"Really?"

Mike nodded, taking a pull of his beer. "I remember some passages in those letters being really eloquent, but in a way even a big lug like me could understand. He wasn't an outwardly passionate guy in person, but on paper it came through.

"When I'd come home from the Coast Guard, and later when I came home from college, he was always here. Always was glad to see me. We'd have beers in the hotel bar or go out on the boat or just kick rocks along the beach. If I had a problem, I dumped it at Byron's feet. Money, girls, anything.

"Meanwhile I watched him with your mother. I don't even know how you fit this into the big picture of what happened but he loved her. Like his love for her was a thing in the air. Shit, I'm not good with words but you could see how he loved being with her best. And I wanted what he had. Byron didn't have grandiose ambitions. He was a smart, well-spoken guy. He could've been a success at anything, in my opinion. But he just wanted a nice life in the town he grew up in. With the woman he loved.

"So he changed my outlook a little. I always figured the definition of success was getting as far away as possible from your hometown and making a new fresh mark somewhere else. Byron made me see nothing was wrong with sticking around and building on top of a foundation already there."

Erik was staring past him, listening as he looked across Riverside Drive to the water. Caught between the past and the present. Mike's description of Byron layering on top of the few precious memories Erik kept locked behind display cases in the gallery of his heart.

His father's desertion had been contained with a triangle: himself, his mother and Pete. Now that triangle was taking dimension and becoming a prism. Mike's stories were refracting the narrative into different wavelengths. Erik had only seen father and husband. Now Byron was colored things like son, nephew, cousin and friend.

"I was a senior at Potsdam when my mom called me," Mike said. "She said Byron was missing. I came home that weekend. The place was…

Police were in and out of the hotel and your house. People went door to door from here to Alexandria Bay. They searched the river front on both sides, combed every island."

"So weird how I don't remember any of that drama," Erik said. "I can remember the emotions from when he left, but I've forgotten the day-to-day events. I can see his truck driving away and making a left turn. Then the chronology just implodes and my next memories come from living in Rochester."

"A year they searched. Your mom hired detectives both in the States and Canada. She starved herself to a thread looking for him. My mother would always give me the latest news, but she had less and less to give as time went on."

"I didn't realize how badly I was traumatized until I was in my twenties," Erik said. "I shut down. And when other traumatizing events happened in my life, I reacted by shutting down. My dad taught me leaving was the solution to things."

"How about your brother?"

"He stopped talking. He wouldn't wear his hearing aids. He didn't want to hear it, didn't want to talk about it. It's a wonder he didn't put his own eyes out."

"Astrid was destroyed," Mike said. "Now both her boys were gone. You knew about your dad's brother, right?"

"Only recently."

Mike's shoulders gave a small shudder. "No parent should have to outlive their child. It's... It's so against the natural order of things that it's offensive. Seeing a parent have to bury their child *offends* me. You know what I mean?"

Erik nodded, barely able to wrap his mind around the amount of loss his grandmother had endured. How the saga of the Fiskares was imbued with so much tragedy.

"For Byron to disappear after she lost Xandro? And then to find out he was alive, he'd just deserted his family? Not only you and your mother and brother, but everyone in Clayton? No doubt in my mind, your grandmother died of a broken heart," Mike said. "And Kennet was never the same. He watched Astrid waste away and frankly I'm surprised he survived her as long as he did. Then in eighty-seven he passed, and Emilio lay down months later and checked out. It was the end. The whole hotel felt lopsided, like it had been through an earthquake and nobody would fix the foundations. Nobody would build on top of it ever again. I think that's why Kirsten sold it off."

"I had no idea," Erik said. "My mom took us to Rochester and my mind hit the reset button. She brought us back here a few times and I can barely remember them."

Mike's hands twisted and he started and stopped a half-dozen times before he next spoke. "I felt bad. I still do. I feel like I could have done more for you."

"For me?" Erik said. "How?"

"I mean the way Byron did for me. Been more of an uncle to you that first year. After your mother took you back to Rochester, I could've made more of an effort to reach out and let you know I was here. I don't know. It was bitter. I don't pretend to have words to describe your experience. For my part, it was crushing, bitter disappointment to find out a guy I admired so much could be such a heartless prick. I hear he didn't even show up at the divorce hearing."

"No, he did," Erik said. "It's when he gave my mom this." He hooked a finger under the gold chain. "Do you remember my father wearing this?"

"God, yeah. Shit, look at that. So he did show up?"

"That's what I was told."

"Huh. What were his reasons? Was it another woman?"

Erik opened his mouth and shut it, shaking his head. "I don't know," he said. "She didn't tell me and I didn't ask. Like I said before, I want to hear about him but not from my mother. And if it makes you feel any better, I have the same kind of regret for not making more of an effort with my grandparents. To see them in their last years. I know about bitter. I was young and punky and self-centered but I could have tried."

"Well, you're here now," Mike said and offered his glass. "Life is full of second chances."

"No shit, cousin."

"Skål"

Erik clinked his glass. "My dad said that."

"I know," Mike said, and drank.

Erik unlocked the hotel room door and let himself in softly. But Daisy was awake, sitting up under the light of the bedside lamp, reading. "Hey," she said.

He smiled with a wave, depleted of words, emotionally exhausted. More than a little buzzed. He brushed his teeth and got into bed, full of thoughts and memories. A confused snarl of rusty barbed wire and beautiful silken yarns.

"I'm going to be all up in my head the rest of the night," he said. "I don't feel much like talking right now. I'm sorry in advance."

She patted him, leaned and kissed his face. "Don't be," she said. And went back to her book and let him be.

He lay on his side, staring at the folds of the covers draped over her hip, thinking about a million things. Barely blinking, he surfed the waves of his breath. Thinking. Remembering. Not remembering. Arranging puzzle pieces.

I hear he didn't even show up at the divorce hearing.

Erik's fingers toyed with the charms. Of course Byron had showed up. It was the story Christine told. The story Erik kept telling when he checked "divorced" on school forms and left "father's name" blank.

My parents are divorced. My father left us when I was eight and Mom divorced him when I was ten. When they signed papers, he gave her the necklace to give to me.

Fred's face swam into memory, looking up at Erik from the bottom of a ladder.

I think she's still married to your father.

"I have my wedding band," Christine said. "Upstairs in my jewelry box."

The way he loved your mother. It was like a thing in the air.

Daisy got up to use the bathroom. Erik kept staring to where she had been, staring through time.

A smart, well-spoken guy.

Listening to music no one could hear.

A secret poet.

Sometimes he'd go away, though...

Daisy came back, slid into bed. Threw the extra pillows on the floor and leaned to turn off the lamp.

"'Night," she whispered.

"I love you, goodnight," he said.

A few cars passed outside.

The lamp made tinny clicks as it cooled.

Daisy inhaled and exhaled.

Erik picked up his head. "Wait a minute, you're naked," he said.

"No, I'm not."

"Yes, you are."

"That's all up in your head. Sorry."

He pulled at the covers. "No, I'm positive about this."

"Oh really," she said, laughing. "In the midst of your contemplative brooding you noticed I was naked?"

"Think you could sneak it past me?"

"In your current state of mind? Yes."

"You have so much to learn."

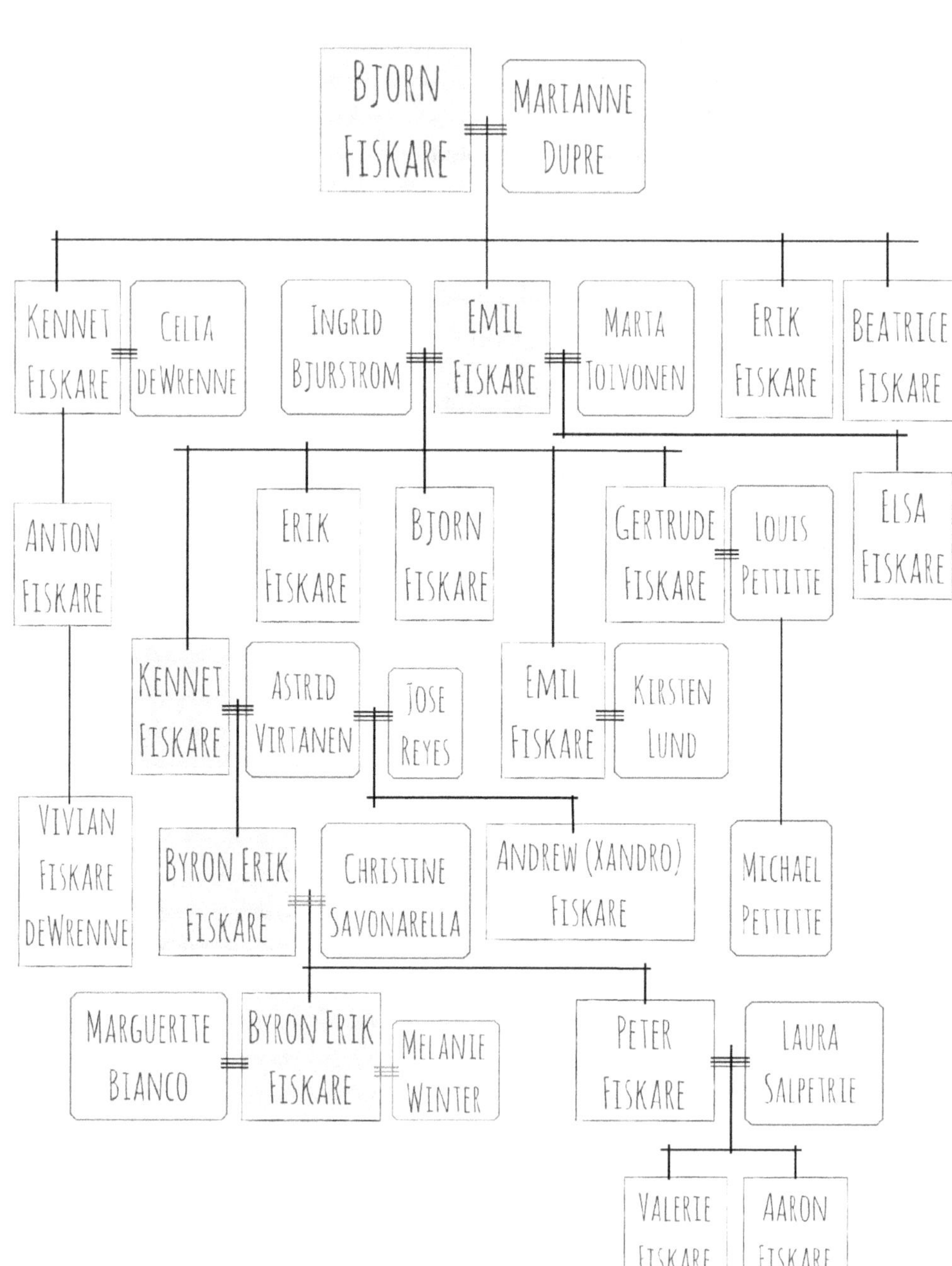

Bjorn Fiskare
Marianne Dupre
Kennet Fiskare
Celia deWrenne
Ingrid Bjurstrom
Emil Fiskare
Marta Toivonen
Erik Fiskare
Beatrice Fiskare
Anton Fiskare
Erik Fiskare
Bjorn Fiskare
Gertrude Fiskare
Louis Pettitte
Elsa Fiskare
Vivian Fiskare deWrenne
Kennet Fiskare
Astrid Virtanen
Jose Reyes
Emil Fiskare
Kirsten Lund
Michael Pettitte
Byron Erik Fiskare
Christine Savonarella
Andrew (Xandro) Fiskare
Marguerite Bianco
Byron Erik Fiskare
Melanie Winter
Peter Fiskare
Laura Salpetrie
Valerie Fiskare
Aaron Fiskare

WITH INTEREST

"HEY, MOM," ERIK said.

"Hello, sweetie."

"Can I talk to your boyfriend, please?"

"Fred?"

"You have another boyfriend I don't know about?"

"What do you need him for?"

"I want to ask him his intentions with you."

"What?"

"I'm kidding, Mom. I just need to ask him something."

"All right, hold on... Fred, Erik needs to ask you something."

Fred took the phone. "I know nothing," he said. "I'm useless."

"Daisy and I have a use for you," Erik said.

"I can't get you out of parking tickets or traffic court, I'm sorry."

"Can you marry us?"

Silence on the other end.

"You there?" Erik said after a moment.

Silence.

"Fred?" Erik looked at Daisy and shrugged. "Hello?"

A scrabble as the phone switched hands. "What the hell did you say to him?" Christine said. "He's crying."

"I asked him if he would marry us."

"Marry...you?"

"Yes. He's a retired Pennsylvania Justice so he can officiate. At my wedding. To Daisy. In Pennsylvania. So I am asking, would he marry us?"

Silence.

"Mom?" Erik rolled his eyes to the ceiling. "Jesus Christ, now she's crying. *Mom.* Would you stop?"

"Oh Erik," Christine said, her voice choked. "You have no idea…"

He smiled. "I know, Mom."

"You don't. You don't know what this means to him. And to me."

"I do. It takes me a lot of years, but eventually I get it. Now will he?"

"Fred? Will you?"

Fred got back on, clearing his throat. "I'd be honored," he said.

"You're listed in the program that way, right? His Honor Fred Williamson?"

"It's The Honorable Frederick T. Williamsen, punk. With an e-n. Get it right."

It was a small wedding, sixty guests, but it was everyone and everything they loved. They wanted no grandiose staging, no ring bearers or flower girls. A simple ceremony with Lucky and Will standing up with them. And the father of the bride would not give her away.

"She was yours when you got me down from the roof," Joe said.

More to the point, the bride and groom had gotten to this day together, goddammit, and they were walking down the goddamn aisle together.

Planning a wedding long-distance while trying to work full-time required massive amounts of organization and trust. Both of which they put in Francine's hands. She took the large, logistic details in Pennsylvania while Erik and Daisy took care of smaller ones in Canada.

They picked gold bands. *Né pour toi* was engraved on the inside of Daisy's. *Née pour toi* on the inside of Erik's.

Born for you.

Daisy and Lucky shopped together for a dress. Will supervised Erik's tux and all the finery was shipped down to La Tarasque. The little party—bride, groom, attendants and children—flew into Philadelphia the Thursday before the wedding.

Vivian would come if her schedule permitted. Mike Pettitte and his wife were definitely coming. The MacIntyres sent their regrets, but Kirsten and Trudy wouldn't miss it.

Erik sat on the porch Friday afternoon, waiting for the Clayton clan. Squinting under the visor of his hand, looking for the dust cloud that signaled a car coming up the road. Listening for an engine the way a child would listen for sleigh bells on Christmas Eve. Finally they arrived.

Mike parked the rental. The back doors exploded open and two ladies got out. Both white-haired: one had a sharp pixie cut and the other a loose bun. Dressed nicely, looking around, pointing, admiring. And as Erik came down the porch steps and along the flagstone path, they caught hands and stared.

"Hello," he said, stopping at the path's edge.

They continued to stare. Mike and his wife hung back by the car, watching.

Erik held still, thinking, *please don't say I look like my father.*

"Cripes," the pixie-cut woman said. "Look at you."

"Look at me," he said, bracing himself.

"Unbelievable." The woman with the bun shook her head, smiling. "You look just like your grandfather."

The first woman put her hand on her heart. "Doesn't he?"

The wind ruffled the sleek cap of her hair as she came toward Erik. Her eyes were pale blue. Familiar, but Erik couldn't say how.

"I'm Aunt Trudy."

"Of course you are," Erik said.

"Do you remember us?" Kirsten asked.

"Not exactly," he said, looking from one to the other. "But I hear I kicked your asses at poker."

Trudy pointed a finger. "Young man, you owe me ten bucks. With interest."

Kirsten laughed and held out her arms. "Come hug me before you get shaken down."

During the rehearsal dinner, which was a casual barbecue at the farmhouse, Erik watched his mother chatting with Vivian, bantering with the two great aunts and howling with laughter when Mike told his stories about her wedding.

Erik's heart swelled from the presence of his extended kin, and the hope he'd returned to Christine some small, joyful part of the past. To Pete as well, whom Erik spied taking a walk with Kirsten around the gardens, offering his arm or hand when the terrain got rough.

"The greatest aunt in the world," Mike said, patting Erik's shoulder as he passed by.

"We may need some bodies buried after this party," Erik called after him.

Daisy came over, curled her hand around Erik's upper arm and kissed the edge of his sideburn. "I'm so happy," she said.

"Me, too," Erik said, looking at Daisy's brother Michel, chatting with Joe and Francine around the fire pit. Michel's wife Anya was deep in conversation with Lucky, while their daughter Kiki was chasing Jack all over the gardens.

Later, when the guests had left and the kids were tucked in, the four friends sat on the porch, drinking the last of the wine.

"We have presents for you," Daisy said, putting a gift bag on the wicker table. Lucky opened hers first and held up a pair of gorgeous diamond-and-pearl earrings. Tucked beneath was a little note, which Lucky read silently. She smiled. Nodded. Laughed out loud. And then caught Daisy's hand in hers, sniffing.

"You," she said.

"You," Daisy said.

Erik took another box out of the gift bag and gave it to Will. "This is for you as my best man," he said.

"Your only man," Will said.

"But it's also a token and symbol of our friendship. Which has no price. Blah blah blah. I love you. Dude."

"Don't tax yourself preparing a statement, Fish," Lucky said.

"Good thing he's not making the toast," Will said, grinning as he opened the box. He looked down and the grin faded.

A long staring moment.

"What is it?" Lucky finally said.

"It's a cock ring."

Lucky laughed. "No, really. What is it?"

"No, really," Will said, turning the box toward her. "It's a cock ring."

"A *sterling silver* cock ring," Erik said. "Doubles as a bottle opener. Only the best for my best man."

The girls were shrieking with laughter. Lucky folded in half, Daisy collapsed on the arm of her chair. Through the cackling, Will just stared at Erik. Erik crossed an ankle over the other knee, laced his hands behind his head and stared back.

"Do you know why I love you, Fish?" Lucky said, gasping.

"My impeccable taste in gifts?"

"You are the only one who can render Will speechless."

Will slowly shook his head. He looked about to say something, then shook his head again, laughing softly.

"Did you engrave it?" Daisy asked Erik, running her fingertips under her eyes.

"I was going to but... Really, you give a guy a cock ring, what more is there to say?"

Will closed the box and set it down on the table. "Thank you," he said.

"You're welcome."

MY BEST FRIEND

DAISY GOT READY IN her old bedroom. Erik used the carriage house to suit up, and it turned into an impromptu stag party. The photographer moved about on invisible feet, taking candid shots. Erik would frame one of the captured moments and keep it on top of his dresser at home. In it, Fred mixed gin and tonics while engaged in conversation with Miles Kelly. Mike, Joe, Pete and Will—all slicked out and looking sharp—stood around chatting while in the background, Kees Justi busied himself with Erik's bowtie.

"I haven't worn a tux since senior prom," Erik said. "And it had a clip-on tie."

"No protégé of mine shows up to his wedding in a clip-on."

"Which is why I needed you here. Among other reasons."

Kees's eyes blinked as he folded and fussed and tied and made it perfect, pausing once to brush away tears.

"Knock it off," Erik said.

"Sorry. You know me. The emotional hamburger. Hold still now."

Erik held his head still and tugged at his cuffs. Will came over and brushed his hands out across Erik's shoulders, picked off an infinitesimal piece of lint, then crossed his arms and looked the groom up and down.

"Look all right?" Erik asked.

Will nodded. "You're hot."

"Isn't he?" Kees said. "Telling you, Fish, whoever fit your tux knew what he was doing. Makes your ass look fabulous."

"Fred, can I get another of those G and Ts," Erik called.

Pete brought it over, clinked his glass with his brother's and they drank. "You all right?" Pete said.

Erik nodded. "Can you hear me?"

Pete lightly grazed his knuckles on Erik's cheekbone. "I always hear you."

Miles came over with the small boutonnière of two daisies and pinned it to Erik's lapel.

"If it weren't for you," Erik said, "I wouldn't be living this truth. I'd be wandering around somewhere, clutching my pearls."

Miles smiled and smoothed down the lapel. Then he reached in his pants pocket and into Erik's hand he pressed what felt like a coin, but was a simple silver disc with the letter F on it. Erik looked up with wrinkled eyebrows.

"It's a fuck," Miles said. "I give it."

Will's phone beeped and he reached in his inside jacket pocket.

"Daisy's coming down," he said. "Drink up, Fish. Photographer's waiting outside to capture the big moment."

Erik took a last fortifying swallow amidst another round of smoothing, tugging and straightening. Through a gamut of handshakes, hugs and ass pats, he went down the stairs. Joe accompanied him as far as the door and gave him a last brushing off.

"That time I came back here with Daisy and you were stuck on the roof," Erik said. "You knocked the ladder over on purpose, didn't you? To make me feel better about my screw up."

Joe smiled. "I wanted to level the playing field."

Erik reached for one of his lapels and turned it out a little. Pinned to the inside was a Purple Heart. Joe had earned it in Vietnam and given it to Erik after the shooting.

"It's what you do," Erik said.

Joe's hand patted Erik's cheek. Tugged his earlobe. "It is, mon pote," he said. "Now go find your bride."

Erik stepped outside, his eyes squinting into the late sun, his heart starting to pound strong beneath his shirt studs.

He crossed the gravel drive toward the house. He heard the soft whirring click of a camera shutter but didn't look around to see where it came from. His eyes were only on the porch. He was two steps up the flagstone path between the garden beds when the front door opened. He stopped. Stood surrounded by wild flowers and dragonflies. He waited, drawing in his breath.

Daisy came out.

The breath caught tight in Erik's lungs.

She came down the steps, a bit of her skirt in her hand, a bouquet of daisies in the other.

"Well, here you are," she said.

The air chugged out of Erik's chest as his mouth began to curve up.

"Here I am," he said.

Her dress was slim and simple. Her shoulders gorgeous in its halter top. Her hair pulled back in a low bun and from it flowed her veil, tumbling like froth over the clean lines of her skirt. As she came along the path through the flowers, her smile was trembling and her eyes shone a blue-green shade he'd never seen before.

Erik's gaze blurred. His feet took him forward to close the gap, his arms reaching. Her arm and its bouquet went around his shoulders. Her other hand wrapped her veil around them. He picked her up, turning in a slow circle until the veil wrapped itself around their legs as well.

"Will you marry me," he whispered.

She nodded against his neck. "Today."

The photographer caught it beautifully, and the picture of them wound up in white against a bright tapestry of wildflowers would forever hang over the fireplace at Barbegazi.

Cool cross-breezes blew through the big barn, yet within it was warm with love and music. At the center of every table was a round sphere vase filled with daisies. A bit of raffia wound around the rim, off which hung a fish cut out of tin.

The band wound up its first set, and as guests drifted back to their tables, Will went up to the lead singer and took the microphone. Through the humming din came a single clink of a fork against a glass. Followed by another. It swelled into a tinkling chorus and broke apart when Erik and Daisy kissed.

"Good evening," Will said. A squeal of feedback and scattered laughter as Jacy began crawling across the empty dance floor, showing her ruffled butt. She stopped at her father's feet and held up her arms. More laughter as she shook her head at Lucky's beckoning. Will picked her up and tried to negotiate the mic, his notes and his champagne glass. "Oh screw it," he said, and tossed the notes aside. "Welcome to life. I'll improvise."

Loud applause. Jacy clapped her hands and blew kisses.

"Most everyone knows I had a front row seat when Daisy and Erik were falling in love," Will said. "People would always ask me... When Dais and I partnered onstage, people would ask, 'What are you thinking up there with her? I mean, do you secretly love her? Do you have a story going in your head? What is that chemistry, what's behind it, what's the secret?'

"And... First of all, anyone who knows me, knows I don't keep love a secret. Second, I only know two men in the world who love Dais more than I do. One's her father and—"

Applause cut him off. Daisy stood up, touched her fingers to her mouth and then flung them out to Joe. Joe caught the air with both fists and pulled them to his heart.

"And the other man," Will said. "The other is her husband over there."

Louder applause. Erik stood up and planted one on his bride and the applause turned to shouting.

"It's so nice I have to say it twice. Her husband. And... What, honey?" Jacy was taking Will's face and turning it firmly to her so she could kiss him.

More laughter as Will hitched Jacy higher on his shoulder. "So the short answer to all those questions about my partnership with Daisy is indeed love. But love is also the longer answer. Because Erik..."

His voice trailed off and the barn grew quiet and still. "Erik's my best friend," he said. "We throw those words around casually. Oh, sure, you're my best friend. But what does it mean? To me, it's the friend who makes you your best. Who makes the best come out in you. Dais made me the best dancer I could be, Erik made me the best man I could be. See what I did there?"

The laughter was soft. All around the tables people reached for hands, drew children onto laps, and looked smiling at each other. Jacy laid her head on Will's shoulder.

"When your best friends are in love, it becomes inspiration. And while everyone knows I had a front row seat when Dais and Erik were falling in love, not many people know I took everything I saw and put it into my dancing. Our best performances together were from me being not a partner, but a mirror." Will looked around, chewing on a bottom lip. "And now you're all looking at me like I'm nuts. Oh, wait, you're crying? Francine, you're crying. That's good."

Francine waved her hands, covered her tear-stained face, then lifted it out and blew Will a kiss. Jacy blew one back.

"I'll wrap this up," Will said, laughing. "Love can bring out the best and worst in us. We've all been a jackass for love. But love makes us do amazing things. And if love drives us away, love is what brings us back. Love makes us pick up the phone. Love makes us listen. Love makes us say I'm sorry. Love makes us forgive. Love makes us better. Love makes us our best. And love makes more love...and...I forgot where I was going with this. Forget it. I'll be in the corner making love, with a front row seat to Daisy and Erik. Raise your glass. I lost my glass. Waiter?"

A new flute was rushed into his hand. "Raise your glass," Will said, meeting Erik's eyes. "And toast to my best friends. To the union of fishes and daisies. To love."

Glasses in hands rose up, a cloud of twinkling golden balloons. "To love."

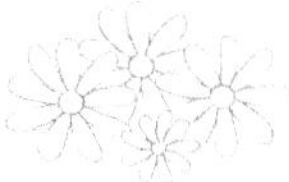

After the reception, they rode from the barn to the carriage house on a tandem bicycle. Daisy skillfully tucked up her dress's long skirt, revealing white Converse sneakers. A sign lettered JUST (STYLISHLY) MARRIED was tacked to the rear seat. With a ring of the bike's bell they were off, the guests lining the road on either side, sparklers in hand and singing "Daisy Bell." The picture the photographer caught would live on top of the upright piano at Barbegazi.

"Hello, wife," Erik said as they braked to a stop.

"Hello, husband."

He got off and held the bike still while she dismounted, then leaned it up against the carriage house wall. He pulled her into his arms and they kissed. His hands ran down her back, along the length of smooth satin. Then a little further and they stopped.

"What are you wearing under here?"

"Not a damn thing," she said, running her finger along his bottom lip.

"Really?"

She tossed her head back a little. "Never wear panties to a party. Have I taught you nothing?"

He looked back at the people lining the road, the last sparklers fizzing out. "Is everyone going home now?"

"Everyone? No," she said. "Private after-party on the porch. Panties optional."

He looked back at her, ran his hand along her cheek. "Did I tell you that you look beautiful?"

She blinked at him and her smile turned down a little. "Not in the last five minutes."

He slid his hand around the back of her neck. "You look beautiful," he whispered against her mouth. He kissed her. Kissed her again. Slower. Her mouth opened to his. Her hands came up to his face. Happiness pulled his chest apart and started stirring things below the belt.

"Get a room," someone bellowed from up the road.

"I'd love to," Erik muttered.

"You will," she said, taking his hand and starting toward the house. "All night long. Or for the rest of your life, whichever comes first."

"You come first," he said, bringing the back of her ringed fingers up to his lips.

Will sent one last text: *Cock ring is a little too snug. Next time get me the extra-large.*

Erik replied. *Sorry. I got myself the extra-large and figured you were one size down.*

Fuck you.

Can't, I'm married. But thanks for asking.

Don't call me.

Believe me, tonight? I won't.

A Different Kind of Hard 

"YOU LIKE BEETS?" Francine said, smiling.

Erik shrugged a shoulder and made one corner of his mouth smile back. He didn't outright hate beets, but they weren't what he'd go for on the buffet line. Still, he'd learned long ago Francine treated picky eaters over the age of five as a personal challenge. Saying you didn't like something was a surefire way to find a boatload of it on your plate later.

"I like anything you make," he said. Which was the truth. Francine could make a bundle of sticks taste good. With unfeigned interest, Erik watched her nature-dyed fingers generously salt and pepper the glistening chunks of red and golden beets.

She reached to her knife block and plucked out her kitchen shears. "Herb garden," she said. "Cut me a big handful of thyme. The lemon kind. You know what it is?"

"I know," Erik said, and shouldered out the screen door with the odd sense of importance he always felt when Francine entrusted him with a kitchen chore.

After a budget honeymoon in Key West—frequent flier miles and the use of Christine and Fred's condo—the newlyweds came back to La Tarasque for two weeks.

"You're supposed to be on vacation," Francine said, protesting as Daisy and Erik pulled on boots and gloves, picked up hoes and rakes and marched into farm life.

"I love it here," Erik said. "It is a vacation."

"When you don't have to do it, you love it," Joe said.

True, they weren't up at rooster crow and heading out to the fields. They slept in and shagged and got up when it suited them. *Then* they headed for the fields and were swept up in the buzzing activity of farm and orchard.

The hard, outdoor work made Erik hungry. Hungry as the summer he was fifteen and had grown four inches overnight. When his young bones ached and his stomach was a constant gnawing knot of hunger. He could feel himself growing, stretching and arranging and shoving things around to make room.

He remembered fifteen being an insatiable year of extremes. He was exhausted, starving, needing, wanting, stretched from one end of his limited universe to the other. A quivering bundle of muscle and nerve, a moody hair-trigger, a speechless porcupine of desires. He wanted his mother then suffocated in her arms. He pushed her away so she would track him down. Girls irritated him to distraction. He fled from their giggling double talk and passive aggressive tactics and then lay awake in the dark of his room, utterly consumed. Hard and frustrated with thoughts of skin and mouths and kissing and sex. And food. Never enough food.

"Good appetite," Francine said, beaming at this man-boy as she filled his plate with more roasted beets.

He liked the beets. He liked growing them and being the "to" in farm-to-table. He knew what lemon thyme was, just as he knew a fresh duck egg had a bright orange yolk and an almost powdery shell. He knew you let the garden dictate what was for lunch or dinner, and La Tarasque in late summer was a benevolent despot. Poached eggs laid half an hour before. Tomatoes still warm from the sun. String beans no bigger than matchsticks. Corn that barely needed a kiss of boiling water. Potatoes dug and scrubbed, then roasted crisp outside and velvet inside. Meatless days passed in simple food of the earth with no violence attached. And then a local cattle farm would butcher and Erik would find himself devouring perfectly-grilled steak and drinking the bloody pan juices like a vampire.

"Good appetite," Daisy whispered in the dark as he took her again and again, his plate un-fillable. Consumed with a different hunger. Marriage was sweet, savory and spicy on his tongue and he couldn't get enough. Couldn't sate the desire to sink into her body and gorge on her attention. To stuff the lost years down his throat and feast on what had been returned to him.

Forever.

He loved his wife. He ate. He cleared the table then he shouldered out the screen door and went back to whatever task was allotted him. He found the work on the farm grounding. A connection to a simpler way of life. It was good work. Hard work, but everything was hard. Erik often paused and looked around at the property, wondering if maybe it were time for a different kind of hard.

Watering and weeding and harvesting, he daydreamed. Imagined a time when Dais would retire, hang up her pointe shoes entirely and she and Erik would move down here to Pennsylvania and slowly take over La Tarasque. He thought how it would be different though, if they had children.

He admitted it freely: whether here or in Canada, being just a couple allowed them to live an indulgent existence. Long hours of uninterrupted work or play. Bedtimes negotiable or ignored. Potato chips and beer for dinner. Sex wherever they felt like dropping their pants. No stopping to feed, change or tend to others. Just them and what they wanted when they wanted it.

I just want us.

I want her to myself.

I want to be the center of her universe and not share her with anyone. Ever.

But little moments kept intruding on the greedy reverie. Sitting around the table with Joe and Francine, Erik would look for a high chair. Or stare at Francine's empty lap. Or look at Joe with a dish towel thrown over his shoulder and think it ought to be a baby.

I want a family. Someday.

We can't wait too long.

But I want her to myself.

Back and forth between the two wants he was volleyed like a ball.

I want so much.

I want everything and I wasted so many years.

I want my youth back.

I hate what I did.

I want.

THEY CAME HOME TO Barbegazi and slipped into their routine. The seasons turned, birthdays and holidays passed. Then came the cold, dark months of early winter.

Talk of children was casual and hypothetical. Couched in somedays, whens and ifs. Truth was, in watching and listening to the men closest to him who were parents, Erik felt in no burning rush to join the club. Pete Fiskare was out of his mind with worry over his son Aaron, whose daily struggles with dyslexia and ADHD were a never-ending source of anxiety. His daughter Valerie, on the other hand, was a Renaissance woman of effortless talents and intelligence, yet she was devoted to being a world-class underachiever.

"Aaron wants the world," Pete said. "Val's pursuing a degree in bare minimum. I want to swathe him in bubble wrap and throw her out the window."

Next door, Will and Lucky were occupied with finding a speech therapist for little Sara.

"Speech therapist?" Erik said. "She never stops talking."

"I know," Will said, his eyes shadowed with worry. "But she's not *saying* anything."

At her kindergarten registration, questions were raised about "developmental milestones" and now the Kaegers were running around getting her evaluated. Meanwhile, Jack's second-grade class was having a bullying issue and Jack was a nervous wreck, often flat-out refusing to go to school.

Lurking behind the promise of day-to-day logistical stress, out beyond the occasional health alarms, the pressing emotional issues and the complex social dramas, was the most sinister threat of all: the phone call.

Joe and Francine, Maurice and Ségolène, Christine and Fred and even Judy Dare—they all got The Call.

There's been an incident.

Your child was involved.

You need to come.

Erik observed, gathering intelligence and analyzing hard truths: to become a parent was to go around with your heart flayed open for the rest of your life. Moving the earth and giving your best for your kids, with no guarantee your best would be enough to keep them safe.

Fuck this, his genes thought. *Me, Dais and the cat. That's enough.*

Except it wasn't.

He chewed at it through the winter, more and more conscious he was chasing down forty now.

"You'll know, mon pote," Joe said.

"You'll know," Fred said. "It's like love. It sneaks up on you."

It's just one of those things, Mike Pettitte texted in one of their frequent electronic exchanges. ***You do it because you know.***

"Dude, you'll just know," Will said.

"I know I'll know," Erik said to them all.

One March morning, they awoke to three feet of snow with more coming down. The roads closed and a bank holiday was upon them. Will and Erik took Jack and Sara outside to build a fort. They fought a merciless snowball war and then trooped back into Barbegazi's kitchen, numb-fingered and runny-nosed and ravenous. Lucky and Daisy were baking. The tea kettle sang. They bellied up to the kitchen table and dug into the bread and treats.

Jacy woke up from her nap and came stumbling in, her blonde curls smashed flat along one side of her head, a blanket dragged behind. She climbed into Daisy's lap and put her thumb in her mouth. Daisy kissed the tousled head and reached arms around to butter a slice of bread. Jacy closed her eyes and rested her temple at the V of Daisy's sweater.

Erik stared, his mug frozen halfway to his mouth.

Daisy kept the child perfectly balanced in her lap as she poured and sliced and arranged for the others, laughing and talking. She siphoned some of her tea into a clean mug and topped it off with milk. Then held the cup for Jacy to sip. Buttered another piece of bread. Like a trusting newborn bird the little girl accepted food and drink, then laid her head against Daisy again.

Erik stared.

Jacy caught his penetrating gaze, smiled around her thumb then reached out her arms.

"Careful, honey," Daisy said, shifting a leg to balance her. "What do you want, you want Uncle Erik?"

Jacy never wanted him. Now her arms reached further across the gap. Erik took her on his lap. She burrowed into his chest, her little fingers curling around his shirt cuff, playing with the buttons.

He was steel. Her head was a magnet. Slowly his chin lowered and he inhaled the smell of her hair. Powder. Sleep. An indescribable sweetness. His heart pounded slow and steady against the plump, warm weight in his lap.

The overhead lamp splashed a circle of gold across the feast. Steam rose from tea mugs, weaving with the talk and chatter to make a wreath around the two families. Jack's arms crossed around Will's neck from behind, chin on his father's shoulder. Will's hand laced carelessly with Lucky's on the table. Sara rocked in Lucky's lap, eating a cookie. Daisy poured and sliced and fed. Her hands busy. Her lap empty.

"Unca fower," Jacy said, her finger now drawing a circle around his daisy tattoo. "Fower pretty."

Erik's hand gently closed around the little girl's wrist as he looked at it all. For the first time in his life, he *saw*.

Later in bed, he lay on his side, resting on his elbow and running his hand over Daisy's body. Fingertips caressing the little red fish, then moving to draw circles around her stomach. He spread his palm wide, fingers reaching, feeling her belly button rise and fall beneath him with her breathing.

Her hand caressed his head. "What?" she whispered in the dark.

He opened his mouth then closed it. "Nothing," he said. And kissed her before she could call bullshit.

He loved her hard that night. With a strange desperation. Throwing himself into her. Even after he came, he kept pushing into her, further and further, gripped in a frustration of inability. His throat was coming apart with it.

"Honey, you're hurting me," she said, hands on his shoulder blades. "Stop."

His body collapsed down on hers. "I'm sorry."

"What is it," she said. She peeled his head off her shoulder and held it propped above hers, running her thumb along his lip. "What is it, what are you trying to do?"

"Make a baby," he said.

She gathered him back to her, winding arms and legs around his body and pulling him close. "You will," she said, rocking him.

"I know," he said, exhaling, wrapped in an assured conviction. "I know."

REVERSAL OF FORTUNE 

HE HADN'T HAD A physical in years. Hadn't even been sick since he moved to Canada, so he didn't have a regular doctor. He went to Will's guy, who pronounced him in boringly good health and recommended a urologist. The urologist took Erik's medical history and immediately referred him elsewhere.

"You're in luck," the doctor said. "Up until now, New Brunswick's best fertility clinic was in Moncton. They just opened their Saint John satellite six months ago. Urology and reproductive services all under one roof. You'll want to get in to see Martin LeBlanc before he accumulates a waiting list."

"Is he good?" Erik said.

"He's the one you want."

Erik called the practice in Rochester to have his records transferred. He sat in Dr. LeBlanc's handsome office and they went through it together. Besides all the obvious questions, LeBlanc seemed interested in the arc of Erik's life story. His bedside manner was so superb, Erik spilled it all out with ease: his youth, the shooting, the aftermath, his first marriage, the fertility troubles, the divorce and finally, the reconciliation with Daisy.

"And you've been married how long now?"

"Almost a year."

Leblanc flipped through his notes. "You're thirty-eight... Your wife is thirty-seven. Do you feel you've spent enough time together as a couple? Truly enjoying each other and the time alone?"

"We do. And we both feel comfortable with it being just the two of us, in case none of this works out."

LeBlanc rubbed his chin thoughtfully. "I'm interested by something you said in passing. How since you've reconciled with your current wife, your cells are happy."

"It's always been that way," Erik said. "Since the day I met her. Like I could feel my atoms lining up whenever I was with her. It's hard to explain."

LeBlanc nodded. "Your cells are happy," he said again. He opened a drawer in his desk and without ceremony plonked one of the ubiquitous specimen cups in front of Erik. "Let's see if that's indeed the case."

Erik raised eyebrows at him and then flicked his head toward the thick medical history file.

"Always look for the simplest solution first," LeBlanc said.

"Well," LeBlanc said at the follow-up. "This isn't a miraculous reversal of fortune by any means. But I wouldn't call you a lost cause."

He turned the lab report toward Erik and pointed with a finger. "Counts still aren't anything near what we want, but you did move the needle. Four years ago, your average sample yielded three million sperm per milliliter which is considered severe. Today's sample shows seven million per milliliter."

"Shut up," Erik said. "Seven?"

LeBlanc's finger circled. "Lucky seven."

"The whole time I was being monitored, I never shot over five." He looked up. "So now my counts merely suck instead of being abysmal. What about the motility?"

"What indeed." The doctor's finger now made a circular motion around the words Type C. "You were Type D before. No motility whatsoever."

"What's C?"

"Your boys are swimming. Swimming a little stupidly— That is to say, they move their tails but they have little to no forward progression."

"I see."

"All the same, I wouldn't discount your cellular happiness theory. Clearly your body is in a better place these days."

"So what's your plan?"

"Most likely we'll have to do a surgical extraction again, and IVF with ICSI. Assuming, of course, your wife has no issues. Given her age, I'm afraid statistics aren't on her side. It's just a hard fact of female life. But we won't know anything until we see her."

The dull ache of regret for the lost years surfaced in Erik's stomach. He managed a small smile. "You could say I was living a Type C life for a bunch of years. Moving my tail a lot but not progressing forward."

LeBlanc laughed and rubbed his hands together with relish. "Well, let's have Madame come in, shall we?"

THE SWEET SPOT

"BUCKLE UP," ERIK SAID as they drove home from the clinic. "The ride gets kind of crazy from here."

"Bring it," Daisy said absently, reading over a pamphlet on IVF. An additional thick sheaf of papers was in her lap. These were the only sources of information she was permitted. Dr. Alibrandi, the obstetrician assigned to their case, was adamant.

"Stay *off* the internet," Alibrandi said. "You have questions, you call us. Any online chat rooms or forums, I'm telling you—you will be a lunatic before we even start. Promise me."

"I promise," Daisy said.

"Don't lose your sense of humor," LeBlanc said when he saw them in the hall.

"I promise," Erik said.

"This is complicated," Daisy said, flipping pages. "Because of how you time everything. A lot of hurry up and wait."

"It is," Erik said. "I feel bad because I'm the one with the issues, but one procedure and I'm done. You get all the hassle and discomfort."

She hummed in her chest then put the papers down in her lap again. "I'm not afraid of physical discomfort. Being a dancer I don't go a day without some part of my body hurting. The shots? I used to cut myself with glass so how bad can shots be?"

Erik gave a small laugh.

"Well." Her shoulders rose and fell as she took a deep breath. "I hope everything's all right on my end."

"How do you mean," he said, taking her hand.

"I'm thirty-seven."

"Which isn't *that* old. Come on, forty-seven would be more of an issue."

Another inhale. "I starved myself for so many years," she said. "All that chain-smoking and starving and abuse. It had to have some kind of effect. It worries me."

They were at a red light. He squeezed her hand and brought it up to his mouth. "We'll find out soon enough," he said. "Try not to worry until we have something real to worry about."

"After everything we've been through," she said. "Who knows? Maybe we'll catch a break."

The light turned green and they both burst into cynical laughter.

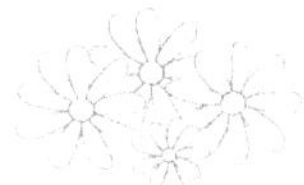

Daisy made big calendars to hang on her office wall and started grooming an assistant ballet mistress who could cover classes and rehearsals when Daisy was at appointments. The first month was mostly reviewing IVF protocol at the clinic. Daisy went in for one procedure where a mock embryo transfer was done. A dress rehearsal to test the size and placement of the catheter which, hopefully, would eventually place a fertilized egg into her womb.

The second month kicked off with birth control pills to synchronize and monitor her cycle. This phase could last up to three months, depending on how her ovaries responded. She was at the clinic every morning for blood work and ultrasounds.

"Nothing like a needle and a trans-vaginal probe to start your day," she said.

Over the next two weeks, the lab relayed good news on Daisy's blood work. "Your levels are perfect," the nurse said. "Right where we want them."

"You have the ovaries of a twenty-eight-year-old," the ultrasound technician said.

"Oh my God, are we actually catching a break?" Daisy asked Erik, who was watching the monitor.

"Let me check." He moved to the window and peeked between two slats of the venetian blinds. "Just as I thought," he said. "The harbor turned to blood, huge cracks in the Earth's surface and big rocks falling out of the sky."

Before Daisy's cycle started again, they attended the injectables class and after a two-hour wait at the pharmacy, went home with a cooler of vials, a case of syringes and another sheaf of printed instructions. Daisy made another calendar to hang on the bathroom wall.

"I got this," Erik said on the first scheduled night. "I used to do this to myself three times a week."

"Yeah, little subcutaneous ones on your legs. Not intramuscular ones in your butt."

"Same principle," he said, flicking the syringe to get the air bubbles out. "And I'd take one in the ass every now and then."

"I'm telling Will," she said.

Erik pulled the cap off the needle. "All right, come on. The trick is to do it fast. The buildup is worse than the shot."

His heart was thumping but he acted cool, remembering the nurse's advice to keep it business the first few times. ("No jokes, no chatter, no ass patting," she said. "Just do it.")

He found the sweet spot ("Stay above the crack, outside half of the cheek") and swabbed it with the alcohol. Spread the skin as taut as he could.

"Take a breath in, on three," he said. "One, two, three."

Like a dart he jabbed. Daisy gave a small grunt and blew her breath out. He pulled the plunger back a hair and then pressed it down.

"Jesus," she said through her teeth.

"Sorry."

"The push burns."

"Done," he said, tossing the syringe in the disposal container they were given and massaging the skin around the injection site.

"All right," Daisy said, pulling her pants back in place. "Nice job, Fish."

"Thanks, Marge."

She crossed out the day on the calendar, kissed him and left the bathroom. Erik exhaled and looked at his shaking hands.

HARVEST

AS HE DID WITH Melanie, Erik had sperm surgically extracted. It couldn't be cryogenically stored, so the procedure had to be done within a day of the egg harvesting. If Dr. LeBlanc couldn't get any viable sperm, the cycle would be lost, but the retrieved eggs could be frozen to use with a later attempt. Or with a donor.

"Who's second banana?" Will asked one night. "You still want your brother?"

"Well, I want you," Erik said. "But your ship has sailed."

"I can't do anything to help?" Will said. "Come and jerk you off? Just once? Please?"

Erik threw a specimen cup at Will's head. "Jerk that, asshole."

Plans B, C and D had been sketched out. If they got both sperm and eggs, they'd proceed with IVF. If they got eggs but no sperm, they'd still proceed, but with Pete donating. If the IVF failed on either account, they'd take a huge vacation somewhere, regroup and look at adopting.

"Thus shall be the plan," Erik said.

"Subject to sudden emotional change and-or life's bullshit sense of humor," Daisy said. "Without warning."

Two weeks passed. Daisy spent her life on the phone. She was on a first-name basis with the pharmacist and already added five nurses to her Christmas card list. Her thighs and glutes were bruised and her breasts ached, which made finding a comfortable sleeping position nearly impossible. She went through her day tired, sore and moody. When Erik called her cell, she answered like a law firm. "Tired, sore and moody, may I fucking help you?"

But the break they seemed to have caught stayed in their hands. After all the shots, the morning monitoring appointments, ultrasounds to measure follicles and blood work to measure hormone levels, finally it was time for harvest.

They arrived together at the clinic for the sperm extraction. LeBlanc encouraged wives and partners to be present at procedures. "You've been robbed of all the fun in making babies," he said. "Nothing sexy going on here. You should be able to be close. Hold hands. At least feel like you're doing it together."

"He's such a sap," one of the nurses said.

"I believe in the power of love," LeBlanc said. "Fine, I'm a sap. It's my downfall."

"Or your saving grace," Erik said. He appreciated having anyone's hand to hold while getting a needle of Novocaine in each testicle. He also appreciated the Ativan they threw in his IV line. Now he was just full of floaty dread, instead of anxious and full of nauseating dread.

"The buildup is worse than the shot," Daisy said, managing to still be adorable despite the blue cap covering all her hair.

"You got it spaced over two weeks," he said, conscious of his tongue and teeth and how his mouth moved. "I get it all in one go." He closed his eyes, hoping he would drift off. Hard to do with his private parts on public display. Everything was so desexualized by now, he was beyond being embarrassed. Vulnerability, however, stuck close by.

I can live without having kids, he thought. *You slip, cut the wrong thing and desexualize* me, *then it's going to get ugly around here.*

Daisy's hand ran soft over his forehead. He smiled and opened his eyes. The room swam a little then focused again. Daisy smiled back and they stared.

"All right, my friend," LeBlanc said. "Let's begin."

"Fuck," Erik said as Daisy took his hand in hers. Then the stabbing pain that burned, froze and ached simultaneously. Something between a kick to the balls and an ice pick to the groin. The air crawled into his lungs and he had to grab it by the ankle and drag it back out.

"Jesus," he said against his fist while his other hand squeezed Daisy's fingers.

"Breathe," she said.

"Doc, you bastard," he said, laughing because it beat crying.

"Sorry," LeBlanc said. "Two more."

"Can't wait."

The second burned and ached. The third was merely pressure that aggravated the ache. In a few minutes, everything below his navel and above his knees disappeared and he could get a full breath in.

"All right?" Daisy said.

He managed a wobbly smile. "Nothing to it."

Her hand caressed him. He focused on his breathing until the nausea dissolved away. Long minutes dripped by. He watched his heart rate on the monitor a while, until the beeps made him sleepy. He turned his head into Daisy's hand and closed his eyes. Then yawned back into consciousness some length of time later. He felt vague pressure and pushing. The click and clink as instruments were passed. Daisy's cool palm on his forehead.

"It's going well, Erik," LeBlanc said. "We've got two vials."

"Really?"

"Yes."

Daisy laid her head down next to his. "Whose balls are better than yours," she whispered.

He chuckled. "I'm afraid my balls won't be much use to you the next two weeks."

"I have other uses for you."

"What, catching mice and killing spiders?"

"It's the main reason I married you. Live-in pest control."

While he rested on ice in recovery, Daisy got a hormonal trigger shot to set ovulation in motion. Erik spent the rest of the day on the couch at Barbegazi, watching TV while he cozied up to bags of frozen peas. Daisy waited on him hand and foot, rotating the cold packs. Twenty minutes on. Twenty minutes off. With eleven Advil for breakfast, he'd be fine.

"I'm pleased with what we got," LeBlanc said when he called that evening. "An excellent sample given your history."

"Are they swimming?"

"Doesn't matter. With ICSI, the first thing you do with sperm is cut the tail off."

Daisy went back the next day for retrieval. Erik wasn't allowed in during her procedure. He sat with his ice packs, reading, until they called him into recovery.

He eased himself into a chair next to the bed. Daisy was still sleeping. Her head drooped to one side and her hands rested on her stomach, the IV line running from the back of one to the pole. A blood pressure cuff on her arm and a pulse tracker on one of her fingers.

He looked at her. Looked into the past. The last time he saw her like this was after the shooting. Today was nothing like then, but still, the clinical smell of the room pressed his memory. The faint beep of monitors echoed in his mind and a sadness filled his chest, remembering how Daisy's face had been so motionless and far away as he stood at her bedside that day. Gunfire still ringing in his ears. Her blood all over his shirt. Caked in his nail beds and smeared on his work boots. His palms and knees nicked and scratched because he'd crawled through broken glass to get to her.

We were so young, he thought, taking her hand. His fingers played with her wedding rings, thumb running along the edge of the diamond.

"Where are you?" Daisy said. Her head lolled and settled toward him, her eyes still closed.

"Here," Erik said. "I'm right here, Dais."

The polite rattle of knuckles on the door and LeBlanc leaned into the room.

"I hear she did great," he said. "Beautiful eggs and lots of them."

"She's generous," Erik said, bringing Daisy's limp fingers up to his cheek.

And forgiving.

LeBlanc stood at the foot of the bed, looking at Daisy. "I'm pleased," he said. "Everything has been absolutely textbook. It's going much better than I expected."

"Dude." Erik reached to knock on the wall. "Are you out of your mind saying that *out loud?*"

"Sorry, sorry, her eggs are rotten." LeBlanc said, laughing and rapping his head. "This is going terrible. You're doomed. I have no hope whatsoever."

Thirteen eggs were retrieved from Daisy's ovaries. Six were immediately frozen. The other seven were injected with a single sperm each.

They lay in bed that night: Erik black and blue, Daisy sore and cramping. They held hands and imagined what was happening in the lab. Two becoming one. Then dividing into two again. Four. Eight. Merging. Melding. Becoming something greater.

"I wish I could watch it," Daisy said. "Wouldn't that be something?"

"I think my head would explode."

The clinic called daily with updates and, to the Fiskares' fascination, even emailed pictures. Daisy printed out all seven and tacked them to the refrigerator.

"I think this one has your eyes," Erik said, peering close at the black-and-white blobs.

"This one has your ass," Daisy said. "It gets my vote."

On day three the lab reported two of the fertilized eggs did not mature to the blastocyst stage. Day four's status was given as "normal."

"We have five beauties," Dr. Alibrandi said the morning of the fifth day. "Given your age, and that this is your first IVF cycle, my recommendation is to implant three and freeze the remaining two."

The next day, Daisy and Erik witnessed as the embryos were selected and loaded into the catheter. They watched on the monitor as the sonogram showed the catheter being placed.

"You so much," Erik said, holding Daisy's hand tight.

"So much you."

He began to softly whistle "Daisy Bell." The nurse joined in. Then Alibrandi. With a puff of air the embryos were released. The catheter was examined under a microscope to make sure they left.

"A successful transfer," Alibrandi said. "Well done."

Daisy rested for twenty minutes at the clinic, then went home to recline as queen for another seventy-two hours. Sara Kaeger took this quite literally and brought over a tiara. Daisy wore it the rest of the night.

Francine called. "How are you, my loveys," she said. "What are you doing now?"

"Hatching," Daisy said.

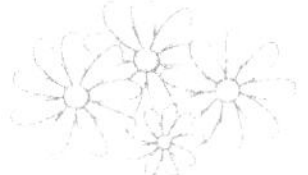

The blood work said yes. The urine tests said yes. Progesterone levels insisted yes. Daisy wouldn't accept anything until she saw it with her own eyes. Even the onset of morning sickness didn't convince her.

"Believe it now?" Erik said as she came out of the bathroom, green and shaky.

"Stomach bug," she said. And continued to say nearly every day, living in benign and superstitious denial until the first ultrasound.

"We could walk out of here the parents of triplets," Daisy said, pausing with her hand on the clinic's door. "I kind of feel like running."

"Go big or go home," Erik said, feeling a little terrified himself, but opening the door with purpose. "After you."

"One," the technician said.

The Fiskares peered closer. "Are you sure?" Daisy said.

"Just one." The technician circled the screen with a fingertip. "And look at that heartbeat. Fantastic."

Daisy started crying.

"Hey, we were braced for triplets," Erik said, gathering her against him.

"I was braced for *none*," she cried. "I can't believe it worked."

"Congratulations," the technician said.

Erik kept staring at the monitor. "Holy crap, I got her pregnant."

Daisy cried harder. Her arms tightened around him and his shirt grew damp under her tears. His hand stroked her hair, but his eyes never left the black-and-white image. He gazed at the little blob with its fantastic pulsing heart. He felt his own heart beat against the wall of his chest as the gold chain around his neck grew heavy and warm.

"Hey, little fish," he whispered to the screen.

THE FAMILY DYNAMIC

IN SEPTEMBER, TRUDY AND Kirsten went on a New England-Canada cruise. One of the ports-of-call was Saint John, and Erik took them to lunch at one of his and Daisy's favorite haunts.

"Well, isn't this nice," Kirsten said, unfolding her napkin.

"We didn't have much time to chat properly at your wedding," Trudy said.

"Which we're still talking about," Kirsten said, patting Erik's hand. "Such a good time."

Trudy was digging in her handbag. "Now let me show you this right away or I'll forget later and be mad at myself." She drew out a small, black drawstring bag. She tipped something out of it into her hand and put it into Erik's palm.

It was another fish charm. Identical to Erik's, save one detail.

"It's silver," Erik said.

"Of course it's silver," Trudy said. "It was for a little girl. This is Beatrice's fish."

"How did she die?"

"Polio. There was an outbreak in eighteen ninety-four. Beatrice died and Major was left with a lame leg."

"Major?"

Trudy squeezed his forearm. "You're the third Erik in the family, honey. My brother was Erik, and so was Emil's brother. But my uncle would punch himself in the nose before answering to Old Erik, so he was called Major and my brother was called Minor."

"What a shame you never met your namesakes," Kirsten said. "Both of them were a couple of characters."

"Neither is buried in the family plot," Erik said.

Trudy nodded. "Erik Major wanted his ashes scattered over the river. Erik Minor moved out west in the sixties. He died in California and he's buried there."

"I see." Erik admired the silver fish another moment, then gave it back to Trudy.

"Shame I have no daughters," she said, putting the little bag in her purse. "And currently, only grandsons. But the fish will stay in the family either way. Now, tell me, what's good to eat here?"

Over lunch, the aunts told stories about the family, Clayton, life in the hotel and on the river.

"Can you tell me about my dad's accident?" Erik finally asked.

The ladies exchanged a glance Erik couldn't interpret. Then Trudy began to tell how Byron and Xandro had been racing their boats in the early morning hours. A foolish stunt on the St. Lawrence River because of the fog that poured off Alexandria Bay at that time of day. The river was treacherous enough with shoals and rapids. The fog made it doubly dangerous.

"Your father knew better," Trudy said. "He was only fifteen, but he grew up on the river and knew the risks."

"A river rat pilots a boat before he drives a car," Kirsten said.

"You learned the rules and got your ass handed to you if you broke them. Both Byron and Xandro knew better."

"Xandro had Elsa in the boat with him," Kirsten said. "She certainly knew better. Then again, she always had a funny hold on Xandro. Something was strange about the whole incident. Like it was a dare gone horribly wrong."

"The accident happened around Fishers Landing. Bunch of little islands clustered in the river there, along with a half-dozen shoals. It's a tricky place. The currents are strong."

"And unpredictable," Kirsten said.

Trudy nodded. "Even my father and Major wrecked a few boats there, back when they were running booze during Prohibition."

Erik made a mental note to circle back to his great-grandfather's bootlegging adventures. "What exactly happened to my father?"

"Well, the thing is, Xandro first said he'd been out in front of Byron's boat and didn't see what happened. But later he came clean and said he'd been behind Byron the whole time and he'd been trying to ride Byron's wake."

"I don't understand."

"River rats had their favorite stunts, one of which was riding the wake of a freighter or some other big ship."

"With a surfboard?"

"No," Kirsten said, "with their boats. You align the bow with the wake just so. If you do it right, you get about six inches of the boat on the crest and the rest of you is floating."

"It's an amazing sensation," Trudy said. "You feel like you're going fast and holding still at the same time. But it's also dangerous and if my father ever caught us doing it, we'd get our fish warm."

Erik laughed. "Your fish what?"

"Få sina fiskar varma," Trudy said. "It's a Swedish expression. Literally translates to 'getting your fish warm' and it's what we kids called a hiding."

"So that's what Xandro was doing?" Erik said. "Riding the wake of a freighter?"

"No, he was trying to ride *Byron's* wake. The trough a motorboat leaves behind is nothing like a freighter's wake. Xandro got too close and he clipped Byron's stern. And Byron lost control and went flying end over end."

"Jesus," Erik said.

A pause while the waiter cleared plates and asked if anyone would like dessert. With glittering eyes Kirsten raised a finger. "I'll see a menu." She smiled at Erik. "Life is short. Have dessert."

"Byron's life should have been short," Trudy said. "Cripes, that he wasn't killed is nothing short of a miracle. You'll never convince me otherwise."

"How bad was he hurt?"

"Cracked his skull. It's a wonder his brains weren't dashed out."

"Or that he didn't drown," Erik said.

"Well, unlike Xandro, Byron had a life jacket on," Kirsten said. "And he ended face-up in the water, not face-down."

"Current took him," Trudy said. "And he floated off into the fog. Coast Guard finally found him in a little cove."

Kirsten frowned. "It wasn't like it is today. With an ER in every hospital and medevac choppers and trauma centers."

"We had a tiny little hospital in Alexandria Bay," Trudy said. "It had an X-ray machine and it was considered high-tech. They brought in our nephew with a fractured skull. All they could do was tell Kennet and Astrid how many cracks."

"What did they do with him?" Erik asked, barely breathing. "The nearest city is Watertown."

"No, Watertown had no help for him," Kirsten said. "Kennet and Astrid took him to Montreal. First to the Royal Victoria, and the doctors there transferred him to the Montreal Neurological Institute. It was the best facility for him. 'Traumatic brain injury' wasn't in the mainstream vocabulary yet, but the Neuro was just starting to study it. They took Byron in pro bono."

"Still," Trudy said, "the doctors didn't give him a high chance of survival. And with the pneumonia he developed on top of the brain bleed, he should've been dead."

"Or a permanent vegetable."

Erik blinked. "Was he in a coma?"

"For about two weeks," Trudy said, leaning her chin on her hand. "I didn't see him while he was up in Montreal, but my brother would give updates. First he said Byron's eyes were opening but he wasn't looking at anything. Then it seemed he was focusing on things. Turning his head to follow noise, looking around the room. But not talking or reacting to people. Not responding to his name. But then one day..." She lifted her head and snapped her fingers. "Opened his eyes. Perfectly lucid. And said hello. As if he'd woken up from a nap."

"Jesus."

"Didn't know what the hell happened to him, but he knew who he was and knew who belonged to him. It was a miracle."

"The doctors were stunned," Kirsten said. "No one had an explanation for how he survived."

"Although he wasn't the same after," Trudy said.

"How so?" Erik asked.

Again, a look was exchanged between the sisters-in-law. This one longer. It seemed to make the air shimmer between them.

"You survived Lancaster," Trudy finally said. "Were you the same?"

Erik gave a small smile. "No, ma'am."

"Nobody was the same," Kirsten said. "Definitely a shift in the family dynamic."

"You mean Xandro was sort of disgraced after the accident?" Erik asked.

"He got his fish deep-fried," Kirsten said. "And deservedly so."

Trudy nodded, the corners of her mouth pulled down. "It didn't help that he lied to Kennet about what happened. Which, of *course* a person will do when they're in panic mode, especially when they're young and terrified and faced with the idea that a brother could die because of their actions."

"But you add the lying to the other broken rules," Kirsten said. "Racing in the fog and not wearing a life jacket."

"Yikes," Erik said.

"Kennet whipped Xandro awful," Trudy said. "Then took his boat license away. To a river rat, it's like losing a leg."

"Xandro must have died a thousand deaths."

"Oh, he wore it like a hair shirt. But understand one thing about how your great-grandfather raised me, your grandfather and my brothers: when we misbehaved, we'd get our fish warm, followed by forgiveness. Even with our most egregious misdeeds, there was never an ongoing harangue or a perpetual grudge. We took our deserved licks, went to bed without supper, and in the morning we never doubted we were still loved and valued. Nothing was held over our heads like emotional blackmail. Understand?"

"Do I ever," Erik said quietly.

"Kennet raised his own sons the same way. He was a firm disciplinarian, but he was fair and forgiving. He forgave Xandro, but I don't think Xandro ever quite believed it. And while he and Kennet were always loving toward each other, you always got the sense that Xandro's love was just the tiniest bit... I don't know. Fearful. Tentative. Like he was still atoning. That's why I say he wore the accident like a hair shirt. And Byron became the center of Xandro's universe."

"To the point where Xandro almost didn't go away to college," Kirsten said. "He had a full scholarship to the Fredonia School of Music, but he didn't want to leave home. He was only the second Fiskare to go to college and your grandparents begged him to go."

"Who was the first Fiskare to go to college?"

"My middle brother Björn," Trudy said. "He went to the University of Vermont for two years, but then he joined the Army. He was killed in Italy in nineteen forty-five."

"The family lost so many children," Erik said. "When Xandro died, my grandparents must have been... I can't even think of a word."

"It changed them," Kirsten said.

"That's the word," Trudy said.

Erik shook his head. "You know, my father-in-law fought in Vietnam, and he always told Daisy, 'We come back from war changed.' More and more, I realize how he didn't mean just literal war."

"So true," Kirsten murmured.

"Kennet and Astrid were once such open, joyful people," Trudy said, "but after Xandro died, they were like snuffed candle flames. They turned inside-out. Or rather, outside-*in*. They pulled inward. Became detached and reserved. They built a little protective fortress around themselves and from within, they merely observed the events of life. They didn't despair and they didn't rejoice. They just existed."

"They aged so quickly in the years after Xandro died," Kirsten said. "But they revived a bit when you were born, Erik."

"A bit?" Trudy said. "They had an absolute golden age because of him."

"Me," Erik said carefully. "Me and my brother, you mean."

"Well, of course, Peter."

"But especially you," Kirsten said. "You were Astrid's darling."

This was so at odds with Erik's personal narrative, he could only gape. He'd been his grandfather's darling. Christine said so. Any memory Erik could scrape up from Clayton had Kennet's presence somewhere. He barely remembered Astrid.

"I was?" he said. "Why me?"

"Because you looked just like Xandro." Trudy reached and touched Erik's necklace. "The boat charm was his."

"It was Xandro's?" Erik said, stunned.

"Technically it was Astrid's first. Kennet had the deWrennes make it for her. When they got engaged, they gave it to Xandro. Like a symbol he was theirs. Xandro had no memory of his biological father. Kennet was the only dad he knew. He wore this little boat his whole life. I don't remember exactly when he had *Fiskare* engraved into the bottom, but it was one of the few times I saw my brother cry."

While listening to her, Erik ran his thumb over the tiny letters etched in the boat's bottom. Nine thousand emotions were piling up in his body, along with a hundred questions in his mind. The waiter came back and the aunts ordered dessert, but Erik passed. He had no room for anything inside.

"It makes me so happy to see you wearing the chain," Trudy said. "I remember playing with the charms when I was a little girl."

"Same," Erik said softly. "I played with it when it was on my father's neck."

He scooped all the charms into his palm and looked at them. "I always thought it was one complete piece," he said. "But it's not. It was assembled. It's a collection."

"It's a story," Kirsten said.

Trudy smiled. "You could even say it's a fish tale."

A COLD BEAUTY

ERIK TOOK THE LADIES to the Imperial Theater to see Daisy and have a little backstage tour. After much hugging and kissing, Kirsten paused with Daisy's face in her hands. She peered close then turned to Erik. "Young man, did you knock this girl up?"

"Oh, you're one of *those* types," Daisy said, laughing.

"Damnedest thing," Kirsten said, her expression smug yet a flicker of sadness in her eyes. "I never got any kids of my own, but I have this weird ability to peg a pregnant woman from fifty yards."

The Fiskares had only told their parents and the Kaegers, cautiously sitting on the news until the end of the first trimester. But the ladies were too irresistible not to let in on the secret, which they promised to keep.

"This was so nice," Kirsten said as Erik walked them back to the pier. "What a beautiful city and what a lovely life you've made."

"And you speak such nice French," Trudy said.

Erik laughed. "My French is terrible, are you kidding?"

Trudy shrugged. "Sounds sexy to me."

"Reminds me," he said. "Was my grandmother born in Brazil? Or did she move there from Europe?"

"She was born in Finland," Kirsten said. "Her family fled the Finnish Civil War, first to Sweden, and then they immigrated to Brazil when Astrid was about five."

Trudy held Erik's arm a little tighter. "You know, dear, the story of you and Daisy is very much like Kennet and Astrid's story."

"It is?"

"Astrid was Marta's distant cousin, and she came to visit us in the summer of nineteen forty-one. She and Kennet fell deeply in love. To be honest, all of us Fiskares fell in love with Astrid."

"Lord, she was so glamorous," Kirsten said.

"She had a figure like a Coke bottle and that white-blonde hair. Pale skin and red lips."

"It was a cold beauty," Kirsten said. "Like a piece of Danish furniture. But she was the warmest, most wonderful person. We had so much fun. And she and your grandfather were just head over heels."

"What happened?" Erik asked.

"Liisa, Astrid's mother, didn't approve. She wanted Astrid to marry Jose Davis-Reyes, who was rich and connected and could keep Liisa in the style to which she was accustomed."

Kirsten held up a finger. "To be fair, Astrid always spoke well of Jose. He was her good friend, not the villain in the story."

"I agree. Liisa was the true villain."

"I hated that bitch," Kirsten said, sniffing. "Honest to God, Trudy and I made a voodoo doll and stuck pins in it."

Erik had to laugh then, though he wasn't satisfied with the story yet. "So what happened?"

"To cut to the tragic chase," Trudy said, "Liisa ripped Astrid and Kennet apart. Astrid played the dutiful daughter and Kennet played the gentleman."

"Which is delightful if you're into eleventh century courtly love," Kristen said. "We Fiskares thought it was a royal crock of shit."

"All this to say," Trudy said, "just like you and Daisy were separated by circumstances, to the point of estrangement, so were your grandparents. They had no contact during the war. Not a word. But then Astrid's husband was killed in Italy and she and Kennet got a second chance."

"Again," Kirsten said, "it sounds like a romantic fairytale ending, but your grandfather was profoundly changed after the war."

"As much as you were changed after Lancaster," Trudy said.

"He had PTSD?" Erik said. "I know they called it differently, but..."

Trudy nodded. "He was haunted. Both by things he saw and things he did. Look up the Chenogne Massacre, and you'll learn a little about what he experienced."

"All right," Erik said, feeling cold all over.

"Chenogne happened in early forty-five. Then right before V-E Day, Kennet's unit liberated Mauthausen concentration camp."

Erik's chill intensified. "Jesus."

"He wouldn't talk about it and frankly, I never wanted to ask what he had seen in that hellhole."

"Me neither." Kirsten gave a little shiver. "You can look it up."

"He kept a diary during the war," Trudy said. "I wish for your sake I knew what happened to it. Isn't it maddening, how you know certain objects exist but you don't pay attention to their exact whereabouts? And then they're lost. Forever. I don't have the slightest idea what became of Kennet's journal." She sighed. "I'm so sorry, honey, it would have been a treasure for you. I feel terrible the important men in your life are such mysteries."

"No," Erik said slowly. "No, don't be sorry. All your stories are treasure. Thank you for telling me. I have more family history today than I had yesterday, and now that Daisy's having a baby, it just means everything." He jostled Trudy's side. "Besides, I'm finding the important women in my life make me who I am."

They had arrived at the pier. At the ship's check-in booth, Erik hugged and kissed his aunts, promised to take care of his wife and to keep in touch.

"Bon voyage," he said. "Try not to get yourselves thrown out of the casino."

"Oh, we've been banned already," Kirsten said, sliding on her giant sunglasses. "Now we pass the time trying to pick up men."

"What do you mean trying?" Erik said. "Fiskares just stand in bars and take numbers."

Kirsten laughed and Trudy reached one last time to caress Erik's face.

"Look at you," she said, her eyes bright with tears.

THE MEN I LOVE

"SO TELL ME FIRST," the technician said, pulling on her gloves. "If you'd like to know the sex of your baby. That way I get my pronouns arranged up front."

"Yes," they said. It had been decided long ago. No surprises. They wanted to know who was coming.

The technician clicked and clacked at her monitor some more. Then she squirted her bottle of gel onto Daisy's stomach and set the ultrasound wand down. "Let's find a baby," she said. "Except you're such a skinny minny, I'll probably find the pattern of the rug under you first."

They laughed. Daisy was fiercely proud of her bump, although what counted as a bump for her was a normal woman's indigestion. Heart thumping with anticipation, Erik caught her hand up in his. She flicked her head over to him and smiled, then turned back with interest to the monitor.

"Hello," the technician said. "Somebody's showing off."

"What," they said, leaning in.

She angled the screen further in their direction. "This would be a boy."

And indeed it was.

"Impressive," Daisy said.

"Well, come on," Erik said, a smile widening his face and a burning pleasure filling his chest. It crackled in his veins on the ride home.

Glowed like a fire died down to red coals as he pinned the sonogram pictures to the refrigerator.

It's a boy.

He went outside, stood in the sun on the concrete slab, golden and warm as he mixed up his face with Daisy's face to come up with a new face.

What will you look like?

Who will you be?

His eyes swept the yard, imagining his son at play. He squinted at the trees, assessing them, coming back repeatedly to the oak and its sturdy branches. It was begging for a treehouse. A really spectacular one. He'd do it right, get a couple of the stagehands to help him. Jack, too. Together they'd build something amazing for his son.

It's a boy.

"What are you thinking about," Daisy said, sliding her arms around him from behind.

"Everything," Erik said, loving the curve of her belly in the small of his back and the news it brought.

"Have you thought of any names yet?"

He smiled as he turned to hug her. "Kennet," he said. "After my grand-father."

"Kennet Fiskare," she said thoughtfully.

"Kennet Joseph? For your father too?"

She gazed out at the lake, her mouth shaping the names with no sound.

"Just a thought," Erik said, his hands spreading wide across her stomach.

"No, I like it. Would we call him Kenny?"

"Well, I thought maybe..." He hesitated, feeling shy. "Kees. For short."

Daisy's eyes flew back to him. Her hand reached up and caressed his face. "I love it," she whispered. She curled into him, her arms going around his waist. "It's perfect."

"Should we tell Mr. Justi now or later?"

Daisy laughed. "He is going to be a *wreck.*"

That night she was on top of Erik in the dark, drawing him up into the depths of all that round, lush magic. Soft skin stretching to accommodate new curves. Her body bursting with an indescribable energy. Tight, hot and overflowing. He put his hands on her stomach, felt that warm, thrumming arc under his palms.

It's a boy.

Kees.

His hands seemed to melt into her. "It's so much," he said, pulled apart with feeling. Mixed-up faces morphed through his head. Blond hair and brilliant blue eyes. Dark hair and deep brown eyes.

Who will you be?

"I'm so happy," she said.

His palms slid up to hold her breasts.

She's having a baby.

It's a boy.

He leaned in. Gave his weight to the joy, let it cradle him in arms. Daisy drew up along the slick length of him, her head falling back and her hair tumbling over his wrists. She was so full of life it made him feel like dying. His heart circled around like an eel. Every cell in his body writhed and stretched out long, yearning, wanting, pushing up into his wife's vital heat.

"It's more than I ever wished for," he said.

"It's everything I wished for," she said. She put her hands on top of his, quieted the vertical pull and push of her hips and settled down on him.

"I have all the men I love inside me," she whispered.

Part Four: Glass

MOMENT

"DUDE," WILL SAID. "Did I tell you about the time Lucky and I ate the pot brownies?"

"No."

"Chick in the corps made them and gave us one. We quartered it. All right? A *quarter* of a brownie each."

"What happened?"

"Monumental, mind-blowing, transcendental sex. Followed by Lucky having a panic attack the likes I've never seen before. I had to scrape her off the ceiling. It was ridiculous."

Erik laughed.

"I mean that real unattractive paranoia. Like she thought I was going to call CPS and have her declared an unfit mother. Meanwhile, the hemispheres of my brain have switched places and I barely remember my kids' names. Parenthood ceased being a concept. It was like being an amoeba." He rubbed the back of his neck. "That was a night and a half."

"Better than banging the manny?"

Will laughed. "You just love asking me that, don't you?"

They were in the parking lot of the Imperial Theater. The curtain was down, the house lights off, doors locked. The last techie had gone home. They ought to have been home for dinner. And they'd meant to. But somehow a fifteen minute conversation tripped and fell down into an hour.

Erik hesitated then pushed a little. "Did you bang him?"

Will gave a last chuckle. "No," he said. "But I had fun thinking about it."

They were quiet. A breeze blew by, clearing the slate.

"When was the last time you were with a guy?" Erik asked.

Will's eyebrows went up. "When I was in Germany. Why?"

Erik shrugged. "You still want to?"

"You mean am I still attracted to men? Sure. But I'm married now. I don't fuck around with either gender."

"I just wondered if the itch was there. I wasn't implying you scratched it."

"Well then, yes," Will said. "I do still think about it. I'm still attracted to it and, on occasion, I outright want it. Wanting isn't having."

"I can't help but be curious why," Erik said.

"Why what?"

"Why you like men. Although I know asking you makes about as much sense as you asking me why I like women. I don't have an explanation for it. It just is."

"It's hard to articulate," Will said. "Women are... They're soft."

"They're pretty."

"Pretty's relative, though. Look at the company roster, you'll see eighteen boys anyone would describe as pretty. Pretty is just what you're hardwired to see as attractive."

"But we are talking attraction. I can comfortably say a guy is good looking. It doesn't suck to look at you. And take that new superstar of yours, Andre. He is one handsome dude."

"That he is."

"So why does it end there for me and not for you? He's not pretty. And he's not soft, either."

"I think that's exactly why it doesn't end for me. Something in me is attracted to familiarity as well as to opposition."

"I don't follow."

"When I love a woman, I love what's opposite of me. With a man... it's what's the same. Kind of like, I love in him what I love in me." He shook his head abruptly. "I don't mean love like *love.* I mean... It's hard to explain."

"No, I get it."

Will chuckled. "Do you? Or are you just sweet-talking me?"

"I'm sweet-talking you. I have no idea what the fuck you mean."

Will ran his hands through his hair. "I wish I had a cigarette. What the hell is up with that? Will a day ever come when I don't think about smoking? It's been three years. I'm not going to start again. But every damn day, I swear to God. I think about it."

Erik yawned, rubbing his tired eyes. He should go home. But he didn't feel like it. Silence had passed between their cars, between their identically-posed bodies: arms crossed, the sole of one foot against a tire. Between his thumb and forefinger, Will was worrying his bottom lip. His expression far off.

Erik looked at him.

He'd never grown his hair back. It stayed short, threaded with silver over his ears now. They and the faint lines around his eyes and mouth were the only things that betrayed his age. He was still fit and built with ramrod straight posture. Dark-eyed, proud and handsome. Larger than life with his physical affection and irreverent humor. Brutally honest yet tender-hearted and protective of the ones he loved.

"You keep staring at me like that and we'll have to take it inside," Will said.

Erik's face was warm around his smile. "What happened in Germany?"

Will blew his breath out, looking up at the skies. "Long version or short version?"

"Short."

"Short version. I lost my shit and went into therapy. And in therapy I finally admitted I'd been in love with you in college. James was simply a means to...divert it elsewhere."

Erik said nothing. Did nothing. Didn't blink, didn't swallow. His pulse neither quickened nor slowed. He went so still, he felt part of the machinery of his car. Cast in steel and polished to a gloss. He went on breathing, knowing it would take more than *he was in love with me* to crumple and bend him.

"What's the long version," he finally said.

Will was staring off again at nothing, but a corner of his mouth went up. "I missed you," he said. "And this time I diverted it with a guy who looked like you. A guy who seriously fucked with my head and left me a crying mess on the floor. Left me wandering around Frankfurt at two in the morning, looking up at his windows like I was James. It had all come full circle. The past was catching up with me, my debts were coming due and I was getting what I deserved because…"

"Because?"

"Because the shooting was my fault. I brought it all down. Just like you said."

"Dude, I feel terrible ab—"

Will put his maimed palm up. "My breakdown, my rules."

"Fair enough."

"Besides, it wasn't anything I hadn't already accused myself of. A thousand times. Ten thousand times. Every day. To this day. James is like a cigarette. He floats in and out of my thoughts. Sometimes he passes through. Sometimes he sticks around for lunch. I find if I just let him come in and touch things, he leaves a whole lot quicker."

"I can't fathom you feeling nothing for him at the time," Erik said. "I know you: you don't do anything unless it feels good. He was more than just a diversion."

"No, you're right. An attraction was there. On a lot of levels. I know it came across as me having the upper hand in the situation and to a degree, I did. But when it was the two of us alone, behind closed doors, in the dark? There he had one hell of a secret weapon."

"Which was?"

Eyebrows wrinkled, Will looked over at him. "You," he said, as if it were obvious. "He knew how I felt about you. Knew I had to keep it a secret so it was fun for him to bust my balls and come close to outing me. Drove me nuts. On the other hand, I hate secrets. It was a relief *somebody* knew."

"But—"

Will's hand went up again. His smile was brave, but weak. "Dude, I've told as much as I can tonight. Rain check on the rest?"

Erik nodded and let it go. They went quiet and he tried to arrange all the pieces. Fit them together so a picture began to emerge. Will loved someone. Circumstances arose where he could feel that love with a little more freedom. He found a proxy to pretend with. The proxy caught onto him and used love as a weapon to get more of what he needed. Will got sucked into a vortex of pain and pleasure.

And then it all went down in gunfire.

"I'm sorry," Erik said.

"You didn't do anything."

"But I'm sorry. Sorry it happened to you. The burden of it must've been fucking horrid."

Will shrugged. "I had a good shrink. He helped me put it down."

"Still," Erik said. "I feel terrible for how I abandoned you. I feel like shit for diverting all my pain onto you and letting you be a convenient villain. I hate what I did. I hate the time I threw away. I wasn't your phone call when you were tanking in Germany. I didn't hold a candle at the memorial in Lancaster. I wasn't here when you got married. I never got to see you and Dais dance together in your prime. I missed her career. I missed all those ballets. All that creative collaboration. I missed it. Those are my cigarettes."

"Put it down," Will said. "You're here now. The past will just give you cancer."

Erik smiled. Closed his eyes and tried to let the jumble of thoughts and feelings in his head fall into their natural resting places. He felt at peace. Yet oddly wistful. With a nagging reluctance to leave. Something felt unfinished. Unsaid.

"I still trust you," he said.

Will rolled his lips in, nodding. "I tell you anything. It's so easy. In my weird head, out my big mouth. And rarely do I worry you'll misunderstand me. I could always be myself with you. It's not a thing to be dismissed." He glanced up. "You know?"

"I know," Erik said. And they looked at each other.

As an acceptable amount of eye contact came and went, Erik felt the air shimmer and tighten. Just as it did when he stared at Daisy.

The night pulled away.

He felt his chest turn out.

Everything in creation seemed to look back over its shoulder at them.

"What?" Will's mouth formed the word with barely a sound.

Erik shook his head a little. "Nothing," he said, equally noiseless.

Creation took a step in. Interested.

"I haven't been in the game a while," Will said slowly. "But I think we may be having a moment." The words were joking, but his voice was laced with a vulnerable heaviness. And his eyes didn't move from Erik's.

They stared. The weighted history of their years sat on its heels, motionless.

Erik's phone chimed from his pocket. Blinking hard, he took it out, knowing it was Dais.

Can you come home? I'm not feeling good.

What's wrong? he typed. "I need to go," he said to Will.

I just feel like I want you to come home. Indulge the mommy-to-be.

"Everything all right?" Will said.

He put the phone away. "She wants me."

"Don't we all?" Will pushed off the side of the car and raised a hand. "Always a pleasure, Fish."

"Hey," Erik said. "Look, I... I mean..."

Will laughed. "I love you more than can be discussed in a civilized manner," he said, opening the driver's side door. "Now get out of here. And no texting me later asking me if I'm all right. None of that shit. We had a moment, that's all."

He drove out of the parking lot, a single toot of the horn in his wake. Erik put his forehead on the steering wheel and took a few shaking breaths before he started the engine and drove home.

"WHAT HAPPENED?" DAISY SAID, before he'd even put his keys down.

"Nothing."

"You're shaking."

"He told me about Germany. I'm a little…upset. That's all. Are you all right?"

"I'm so tired," she said. "I haven't felt like myself all day. Either I'm anxious or I'm coming down with something."

He ran his hand over the hard curve of her belly. "I feel a little unsteady myself. Maybe you're picking up on my shit."

She smiled and went into his arms. "Don't know where I stop and you begin."

He took her face in his hands and kissed her. "I'll make dinner. Go lie down a bit."

He threw together some pasta, keeping a portion plain for her. Now in her eighth month, it seemed anything rich or spicy gave her heartburn. Wiping his hands on a dishtowel, he went out to the living room where she was asleep on the couch. She looked so thoroughly out, he decided to let her sleep. She could eat later. But as he went to cover her with a blanket, he felt the heat radiating off her.

"Dais?" he said, reaching a hand to her face. It was flushed and she was hot. "Dais." He crouched down, gently shaking her shoulder.

"Wha…"

"Honey, you're so hot. Are you running a fever?"

She picked up her head, put a hand to her cheek. "Am I? Oh. I am hot."

"You feel all right?"

"I just feel so tired."

"Go upstairs," he said. "Get in bed and I'll call the doctor."

"It's probably nothing."

"Indulge the daddy-to-be," he said, kissing her flushed face.

The on-call nurse didn't seem over-concerned. He asked if Daisy was experiencing any bleeding or contractions. She wasn't, just the 102 temperature and the extreme fatigue.

"Is the baby moving?" the nurse asked.

Erik relayed the question.

"He's not moving now," Daisy said, her hand going to her belly. "But he was kicking me all day. Even when I was driving home, a couple hours ago."

"Then take two Tylenol and go to bed," the nurse said. "Rest. Plenty of fluids. Likely it's just a cold or virus, but if the fever persists into tomorrow, come in. Any bleeding, any cramps or contractions, go directly to urgent care."

Erik ate alone at the kitchen counter. He cleaned up then went upstairs. His mood was still anxious and he bit half a Klonopin into a sloppy quarter and swallowed it. Just to take the edge off. Or give him a placebo effect.

No sooner had the bitter taste left the back of his throat when his phone pinged. It was Will.

You OK?

Erik gave an eye-rolling grin. *I thought we agreed not to do this?*

You agreed, not me. And you're answering, aren't you?

Fuck you.

Didn't see THAT coming, didya?

Erik chuckled in his chest. *Get out of here.*

Don't fucking call me.

Erik set the phone back on the bedside table. "My life is so weird sometimes," he said.

Daisy made a noise in her throat.

He stacked the pillows against the headboard and opened his book. Daisy rolled and curled against his legs.

"You all right?" he said, stroking her hair.

She made a small sigh but said nothing. He laid his hand on her cheek. It was warm, but not as viciously hot as before.

He read. Time dripped by, measured in pages. The knot in his chest and stomach loosened. His eyes began to feel a little heavy.

"I don't feel right," Daisy said, startling him. She sat up, pressing the backs of her hands into her eyes.

"What's wrong?" Erik said.

"I have to pee." She got up, tired and clumsy. She stretched, pressed her hands into her back. She walked three steps and then let out a gasp, then a cry, and lurched into the dresser, clutching its edge.

He was out of bed and moving to her. Warm, stringent liquid ran down her legs, making a puddle on the rug and spreading onto the hardwood floor. Clear at first. And then tinged pink. Then red.

"Oh God," Daisy said. "What's happening?"

 TROUVER UN BATTEMENT

DAISY LAY ON A bed in an exam room of the ER, her bared belly glistening with gel. Erik sat in a chair next to her. The sonogram technician stared at her hands. Frozen on the monitor in black and white was the baby. Whole. Perfect.

"Are you sure?" Daisy said again. "He was moving all day. Moving and kicking."

"I'm sorry," the technician whispered. "Something must be wrong with the machine. Let me get someone."

She got a lot of someones. The attending doctor came in, followed by a social worker and a pediatric nurse. The room filled with an ominous, heavy energy as the doctor pulled on gloves and set the ultrasound wand down on Daisy's stomach again. The image on the screen morphed in and out of view. Settled back into focus and held still. Erik's eyes volleyed back and forth, looking from one grim expression to the next, waiting for an answer that wasn't coming.

"I don't understand," he said. "What is happening?"

"Is there someone we can call for you?" the social worker asked.

Erik looked at her as if she were speaking another language. "We called *you*," he said stupidly.

"Madame Fiskare," the doctor said. Tall and black, he looked no more than nineteen in Erik's bewildered eyes. His dark blue scrubs barely reaching his ankles. Gangly arms and knobby wrists emerging from a too-short white coat. A strong accent garbled his French into a soup as he said, "Je suis désolé. Je ne peux pas trouver un battement."

"Speak English," Erik said, his voice cracking through the dense air.

The doctor's high cheekbones winced. "I cannot find a heartbeat, sir. I'm sorry."

"No," Daisy said, reaching fingers toward the screen. "No, he's right there. He's right there. He was here all day. I felt him."

Erik stood up and put his arms around her. She fought through them, actually slapped one of his hands away.

"You're wrong," Daisy said.

Erik turned his head, looked at the wall and wished to disappear.

"He's right *there*," she said.

"Madame Fiskare," the doctor said. "I am truly sorry. Under different circumstances, I could let you go home and take your time with the decision. But look here. Please. The sonogram shows the placenta is beginning to detach. You are running a fever and this can only get more critical."

"What are you saying?" Erik said, turning around, unable to grasp what this *kid* was telling them. "I don't understand."

The nurse moved closer to the bed and took Daisy's hand in both of hers. "You're going to have your baby," she said, speaking slowly and clearly. Her soft voice full of kindness.

She looked at Erik. "We're going to put her into labor. She has to deliver."

"But the baby is…" And finally it clicked. His head spun as realizations crashed one into the other like a multi-car pileup on the freeway. It wasn't going to disappear, be absorbed back into Daisy's body or bleed quietly out of her. It wouldn't just *go away*. It was a thirty-week pregnancy. It was a baby. The baby was dead.

And Daisy had to bring him out.

She has to deliver stillborn.

"I can't." Daisy was crying into her hands. "I want my mother," she said, her voice squeezing through her fingers. "I want my mother. I can't do this without my mother."

"Where is she?" the doctor said.

"Pennsylvania," Erik said, feeling he might throw up. He kicked one toe hard into his other calf, sending a bolt of pain up the back of his leg. He caught the sensation in his teeth and bit down.

Get. It. Together.

The nurse had Daisy's face in her hands. "My name's Lee," she said. "I'm going to stay with you. I'll help you have your baby." Lee looked at Erik, pale beneath her copper-colored freckles but her eyes were clear and unblinking. "I will help you do this," she said.

Erik pushed all his feeling into a far room and slammed a door on it.

Feel nothing, he thought. *You will feel nothing.*

He gathered Daisy up in his arms, gathered his strength and his wits. Over the top of Daisy's head he looked at the black doctor, then back at freckle-faced Lee. "Tell me what's going to happen."

They began to tell him, but he was only half-listening. From within his heart, he heard fists pounding on a door as the cowering ball of emotions yelled for him.

You left us here once, they cried. *We grew big and hairy in the dark. We became monsters and you thought we forgot about you. We don't forget. Slam the door hard. We'll still be in here. Remember.*

He remembered.

He cracked the door, let the hallway light shine a little inside.

He promised to come back and feel it later.

BRING EVERYTHING

FOR ALL HIS YOUTHFUL and gangly appearance, Dr. N'Dour, the Senegalese resident, was poised and attentive. He waved nurses away and set Daisy's IV port himself. His giant hands were deft and sure, his thick French soft and hypnotic. The sonorous voice seemed to fold Daisy into an envelope of shocked calm. Her weeping hushed into chopped, hitching breaths and her swollen, stunned eyes went far away.

While they were getting Daisy settled and prepped in a room on the maternity ward, Erik stepped into the hall with his phone. It was one in the morning now. People needed to be woken up.

Will's cell rang twice. A scrape and scrabble and a thick inhale of half asleep breath. "Hey..."

Erik opened his mouth and tried. Failed.

"Fish?"

Erik tried again. "The baby died," he said, a hand over his face, screening the world away.

"What?" Will said, his voice coming into focus.

"We lost him."

"What the f— Where are you?"

"At the hospital."

"Oh my God. Fish, what happened?"

"I don't know. She started running a fever. Her water broke. They couldn't get a heartbeat. He's gone."

"Jesus fuck, are you kid— Fish, I'm so sorry."

"They're putting her into labor. She's going to deliver in the next few hours."

"Oh God. Fish, I'm sorry. I'm so sorry."

"She has to deliver stillborn." His voice was rising up and getting away from him. He swallowed hard, pulled a long breath through his nose to keep it all back.

"Where are you?" Will said, sounding both awake and on his feet. "SJ Regional?"

"Yeah, I—"

"I'm leaving now," Will said. "I'll be there in twenty minutes."

"You don't—"

"Shut up. I'm coming." And the line went dead.

Knowing Will was coming stuck to him like a bit of armor. It stiffened his spine for the next two calls.

My biggest fear about parenthood was getting the call, he thought, staring at his phone display. *Instead, I'm making it.*

Irony, go fuck yourself.

He woke up Joe first, then Christine, using variations of the same words: "We lost the baby. You need to come."

The phone grew hot in his hand as the shock rebounded over the line. Hearts shattering into pieces hundreds of miles away. Followed by the saddling up. The circling of the wagons. Torches and drums in the distance. The cavalry on the move.

"We're on the way," Joe said. "We love you."

"I'm coming," Christine said. "I love you."

It couldn't be made easy, but the staff turned themselves inside out to make it as peaceful as possible. Daisy's room was far away from the other delivery suites, and apparently some cryptic signal or sign was at the door, indicating to the ward a stillbirth was happening. Everyone who came in treated them with the utmost respect and compassion.

They gave Daisy an epidural for the physical pain, and Fentanyl to take the edge off the mental pain. They turned off the drugs that were meant to stop contractions, and started drugs to precipitate them. Then they had nothing to do but wait.

Daisy drifted in and out of sleep, occasionally rambling under her breath. Snippets of conversations with no one. Sound bites from her stream of consciousness.

"And I'm done now," she said.

"It's the Fentanyl," Lee said. "You have no filter when you're on that stuff. And the fever isn't helping either."

"I'm sorry about David," Daisy mumbled.

Erik drew back a little. Her eyes were closed and her face was expressionless, but she said it. It slipped past the filter.

Did it still haunt her?

He laid his hand on her forehead. "It was long ago," he whispered. "I forgave you long ago for that, Dais."

A nurse came in and said Erik had a friend in the waiting room. Lee nodded at him and drew her chair a fraction of an inch closer to the bed, indicating she was on watch.

Sandy-eyed with fatigue, muscles aching, Erik walked the short hall down to the waiting area. Will stood up from the couch and came striding to meet him. His arms reached and Erik fell into them.

"Give it here," Will said, holding him tight, a hand on Erik's head. "Give it to me. I'll hold it."

Erik let go, let the load slip off his shoulders. He shoved it all at Will and let him take it.

"I'm sorry," Will said.

"I can't believe this is happening."

"I know. Sit down and don't do anything right now."

"Where's Lucky?"

"She's waiting for the nanny to come and then she'll be here. You tell Dais she's coming. Now come on, sit down. Shut your eyes."

Erik did, and was surprised when the edges of his mind blurred out and he snoozed briefly. A quick catnap with Will standing guard. His phone buzzed in his pocket. Once. Twice. With a low cry he sat up, his body electric with adrenaline.

"It's all right," Will said. "You were out fifteen minutes. That's all."

Erik shook his head hard.

"A nurse came by," Will said, a soothing hand on Erik's shoulder. "Said Dais is still asleep. You didn't miss anything. I'll get you a soda." Will stood up and went to the vending machines, reaching in his back pocket for his wallet.

Erik checked his phone. It was his brother texting.

Mom, me and Fred will be on a 6AM flight. We're coming. I'm so fucking sorry. Whatever I can give you, it's yours. Yesterday.

Erik started to text that Pete didn't need to come. Then he backspaced all the letters out and typed, *Thanks. I got nothing. Bring everything.*

I will. You don't fall apart until I get there. Hear me?

I hear you.

"I let myself into your house and threw some shit together," Will said, kicking a backpack by the leg of the chair. "Some clothes, your phone chargers. I grabbed both toothbrushes on the sink and then just stuffed your whole shaving kit in there. Lucky can bring whatever else you need."

"Thanks."

Will twisted the cap off the soda bottle and handed it over. "Who do you need me to call? Give me numbers. I'll take care of it later in the morning."

Primed with caffeine, Erik scrolled through his contacts and calendar. "I had a dentist appointment tomorrow, cancel that. Car was supposed to go in for an oil change. You need to call the garage for me..."

Will wrote down the numbers. "What else?"

"Feed the cat at some point." Erik exhaled and ran a hand through his hair. "The Biancos are coming. And my mom and Fred. They'll need to be picked up."

"I'll do it. Don't give it another thought. I'll take care of everything."

"And call Mike Pettitte for me."

"Your cousin? Sure. I'll call him first."

Erik almost asked why, then realized of course, because Mike was family.

Erik closed his eyes. More wagons appeared on the southern horizon. Clayton would be woken up. Mike would know soon. He'd call Trudy and Kirsten and then tell the MacIntyres. By tomorrow Vivian would know. Erik looked to the rear of the gathering forces, beyond the village to the cemetery. The stones turned toward him, attentive, supportive, reaching ghostly hands back to him. The clean white grave of Beatrice Klara sharp in his mind. Elsa and Xandro in the shadow of the pine trees. The young soldier Björn under bronze. Lost children.

Lost fish.

We're here. We feel terrible. These things happen and they are terrible things to bear. We bore them. We know. We're here.

You're not alone. You found your tribe. You will survive this.

"I can't," he whispered, knowing he could, but wishing with every fiber of his being he didn't have to.

"You can," Will said. "You don't have to do it well. You just have to do it."

"All right," Erik said, standing up. He held out his hands to Will. "Give it back."

Will stood up and made a pouring gesture into Erik's palms. Then he hugged tight and kissed Erik's head. "I love you," he said. "I'll be here the whole time."

Erik sank his teeth into that. Fists and jaw clenched, shoulders set, he nodded against the broad hard plain of Will's chest. Then he pulled free and went back to Daisy.

BORNE

"WHAT WILL HE LOOK like?" Erik asked, afraid he would recoil.

Lee touched his arm. "Like a baby. He'll be beautiful to you. He won't be a monster or an alien, I promise. You can hold him. Bathe him. Dress him. As long as you want. You'll have complete privacy and complete freedom. We're here to make you as comfortable as possible."

He looked away from her and fought the urge to throw off her touch. No comfort could be found here. Nothing was private or free. Who did Lee think she was, telling him he'd hold a dead baby and find it beautiful? That he could dress it up like a doll and pretend everything was fine?

Somebody help me, he thought. He couldn't see the wagons coming. Will's embrace had long slid off his back and he was exposed to the enemy and alone.

Daisy said something under her breath. Her fingernails drew along her skin. Slower. Deeper. Pink, raised welts began to emerge on the inside of her forearm.

"Stop," Erik whispered, putting his hand on top of hers. "Don't hurt yourself. It's not your fault."

He held her tight, willing to do anything—*anything* to get her out of this. If it meant lying down and letting someone sledgehammer his legs, he'd do it.

Leave her alone. She's been through enough.

"He shot the glass," Daisy said, her head moving side to side, her eyelids fluttering.

"I know," he said against her hair. "I know, honey. It wasn't your fault."

It's never anyone's fault.

It's just fucking life coming in to backhand me as soon as I lean into a moment.

It wasn't supposed to be this way. Mike Pettitte was right. This was against the natural order of the world and it was offensive. Mike would be livid when he heard the news. Primed with outrage and justice, he'd tear this place apart and make it all right again.

Except he couldn't.

Nobody could make this right.

Erik shut his hot wet, eyes and turned his face into the pillows above Daisy's head. His mind swirling with fatigue, his back and legs aching. Weak, but resolute, he stood in the arched doorways of his beloved cathedral, armed with nothing but his bare hands.

Fuck all of you. I hate your fucking guts. Get out of here and leave me and my wife the fuck alone.

He brought Daisy's hand with its crooked fingers and ragged nails up to his mouth. He closed his teeth on Astrid's diamond and bit.

Help me, he thought. *Somebody help me.*

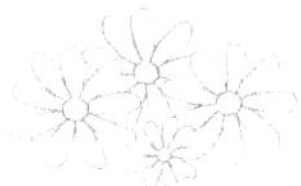

The Fentanyl wore off as the contractions grew more intense. Daisy was down from the high and reeling in reality, fighting against her body, fighting the inevitable.

"I can't do this," she said. "Don't make me do this."

"You have to," Lee said. "No one else can do it. You can and you will."

"All right, Dézi, you're going to push now," Dr. N'Dour said.

She was shaking her head, her voice swelling like a balloon. "I can't. I need my mother. I can't. I can't do this." Her voice stretched thin until it was a hoarse squeal.

"Dais," Erik took her face in his hands. "Look at me."

"Don't make me," she said.

"Look at me," he said. "Look only at me."

Her eyes settled on his. Then they settled into his. She exhaled.

"Only me," he said. "Remember?"

Her chin rose and fell.

"You can do this," he said. "You can do it for me."

She nodded again, biting her lips.

"Will you do this for me?"

Her eyes closed then opened. No green was in their depths as she breathed in through her nose and whispered, "Yes."

"I want to see him," Erik said. "Let him come out so I can see him."

She touched his face. "All right." She pulled in her breath again and her expression settled into the cold, determined look of a soldier. "All right," she said, louder, sitting up.

"You are a mother now," Lee said, helping her. "You're part of a great chain: you, your mother and grandmother and great-grandmother. They're all with you now, Daisy. They'll help you."

It took three sets of three pushes and the baby crowned. Erik held Daisy the whole time, his face close by hers.

"I love you so much," he said. "I swear I've never loved you more."

Resting between contractions, she turned her face into his neck, breathing hard.

"You're so strong," he said, his heart full of pain and pride. "You're the bravest person I know."

"It's almost over," Lee said, giving her some ice to chew. "You're doing beautifully."

"This is the most beautiful thing I've seen you do," Erik said through his teeth. "Ever. This is the most important thing you have ever done."

"One more push, Dézi," N'Dour said.

"You got this," Erik said, sliding his arm under her shoulder blades. Her head dragged over his forearm and then lifted. Her eyes blazed like steel.

"One more," she whispered and rose up to finish.

Erik turned his head then, and watched his son be born. As if in an underwater dream, he saw Kees emerge. Saw the doctor's hands turn him prone, the cord trailing behind, and for a moment Kees was held aloft like an offering.

Born.

And borne.

His face was turned away and something about the tiny pale back curved over N'Dour's blue-gloved palm stopped Erik's breath. The fragile spine visible through translucent skin. Wet whorls of hair stuck down to the eggshell skull. He looked neat and tidy in the doctor's hands. He was perfect.

He's alive.

It was a mistake. A bad dream. He's alive.

Then the baby's limbs flopped out, dangling over N'Dour's forearm and the moment shattered. A sound escaped Erik's chest. He was filled with a stunning sense of finality at the sight of those limp, lifeless arms and legs. As if there had been a flicker of hope, a valiant attempt to try, but then everything gave out. And Erik was awash with a sudden and sorrowful blame.

I'm sorry, he thought. *I let you down. Oh, Kees, I'm so sorry...*

He swayed and wobbled on his legs as the doctor brought the baby up and onto Daisy's chest. Lee smoothed a blanket over.

"Un beau garçon," N'Dour said softly.

Erik put his hands over Daisy's, their fingers piled on top of the tiny infant. Daisy didn't move. Her eyes were closed, her face a pinch of chalk.

An undeterminable length of time unfurled. Then a soft hand settled on Erik's shoulder and Lee asked if he would like to cut the cord.

"Go," Daisy said, her eyes still closed. "Do everything."

The cord was clamped in two places and N'Dour showed Erik where to cut between. The blades felt flimsy and inept, chomping and hacking through the last lifeline. Cutting all hope.

Vaguely, from some past conversation, he recalled Daisy telling him about a book and soulmates being severed. A blade slicing the bond and releasing enough energy to rip a hole in the sky.

He gritted his teeth and cut through. The air around him remained intact. He let the scissors fall from his fingers and went back to Daisy's side. He put his hands on top of hers again.

He didn't cry. He was too confused.

He was waiting for the sky to tear open.

THIS IS MY SON

THEY GAVE HIM A bath together, dressed him in the onesie and cap the hospital provided and carefully wrapped him in the swaddling blanket. Daisy was shaking by then, limbs trembling as the excess adrenaline poured out of her body, skin shivering with another low-grade fever. Fluids and antibiotics hung from her IV pole. Dr. N'Dour ordered a bit more Fentanyl and, once back in bed, Daisy fell asleep.

"I am so sorry," N'Dour said, one of his hands swallowing Erik's and the other clasping Erik's upper arm.

Erik could only nod and touch the kind doctor's arm in return. Mute with gratitude, he then turned and hugged Lee Malone harder than he'd ever hugged a human in his life.

"You're so good to her," she said, swaying side to side with him. "You are an amazing husband."

"Thank you," he managed to whisper.

She stepped away and put her hand on his face, bright tears rimming her eyes. "Go lie down now. Hold her. Don't let go."

After she and N'Dour left, Erik heeled off his shoes, picked up Kees and settled next to Daisy in the reclined bed. The baby's tiny capped head was no bigger than a baseball in Erik's palm. The point of the swaddled bundle barely made it to his elbow. He could tuck Kees against his chest like a football and make a dash for it.

Daisy nestled closer to him, mumbling something. Erik brushed her head with his mouth then turned eyes back to the child in his hand.

This is my son.

He stared at the wizened little face. Two lines for eyes. Tiny hairs for brows. A mouth set in a serious straight line. Gently Erik moved the cap back. He had hair. Not a lot, but enough for Lee to clip some. She'd wrapped the minuscule lock with thread and put it in an envelope for them to keep.

He remembered Daisy had kept a lock of his own hair all those years they were apart.

"Because it's what you do," she said.

Erik carefully pulled the cap into place. His fingertip traced the delicate curve of Kees' cheek. He looked so solemn. So contemplative. Occupied with deep, important thoughts.

This is my son.

"It has no name," Daisy said, her eyelids fluttering. Her hand lay small and limp against his shirt. The gold of her rings dull in the room's flourescent light. Her wrist slender within the hospital bracelet. Erik blinked as its typed letters swam into focus.

FISKARE, MARGUERITE B.

He tilted his head, reading, as if only now realizing who she was.

"Marguerite Fiskare," he mouthed.

He eased Kees's tiny wrist from the blanket, the little slip of plastic fastened about it.

FISKARE, KENNET J.

On his own wrist, the documentation officially linking him to the other two.

FISKARE, BYRON E.

He clenched his fingers in a fist, the tendon in his wrist making the bracelet rise up and down. A heartbeat beneath his name.

They belong to me. This all belongs to me.

It belongs to my name.

His throat melted and his eyes bubbled over as he gathered Daisy closer. He laid the baby on his chest and curved his arms around both bodies. His wife in a drugged, fitful sleep. His son in an eternal sleep.

It does have a name.

This is my family.

And he clutched it all and wept for it.

IT'S WHAT YOU DO 

"I KNOW IT SEEMS odd to take pictures," the social worker said. "Sort of irreverent. Even macabre. But it's not. Please don't think anyone will think strangely of it. However you want to remember your baby, do it."

Erik tried to relax into instinct. Holing up alone with Daisy and grieving privately seemed the thing to do. But it felt wrong. It was making everything worse.

"Is it all right with you if Will and Lucky come in?" Daisy finally asked. And it was all right. More than all right. Erik wanted them badly. Wanted friends close by until his mother and the Biancos could get there.

So they gathered in the little room, the four of them. They took turns holding Kees, took turns holding each other. Lucky had brought her camera and discreetly took some pictures. Just a few. Just to remember.

Lying beside Erik in the bed, Daisy touched his necklace. "Put it on him," she whispered. "Please."

He unclasped it and put it around Kees's small head. Arranged the charms so they clustered together on Kees's heart. He and Daisy held him.

Lucky took a picture.

Will and Erik sat side by side in chairs. Will held the baby and they stared across the room at Daisy and Lucky in the hospital bed, curled up together like sisters.

"She did that the night you left Lancaster," Will said. "Got right in the bed with her. Held onto her all night."

"It's what you do," Erik said. He could barely move his jaw he was so tired.

"I envy that about women. No taboo rules or bullshit when it comes to physical comfort. Your best friend is smashed in pieces, you get right in bed with her and hold the pieces together."

"Want to sleep over tonight?" Erik said. "Hold my pieces?"

Will slowly turned his head. "Did you actually just make a joke?"

Erik closed his eyes and managed a weak smile. "No."

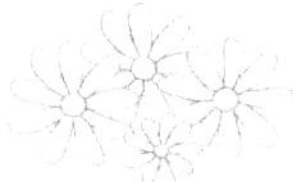

The inability to get to Erik immediately after the shootings had always haunted Christine. She all but loaded herself into a slingshot and flung herself toward Canada. She was there now, with Peter, while Fred had gone with Will to the airport to get the Biancos.

Christine rocked Kees in the cradle of her elbow, her finger tracing the little face.

"Look how thoughtful he is," she said, blinking back tears. "You looked like this after you were born, Erik. Just like this. Thinking, thinking, thinking." She sniffed hard and held the bundle to her breast. Her other arm reached to pull Erik close.

"You looked just like this," she whispered.

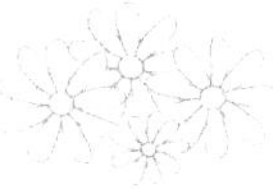

Francine and Joe put their hands together and held their grandson, heads bent low. After a while, Joe moved to sit on the edge of the bed where Daisy had dozed off. He stared at the wall, a silent soldier, stroking his daughter's forehead. Fred sat on the wide windowsill, hands laced around a knee, looking out at nothing.

Erik sprawled in a chair, his temple on Christine's shoulder. Her hand caressed his hair. His neck began to ache but he didn't want her to stop. He slid down to sit on the floor, put his face on his mother's knee. She rubbed his back. Pete came to sit where Erik had been and put a rough hand on his brother's head.

Francine continued to hold Kees. One loving, fearless fingertip stroked between his eyebrows and over the fragile crown of his head. She sang a little song in French.

The fever persisted and, worried about infection, the hospital kept Daisy another day. She spent it in bed, dozing and waking, holding Kees while curled in her mother's arms.

Erik shied from anyone touching him now. He paced away or slumped through the prickling, shapeless hours, feeling more and more caged. He wanted to go home.

Texts and voicemails piled up on his phone. Most he let go. Some he returned.

"I'm so sorry," Mike Pettitte said, his voice tight and gruff. "I'm here for you. Please know I'm here. If there's anything I can do, Erik, you call me."

"Oh my dear, I feel terrible," Vivian said. "I'm so sorry. I'm thinking about you all the time."

"Sweet boy," Aunt Trudy said, with Aunt Kirsten on another extension. "Our hearts are broken for you."

"Thank you," Erik said over and over to his people. "Thank you."

"I can't put him in the ground," Daisy said. "I can't bear the thought."

"No," Erik said. "I can't either."

"He needs to be near us." Her voice was syrupy with tears and pain. "He's so little. I want to keep him."

"I do, too."

The arrangements were made for them. They didn't have to lift a finger or make a call. Their sole task was to hold Kees and press him into their memory before they took him away.

And sign the certificate of stillbirth.

And remember to take it to the registrar at some point.

And collect his ashes.

And...

PEOPLE WERE UNBELIEVABLY KIND. The house filled with food: casseroles, soups, pies. The counters creaked under the offerings, the fridge exploded with sympathy. Flowers filled every room. The fruit bowl overflowed. A waterfall of envelopes spilled from the mailbox. Cards, notes, letters. Donations were made to charity in Kees's name. A Jewish family in the neighborhood had a memorial tree planted in Israel. Another had a star named for him. Every deed was accompanied by beautiful loving words. *You're in our thoughts. In our prayers. We're broken-hearted. I'm sending you my love. I'm lighting a candle.*

A package arrived from deWrenne Atelier and they unwrapped a beautiful silver hummingbird with a jeweled eye. A note from Vivian read: *In the spirit world, hummingbirds are messengers of joy. But they are also known for the ability to get in and out of small places, and their ability to heal. I send you all my love in this little bird, and hope it can hover in the small dark places of your hearts and help heal you.*

The MacIntyres sent flowers. *Come to Clayton anytime you wish. Come home and stay with us. We'll take care of you.*

Mike Pettitte texted often. ***Hey buddy. I'm out on the boat. I'm thinking about you. I'm here if you need me.***

Love came from all directions. On paper, on screens, in dishes and words and deeds.

We're thinking of you every minute.

I'm sorry.
We're sorry.
We're so sorry...

Kees came back to them as a few cubic inches of ash. Most of the cremation urns offered by the funeral home were cloyingly kitschy. They picked the simplest one available for the time being.

They didn't quite know where to put it. The mantelpiece seemed too obvious and lonely. The kitchen was the center of their household universe, but it seemed an odd location to keep an urn. They took turns keeping it on their bedside tables for a week until Daisy placed it on top of the upright piano. Erik took the black and white picture of four Fiskare generations from his desk and set it beside his son.

And baby makes five.

He fussed and arranged the composition of picture frame and urn, trying to get it perfect. Wishing he could reach fingers into the photograph, rip his infant self out of his great-grandfather's arms and put Kees there.

"Take care of him," he said under his breath, meeting Emil's eyes. He imagined the old man, who had lost a son in the war, nodding as his arms tightened protectively.

These things happen and they are terrible things to bear.

Erik sat and played "Twinkle Twinkle Little Star." Then he felt dumb and closed the lid over the keys.

"Play the Prelude in C," Daisy said. "It's a lullaby." She sat on the floor and he noticed she was working a jigsaw puzzle on the coffee table.

"Why are you doing that?" he asked, feeling dumber, as if he ought to know why.

She looked at him as if she thought the same. "I just want to put something together."

He nodded and opened the piano's lid again. He played a flat, soulless version of the Bach prelude. Started a Mozart sonata but stopped for no reason and went to sit on the floor by Daisy. He poked a finger through the box of pieces, looking for the borders, which he slid across the table to her. Her thank yous were clipped and businesslike, as though he were passing her instruments during a surgery.

He helped her for half an hour, not speaking. Then he got tired and lay down on the couch. His hands were ice cold and he held them tight between his knees.

He thought of the time he was eleven and had watched the movie *Poltergeist,* which had scared him past healthy terror into a unshakable, manic upset. The only thing that could assuage the freaked-out distress was bodily contact with his mother. He slept in her bed for nearly three months.

Christine was patient with the obsessive rituals he insisted on. He had to sleep on the left side of the bed, far from the closet door. The closet itself had to be scrupulously inspected and then remain wide open. In bed, Christine's back needed to be tight against his back, no gaps. Above all, his hands had to be between his knees. Only then was he safe against the fiery, preternatural *thing* that lived on the other side of a too-tenuous border between real and unimaginable. A nameless predator that made maggots erupt from steak and made you want to claw your own face off.

He closed his eyes, his hands safely tucked in. A light doze and a foggy wakefulness passed him back and forth. He opened his eyes and Daisy was still at work.

"Are you getting tired?" he asked.

She shook her head. He fell back asleep, woke again later and she was sitting still, her hands motionless among the colored pieces. Bastet perched on the table, her silvery neck stretched out long and she was licking the tears off Daisy's face.

Daisy's mouth trembled between a touched, grateful smile and a grimace of despair. "You funny little thing," she whispered. "You're so sweet to Mommy." Her voice broke apart on the word and her chin dropped between her shaking shoulders.

Erik touched the back of her neck. "Do you want to go to bed?"

"No." A world of hurt packed into the single syllable and a surprising amount of force behind it. It slapped his face. Bastet jumped off the table and pattered away on silent paws.

Erik stared at his wife, back at work now, her jaw tight and her brows pulled down. Into the soil of his broken heart a seed fell: *This is going to change us.*

It's already changed us. It will never be the way it was before.

He looked around the living room. Looked at the picture of them over the fireplace, wrapped up in Daisy's wedding veil. Looked at their son's remains on the piano top. Looked at their house, their life, their doing and their making. It all gazed benignly back at him, eyebrows raised.

Well?

He slid his fingertips along the tender bumps of Daisy's spine, then flattened his hand across her nape. "If I lose you, I will die," he said.

Her hands went still. She turned her head toward him. Her eyes were closed, her thick lashes damp and spiked. "I need to put this together," she said through the wall of her teeth. "Or I will start breaking things."

He had an intense vision of maggots and he squeezed his eyes shut. "I'm scared we're going to break."

"I'm scared for us, too," she said. "Let me do this."

He let her. It was how she was keeping the closet door open. Keeping the face-clawing demons on their side of the boundary. He would be patient and keep his presence against hers. No gaps.

He dozed off again. When he woke, it was done. The puzzle was complete and Daisy had her head pillowed on her crossed arms on the table, fast asleep. Bastet was curled in a neat, precise ball inside the puzzle box's lid.

Erik woke Daisy just enough to get her on her feet. Then he picked her up like a child and carried her upstairs.

"Good job," he whispered, strangely proud. "You did it."

MILK

EVERY DAY HE BECAME more and more aware how the past was made up of stepping stones to now. No coincidences. No accidents. You gravitated toward and attracted the people you were meant to have in your life. They belonged to you, they were precious to you. They deserved to be told so.

John Quillis called. "Oh God, Fish," he said, his voice soft but strong. "My heart's broken for you guys."

"I never thanked you," Erik said, "for what you did for Daisy."

"You don't have to—"

"I do have to. Because too often these things go unsaid and it ends up being too late. Not a day goes by I don't look at her scars and think she wouldn't be here if it weren't for you. I mean it. I owe you an apology for the past. And I owe you my gratitude for... Forever. If you'll have it."

A small pause on the other side of the line. "I'll have it," John said. "Thank you. It means a lot. Honestly, Fish, I only did what any man would've done."

"But you did it when it mattered. I left and you stayed. You were more of a man than I was and I won't ever forget it."

Erik's ex-wife called. "Miles and Janey told me," she said, her voice trembling. "Oh baby, I'm so sorry."

Her ubiquitous use of baby used to grate on his nerves. Now it settled like cool water on a burn.

"And I'm sorry," he said, setting his forehead against the cold refrigerator door. "I understand so much now, Mel, and it's making me think of when... I mean, I..."

"I know," Melanie said. "I know, baby. You don't have to explain. I put you and Daisy on the prayer board of my church. We're holding you tight. Now you rest and take care of yourself."

Daisy's ex-boyfriend, Ray Bonloup, who had lost a child of his own, sent a book of Mother Goose rhymes with breathtaking watercolor illustrations. *It was going to be a birth gift,* he wrote. *And I've been agonizing what to do. I send it with my love and my compassion. I know you think nobody understands. Please know I do. And know I will tell you the truth. One day it will hurt just a little less. One day, you will smile again. Beauty still exists. Joy still exists. I promise, you will find them again.*

Kees Justi sent flowers with a note. He couldn't call yet, it said, because he couldn't stop crying.

They stuck the cards and letters on the refrigerator door, making a colorful, layered collage. Unlike the urn, all the beautiful words and sentiments belonged in the kitchen. They ate them for breakfast and nibbled them as a last, late-night snack.

One day, in the mailbox, an envelope postmarked from Virginia Beach arrived. Addressed to Erik this time. Inside was a single sheet of paper, a clipped verse from the Bible taped to its center. Psalm 41—his and David's old battle cry in the wake of the shooting.

> *All my enemies whisper together against me; they imagine the worst for me, saying, 'He will never get up from the place where he lies.'*

David's handwriting beneath in blue ink.

> *Opie called to tell me what happened. God, I'm sorry, Fish. I can't imagine the place you're in. Can't wrap my mind around this kind of loss. It's beyond words. Beyond everything. My heart hurts for you and Dais. It's not fair.*
> *I wish I could do something to help you get up.*
> *I'm thinking about you guys all the time.*

> *I'm so sorry. For everything. It never stopped matter-*
> *ing to me. I never stopped missing you.*
> *Dave*

Erik made to fold the letter back up but then smoothed it out instead. He took it inside, to the kitchen, and stuck it on the fridge.

"Thanks, man," he said, touching the bible verse with his fingertips.

Daisy's milk came in. She arm-swept the vanity in the bathroom and fell on her knees on the rug, her face in her hands. Rivulets of pale gold spilling from her breasts and making tracks along the loose skin of her stomach.

"It's just coming," she said, weeping. "I'm not doing anything. It's just wanting to come out for him."

It was her ugly cry. Brayed, choking sobs and her skin filling with heat. Her fingers hooked in her hair. Erik held a towel to her chest, held her head against him and rocked her until her body trembled into still-ness.

She went tight and quiet after that episode. He found her at the end of the dock the next evening, smoking cigarettes, nearly five years after kicking the habit.

"I don't want to hear it," she said. "I'm going on a bender. You can join me or you can clean up afterward."

He went back to the house for a bottle of wine and joined her in the Adirondack chairs. They smoked clear through the pack, butts piling up around their shoes. They chugged straight from the bottle, passing it back and forth, and when it was killed, they opened another one. Then another. They got disgustingly, sloppily shitfaced and woke up the next morning feeling like a collective ash pit. A pair of festering dumpsters.

Because why be miserable when you could be wretched?

"Are you all right?" he asked every day.

"No," she said. "I'm not. I don't know what to do with myself."

Indeed her entire presence seemed confused. She walked into rooms and stopped cold, looking around like she didn't recognize her own house. She paused in the middle of a sentence, searching for a word, perplexed it wasn't there. Her eyes looked either stunned or exhausted. She held a book in her lap but turned no pages. She said she wanted to go to bed. Then she tossed and turned.

"I keep thinking it was something I did," she said in the dark one night.

Startled, Erik picked his head up off the pillow. "Something you did?"

"He was kicking me all day. He was trying to tell me something."

"No, honey," he said, an entirely different narrative in his mind. He'd been kicking himself for days, full of recriminations for trusting the nurse and not taking Daisy to the ER as soon as she'd spiked that fever. For not being *that* husband—the one who didn't take chances with his pregnant wife's health. Medical attention a couple of hours sooner and they wouldn't be in this fucked-up mess. This was a test to see what kind of father material he was and he had scored an effortless F-minus.

"It wasn't your fault," he said, his stomach cowering in a corner, positive she was going to figure out it was his fault, pack up and leave him.

"Yes, it was," Daisy said. "I should have paid more attention. I should have *known*." Her voice cracked open and she dissolved into weeping.

"No," he said, wrapping his arms around her. "You couldn't have known, Dais."

"He died in me," she said, her voice elbowing its way through the harsh sobs. "He was kicking me all day because he was *dying*. I just went around like nothing was wrong and all the while he... What was happening to him in there? I can't stop thinking about it. Was he drowning, was he choking? Was he being strangled or smothered, thrashing around in there trying to breathe while I—"

"Dais, don't do this to yourself," he said, tightening the circle of his arms.

"I couldn't help him," she said, nearly incoherent now. "I feel like my own body killed him. He was supposed to be safe inside me and he died in there. I was his *mother* and I couldn't..." She broke out of Erik's embrace, grabbed one of the throw pillows and hurled it at the far wall. "Why," she screamed into her hands. "I want to know *why*."

She fell down in the mattress again, curling into a ball. Erik pulled her in. Her back seized and shook against his chest. He held her tight and let her cry the poisoned thoughts out.

I can't take this, he thought. *It's going to kill me this time.*

Yet he lay there and took it, alive and wretched. A mirror of all the impotent helplessness Daisy felt for Kees. His wife was strangling and smothering in front of him and he had nothing to offer, no way of helping her, powerless to explain. He could only hold onto her, make his arms into a womb where she would be safe. All the while his heart flailed against his ribs, griefstricken, worthless and ashamed.

Daisy shivered, finally going soft in his grasp. He got out of bed and went to run cold water on a washcloth.

"It wasn't your fault," he said, wiping her puffed face. "I will never blame you for this."

She sniffed hard behind the cloth, nodding.

"I'm getting you a Klonopin," he said. "No more tonight. I want to shut your head off so you can sleep."

She took the pill, tossed the wet washcloth on the floor and lay back down. He gathered her against him and the minutes ticked by in brooding silence.

"And who are we kidding anyway," he said. "If anything's to blame, it's my stupid sperm. They probably showed up with only half the blueprints. Jesus Christ, I can't do anything right."

He crafted the words as a joke, but they got tangled up in the tight passage of his throat, splintering his voice in half. Daisy turned to him, grabbed at him with frantic hands. "No, Erik."

"I'm the why. Blame me. I'm useless."

"Useless?" Her arms went around his neck. "You think this is being useless? You're letting me throw every ugly thing inside me onto you. You're letting me scream, letting me cry, letting me be weak and broken and defeated. This is everything I couldn't do after the shooting. This is the side of me I was terrified to show you. But I'm showing it now and you…"

"And I'm not leaving," he said. It was the most vulnerable and skinless he had ever seen her and he took the time to chisel it into his experience. "Whatever you have, you give it to me. Whatever you put in my way, I will move it. I'm not afraid of anything you show me. I'll never leave you."

She took his head and pressed her brow tight to his. "You're my husband."

At the simple declaration, his eyes blurred hot and he hugged her hard.

"You're the father of my child," she said. "You're my life, you're helping me breathe, you're keeping me alive. And I swear you are the only thing I love in this fucking world right now."

His body shuddered in her arms. He dug his fingers in the stale tangle of her unwashed hair and tasted the misery on her skin.

"God, I hate everything," he said. "I love you and hate every fucking thing else."

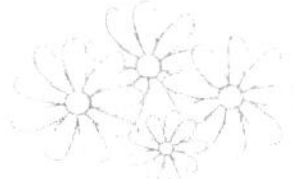

The fertility clinic put them in touch with a support group for parents of stillborn babies. Daisy found some comfort in the meetings, but Erik was strangely untouched by them. The horror stories shared around the circle beaded up on his skin. Nothing stirred his empathy or validated his feelings. He sat through the sessions with an attentive expression, surrounded by people in the best position to understand him. Yet he felt utterly misunderstood.

Worse was having to see marriages straining and crumbling before their eyes. People attending solo because their spouse wouldn't come. On more than one occasion, Erik was the only male present in the circle of chairs, listening to women grieve not only for the loss of their child, but the loss of communication, of support and intimacy. He felt the eyes on him as if he were the representative of the absent men. Tearful glances asking, *what's wrong with him? What am I doing wrong? Tell me.*

He had neither answers nor understanding. Overnight it seemed he and Daisy had crept into a new phase of mourning and they couldn't bear being apart. They followed each other everywhere. One's five-minute errand was cause for the other to get in the car.

"I'd like to be alone."

"Fine, I'll come with you."

It got slightly ridiculous. He sat on the bathmat waiting for her to finish showering. She waited for him outside the men's room at restaurants. They stopped what they were doing eight times a day to put arms around each other, helping each other limp and hobble toward an unreachable finish line.

Barbegazi had never been such a mess. They let the food spoil, the dishes pile up and the laundry go undone. The garden beds fell to weeds and the clutter accumulated. It could all be cleaned up later. Right now, they put their feeble energy into each other. All the little triumphs of their love story had been banked away over the years, accumulating interest. Now they made lavish withdrawals, cashed in every bond, every insurance policy.

By day, they spent their emotional capital hand over fist, each splurging on silly necessities the other needed.

"You're the strongest wreck I've ever known," he said when she succumbed to tears.

"You're the most useful person in my life," she said when he gnawed mercilessly on his heart.

At night, they lay down together, pulling marriage over their tired, aching bodies like an extra quilt.

"Fuck everything else," they whispered. "I just need you."

Erik woke up to find the other side of the bed empty and piano music tinkling from the room that was once the office and meant to be the nursery. Peeking in, he found Daisy doing a barre, holding onto the side of the crib. Stretching and limbering. Doing her core exercises.

"Does it make you feel better?" he asked, sitting on the floor to watch.

"First position is always first position," she said, smiling. Then slowly her outstretched leg touched the floor again. The smiled dissolved and her gaze went far away. "No, it doesn't make me feel better," she said. "I'm so confused. I can't find my center. I can't balance. Everything hurts.

And I don't know if I should get back in shape or just screw it because I'm going to try to get pregnant again anyway. I don't know what to do with myself. So I'm going through the motions of what used to make me feel better."

She returned to her routine but stopped after a minute.

"Do you want to try again?" she asked.

"Not now."

"I meant one day."

"Yes," he said. "But not now. Right now I'm taking care of you."

Elbows on knees, he sat and watched, letting the strains of Chopin fill his chest with a dull melancholy. Letting Daisy fill his eyes with her beauty and her pain.

You are my wife.

He turned his wedding band around and around his finger as his sole purpose rolled cool and solid in his mouth like a piece of ice.

I will stay here. I will watch over you.

I will protect you.

YOUR SIDE WARM

THEY CLEANED UP THE house and sank a little more conviction into the future. Yes, they would try again.

"But take the time to mourn," the doctors said. And the counselors. And the people they met at support group. They were doing it right this time. Perhaps over-doing it, but both had learned the hard way it was no good toughing it out alone. They went for counseling separately, and together. They read books. They threw information at it.

Grieve and celebrate, the popular opinion seemed to be. Celebrate and grieve. Feel all of it.

The handful of pictures Lucky took in the hospital were beautiful, but one was especially so. Erik lying in the hospital bed with Daisy's head on his shoulder and Kees on his chest, both their hands cradling him. The gold chain around Kees's neck and the charms resting on his back. The light was soft. The composition was peaceful and dreamy. The baby looked almost ethereal. Framed in silver, it was lovely. They put it on top of the piano, keeping a lit candle on one side and Vivian's hummingbird on the other.

They got a special box and put away the lock of hair, the hand and footprints, the hospital bracelet, the baby cap and the swaddling blanket. Daisy added the lab photos of the fertilized eggs and the sonogram pictures. Will came one day to disassemble the crib and put it in the attic. They kept the door to the empty nursery open and wandered in and out as it moved them.

They tried to build it into the matrix. To let it hurt. To lean into it and feel it so they could make it part of them.

It sucked.

The rush of confused, post-partum hormones gave Daisy horrible night sweats. She woke up soaked and shivering, the sheets and the comforter cover sopping wet. Erik laid down beach towels and flipped the duvet over while she changed into dry clothes.

He felt helpless as the loss manifested itself in other cruel ways. The bloodied pads in the bathroom wastepaper basket made him angry. Daisy's breasts were rock hard and burning. The pain of her milk drying up made her face twist. It shot up into her armpits, throbbing and pulsing. She bound herself into tight sports bras, but sometimes the milk came down anyway, soaking through to her shirt. Or spilling through Erik's fingers as he cupped those heavy, grieving spheres in his hands.

Leave her alone, he thought, furious his wife had to bleed and sweat and leak this way, as if she needed a constant reminder of the loss.

Let me take some of this away from her. Give me some of it.

Make it fair.

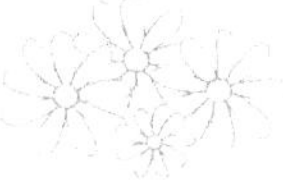

"It's so unfair," Lucky said. She had brought over a pot of chicken soup, pantry provisions and Jack.

Jack put his arms up and Erik hugged him.

"No, pick me up," Jack said. Erik counted off and swung him onto his chest. Jack wrapped arms and legs around and squeezed. "You need an extra hard hug."

"And you're so good at them," Erik said from under young boy bones and muscle. He stretched out his arms, leaving Jack clinging like a monkey. "Look," he said to Lucky. "No hands."

"He's a clutcher," Lucky said, smiling. "From day one. Just wanted to be held."

Erik set Jack down. The boy went upstairs to the bedroom where Daisy was reading. Erik peeked under the pot lid at the soup. It looked delicious but he wasn't hungry.

"I hate this," Lucky said, stacking rolls of paper towel under the sink. "I mean honestly. Fucking enough."

"Is this where I say something about everything happening for a reason?"

She shut the cabinet and got up, the tendons in her knees popping. She crossed her arms and looked at Erik. "We never talked about it, did we? You and I."

He shook his head. He hardly ever thought back to the night Lucky miscarried at Jay Street. When he walked through the drips of blood on the bathroom floor. Crouched down shivering to gather Lucky up in his arms, pull her into the safety of his embrace and get her to let go of what was already lost.

Lucky reached to fiddle with the collar of Erik's shirt. "Will always said, 'If you can't find me, get Fish.' And that night... If he couldn't be there immediately, I can't imagine anyone else but you coming to the rescue."

"I didn't do..." He let the words go. They weren't true. And this wasn't about him. He opened his arms and she hugged him tight.

"Thank you," she whispered. As if it had happened yesterday. "And if you ever can't find Dais, you get me."

He let his forehead sink onto her shoulder. His body trembled with a weary sadness.

The four of us need each other.

We're not weird. We're nothing but typical.

"You're tired," Lucky said. "Go rest. Send Jack down."

Erik went up and peeked politely through his own bedroom door. Daisy was asleep. Jack sat up against a wall of pillows, looking at the pictures in Erik's book of Swedish folk tales. Feet making twin hills in the quilt. His expression serious as he turned the pages.

"Taking care of my girl?" Erik said as he went in.

Jack closed the book and put it down on the nightstand. Swung his feet to the floor and got up.

"I made your side warm," he said. "I'm good at that, too."

His arms went around Erik's waist, squeezed once. Then he slipped like smoke out the door.

He moved as noiselessly as Will.

EVERY MAN'S LIFE

UNDER CANADIAN LAW, a child born after twenty weeks gestation—alive or dead—guaranteed full parental leave. Both the Fredericton Playhouse and New Brunswick Ballet threw compassionate leave on top, giving the Fiskares fifteen weeks to grieve.

"Get out of here," Will said to them. "Just go somewhere. Go around the world. Fuck it."

They didn't want to go anywhere. They stayed put, wandering around their life, getting through the structureless days. Picking things up and putting them down again. Eventually, cabin fever settled in, and they headed outside in an orgy of yardwork. Dawn to dusk they labored, cleaning up the world with a feverish energy. The lawn and garden beds were immaculate, the garage sparkled and the shed boasted a new paint job. Out of chores, they began walking long miles together: loops around the lake and treks through the woods. On stronger days, they drove to parts of the Trans Canada Trail. They tramped and trudged along the pathway, not to enjoy the scenery, but to wear themselves out.

Erik kept hypervigilant eyes on his wife's skin. "Promise me," he said. "If you start thinking about glass, start even entertaining the idea of hurting yourself, you tell me."

"I promised to stay alive for you," she said. "A long time ago."

"Promise this for me now."

"I promise," she said. "It hasn't entered my mind. It's not who I am anymore."

"All right," he said. "But if you feel like you're spiraling down into the dark, you're going on the meds. It's not even a question."

She touched his face. "I know."

"I mean it," he said, his voice shaking. "Your mental state is more important to me than anything else. Don't tough it out, Dais."

"I don't have the strength to tough it out," she said, a tiny, sad smile trembling beneath her damp eyes. The green was gone from their depths. She was a woman at war.

Erik felt battle-weary and defeated. He hadn't cried since Kees's ashes came back to them. He walked around with a constant lump in his throat, but the tears wouldn't come. Woven in with his stopped-up grief was an enraged fury and the occasional, twisted urge to either trash his workbench or kick a small animal to death.

He found himself frequently visiting his bedside table drawer, taking out the leather case with his Purple Heart, peeking beneath the inset where a flattened copper penny lived. Fighting a strange urge to put it in his pocket.

He passed long stretches of time gazing at the coin, remembering the power it held over him for so many years. He looked the compulsion in the eye. Acknowledged and felt his way through the need as he peeled his fingers off it.

It wasn't your fault.

It wasn't wood un-knocked, it wasn't superstition ignored, it wasn't you flaunting your happiness and inviting James to come back and shoot it down.

It was nothing you did or didn't do.

It's something that happened to you.

He kept waiting to either cry or erupt. Anything to break the stalemate. Grief was an iron collar. Anger was barbed wire in his guts.

It hurt like hell.

He wondered if he was dying.

"Can you die from not crying?" he asked.

"I'm tired of crying," Daisy said through her clenched teeth, her forehead against the window pane. Outside was torrential wind and rain.

"I'm so fucking angry. I want to smash something. I want to kill something. It's not fair."

He put his arms around her from behind. "Nothing's fair."

"We got sucker punched. All that joking about us finally getting a break and fate was just off in a corner fucking laughing. Waiting to backhand us into misery. I am *sick* of life doing this to you and me..."

Will and Lucky were renovating their kitchen. They invited the Fiskares over, gave them each goggles and a sledgehammer and pointed toward a wall marked for demo.

"Remove that," Will said.

They destroyed it. Reduced the entire thing to a rubble of sheetrock and studs in under five minutes. Then pounded the pieces into dust because fuck everything.

Breathing hard, Erik looked over his shoulder at Will. "Got anything else you want taken out?"

Eyes wide at the kill, Will slowly shook his head. "No, but I got some wood you can split?"

"I'm taking your wife," Lucky said. "We're going for a spa weekend. Make sure Will doesn't burn the house down."

"I heard that," Will yelled from the living room. "We're having our own spa weekend."

"We are?" Erik said.

"No," Will said. "I have to work."

But he left the kids with the nanny and spent the better part of Sunday afternoon with Erik. Just hanging out playing video games. It was like college, Erik thought, sitting on the floor next to Will, their backs up against the couch. Sweatpants and ball caps. Unshaven and scruffy. A pizza box and empty beers on the coffee table.

He felt old all of a sudden.

"I just hit the wall," he said, an immense surge of emotion pressing against the back of his eyeballs. He wanted Daisy to come home. His heart hurt, as if she had left forever.

Will tossed his remote onto the table. "You all right?"

"I feel like ten kinds of crap."

Will put an arm around him. "Dude..."

Erik sniffed hard. Tried to laugh it off. But it hurt today.

"I still got Dais," he said. "I threw all those years away but I found her again. I still got her. I'll never let her go. I need her more than I need any of the rest of it."

"Fish, what are you trying to do, find a bright side? You got no silver lining. You lost your baby, all right? You lost your son."

Erik pressed his forehead against the heels of his hands. "I lost my Dad," he said. "And I lost my son. I'm abandoned from both fucking sides now. What the hell is the world trying to tell me? What, Will? What's it going to take? How much do I have to take?"

His entire life burst through his eyes and he was crying. The collar slipped from his throat and all the furious hurt in his heart boiled up. With a grunt of rage he shoved the coffee table, tipped it over in an avalanche of magazines, electronics, pizza crusts and tin cans. Then he fell back, his face in his hands, weeping.

"Come here," Will said.

Blind with hot tears, Erik stepped off the edge of himself, stepped over the line and turned toward Will. He rolled on his knees and down on the other hip so he could slump in the circle of those tattooed arms, bury his face in the wall of Will's chest and let it go. The river of grief burst its dam and ran free, pouring out like thunder.

"I got you," Will said over the roar. "Give it here."

Erik cried hard. Cried for all the joy in his life that had been yanked away, shot down and burned up. He cried as both angry man and frightened child and the combined hurt was suffocating. He could grieve as an abandoned son or grieve as a bereaved father, but the bi-fold pain of both at the same time was drowning him. It sank sharp, icy nails into his skin. A lament so old, so familiar, it seemed slightly ancient.

You left me. Why did you leave me?

Red tail lights of his father's truck making a left onto Webb Street.

The squeak of the bassinet wheels when they took Kees away for the last time.

Ashes on top of the piano.

Gold around his neck.

Come back.

Daisy crying in the night. Crying for him out loud in the dark with no arms to hold her.

Don't leave me. Come back.

He was swept along until he thought he would die, coming to a slow stop and finally left floating in the shallows, spent and exhausted.

"I can't take any more," he said.

"I know," Will said. "I can't watch you take any more."

Erik freed a hand and wiped his face. "This is karmic debt coming due, isn't it?"

"What do you mean?"

"It's what I did to Dais. This was her, crying on the floor every night for me. I made her feel like this. I made both you and her feel like this."

"Don't. It's old pain and it's forgiven. It has nothing to do with now."

"I fucking hate now."

Will held him tight. His heart beat slow and steady in Erik's ear and his jaw rested on the top of Erik's head.

"I hate it too," Will said. "You don't deserve this shit."

Erik exhaled and they sat still a few minutes, breathing. Then Will's hands patted Erik's back and squeezed his shoulders. "You all right?"

"I'm tired."

"Go lie down. I'll clean up. Go on."

Wobbling like a newborn foal, Erik slowly got to his feet, needing the crutch of the toppled coffee table to help. He stumbled upstairs and lay down. His head ached and his eyes burned. Yet within minutes he plummeted into a coma-like sleep, emerging when Daisy slipped in beside him and curled up in his arms.

"I'm home," she whispered, her voice blowing away the fog.

He held her, breathing deep, assessing himself. The headache was gone. His throat was open, his chest peaceful. He felt husked out. Sort of...clean. The grief was there but it wasn't so slimy.

"Feel okay?" he asked, sliding his hand along her neck and into her hair.

"I do now," she said. Bastet jumped up onto the bed and curled herself into the tiny space between their bodies. They laid their hands on her silvery fur and rested.

Later, Will texted a black and white picture. A soldier sitting on the ground, crumpled weeping in the arms of a mate. His face pressed, hidden, against his friend's chest. Every line of his body utterly defeated. The soldier who comforted stared straight ahead, his face a stone. Taking in the horrors of combat as if nothing surprised him anymore. But the hand on his shattered friend's head was soft. Gentle. Erik could almost see it moving there. Could almost hear the repeated, murmured litany: *It's all right. Let it go now. I got you.*

Story of every man's life, I guess, Will texted. ***At one point or another.***

Erik replied. ***The thing you said about loving in a guy what you love in yourself? I get it now.***

A bit of silver had peeked through the clouds over Erik's heart. Kees's death would never be justified. It would bewilder and anger Erik all the rest of his days. Yet it had shone a light on bit of truth. At just the right angle to kindle a sudden insight.

"I only did what any man would've done," John Quillis said.

Not any man, Erik thought. *Exceptional men.*

His life was filled with them.

The moment with Will in the parking lot, so foreign and strange at the time, shimmered in Erik's mind like a miracle. It wasn't a thing to be dismissed. Without it, Erik would still be trapped in the agony of unexpressed grief. Dying from unshed tears.

It wasn't the first time he and Will had been in a foxhole with a battle raging over their heads: in the hospital after the shooting, Will had been the weeping soldier, his face crushed into Erik's chest, shell shocked and stricken, hiding from the world. Now Erik was the broken one. And Will was on the lookout.

I trust him with my life. I trust him with my pain. He can't make it go away, but I can give it to him to hold for a while.

He knows me.

I see in him what I like best in me.

Life was war. Life would go on doling out what it saw fit, and he and Will would just keep switching roles. The rock and the wrecked. Each being what the other needed, knowing they could never be misunderstood.

And if that wasn't love, Erik had no idea what was.

Dave,

Thanks for your note. I won't lie. It's hard. It hurts like hell. We're just getting through the days. Most of them suck, some are merely numb. The rest aren't worth getting into. You'd think what we went through at Lancaster would prepare us better. Maybe it's best not to think the worst has happened to you.

I know you and I still have a lot to say to each other. Or maybe not. I'm too tired to hold onto stupid shit anymore. Too sad to cling to what happened back when neither of us knew any better. It was nobody's finest moment. What happened that day is on you, but what happened the next twelve years is on me. It's too much weight. And it doesn't fucking matter anymore. It did at the time, but now I can't stay in that bitter place. I'll never get up if I do.

I've been thinking a lot about the night of the shooting. At the hotel. I remember I talked to my mom before I fell into bed and she told me, "Put your head down. Stay with David." Then you handed me a valium and stood watching until I swallowed it.

You didn't go to sleep. You were in the chair in the corner, reading the bible, reading Psalm 41 out loud. Keeping watch until I was out. You stayed with me. You set me in your presence.

I can't say I'm ready to see you. But I can say the night of the shooting was, without question, your finest moment. And I'm keeping it. I'm keeping the moment and letting go of the rest. It's a better place.

I'm letting go of it. All right? If it's weighed heavy on you these years then put it down. Leave it in the corner. Go to sleep in a better place.

We own this place.

Take care of yourself. Take care of your family. Hold them tight.

—E Fish

"HEY BUDDY," MIKE SAID. "How you doing?"

"Hanging in there," Erik said. "Listen, I wanted to ask you something."

"Shoot."

"You said my dad wrote you letters. When you were in the Coast Guard or at college."

"That's right."

"Did you keep any?"

A thoughtful silence in which Erik could see Mike pulling at his beard. "Well, that's a good question," he said. "I don't remember having a ceremonial disposing of them, but that's not to say they didn't get scooped up and tossed during one clean-up or another."

"I just wondered," Erik said. "You told me in one of them he talked about the struggle after Pete went deaf. How hard it was when things were beyond your control. I don't know. I got to thinking I'd like to read that if I could."

"Well, I'll tell you what, I'll look. I have some boxes in the attic with old papers and such. I'll certainly look and if I find any, I'll send them to you."

"Thanks," Erik said. "No rush. I'm not expecting you to have kept them, but I thought I'd ask."

They chatted a little and then hung up. Erik laced his hands behind his head and gazed up at the ceiling. Footsteps came into the living room behind him and he extended his fingers out. Daisy took them in hers.

"Do you want to go for a walk?" she asked, leaning over the back of his chair.

He didn't. Then her perfume curled around his nose and he looked up. She was wearing her favorite black cashmere sweater, her necklace with the gold fish and the pearl and the matching pearl earrings. Her hair was fixed and she had a little lipstick on. She looked pretty and Erik could see the effort it took. He ran wet hands through his hair and put on a clean shirt before they left.

They parked in town and walked. No destination, just crisscrossing the grid of Saint John. Watching boats come in and out of the harbor, watching people going about their business, watching the world continuing to spin.

Hunger made a surprise appearance so they went into the Wharf Tavern. Nick behind the bar came around to hug them. "It's good to see you out. I've been thinking about you guys. Come sit down."

They sat kitty-corner at a little table with a bottle of wine and shared an order of fish stew, hot and creamy and loaded with good things. They dunked bread and fed each other shrimp and scallops and haddock. Not saying much but never breaking physical contact, their ankles woven under the table.

And over the rims of their wineglasses, they stared.

"I love nobody and nothing," Erik said, "the way I love you."

They ambled down Chester Street. Stopped in A Drink With Bread and Jam and bought a half-pound of their favorite loose leaf tea. Wandered through a bookstore. Looked in windows. Looked at each other.

"I'm having a good time," Daisy said, picking a bit of something off his jacket then smoothing her hand down his chest.

He hooked his arm around her neck and inhaled deep on the crown of her head. Breathed in fresh air and the warm, clean scent of her hair.

"So am I," he said.

They walked around a flea market at Lalille Pier. One booth had the perfect little silver box for Kees's ashes. Sleek and handsome and simple. When the vendor learned what it was for, she pressed it into Daisy's hands and wouldn't take their money.

"Que Dieu vous bénisse," she said, kissing their cheeks.

Her blessing on their faces, they turned down Palace Avenue. The sleek black awning of Ink & Think, the tattoo parlor, beckoned from across the street. Not a glance or a word was exchanged as they crossed over.

Just a K, they decided. The artist copied the letter's style straight out of Daisy's fish tattoo and inked it into them in black. Erik's on the inside of his right wrist. Daisy's in the hollow of her left hip bone.

She came to him that night. The tiniest green flicker in her eyes as she wound her arms around his neck and found his mouth with hers. He slid his hands up the back of her sweater and unclipped her bra. His touch was careful, knowing her breasts were still sore. Their sorrowful weight filled his palms but they stayed dry.

Her hands trembled as she pulled his shirt off and pushed his jeans down. She eased him to the bed and lay on top of him, the full length of her body all along his. Her head on his chest, her toes against his ankles. Naked save for her jewelry. Every bit of adornment she wore was something Erik had given her. On her finger. At her ears. Nestled in her throat.

He held her, thinking he was in no mood for sex, but then he was growing hard under her empty belly and filling up with a hungry and desperate mood to connect.

"Can we?" he asked, his hands buried in her hair. Wanting to be inside her skin and her body and her heat.

"Not yet," she said, sliding down the mattress. "Soon."

"You don't have—"

"Shh. I want to."

Her hair fell over his chest and stomach and her arms curved like wings over his legs. He hadn't the strength to savor her touch, instead he gave in, gave over and she quickly brought him around with her soft hands and her warm mouth. He came with a thunderous shiver through his chest and a wet hiss of air through his teeth.

"Dais," he whispered, another shiver going across both shoulders. Then one more out his ears and he was still.

She pulled the covers over them. They fell asleep side-by-side. Shoulders nestled, his right arm along her left flank, the tattooed K's pressed tight together.

"COME HERE," CHRISTINE SAID from Key West. "It's beautiful. You can take the studio apartment and live on the beach. Come here and be in the sunshine. Fall into the ocean. Do nothing. You can come here."

"Come," Francine said. "It's beautiful here. It's apple blossom time. We're rolling in eggs and strawberries. You can be in the carriage house. Come here, darlings."

"I guess we could," Daisy said, washing dishes.

"If you want to," Erik said absently.

"I don't know. I mean— Shit..."

A wine goblet slipped out of her soapy fingers and smashed in pieces on the tile floor. She jumped away, screwing up her face. "God dammit, I *hate* that sound," she said.

Erik froze, staring at the glistening shards.

He was remembering another time. Another broken sound. A plate flung against the wall. A jagged rubble falling at his feet. His first marriage in pieces.

"You don't fight for anything you love," Melanie cried. "I can't stand your complacency anymore. I plan our vacations. I plan our time and you just show up. Without an impassioned opinion, you just go where I tell you."

Erik stared with a dawning realization.

She's waiting for you.

Make a decision. Do something.

Lead your life, don't just follow it around.

"Let's go," he said, opening the cleaning closet door and reaching for broom and dustpan. "We're going. We're getting out of here."

She looked at him, her eyes brimming as he crouched down and started sweeping up the mess.

"Let's just get in the car and drive," he said. "Drive down the coast. We'll stop in Maine, we'll stop in Boston, we'll stop in New York. We can make it up as we go along. Let's head for La Tarasque and take it from there."

"All right," she said. "I want to take Kees with us."

"So do I."

"I can't leave him alone in the empty h—"

"We'll take him with us," Erik said. "Not everything has to be a thing."

The dustpan filled with broken glass, he stood up. He kissed her. Took a step away but then stopped and kissed her again.

"Go pack," he said.

Friends offered their lake cabin outside Bangor, Maine so they made it their first destination.

They had been easing back into sex for a little while. Slow and careful and conscientious. Tonight they coupled with a savagery. It wasn't making love. More like trial by fire.

It burned bright in the hearth, the charred logs slipping and crackling and popping. The clear yellow flames throwing shadows on the walls and the shadows throwing waves of heat onto the bed.

The bed was dead center of the cabin, like an altar. Erik lay on his back and Daisy was on top of him, going at him with a vengeance. They were still fully dressed, only what was necessary had been bared or undone. Over him, she was burning, too. Burning hotter, harder, and he was buried in the immensity of her need. She writhed under his touch, a wild and dangerous thing. Her lips were open, her throat strained, but still no sound came from her. Under normal circumstances, this would indicate she had reached the pinnacle of pleasure and he would coax her with his voice.

Come. Come to me.

But now the soundlessness only signaled how desperately she was still trapped in grief.

He took her hands in his. "Cry," he whispered. "Cry to me."

Her head lolled, her skin burned, something in her seemed to crumple and she came down off him, crashed gently down into the pillows. He rolled to her, ignoring the tangle of his clothes, slid his hand to the back of her neck, into the hot dampness of her long hair. His mouth found hers. He pulled his arms from his sleeves as she unbuttoned him, lay back long enough for her to pull his pants off. Then he was on her again, her mouth in his again. His hands were stripping her clothes off sure and strong. He wanted to throw them at the hearth, consign them to the flames and burn them. Burn all of the hurt away, reduce it to ash so he could show her who he was.

On fire with fearless purpose, he moved over her, held her down and pushed deep into her, kissed her open-eyed.

"I need you," she whispered against his mouth.

"I'm here."

"Help me." Her teeth chattered by his ear. She clung to him, her face in his shoulder, limbs trembling as the storm rolled through.

"I've got you, Dais. I'm not afraid of what you're feeling. I can't love you without loving this too." Gently but firmly he took her head in his hands, took it off his shoulder and made her face him. "Look at me now."

She tried but could not focus on him.

"Look at me," he said. "Look in my eyes."

She breathed in, deep, held it a moment, her eyes trying to settle on his.

"Look at me," he said again. "Look only at me."

It took a few minutes, her breath hitching in and out of her lungs, but gradually her eyelids ceased flickering. Her gaze locked into his and her body grew still. His hand caressed her face, thumb running beneath her eyes and over her mouth.

They stared. They breathed. The heat of the room coalesced into a bubble, sealing them up in peace. Time relaxed. The flames were dying down to embers. The cool blue of a fire a thousand times more powerful. He kissed her, nudged her lips open with his and moved into her mouth, finding her tongue. He grew hard inside her again, reared his hips back a few inches and then settled deeper into her. She spread her legs further and her hand pressed the small of his back. He slid into her, out of her, feeling himself disappear into her body, down into the core where their halves had made a whole.

It was the most love we ever made. A new spire on our cathedral. I don't have to tear it down. It can stay there and be beautiful.

An almost triumphant desire surged in him, strong, bright and true. It crashed through the roof of his mind and the fabric of time slowly split down the center.

"Come back to me," he said, throwing out the hook.

"You," she said, caught and drifting toward him. "Only you."

He tried to keep looking in her eyes as she rumbled beneath the plate of his desire and bucked him up. He held on until the long line of her throat opened to the ceiling and her edge touched his. They came together, and this time it was her voice that turned inside-out and ricocheted off the walls, while he threw back his head and made no sound at all. His voice retracted, coiling around the inside of his skull. An enormous noise. Like a cathedral bell ringing.

Daisy. Daisy. Daisy. Daisy.

He fell down by her, his chest heaving, eardrums pounding. Her hand dropped heavy on his head. They were both soaked, salty and dripping and spent in the damp, twisted sheets. The windows were opaque with steam. The air of the cabin pressed down on them from all sides as the edges of the universe wove back together.

Slowly she got up, came around to his side of the bed, beckoning. He took her hand and followed her to the door. They stepped onto the porch and gasped together with visceral relief as the cool of the evening swept over their bodies.

Outside was purple, velvety twilight. The air was a soft towel blotting away the sweat of their lovemaking. They were isolated deep in the woods, not a human soul around and only the sounds of nature creating a low background hum. Hand-in-hand they went down the short path to the edge of the lake and waded into its cool depths.

As the water closed over his head, Erik's skin and bones dissolved. He couldn't tell where he stopped and the lake's embrace began. He came up, raking his fingers through his hair, running them over his face, then toppled back into the drink. Over and over, they both sank beneath the surface, rinsed themselves clean, wrung themselves out, then dropped under again.

Suffused with a beautiful weariness, he moved to a shallower place where he could kneel in the soft sand. She swam up to him, floated into his lap, her arms around his neck.

"I'm so happy right now," she said. "I didn't think I ever would be again."

He cradled her to his chest, fell into the green of her eyes as he went looking for her mouth again.

"I love you," he said. "You're the love of my life."

He turned in the silky circle of her arms, drawing them around him from behind. "Hold on."

With her cheek snugged tight against his, he pushed off and glided toward the middle of the lake. She streamed out behind him like a cape.

Hold on, his heart sang. *Hold onto me.*

DAISY'S ORIGINAL DUE date arrived. Kees should have been born today. Or perhaps he would've been born already.

The day bristled with a strange longing, looking from Daisy to Erik and back like an expectant puppy with a leash in its mouth. They took themselves for a long walk down country roads. They sighed a lot but didn't say much.

In the late afternoon, they lay in the hammock at the far end of the porch at La Tarasque.

"What are those flowers?" Erik asked, pointing to the drifts of magenta pom-poms on the other side of the railing.

"Monarda," Daisy said. "Bee balm."

The fluffy flowers were thick with bees. And as Erik and Daisy lay still, hummingbirds began to approach. First one. Then two more. Hovering with blurred wings as they fished for nectar.

"Messengers," Daisy said. "They get into dark places and heal."

"I've never seen them this close," he said.

"Maybe they have a message."

They swung a while in silence.

"It's not like he had a personality yet," Erik said. "Although when I saw his face and he looked so serious... And my mother said it was how I looked. He became a person to me. Like I could see that would be part of who he was. Or who he was supposed to be."

"Do you believe in reincarnation?" Daisy asked.

"I don't know. Why? Do you feel like he's gone to be born somewhere else? As someone else?"

"He was ours," she said. "I mean, we made him. We shared him. He was born of us."

"Our cathedral," he said, seeing the new spire rising above stained glass and bells.

"I've always gravitated toward the idea that souls are an eternal source of energy and these bodies of ours are just shells," Daisy said. "Going through IVF really solidified it for me. Seeing pictures of the dividing cells and it was all happening in a dish, in a lab. Was Kees's soul present at that time? What about those embryos we froze—is the soul frozen inside them? I can't believe it is. Bodies are just the shell. Gender is part of the shell. The soul comes along later, by choice. I really believe this. Souls have a purpose and their energy belongs with a certain other energy. They go where they belong. It's not random..."

Erik closed his eyes, perched on the edge of whatever she was going to say next. "Go on."

"Kees was supposed to be ours. That soul belongs to us. It just caught a bad ride this time."

"A bad ride?"

"A body that didn't work out. A defective shell. The soul is still ours. It'll come back. Maybe as a boy again or maybe as a girl. But it'll come back to us." Beside him, he felt her shrug. "I don't know. Maybe it's dumb, but it makes me feel better. I can believe in it. I mean, you came back to me. So Kees will, too. Somehow."

Erik was quiet. As she spoke, a cloud of sparkling yellow lights began to creep across the inside of his eyelids. Moving left to right like fireflies. Something loosened in his chest. Daisy's words fell into place like Tetris blocks, each one turning and rotating to accommodate the next, assembling a greater structure.

The soul caught a bad ride this time.

It'll come back.

It's ours. It belongs to us.

"I believe it too," he said. "I didn't know I believed it until I heard you say it."

For the first time since the stillbirth, Erik felt a flicker in his heart. A tiny spark of hope. He cupped his hands around it. Breathed gently. Treated it like a feather of memory. Or a newborn baby. He couldn't grab for it. It had to come to him.

"I can still feel him in my hands, Dais," he said.

"I'll always feel him in my hands. Our hands were born to feel that soul."

"It'll come back then."

"It will."

Daisy curled into him. He ran his mouth over her hair.

"When we get home, let's finish that damn screened-in porch," he said. "And then plant bee balm all around it."

THE RIVER WORLD 

DOWN IN KEY WEST, Erik dreamed often of his father. It was a dream he'd had for fifteen years. In a golden boat, on a lake, hauling in golden fish, while Byron stood on the shore, cheering his son's catch.

Who do I look like? Erik yelled over the water.

And Byron called back, *You look like me.*

"Come take a walk," Erik said to Christine.

It was an overcast day. Every now and then a bit of lazy rain came through. But the air was soft and the waters of the Gulf were warm. He and Christine gathered a few shells, then sat on the beach to talk.

"You told me once," Erik said, "you'd never forgive the father of your children. But you'd listen to the man you loved."

"He was the love of my life," Christine said, arranging her shells on the sand in front of her.

"You also told me he gave you the necklace when you signed divorce papers," Erik said. "But that's not what happened. Is it?"

Staring at her collection, Christine shook her head.

Erik set the backs of his fingers on her cheek. "I'm not angry and I'm not accusing you of anything," he said. "I just want the story. Nothing will upset me now, Mom. Nothing."

"It was the only lie I told you," she said, hugging her knees.

"You were protecting me," he said. "I understand. Did he leave it behind?"

"On the bedside table," she said. "I never saw him again."

"But why…" He took his cap off, scratching his head then replaced it. "Why pass yourself off as divorced? Why not just let him be missing? Or say he was dead?"

"Missing was too hard to explain," she said. "I couldn't tell you and Pete he was dead because what if he showed up again? Missing was cruel and left the door open for too many questions. Divorce worked best. You boys could accept it and it got everyone else to shut up and leave me alone. I was slightly out of my mind at the time. Deep in survival mode. I got us out of Clayton, slapped together a skeleton story and beefed it up by saying I didn't want to talk about it."

Erik wrapped arms around his knees as well. "And the child support payments for me and Pete?"

"That was Farfar," she said. "He sent those. He helped me keep up the pretense until you were both eighteen."

The shoreline blurred as Erik's eyes welled up.

"You naming the baby after him," Christine said, touching his arm. "He would've been so proud."

Erik sniffed hard, turned his head to wipe his face on his windbreaker. "What do you think happened to Dad," he asked. "If you never saw him again, if the divorce was a fabrication, then in your heart, what do you believe? Do you think he's dead?"

"No. He's alive."

Erik reared back a hair. "You believe or you know?"

"I believe."

"So…?"

Christine didn't say anything. She sat cross-legged now, her hands twined against her ankles. The wind blew wisps of her silvery-blonde hair around. Her face was tanned, lined and far away.

"You kept his ring," Erik said.

She nodded.

"And you kept his name," he said, the revelation dawning as if the clouds parted to let a sunbeam through. "You won't marry anyone because he wouldn't be able to find you."

She smiled at the waves. "We all have our weaknesses."

"You could marry Fred and not change your name."

She didn't answer. Her smile hinted Erik was sadly missing the point.

"Do you think it was another woman?"

"It was the river world." She looked at Erik then. "It gets touchy-feely from here," she said. "You don't have to believe what I believe. I'm just telling you the context I had to put it in."

"Something happened after the accident," Erik said. "Didn't it? Trudy and Kirsten told me he was never the same after."

"But they knew him before," Christine said. "I didn't." She drew a deep breath, running a hand through her damp hair. "We didn't have the knowledge back then, Erik. It was nineteen sixty-two. Trauma was barely a concept, much less a medical condition. The terminology to address traumatic brain injury didn't exist, let alone treatments. I don't remember even hearing the diagnosis of TBI until the Iraq War. Back then, the diagnosis was one word: lucky. They said he was lucky simply to be alive."

"But something was changed."

"So many words for it now," Christine said. "Pick one. PTSD, you know about it all too well. Or you could say he suffered absent seizures. Or he had problems with emotional processing. An empathy deficit or a depersonalization disorder. Alexithymia—that's a word and a half, it means you have difficulty recognizing or describing emotions."

She picked up one of her shells and flung toward the waves, watched it plop in the shallows. "Your father called it the river world. Because it all started when he was floating in the river. After he was thrown out of the boat."

"When what started?" Erik said, confused.

"He would turn off. He had episodes when he would be present and cognizant and functional, but he had no emotional connection to anything. He felt nothing. He said the color would go out of the world. His *adjectives* would disappear. Like he was a harp and one by one his strings were unplucked until he was just a hollow frame. An empty shell, standing in the center of his life and none of it meaning anything to him."

"For how long?"

"Sometimes minutes. Sometimes hours. Then he'd come back. He said coming out of the river was the reverse of strings breaking. Instead of one at a time, he came back with a glissando." Christine's hand fanned through the air, sliding along the keys of an invisible piano. "He'd *slam* back into himself, as if being concussed again. It was terrifying. It would leave him in tears."

Erik flailed for a question. "Did his parents know?"

"They took him to doctors," she said, nodding. "They did a lot of studies up in Montreal. But not much could be done for him. It was episodic. And between episodes, he was completely functional. While having them, he didn't become psychotic or catatonic. He didn't convulse on the floor or pass out. He just..."

"He'd get a faraway look in his eyes," Erik said softly. "Like he was listening to music no one could hear."

Christine leaned away a little. "Who said that?"

"Mike Pettitte."

She blinked, her chin nodding a little. "I wonder if he knew. Of course Farmor and Farfar knew, but they didn't discuss it. They felt lucky their son was alive. If this occasional detachment issue was the only after effect, so be it. They took it in stride, carried on and kept it to themselves. It was their way. Your father said it didn't bother them when he was in the river world. Coming out with a huge outburst of emotion was what upset them. As he got older, he learned to hide the returns. Or at least manage them."

"When did you find out?"

She drew patterns in the sand. "I saw it for the first time at Xandro's funeral. Everyone went back to the hotel afterward for coffee. I didn't know anyone. I felt awkward and shy so I went for a walk by the river. I saw this boy sitting on the rocks and he was crying. Crying with his whole body. I recognized him as Xandro's brother. I don't know why I... You'd think I'd have gone away and given him some privacy. Instead I went up to him. I sat on another rock and... I just sat. Because next to him was where I was supposed to be."

She touched Erik's arm, a small smile on her lips. "You of all people know what it's like when you find a soulmate."

"He was coming out of an episode? Right then?"

"Yes," she said. "I didn't understand what was happening. I thought he was crying for Xandro. Not long after, he told me about it. When it was clear what was happening with us, he told me everything."

"It didn't scare you?"

She shook her head. "It was the only way I knew him. I didn't have an old Byron to compare to. I was never afraid, even when I watched it happening. It scared him, though. When I got pregnant with you, he was beside himself. He was already terrified he'd one day go into the river world and never be able to come out. With a family, there'd be so much more to lose."

"But you had me anyway," Erik said, his voice gruff.

"Nothing could stop me," she said, running her hand along his cheek. "When you were born, it happened. In the hospital, when you were just hours old, Byron went into the river. I put him in a chair and put you in his arms. I said, 'You hold onto him. You look at him. He'll keep you afloat.' Then I watched.

"It was a long episode. I didn't take my eyes off him. He didn't take his eyes off you. Finally I could sense it was coming around. He was going to slam back into himself. And when he did..." Christine's arms curved, cradling an invisible baby. "He never let go of you. I could see the amount of effort it took for him to control the glissando. To let it all sweep through him and back into him without letting go of you or waking you up. The tears slid down his face and dripped onto your little mouth. Then he laughed. He came out of that one laughing at the end..."

Erik dropped his head onto his forearms. Christine's hand settled soft on the back of his neck. "It always stayed in my mind," she said. "How the first thing you ever tasted in your life was your father's tears."

Slowly Erik leaned until he touched his mother's side. She put her arms around him.

"You're so strong, Erik," she said. "You're the strongest person I know. Stronger than a river. You asked me and I told you the truth. I believe in my heart your father went into that world of his one last time and couldn't come back. Something happened. He sank this time. He drowned. It was the only thing that would make him leave. It's what I believe. It's what I have to believe."

She went on holding him. Erik lifted his eyes and over his kneecaps he looked out at the ocean.

"Believe me," Christine said. "Believe when I tell you he loved you."

"Why didn't you tell me the rest," he said, already knowing the answer.

"Because my heart was broken."

Erik stared as wave after wave hit the sand. Relentless. Eternal. They'd been crashing onto shores for millennia and would go on doing so long after Erik was gone.

He loved me, Erik thought, staring at the water, defying it to disagree. *You heard her. Him leaving had nothing to do with me. I was his son and he loved me.*

The tide laughed as it advanced and retreated.

I don't care, it told him.

The ocean had ceased being emotional eons ago. Its majesty lay in its aloofness. It didn't care about your problems or your grief. You were nothing to the waters. They took your troubles with an almost cruel ambivalence, knowing they would outlive you forever. Whether you broke or fixed. Whether you stayed or left.

Erik stared at the rising walls of water, the frosting crest as each rolled over, like fingers folding down into a fist around the shore. Their cadence, so mocking before, turned soothing.

Give it here.

Give it to me, I'll hold it.

The waves didn't care. Their rhythm would never be interrupted. Their purpose would never be lost.

The ocean was forever.

So was the river.

He went to forever.

Where nothing feels.

He rolled up his left wrist and gazed at the daisy tattooed there. He remembered the day he had it inked. And remembered a dark night when he pressed the blade of his jackknife to its petals and almost cut it out. He turned up his other hand and looked at the black K.

These things happen and they are terrible things to bear.

Still the waves kept coming.

Give it here, they said. *Live your life. Feel your life. Or else go to your father's forever and feel nothing. It makes no difference to us.*

He looked at his wrists and the ink permanently in his skin. He would die with these. *I will set you in my presence forever.*

Dais is forever.

I go to her.

A break in the ocean's sound made him look up. The water seemed to be drawing back, as if waiting. The shoreline in its wake glistened and bubbled.

Your father broke and left. You broke and left, but then you came back.

You stayed and fixed.

You are not him.

Give it here now and feel your life.

Let him go.

"All right." Erik's mouth shaped the words with no sound. A large wave crested and fell, rolling up the beach. Nearly reaching his bare feet before melting into the sand.

"I feel like I've given you nothing to make you feel better," Christine said.

He put his hand on top of hers, twining their fingers. "You gave me everything."

Part Five: Silver

THAT GUN IN HIS HAND

WILL TEXTED ERIK on a Monday afternoon: ***Come over to the theater. Dais and I want to show you something.***

"This is romantic," Erik said as they led him into one of the studios. The lights were dimmed and votive candles lit all around the perimeter of the space. "Am I overdressed?"

"Terribly," Will said. "Take your pants off."

"Quiet, you," Daisy said. "Take a seat, honey."

Curious, Erik sat on the floor beneath the barres. "What's going on?"

"Professional consultation," Daisy said.

She hit the music. Three precise guitar chords, a single drumbeat and the hair rose up on Erik's forearms. It was Jimi Hendrix's "The Wind Cries Mary."

He set his chin on his kneecaps, hugging his shins. He hadn't seen Will and Daisy dance together in over fifteen years. His stomach curled in anticipation, mixed with an odd fear they wouldn't be what he remembered. But of course, they were.

Complex and percussive phrases layered on top of the lazy, syrupy music. Quickly, Erik was drawn in, tasting the flavor Will and Daisy were going for. It wasn't romantic. They danced primarily in unison and the partnering was about mutual strength and support. As usual though, Erik was pulled into Will's movements. Through Will he felt Daisy's hands, limbs and weight. He watched her, but he *was* Will.

Our best performances together were from me being not a partner, but a mirror.

Floating in the flickering candlelight, absorbed mind and body in the dance and mesmerized, Erik realized what a gift they were giving him. Or returning to him, rather: all the lost years of their partnership. The collaboration he had missed. By letting him watch this embryonic version of a pas de deux, he felt the last, small sins of the past finally forgiven. Set free on the wind and let go forever.

They ran out of choreography at the end of the bridge. Will set Daisy down and they became human and ordinary again.

"What do you think?" Will said, breathing hard.

"I think it sucks," Erik said, wiping his eyes on his shoulder. "Where's the rest of it?"

Will tapped the side of his head. "In here. Meanwhile, I need you to build a set."

"Not a set," Daisy said as she toweled off her face. "An experience."

"Something wild," Will said.

Erik rubbed the back of his neck, chewing on a germ of an idea. "How wild?"

"Woodstock wild."

"Let me drop acid and think about it," Erik said.

It helped the Fredericton Playhouse was doing a run of the 60's musical *Hair* and Erik's mind was already in an expansive, let-it-all-hang-out mode. He came to the ballet's early rehearsals and took copious notes. He played Hendrix in his car and through his earphones while running. He pored through production books, leafed through Daisy's photo albums from her days at the Metropolitan Opera House. He researched the hazards of a multi-storied, vertical set and how to overcome them. He quizzed every member of New Brunswick Ballet on what would make them feel safe and what would get in their way.

"This isn't going to be a nude ballet, is it?" he asked.

"Yes," Will said.

"No," Daisy said.

"Maybe," Will said.

Erik made a careful note. "No splinters, no sharp edges, no sticky surfaces."

He threw all his ideas and concepts into the stockpot and stirred in the memory of the forest scene his father once built in his bedroom. The result was a cross between construction scaffolding and a psychedelic playground. Three levels of space for the dancers to move in, on, under and through. Steps, ropes and cargo nets bridged the gaps between.

He brought the final sketches next door and sat at the kitchen table with a beer while Will went through them.

"I should be able to make a model this week," Erik said.

Will hummed absently, his eyebrows pulled low, his fingers running along his hairline. Erik smiled as he caught sight of Will's new tattoo: a small, black fish on the inside of his forearm, leaping ahead of a cresting wave.

"Why?" Erik said, when he first saw it a few weeks ago.

"Because I hate your guts," Will said, which was the extent of the conversation.

Erik watched now as Will unconsciously folded his fingers into a fist and relaxed them, over and over, making the fish ripple. He set aside the last sketch, exhaled heavily and looked at Erik.

"What do you think?" Erik said.

"I think I'm in love with you again."

"I know, but what do you think of the set?"

Will slid the drawings across the table. "If you build it, I will come."

Daisy was deep in a creative zone as well. The first time Erik saw her dance "Hey, Joe" was in the empty nursery at Barbegazi. It brought him to his knees, staring open-mouthed and stunned at the raw emotion. One minute her body was a mirror of Hendrix's signature guitar sound, the next it was the undercurrent of percussion. Barefoot, strong and glorious, dancing from her unapologetic guts, she squeezed the music tight in her limbs and wrung a story out of it.

"Has Will seen this?" he asked when it was over and he felt like a truck had hit him.

She shook her head, sucking wind. Hands braced on her knees, back and chest heaving and sweat dripping onto the hardwood floor.

"You have to show him," he said.

"It needs a little more work."

"No," he said. "It doesn't need anything except Will's eyes."

The three of them went over to the quiet Imperial Theater. Daisy wanted to try the solo on the stage, to see if it translated from a small space to a larger one. Erik sat with Will in the back row to watch. At the end of the second verse, Will dropped his head in his hands, fingers clenched tight in his hair and shoulders quivering.

"Fuck. Me."

"I know," Erik said.

"Jesus Christ, Fish."

"I know. It's so many things. It's her after losing Kees. Or it's me after she slept with David. Or her father trying to get his son back."

Will's dropped his hands and his face flicked to Erik with a look that was almost angry. "The fuck are you talking about?" he said, eyebrows pulled in a single straight line. "It's *James*."

Erik felt his face widen as his brain scrambled, rewound and started over again with fresh perspective. He looked at the stage, looked back at Will. "Oh my God."

"You see it?"

"I see it."

"Where was he going with that gun in his hand?"

Erik folded his arms on the seat back in front of him and set his chin down. "Unbelievable it wasn't the first thing I thought of."

Will hitched forward as well. "Don't take this the wrong way, but I'm kind of glad it wasn't."

Erik glanced at him. "You mean the shooting's been replaced by better tragedy?"

Will smiled and shrugged. "Maybe that's life. Trading in one tragedy for a better tragedy."

Erik looked back to the stage where his wife was dancing and had to agree.

Being part of *Experience* helped heal Erik's soul like nothing else. When the company took to the set in a rough, technical run-through, a pure, clean delight swept through him. The first unadulterated happiness he'd known since they lost Kees.

The rock ballet was a smash, selling out its three-week run. It earned Daisy and Will a prize for choreography at the Canadian Ballet Festival. The gala performance was staged at Fredericton Playhouse. From the lighting booth, through a raucous, standing ovation, Erik watched his wife and best friend collect their award.

He reached and pressed his palm flat to the glass. From the stage, Daisy touched her fingertips to her mouth and turned her palm back out to him.

Erik leaned his elbows on the console and leaned hard on the moment. Filled with the unwavering certainty that if life were going to throw tragedy at him, it would whether he embraced the joy of right now or not.

He might as well make out with it.

Take it to bed.

Get it pregnant.

Later that night, he told Daisy, "I want to try again. I'm ready if you are."

She drew her breath in, slowly let it out. "If something happens this time," she said. "I mean, if it doesn't work, or we lose it... I think I'll be done. I think my heart will have taken all it can."

He nodded, brushing her hair back from her face. "I'm ready for that, too."

"Of course, if nothing happens, if it all goes smoothly... I'll be a fucking lunatic anyway."

He gathered her close and smiled against her head. "Count me in."

SALT AND PEPPER

TRUDY DIED IN THE spring of 2010. A stroke took her fast. She didn't suffer, Mike said.

Erik and Daisy drove to Clayton for the funeral and stayed at the Saint Lawrence Inn. Trudy was buried in Pettitte family plot in the village cemetery, next to her husband, Louis.

Kirsten looked stunned at the service. Her face gaunt, the vivid blue of her eyes cut in half. Erik could feel her bones when he hugged her. Beneath his chin, the tender pink of her scalp showed through her white hair.

Kirsten hugged Daisy then took her face between her wrinkled hands. She stared a moment. When she looked up at Erik, a bit of mischief was back in her expression.

"You did it again, didn't you?" she said.

Erik ducked his head, acknowledging guilt.

"We were thinking," Daisy said. "If we have a girl we—"

"Don't you *dare*," Kirsten said, her eyes flaring to life. She raised a warning finger, looking from Erik to Daisy and back. "Trudy hated her name. You name your daughter Gertrude, you will answer to *me*."

Chastised as young children, they scrapped the idea and promised.

The summer passed in construction. Giving fate, fear and superstition the finger, they blew out Barbegazi's south wall and built a family room, with a new bedroom and bath on top of it.

In mid-October, a heavy package was delivered to Barbegazi, post-marked from Mike Pettitte. Erik opened the box to find it full of silverware.

"Holy shit," he said under his breath, holding up a fork. The handle was shaped like a fish. The tail was situated beneath the tines, the body curving out and in, to fit comfortably in the eater's hand and provide resting places for index finger and thumb. At the bottom of the handle, the fish's mouth opened to hold a perfect scallop shell, tiny balls like pearls set delicately between each ridge.

In a plastic bag were eight napkin rings, also silver, adorned with the same scallop shell. And tucked among the silver was a thick envelope with "Erik" written on the front. Inside, a bundle of smaller envelopes, held together with a paperclip and a note:

Erik,

Surprise! Congratulations on a handsome inheritance. This fish silverware has been on my Mom's table for as long as I can remember, and I never gave a thought to where it came from. Turns out, your grandfather acquired it when he was serving with the Army of the Occupation in Austria. His unit was billeted in some huge monastery full of Nazi wealth. Many GIs did a little shopping—(cough) looting(cough)—and sent the treasure home. Kennet found this silverware, shipped it home, and it's stayed in the family since. In her will, Trudy specifically left it to you and Daisy, which seems to me a perfect bequest. It took a roundabout way from Kennet to you, but it's yours now. So throw a dinner party and raise a fork to your ancestors, I know they'll be raising one back.

You'll see a little something else in the package: cleaning out Mom's house, I found an old box of my papers. In it were three of the letters your dad wrote me. Reading them was bittersweet. But in a weird way, it felt like closure. I hope some of the same is in them for you.

I'm doing all right. Strange to be an orphan. It hits you at weird times, like on Sunday nights when you're used to checking in. I still keep Mom's number in my phone. Sometimes I send her a text. Hey, you never know...

Kirsten was up visiting a couple weeks ago. She seems diminished. One lonely pea in a pod. She and Mom really had an extraordinary friendship and I feel terrible for her. But she's bravely planned a European cruise and even made a crack about having no competition in the casino. Maybe she'll meet a nice fellow she can travel with. She deserves companionship. Someone like her isn't meant to move about the world alone.

Give Dais a hug from me and I'll talk to you, hopefully sooner than later.

Love ya,
Mike

Erik sat on an overturned bucket on the concrete slab to read his father's letters. All around him were raised the studs of the new screened-in porch, which he was building himself. Red, yellow and orange foliage ringed the lake's shore and reflected in its surface. He'd have to hustle to finish before cold weather came, seal it up and nail weatherproof plastic over the mesh openings.

May 17, 1974

Dear Mike,

Sorry I haven't been in touch, but you probably heard the news from Trudy. Pete's gone deaf. Apparently it was him having the mumps last year that did it. I had no idea it could affect your hearing. I thought it just one of those nuisance childhood illnesses you suffered through and came out the other side.

Anyway, we saw a half-dozen specialists in Rochester and the unanimous verdict is the damage is near total. As far as they can tell. A one-year-old can't exactly raise their hand when you play a tone. They do turn their head toward sound but it's not too scientific. We have to wait and see how bad it is. It kills me. Waiting for what you already know is bad news.

It's devastated Chris, but Kirsten and Trudy have been shoring her up, alternating tea and booze. Listening and talking. One last, long cry in the bathroom and the next day Chris emerged like Clark Kent transformed into Superman. Cape on, head down, in pursuit of knowledge. She's been at the library and on the phone finding out everything she can. She's driven from Watertown to Potsdam, brought home fifty books and pamphlets on deaf education, hearing aids, speech therapy, sign language.

Meanwhile I'm angry.

Man to man, Mike, I'm so pissed off I'm useless. I feel like the floor had just gotten assembled under our feet after Xandro and Elsa died. Now this. My parents finally coming back to life a little. Now this. I'm caught between being a good father—hauling up roots and going back to Rochester where they have the best Pete could have... And being a good son and staying put to take care of my parents because I'm all they have. I end up being no good to anyone.

It's not all grim. Dad's been surprisingly helpful to me. We know he's economic with words, even more with emotions. But we've had some good talks and he's made me feel better. Which was a pleasant surprise—comfort coming from where you least expect it.

Mom...well, you know Astrid. She does, not says. I don't think Chris has made dinner once since we got back from Rochester. We don't run out of milk or eggs, the wash gets done. Without a word. Astrid works invisibly. You try to thank her for it and she brushes you off. "It's nothing, älskling."

It's everything.

We'll be all right. Pete's still a happy kid. Follows Erik around everywhere. Reminds me of you.

You take care, cousin.
Byron

July 1, 1976
Dear Mike,

You've got to get a trip home. Clayton has been transported 200 years back in time. It's unbelievable what the historical society has done for the bicentennial. Trudy says the atmosphere reminds her of when the war ended. Every night some kind of party, either planned or spontaneous. Music is playing constantly at the gazebo in the park. The river looks like a regatta. Little boys in tricorn hats, running around with their pants tucked into their socks. Fireworks every night on the river. You just go down around sunset and wait and eventually, they start going off. Pete loves them. Cripes, you never saw anything like his face with the colored lights in his eyes, and those little hands signing away. "Look, Mommy. Stars."

Erik marched in the parade with his gang. Full colonial dress, tugging a cannon. The cannon was our masterpiece—we rigged it up to shoot candy into the crowd. Erik had a pack of girls in petticoats following him the whole route. He better get used to that. Hell, I should get used to that. Chris is going to be beating them off with a stick.

Pete's doing well. He started nursery school two mornings a week and has an aide with him the whole while. He actually calls her his assistant. Ever hear a three-year-old bust out that word?

He wears a real strong aid in the left ear and a slightly less strong one in the right. They're wired to a clumsy contraption that has to strap on his chest. It's temperamental to moisture, gets full of static if you even think damp thoughts. But Chris is on top of all the latest research and says big advances have been made. They're devloping multi-channel aids so you can change the amplification to match whatever environment you're in.

Chris drove down to Syracuse back in June. She attended a talk given by some guy named Daniel Graupe who's at the forefront of all this technology. Computers and microprocessors mean eventually, aids will be more powerful, but smaller. She saw a few prototypes for ones that fit inside a person's ear rather than behind it. No trailing wires to a central device you have to haul around with you. Sounds all space age and far in the future. I want Pete to have these things now.

It's hard.

But Pete's signing all the time and thanks to speech therapy, he speaks well. Chris stays on top of him with diction. Erik, naturally, picked ASL up in about an hour. All right, I'm exaggerating. A week. Now I think he and Pete are devising their own secret version. They have each other.

I got all moody and despairing the other night, wondering what kind of life Pete is going to have, always dependent on others when others aren't always dependable. Or even kind. Erik is both, though. He has my father's dependability and his kindness reminds me of Uncle Emilio. Emilio and my dad always had each other. Peter will always have Erik. And that comforts me like nothing else.

Anyway, come home if you can. This place is fantastic this summer.

Miss you, kid
Byron

August 1, 1976

Dear Mike,

What started out as a celebration summer has turned bitter. I've had it. I tell you, Mike. I can't take one more helping of shit served up on a plate and thrown onto my family's table. And be expected to choke it down...

Pete has meningitis.

He's so sick. So little.

He's fighting, but he's so little and

Plates get thrown down on your table and it's

Sorry I was short on the phone. It wasn't me. I'm not angry at you. You know that.

It's not who I am. I can't explain just

Sorry, Mike.

Sorry about that, kid. It was a tough night. I'm going to try to finish this.

I tell you, Mike, it's hard to be a man when your child is suffering. Pete's getting better—the fever is coming down which means the infection is clearing up. He smiled at us the other day. He's alert and aware and he's with us. But whatever hearing he had is gone. Left ear is now a total loss, and he hears only the most high- or low-pitched sounds in the right. He's in silence now. The river got him and my heart's broken.

You do everything and anything, Mike. You look at life as a system of points. I suffered X so I'm owed X amount of reprieve. The scales should balance. It's only fair.

Nothing's fair.

I lost my brother and Elsa to the river, the same river that took so much of my life away. I keep getting dragged back into the water, feeling I'm meant to pay for something I never bought. I paid. I still pay. We Fiskares paid, goddammit, but the bills keep coming. It's never enough.

What I did and what I do isn't enough so now Pete has to pay. I can't do

I got interrupted. Pete had a bad day. He's in pain and I want to tear the world apart to stop it.

Chris is sleeping at the hospital tonight. I came home and talked with my dad a long time. Again and again, he surprises me. Comes through for me just when I think I can't do anymore.

We sat on the veranda and he had Erik asleep in his lap while he talked. He loves that boy. But Erik is easy to love.

Dad told me something I didn't know: his army unit liberated Mauthausen in the spring of '45. I was astounded not to have known this, and almost a little put-out he never told me. But when I stop to think about the scale of the atrocity, I realize it's not something you can touch on a little. You either have to tell all, or tell nothing. And what went on in those camps... Cripes, even if you wanted to tell, it seems the words just don't exist.

Dad said what he saw at Mauthausen made him realize the pursuit of perfection is a dangerous thing. He said Mom saw it to a lesser extent when she was growing up in Brazil. Those crazy Finns trying to build a perfect paradise on land all but barren. At least they turned it around and turned a socialist commune into a profit. They didn't turn it to smoke up a thousand chimneys. They made it good for something.

Erik is under the table while I'm writing. He plays beneath things—the piano, my workbench. Chris says he's happiest when he's underfoot. Always tinkering with something. I wonder where it will take him in life.

I worry for Erik sometimes. He wants to know how things work and then always wants them to work that way. He gets it from me. It's such a miserable day in a man's life when he realizes he can't always control what life plates up for him. But I guess we sit and survive at the table with whatever tools we have. Pretty china and fish-handled silverware. Candles and good manners. Salt and pepper.

Life isn't perfect, Mike. I guess the best you get is a collection of perfect moments.

You have to somehow turn a profit when the land is barren.

You have to be good for something.

Take care and come see us soon.

Be good,
Byron

Erik folded the letters back into thirds and set them down on the rough, sawhorse table. Thoughtless, his elbows on his knees, he stared out at the lake's smooth, multi-colored surface.

"Erik?" Daisy's voice floated from one of the upstairs window.

"Yeah," he said, fingering the charms on his necklace.

"Erik?"

He turned and called over his shoulder. "I'm right here. What's up?"

"My water just broke."

PULL

"THE NEXT PERSON WHO tells me to push is getting kicked," Daisy said, falling back onto the inclined mattress, breathing hard.

Quiet, appreciative laughter from the nurses as Erik wiped her face with a cold cloth. Her cheekbones had a yellowish cast from tiny blood vessels breaking in her face. Likewise her irises were pink and blood-shot.

"I mean it," Daisy said, holding up her hand. "Too many people yelling push. I know to push. I can't stand that fucking word anymore so say something else."

Erik sponged the back of her neck, knowing the less he said the better. Daisy was already unnerved from giving birth in front of an audience. She didn't need him giving more stage directions.

"It's close, Daisy," Dr. Alibrandi said. "Another good set and the baby will crown."

Daisy's hand curled around the front of Erik's T-shirt and squeezed.

"Entre nous, this sucks," she said.

"I know," he said, giving her some ice. "You're amazing."

"God, here comes another one," she said, her face going tight as she sat up.

Erik took up her leg. Across the bed, Lee Malone winked as she took the other leg. He smiled back, thanking whatever divine, karmic forces had been at work to make Lee on duty when they came in today. It was like an omen. Or a gift.

"Let Lee talk," Erik said. "Everyone else just back off. Let's try it this way."

"Deep breath in, Daisy," Lee said. "Hold it tight and *pull...*"

Even Erik felt a difference with this set. More power was in the foot against his shoulder. Something in Daisy's body seemed more controlled and efficient and her face was narrowed into a pinpoint of focus instead of being scrunched in desperation. When the contraction ended and she lay back, she was panting but she didn't seem as defeated.

"That was tremendous," Dr. Alibrandi said. "She's crowned, Daisy. Right at the door. One more set like that and you'll have her out."

"Pull works," Daisy said. "I pull better than I push."

"Story of my life," Erik said.

She barely got her breath back before it was on her again. The intensity of the room rose up. Voices and sound meshed into a dull roar behind the heartbeat thudding in Erik's ears.

"This is the one," Lee said. "Ring of fire. Just pull as hard as you can to the other side. Don't back down, don't be afraid. You have to be bigger than the pain."

Daisy's face went pink. Then red. The sweat beaded up on her forehead and dripped down her temple. Erik couldn't take his eyes from her. Never in his life had he seen her so concentrated.

"That's it," Alibrandi said. "That's it, keep up the intensity. Again."

"Don't lose the breath," Lee said. "Pull your breath in. Pull hard."

"That's it that's it that's it that's *it.* You're done."

"Is she out?" Daisy cried.

"Her head is out. Rest. Rest, Daisy. Don't push *or* pull."

She collapsed back, gasping. Her hand seized Erik's shirt again and pulled his brow to hers. "Is that it," she whispered. "Am I done?"

"You did it," he said, holding her face, kissing it all over. "You did it. It's done."

"Oh thank God."

"I love you so much." He smoothed her hair back, couldn't stop kissing her. "Jesus Christ, that was incredible."

"Holy crap, I think I'm inside-out. Permanently."

"No, no," Lee said, laughing. "Everything will go back the way it was. I promise."

Daisy's clamp on Erik's shirt relaxed. "Do you see her," she said. "Are you going to look?"

"I can't look," he said. "Not yet."

"Stay relaxed," Alibrandi said. "We're just suctioning out her little nose here."

Cry, Erik thought. Not looking. Only listening. *Cry. Please cry. Come on. Cry for me. Please.*

Silence through the din. Too much like Kees's deadly silence.

Cry, honey. Take a breath. Cry. Please. Don't do this to me.

"Let's try a push without contraction, Daisy," Alibrandi said. "We're going to get her shoulder out. Strong and easy push."

As Daisy bore down, Erik kept his brow on hers, their eyes and hands clenched tight.

Cry. You can do it. Please cr—

"Stop," Alibrandi said.

A cooing hiccup. And another. Stuttering like a cold engine trying to turn over.

"Oh," Daisy cried.

The stammering sound gained strength and grew into a shrieking wail.

"Yes," Erik whispered, the breath collapsing out of his chest, a load of prickling adrenaline coming to replace it. He picked up his head and looked around.

"Daisy," Alibrandi said. "Sit up and reach down here. You too, Dad. Take her."

"Come on." His brain flying, Erik scooped up Daisy's shoulder blades. His other hand slid along her forearm as she reached, gasping and crying, down between her trembling thighs to that screaming form still partly inside her.

"She's all yours," Alibrandi said.

Daisy took the baby under the arms. Erik's hand slid under that tiny little butt and together they drew her out and up, the cord trailing behind. Up and onto Daisy's chest they pulled, Erik shouting, Daisy laughing. Lee followed, wrapping baby and arms in a warmed blanket. "Well done," she said. "Congratulations."

Erik put his spinning head down, at eye level with his daughter, who continued to cry. A tunnel from mouth to lungs filled with the most beautiful sound.

"Oh," Daisy said softly. "Oh it's *you*."

Kirsten Francine Fiskare cried louder.

I can hear you, Erik thought, laying a hand on top of the baby's head. Slick and gooey and red-faced, she stared back at him and shrieked. Her midnight blue eyes were wide open. Her voice stretching and unfolding. Straight at him she stared, as if testing how much he could take.

Eyes locked, Erik set his wrist and its tattooed K gently on his daughter's forehead. A forehead, he noticed, shaped just like his.

"Hey, little fish," he said softly.

Lee ran a cold cloth over Daisy's face and neck. "Relax as much as you can," she said quietly. "Relax and breathe. You did great."

"You're so beautiful," Erik said, leaning to press his mouth against Daisy's cool, damp cheek. She smiled beneath his kiss, her eyes closed and her chest rising and falling in deep, measured breaths.

After a few minutes, Dr. Alibrandi called to him. "Got a job for you, Dad."

The scissors seemed to move easily in his fingers this time. A strong, decisive snip through the cord, not severing hope but freeing his daughter to come home.

"Take a seat, Erik," Lee said. "Have a breather."

A wheeled stool was rolled over. He sat, his head nestled by Daisy's shoulder, his finger in Kirsten's loose fist. Her crying had diminished to small coos. Her little mouth opened and closed against Daisy's skin.

"Your mom smells good, doesn't she," Erik said. A single chuckle in Daisy's chest. Erik's smile widened until it hurt. The triangle of his little family pulled tight, a bubble within the medical ballet still buzzing around them.

This, he thought. *This and only this.*

Thank you for this.

He let go of time and floated on the moment. Not quite leaning into it. Not yet.

"Oh God," Daisy said. Her face was twisting and she bit down on her bottom lip. "Erik."

He picked up his head, a stab of adrenaline in his chest. "What's happening?" he said.

"So much for a breather," she said, gasping.

A second nurse reached gloved hands in to take Kirsten. Lee spooned some ice water into Daisy's mouth and then helped her sit up. "Let's go, Mama."

"All right, Daisy," Alibrandi said. "I know you're tired. You have to dig deep now."

"You got this," Erik said, standing up and getting a hand under Daisy's bent knee. His other hand reached to touch her face. "Look at me."

Her eyes met his. "You told me I was done."

"I lied."

Her chin gave a short nod. "I'll get you for this, motherfucker."

"It's now officially what I do," Erik said.

She let out a sharp cry and her eyes doubled in size. "Oh my *God*, he's right there."

"Let's do this," Alibrandi said. "Put him in my hands."

"Show me a beautiful boy," Lee said.

From somewhere across the crowded delivery room, Kirsten was crying again.

"It's all right, honey," Erik said under his breath, braced against Daisy's strength. "He's coming, I promise. Give your mother a minute…"

LOVING YOUR AUNT

THE SCREENED-IN PORCH was finished. Down to the cushions on the wicker seating, the lights around the large window openings and the three ceiling fans. They made a low purr and the occasional squeak as they kept the breeze moving through.

Erik and Daisy lay together on the double-wide chaise lounge, a bit of extravagance they felt was vital to their existence. In good weather, it was always in use.

Today was good. The sun moved in and out of the clouds, glinting off Astrid's diamond on Daisy's hand and flinging tiny rainbows around the white woodwork. The May air was warm enough for short sleeves and bare feet. Cool enough for a throw blanket across their legs.

At the end of the dock, Will and Lucky sat in the Adirondack chairs, holding hands, their faces turned up to the sun. Sara's sing-song chatter ebbed and flowed as she swung on the tire suspended from the oak tree. At the play kitchen at the base of the trunk, Jacy banged pots and pans, stirring mud and leaves and flower buds.

"Uncle Erik," Jack said, appearing on the other side of the screen. "Let's go fishing."

"I can't," Erik said, his eyes closed.

"Why not?"

"Because I'm loving your aunt right now."

Jack sucked his teeth. "You can love her anytime you want."

"But I want to love her right now."

Daisy turned her head on Erik's chest and smiled at Jack. "I'm being loved."

Jack kicked at the ground. "I'm never loving girls when I grow up. You waste so much time."

"Good plan," Erik said, yawning. "It's too late for me. I ruined my life loving girls."

"I'll fish with you, Jacques," Joe said, coming around the side of the house. "You want to cast from the dock or take the boat out?"

They ambled off, discussing a plan. Erik's hand moved along Daisy's back.

Francine came out the kitchen door with Kirsten.

"Look how beautiful," she said.

She came over and laid the baby on Erik's chest. Just bathed, Kirsten was cool and soft in a striped sailor shirt and little blue jeans, the damp wisps of her light brown hair drawn aside and clipped with a bow. The sleepy, blinking eyes above her pacifier were dark blue. None of the Bianco green in their irises. These were her Uncle Peter's sapphire eyes.

Byron's eyes.

Francine shook out a receiving blanket and smoothed it over Kirsten, then went back inside and returned with her grandson, who had been named Kennet William.

"Why?" Will said when he found out.

"Why?" Erik grabbed Will's wrist and turned it up to show the tattooed fish. "Why'd you do that?"

Will pressed his mouth in a tight smile and said nothing.

"You set me in your presence forever," Erik said. "I don't want any more tattoos so I set you in my presence this way." He dropped Will's arm and swatted the tear-streaked face. "And Kennet Asshole doesn't have as nice a ring to it."

They tried calling him Kenny, but it never rolled easily off their tongues. They tried Kees, but it made their hearts hurt. For a couple months it was KW, which was cute, but a mouthful. It truncated to K-Dub and finally became Kade.

Wearing only a onesie, he wiggled in Francine's arms, eyes wide above a damp slick fist in his mouth, his sturdy legs running in the air.

"Where's Mama?" Francine said. "Look, there she is."

Kade thrust his arms out, nearly toppling from his grandmother's grasp.

Daisy reached up. "Come here, Godzilla."

"I couldn't get his pants on."

Erik raised a hand. "I taught him that," he said. "Sorry."

Laughing, Francine got another blanket. She leaned and kissed all four heads, then let herself out the screen door to wander around the gardens.

Daisy's hand moved in circles on Kade's butt. He looked this way and that, kicking at the blanket. He gnawed his fingers and bopped his forehead against Daisy's collarbones, gurgling all the while.

"Dude, you're a lunatic," Erik said softly. "Chill."

Kade waved a wet hand and blew bubbles, his face unfolding in a toothless grin. Bald for the first five months of his life, fine blond hair was beginning to cover his head. His eyes were somewhere between grey and green, with the Bianco blue rim around the iris.

"Look," Daisy said. "Look who's here, Kade."

Outside the screen, a hummingbird hovered above the masses of daisies planted around the porch. It levitated up, down, then zoomed toward the magenta pompoms of the bee balm. It swooped and darted, squeezing in and out of small places. Looking for sweetness.

"It's Trudy," Daisy said. "She came to say hi."

Kade wasn't interested. He arched up like a lopsided sphynx, his chubby hand reaching toward his sister. Daisy leaned a little to close the gap. Bubbling and cooing, Kade touched Kirsten's shoulder and gave one last questioning croon.

Kirsten turned her head as if to answer, but her eyes were closed. Her downy eyebrows slightly furrowed, as if in deep thought. One little fist tucked by her chin, the other curled tight on Erik's finger. Around her neck on the tiniest of chains slid the silver fish.

Erik sighed under his daughter's placid weight and regarded his wriggling son. "Go to sleep," he said.

Kade gave a small bark of laughter.

"Fat chance," Daisy said. She ran her fingernails lightly along Kade's limbs. Sometimes this got him to settle down.

"Good thing you're cute, kid," Erik said, yawning. All he did these days was stumble around and yawn. He'd feel more alert on a Benadryl drip.

"Da," Kade said.

"Yeah, yeah," Erik said. "Don't sweet-talk me."

"Da da da," the boy sang. He put his cheek on Daisy's chest and she scratched his back.

"This is nap time," she said. "We love nap time."

"I see Kirsten napping nicely," Erik said. "Who else is napping nicely?"

"Da," Kade said.

"Da is not napping," Erik said. "Because Kade won't go to sleep. Ever."

But then, thank God, Kade yawned and pressed a fist to his face.

Erik reached to curve his hand around the baby's head, stroking a thumb between his eyes. "You just think life is amazing, don't you?"

"He's too happy to sleep," Daisy said, yawning.

Erik went on caressing his son's forehead, suffused with an exhausted, content peace. Knowing now the first soul had been too big for one body. Nothing was wrong with Kees's ride—it just didn't have enough seats.

You broke and left, but then you came back.

Because you were meant to be mine.

On top of his heart, Kirsten sighed.

"Da," Kade said.

Your heart is huge, Erik thought. *Your love will be amazing.*

Feel all of it

Kade smiled. Under his father's touch, the tiny eyelids closed for longer and longer until at last, they stayed shut.

Erik's own thick eyes drooped as he looked at Daisy. Her shirt stained with milk, drool and bits of lunch the twins had thrown at her. Her hair half-falling out of its bun, an earring missing, her eyes smudged with fatigue. The gold fish and the pearl neatly nestled in the hollow of her throat. Kade's mouth moving against her collarbone, sucking in his sleep.

This is my forever.

"You so much," he said, drifting off.

A last flash of blue-green before she closed her eyes, tilted toward him and rested her head on his shoulder. "So much you."

The hummingbird zipped past the porch again. It floated on the air, its sleek body suspended between blurred wings. For a moment it gazed at the sleeping Fiskares through the screen. Then, with a last green-gold flicker, it flew away toward the lake.

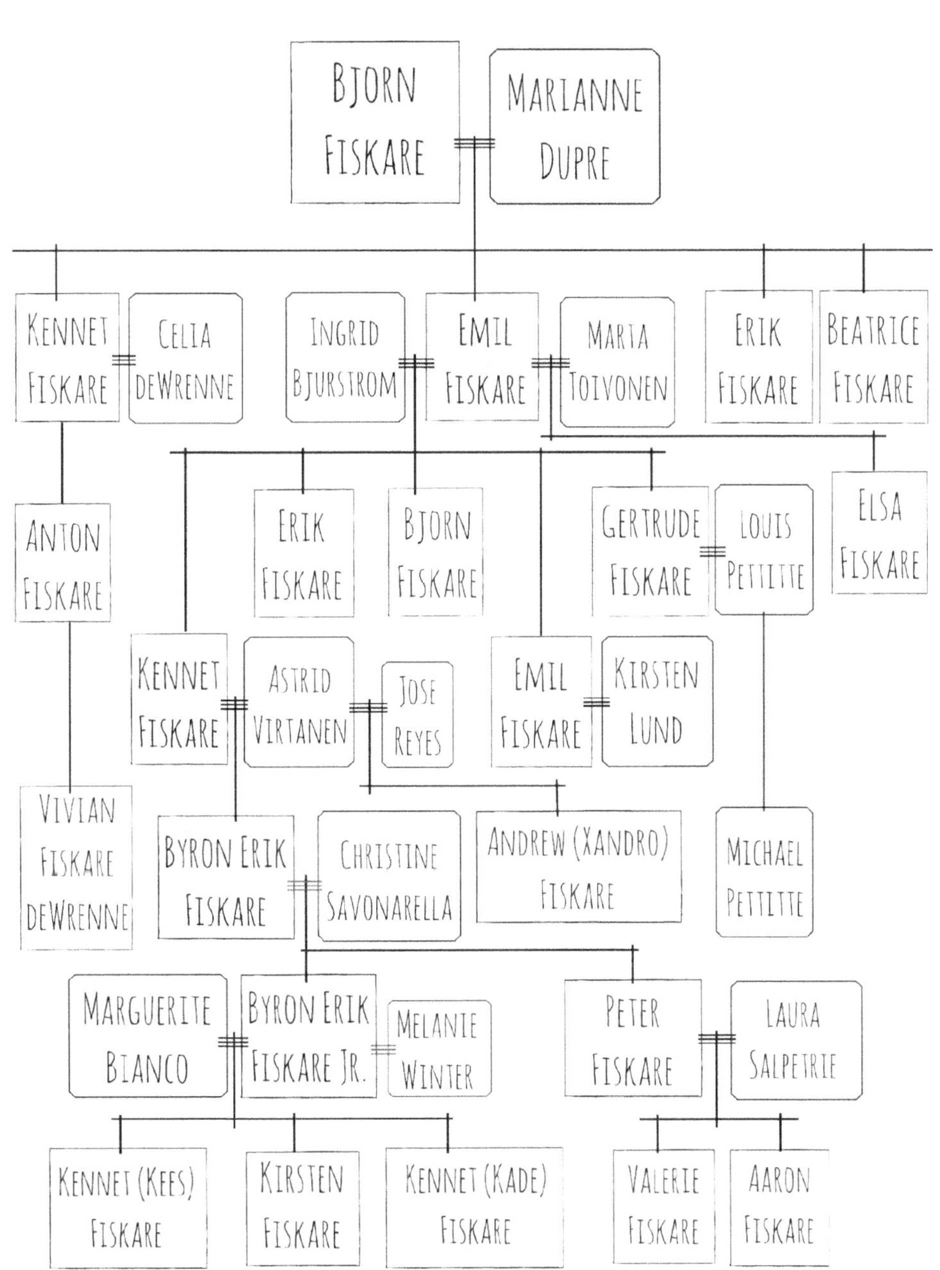

Bjorn Fiskare
Marianne Dupre
Kennet Fiskare
Celia deWrenne
Ingrid Bjurstrom
Emil Fiskare
Marta Toivonen
Erik Fiskare
Beatrice Fiskare
Anton Fiskare
Erik Fiskare
Bjorn Fiskare
Gertrude Fiskare
Louis Pettitte
Elsa Fiskare
Kennet Fiskare
Astrid Virtanen
Jose Reyes
Emil Fiskare
Kirsten Lund
Vivian Fiskare deWrenne
Byron Erik Fiskare
Christine Savonarella
Andrew (Xandro) Fiskare
Michael Pettitte
Marguerite Bianco
Byron Erik Fiskare Jr.
Melanie Winter
Peter Fiskare
Laura Salpetrie
Kennet (Kees) Fiskare
Kirsten Fiskare
Kennet (Kade) Fiskare
Valerie Fiskare
Aaron Fiskare

ACKNOWLEDGMENTS

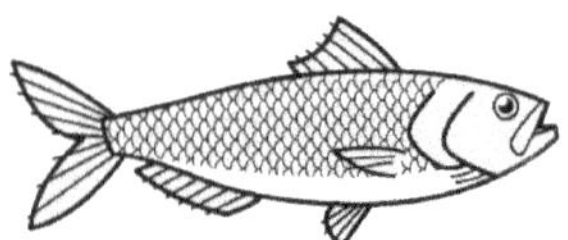

I WRITE STORIES FROM LIFE, and the following people may or may not be aware they contributed to this book:

Dawn Valzania, who suggested less angst and more banging the manny.

Julianne Pressman, who drew a line and is always on my side.

Amy Alt, who helped me get Erik to Canada.

David Cramer, who ate all the maraschino cherries at Mary Laqueur's wedding.

Mary Laqueur Holt, who was a vision in her wedding gown.

Christine Wiita, whose copy of *National Geographic: Drives of a Lifetime* introduced me to the Finnish colony of Penedo and gave me an idea.

Bill Webb, who showed me how to set the proper DMX value for the automated lighting fixtures.

Rob MacKechnie, for his impeccable taste in wedding favors.

Dawn Curran, who did amazing damage control after *Poltergeist*.

My sister-in-law Janine, for her patient answering of a thousand IVF questions.

Corinne Videla, who had a Lucky to get right in bed with her and hold the pieces together.

Kathy McNamee, whose voice is set in her son's presence forever. Her dignified grace and courage and her fierce love for Matt shaped Christine Fiskare like nothing else.

The SLQR Advance Read Army. If I lose you, my stories will die.

My editor, Becky Dickson. When I write, I can hear you.

My stylists: Tracy Kopsachilis, who makes my books beautiful on the outside and Colleen Sheehan, who makes them beautiful on the inside.

The IABB community who is a priceless source of support, humor and friendship.

Emma Scott, author and friend, whose sound, fearless feedback made me dig deeper.

Alleskelle Fraser, for pardoning my French.

Rach Lawrence, for reading what I write.

Ami, because not everything has to be a thing. (Literally.)

Stacie, my gold medal wingman.

My irrefutable fract, Fank.

My grandfathers Ernest and David. My grandmothers Lena and Clara.

My parents, for life and its collection of perfect moments.

My brother, whose saving grace is believing in love.

My husband JP, who proposed in the kitchen. (Him so much.)

My daughter Julie, who looked into my eyes while she was being born and made me see the past and future.

And my son, AJ, who was meant to be mine. He just caught a bad ride the first time around.

THANK YOU

IF YOU ENJOYED *Here to Stay*, I'd love to hear about it. Please consider leaving a short review on the platform of your choice (Amazon, Goodreads, B&N, etc). Honest reviews are the tip jar of independent authors and each and every one is treasured.

If you're a Facebooker, join others who enjoyed my books in the Read & Nap Lounge:

LQRWRITES.COM/LOUNGE

Stop by my website at

SUANNELAQUEURWRITES.COM,

OR INSTAGRAM AT @SWAINBLQR

Wherever you find me, all feels are welcome. And I always have coffee.

ALSO BY SUANNE LAQUEUR

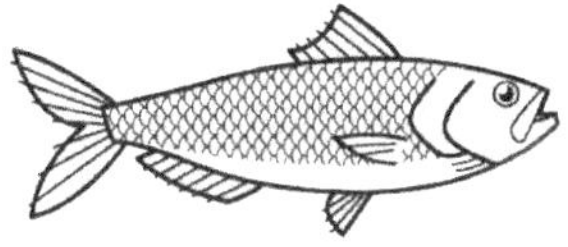

A Small Hotel

THE FISH TALES

The Man I Love
Give Me Your Answer True
Here to Stay
The Ones That Got Away
Daisy, Daisy

VENERY

An Exaltation of Larks
A Charm of Finches
A Scarcity of Condors
The Voyages of Trueblood Cay
Tales from Cushman Row
A Plump of Woodcocks

SHORTS

Love & Bravery: Sixteen Stories
An Evening at the Hotel

ANTHOLOGIES

Flesh Fiction

ABOUT THE AUTHOR

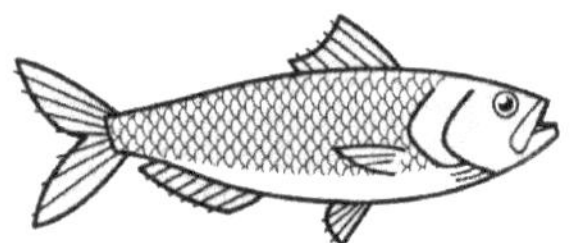

A FORMER professional dancer and teacher, Suanne Laqueur went from choreographing music to choreographing words. Her work has been described as Therapy Fiction and Emotionally Intelligent Romance. She prefers Contemporary Train Wreck.

Laqueur's novel *An Exaltation of Larks* was the grand prize winner in the 2017 Writer's Digest Book Awards. Her debut novel *The Man I Love* won a gold medal in the 2015 Readers' Favorite Book Awards and was named Best Debut in the Feathered Quill Book Awards. Her follow-up novel, *Give Me Your Answer True,* was also a gold medal winner at the 2016 RFBA.

Laqueur graduated from Alfred University with a double major in dance and theater. She taught at the Carol Bierman School of Ballet Arts in Croton-on-Hudson for ten years. An avid reader, cook and gardener, she started her blog EatsReadsThinks in 2010.

Suanne lives in Westchester County, New York with her husband and two children.

www.ingramcontent.com/pod-product-compliance
Lightning Source LLC
Chambersburg PA
CBHW072045190726
48294CB00005B/1411